'Matilda Leyser's mythic characters are gods and humans all at once; her tale of love and destruction is fuelled by ancient power and rich with contemporary resonance. And what beautiful writing! This striking novel conjures our deepest emotions — our feelings for each other, for the imperilled planet that is our only home. *No Season but the Summer* is a memorable debut.'

ERICA WAGNER, author of *Mary and Mr Eliot*

'Matilda Leyser's novel takes the eternal polarities — love and hate, life and death, summer and winter, possibility and impossibility — and brings them crashing together in a tumultuous story of gods living alongside humanity, mother-daughter love and loss, and a glimmer of hope despite it all. In *No Season but the Summer*, our world is still dying, but it is putting up a hell of a fight as it does so, reminding us that we can fight too, and that fighting for our lives might start with listening to the earth.'

STELLA DUFFY, author of *Theodora*

'What a wonderful writer. Matilda Leyser's work is precise, poetic, hard-edged, rhythmical. It seethes with life, and feels both ancient and brand new.'

DAVID ALMOND, author of *Skellig*

'This novel did all of the things that I wish mythic reimaginings would do ... This one is heartily recommended. It's masterfully constructed, moving, and strange in all the right ways. It's carefully and poetically written ... There are very few writers who have succeeded in bringing an ancient myth into the contemporary world with such profound resonance for the issues which concern us. Matilda Leyser is one of them, and I'm very much looking forward to what she might do next.'

SHARON BLACKIE author

'As you climb to earth with Persephone, you know you are in good hands. Leyser has an uncanny ability to make the mythic intimate and the timeless timely. She takes an ancient tale of goddesses and furious wrongs and fashions it into a passionate contemporary story that will resonate with mothers and daughters everywhere. Oh — and she writes like an angel. Her prose at once precise and lush, you can taste and smell and touch every bit of her thrilling, sensuous world. *No Season but the Summer* is an everyday epic with an invitation to ride.'

NICKY SINGER, author of *The Survival Game*

'Artfully transporting classic myth to the present, this is the tale of Persephone, of the stories behind why our seasons change, and "how climate change is stretching and breaking the rules that have long kept the natural world in rhythm".'

The Bookseller

'Deeply elegant and immensely compelling ... the writing is exceptional — every word feels chosen with care, every sentence balanced and the imagery, metaphors of ancient Greece renewed in the modern world ... are breathtaking. I am genuinely astonished that this is a first novel. It feels like the work of someone who's been doing it for decades and has found the freedom to explore the nature of our world along with the mastery of language that such depth of exploration demands. It's utterly beautiful: a jewel of a book. Totally recommended.'

MANDA SCOTT, author of *A Treachery of Spies*

'This is a beautifully written retelling of an ancient myth. It deserves to be widely read and enjoyed ... The writing is lyrical, the characters strong, and the story carries you along.'

ANNE CORLETT, author of *The Space Between the Stars*

NO SEASON BUT THE SUMMER

MATILDA LEYSER read English Literature at King's College, London and then ran away to join the circus. She trained as an aerialist, working up a rope, collaborating with dance and theatre companies, making her own work, and performing in diverse venues, including the National Theatre, Shakespeare's Globe, and the Royal Opera House. After ten years in the air, she decided to come down to earth and take up the far more dangerous act of writing on the ground. She has two children, and is the founder and director of an international movement for creative mothers and carers called M/Others Who Make: www.motherswhomake.org. She also works as an associate director with *I*mprobable, a world-renowned theatre company: www.improbable.co.uk.

NO SEASON BUT THE SUMMER

Matilda Leyser

SCRIBE

Melbourne | London | Minneapolis

Scribe Publications
18–20 Edward St, Brunswick, Victoria 3056, Australia
2 John St, Clerkenwell, London, WC1N 2ES, United Kingdom
3754 Pleasant Ave, Suite 100, Minneapolis, Minnesota 55409, USA

First published by Scribe 2023
This edition published 2024

Excerpt from 'The Trees' by Philip Larkin from *High Windows*,
1974. Used by kind permission of Faber and Faber Ltd.

Typeset in Fournier by the publishers

Printed and bound in the UK by CPI Group (UK) Ltd, Croydon
CR0 4YY

Scribe is committed to the sustainable use of natural resources and
the use of paper products made responsibly from those resources.

978 1 915590 19 0 (UK paperback)
978 1 957363 68 4 (US paperback)
978 1 922586 97 1 (ebook)

Catalogue records for this book are available from the
the British Library.

scribepublications.com.au
scribepublications.co.uk
scribepublications.com

For my mother, Henrietta.

The trees are coming into leaf
Like something almost being said;
The recent buds relax and spread,
Their greenness is a kind of grief.

From 'The Trees', Larkin.

1

PERSEPHONE

It is dark down here. Not bright night dark. Thick through and through dark. I scramble up tunnels, squirm through crevices, and crouch on boulders in the blackness. I feel the fine grain of the limestone under my hands — soon it will soften into soil and I will know that I am near the surface.

No sound but my breath and the rush of the stream, which I have followed, against its downward flow, since I left the river far below. I brace myself, arms out against the tunnel walls as the slope steepens, and press on. At last, it levels. I pause inside the hug of the rock.

When I arrive, I will again become fair-haired, grey-eyed, tall, slight — an identity of colour, height, weight, which I left up in the light. Down here, I am as dark as stone. I never understood how luminous the night was as a child. I used to fear it — the dark that was not truly dark — yet now, for years, I have recoiled from the light on my return. Each spring creation blooms, the birds sing, and I have migraines. No one was ever meant to travel this way, climbing against the gradient of ground and spirit. None of them considered this when the deal was made. I have often thought it would be best if I could stay down with the dead. But not this year.

The river has been rising. This year it was higher, wider, swifter than ever before. It burst its banks. It slapped and crept its way into my husband's cave. He had to rescue his tools — hammer, chisels, tongs. There is a sculpture of me with emerald eyes — one of many he has carved out of the limestone — she lies, reclining between rocks, near the entrance to his workshop. This year the waters covered her. We had to wade past her to reach the ferrywoman. Water over our ankles, calves, knees. Up to our thighs by the time we stood where the shoreline used to be.

We waited — the boat was a speck of light out across the water, unsteady, and distant as a star.

'It isn't safe to cross this year. You'll have to stay here,' my husband said. He squeezed my hand.

I should have pressed his hand back, soothed him. But I was surprised by the panic that flashed through me. For nine thousand years, I have feared crossing that river. I have climbed up to the earth, bringing spring, but feeling like winter. I have dreaded the keen blue sky, the hopeful green. Most of all, I have dreaded the return of hunger.

I do not feel hunger under the earth, but I know it from the world above. I know how deep it can bore into your body. I know the hunger that hunches like an animal in your stomach, gnawing at you from the inside. I know the kind that makes you shrill, translucent as glass, and as fragile. I know the kind that slits you like a fish, from head to tail, leaves you raw, exposed. And I know the kind that seals you like a secret no one can reach, not even you. I hate how hunger seeps into me as I cross back up to life.

But this year, thigh-deep in that wide river, I was hungry for hunger. I have never felt this before. Or if I did, if I ever have, it was more than nine thousand years ago. That time, it led me the other way, down, underground, and nothing was the same again. And now there it was, amid the flood, that feeling, this time tugging me up. The wild water made me want to cross

2

it. So I said it, before thought could catch it back, already with the edge of hunger in my voice: 'No. I have to go.'

Hades, King of the Dead, let go my hand.

I tried to reassure him. I turned and lifted my hands to find his forehead, cheekbones, jawline. This is what we do, what he first taught me to do — how to feel for the rock in each other. How to reach underground, even in the body, to what will last forever.

'I have no choice. You know this.' Every year is shared — spring and summer are my mother's time, autumn and winter are my husband's. Nothing left for me. But it was for the best, they said.

I slipped my hands down to Hades' shoulders, to his spine. To face him, I'd had to turn upriver, so the water pushed against me as I held him. The press of it, the swirl of it around me, was disturbing, thrilling. How it surged on, careless of its course, persistent and yet fluid — so different to the hardness of my husband, to his kingdom of stone. It made me restless.

'You will come back,' he said into my ear.

It was more statement than question, but still he wanted it confirmed. In other years I have been glad of his need, but now it irked me. I sensed the dark mass of water, flowing sideways.

'I have no choice about that, either.'

As soon as I had said it, I regretted it.

His hands dropped away from me.

I told him I was sorry, but he would not kiss me goodbye. When the boat arrived, he would not help me into it. So I stepped in by myself and left.

It was horrible to pull away across the water, to know he was there, standing in the dark, alone, shaking with fright and fury. We never argue. Once before, right at the beginning, I

3

said something that disappointed him, gave him an answer he did not want — but never since. I blame the river. It was as if some fragment of me had been dislodged by the rapids. Something had come loose.

I sense the push of the water in my body still as, at last, I pull myself up from the damp stone into the hollow underneath the woods. I am hungry enough now that I could eat the soil, just like my mother did when I was in her. Dropped down on her knees in the field before the house and stuffed handfuls of the damp, black earth into her mouth. She could have eaten the whole field, she told me, when I was a seed inside her. She wanted to grow me, plant me well. She never understood that I was not like the corn she tended, and for which she was famous, loved, worshipped.

Now here I am again, under the earth, under the yew. Here I part ways with the stream. It slips under a shelf of rock and runs beneath the fields, below the house, where it used to feed our well, and on to join the River Ray behind it. But I must surface now, following these roots against their line of growth into the light.

My mother will be waiting.

DEMETER

Still no sign. Or rather, a thousand signs, but none of them are her.

Celandine, in a vase on the desk, keeps vigil with me as I sit upstairs, beside the study window. I can hear the robin round the back — 'Tic, tic, tic,' — singing for a mate, almost as impatient as me. Nine thousand winters have taught me nothing but to wish the wait were over quicker.

It is not only the celandine that keeps me company — everything waits with me. The gibbous moon lingers in the grey sky. The pussy willow buds are tight with hope. I feel them in my knuckles. In the hairs along my arms, I feel the catkins slanting through the air. In my chest lie the bulbs — daffodil and crocus — lumpy, laden, ready to break open. In my feet I feel the ragged roots, reaching out from tree to tree, from tree to field, in readiness for her.

I remember I waited for her even when she was a child. Waited for her to come in from her reverie, down by the well. To catch up in the fields, press the holes for the corn. She was not a fast worker. Slow to learn, quick to dream. Sometimes I felt as if she were a fish, down in the depths of the river, hard to find, fathom, reel in, and I left on the bank.

There was that wait too when she swam in my belly, for she swelled it beyond nine moons. It was not till the tenth that I began to tighten. She was buried fast and slow to crown. Such strange reluctance for life, or so it seemed to me in those long days of light before the deal. There was no season but the summer then — one time, billowing out like a washed sheet on a blue day, glorious, confident. Harvest followed harvest — nothing stayed underground for long. There were no years to tally up — the sun was always keen, and we were ageless. Full of zest, vigour, lust, love.

This morning the sun is struggling. The winter was so wet it nearly washed it from the sky. It has yet to clear the distant Oxford spires on the horizon. I look out across my front garden, over the empty fields, towards the woods. I am on an island called England now, but I never moved. It was the land that cracked and drifted when the cold came. Even the continents were grieving, brittle, sent adrift.

That was that worst wait of all. I try not to think of it — when Persephone went missing. I sat by this window then, before winter had a name, when it seemed not like a season, but the way the world would be from then on — endlessly hard and bitter.

But she came back. I brought her back, half back. Yet year by year I have the feeling that less and less of her arrives. One year it will be a ghost, or only a girl who looks like her that I greet at my door, not Persephone. I blame the months of dark, the wear on the soul.

A crow clatters across the sky to the stile at the field's end where she should be. The only time I was not waiting for her was when she first began. I'm used to planting things on purpose, but I never meant to grow her.

It happened by the river behind the house. I had held a party and my brother Zeus was the last guest left. We wandered from the house, through the back garden, out into the meadow, to the river. We sat with our feet in clouds flecked with willow leaves. He was gentle for once. Quietly thrumming with power but not trying to prove anything to anyone. There was no hot chase. No cunning transformation. No bolts of passion. Instead, a moment of kinship. A brother and sister side by side. Arriving like one of the lilies, a simple opening that could not be resisted. There we were, dangling our wet legs, thigh to thigh, and then his head was on my shoulder and then we were kissing and then lying before it occurred to me to stop. And then I had no wish, no reason to pull away from him.

When afterwards Zeus rolled over, snored, then woke and

walked away, I was neither surprised nor sad. Given my start in life, I have good reason to mistrust men.

I thought we were safe, my daughter and I. My three brothers were far away — Zeus blazing blue over us, Hades buried down under us, Poseidon submerged in the sea. The earth was ours. The men on earth were different: they were vulnerable, their stay brief. I had nothing to fear from them. I was wrong — both about my brothers and the men on earth.

But there were no bad omens on that day beside the river. I was mother to the earth, to its fields, grains, and fruits. What was one little girl compared to a hundred fields of corn?

I frown at the field, remembering my brothers, not yet seeing my daughter — I stare at the stile, as if the simple act of looking hard could conjure her.

PERSEPHONE

I approach the surface from beneath the life and death tree — my mother's name for yew.

One dusk, nine thousand years ago, Hades cut the ground open here to find me searching for him by this tree. Since then, its trunk has thickened and split, so that when I pull myself up onto the earth, I will be inside it.

Needles and soil block the way. I dig upwards, feel roots holding, snapping, until my hands unearth a faint light and I see them — my hands — for the first time in many months.

I wrestle myself through the crack — head, torso, legs — and then I'm out, on the ground, inside the tree. I remember leaning on it, hungering for Hades. The utter dark of him is in my body as I crawl forwards like a baby, through the split in the trunk, over the yew-needled earth, emerge into the woods, and look up.

A man is standing in the sky. I kneel, put my palms over my eyes, give them back the dark, because I think the shock of light and colour must have made this vision. I take my hands away and look again. He is still there.

He is tall. Big-booted. Big-bearded, wearing a thick coat. He has no wings. There is nothing light about him and yet he is high up, level with the topmost branches of the oak trees opposite. The only man I know who belongs in the sky is my father. Father Sky, they called him. To me, he was as absent as air. I used to stare up at the sky and imagine he was watching me with eyes so wide and blue I could not see them. He was the opposite of my husband, who is all touch. My father was all eyes, no body. No body, that is, until the rare times when he rolled up in a flashing rage, thunderbolts at the ready. Crack. Boom. All eyes on him and on his electricity. Then he would be gone again. Vanished into blue. This quiet, heavy man is not my father.

Now, as I remember how to look, I can see that the man is standing on a thin rope, holding another in his hands, and that these extend between the two oak trees in front of me. He slides sideways with feet and hands along these lines. I see too where he is heading, for in the arms of the oak is a structure like a huge nest, as if a species of giant bird has come to land here. The nest is dome-shaped, a great green covering over it, resting on a wooden platform strapped between the branches. I see more of these structures — another in the other oak. One in the pine. One in the ash to the right of the yew. I look further through the woods — something has happened to the trees.

Someone has wrapped them up. Huge white nets extend from their trunks, swaddling their branches, covering their crowns. A beech, a silver birch, another oak — each have their branches bundled up. They look like ghosts. Branch, bud, first leaves, seen through a veil. As if someone were trying to stop the spring by bagging up the trees. I hear a woodpecker in the oak opposite, but otherwise the woods are quiet. Usually, the birds are jubilant. Here I am, keener to return than I have been for years, and I have stepped up into a world where it seems trees are not allowed to leaf, birds to land, and men may not walk freely on the ground.

I look back at the sky man. He is nearly at the oak nest now. He turns for a moment, looks down at me, frowns. It is hard to make out his face against the glare of sky. He lifts his hand in greeting but says nothing. I raise a hand back in return. He reaches the oak and stoops to disappear inside the green shelter on the platform.

I walk on, through the woods, past more captured trees who can no longer whisper in the wind, though whoever tried to stop their tongues this way knows nothing — my mother taught me long ago that trees talk underground.

DEMETER

There was one other wait.

Years before I had Persephone, when I was still a child — the second-born, the second to be swallowed.

I look up at the lightening sky, remember my first sight of

it, the dive out of my mother, the screaming thrill of breath. My mother Gaia's shining face. Then already I was in Cronus' hands, level with his titanic eyes: his baby girl. I looked good enough to eat, and so he did — opened his mouth, huge as a cave, and thrust me in. My father had been told his children would be his downfall. He was trying to avoid trouble, so he ate it. The fool. He did the same with all of us but Zeus, whom my mother swapped for a stone, big as a baby. Cronus ate that instead. It sank down inside him and we leant on it. It was a heavy hope, the only one we had. I grew from a tiny girl to a woman in the pit of my father's stomach, waiting to be freed.

His stomach stank. It was pock-marked as the moon, unfit for life. I had to eat what he had already eaten, to pick among the remnants of his meals. The days were no more than a faint reddening of the dark. He lurched about the skies, thrashed even in his sleep, so that we were thrown against each other, the stomach wall, the stone. At last, after a lifetime, Zeus brought Cronus a honeyed poison, and it poured down his throat. The muscles that had held us trapped, contracted, thrust us out.

I was born twice. First from my mother's womb. Then from my father's mouth. The world was still there when he threw me up — I fell into its wide, green arms. I swore I would never go into the dark again. I had been eaten. I wanted to be fed, to feed, to bring things to life, fiercely and forever. I taught the people how to farm, to grow instead of gather. I tried to teach them how to settle, though in truth they never learnt. Look at them now — planning yet another road, an expressway — they're still desperate to move on.

I stand, now worried. She should be here already. The sun has cleared the city's spires.

PERSEPHONE

I think of my mother as I walk through the netted trees, towards her house. There was a time when I believed that she knew everything. Many people made the pilgrimage that I am making now to see her. She was as tall as the apple tree, towering above most of her guests. They fell in love with her and with our house, with its sacks of flour, larger than me, lining the hall, with its long kitchen table, laden with gold-bellied loaves. She used to sing as she made bread — a list of yellow things: sun, corn, celandine, my hair — though my hair is almost white, not yellow.

I leave the woods, step out into the fields, and stop. They are bare. Usually, the winter wheat is already ankle-high when I arrive. No crops. I have never seen the land like this before.

When my mother was in charge, every field was full — corn, wheat, barley. Each afternoon she strode out to help the labourers. She would scoop me up into her arms as if she were gathering a bale of hay. She took me even beyond the fields, down by the river in which the trout swam, ready for her hands to stroke them, lull them, lift them gleaming from the water and bring them to her table. I understand why they gave themselves over to those hands. They were as large and warm as the fields, and on the back of them her veins ran like rivers.

It must have rained in the night. The earth is clinging to my feet in heavy clumps by the time I reach the stile into the final field. The first field, my mother calls it, because fields were her invention. I scrape some of the mud off my boots onto the wooden step. A blackbird in the bush has spied me and is sounding out a warning. For years I've wished I could arrive

11

unseen, but this morning I am glad that the hawthorns at least are still noisy with song and not bound up in nets.

No use in hiding now — I step up on the stile.

DEMETER

She's back. The blackbird sings, the morning breaks. She has appeared at last — upright as a hare. Nine thousand years old — still my girl.

I stand at the front door as Persephone comes in through the garden gate.

'Welcome home.'

I hold her, and for a moment she holds me back. Returned from the dead, still in the duffle coat and jeans in which she left back in September. She pulls away.

'Love, you're soaked.'

'What's going on in the woods?'

'I've towels ready.'

'But there was a man. In the trees.'

'Come in. Let yourself arrive.'

I lead Persephone down the hall into the kitchen, pull out a chair for her. I kneel and ease off her walking boots and socks. She lets me, because this is what we do when she arrives. The first winter, she was barely conscious by the time I got her back. I had to bathe her thin body while the fever raged in her. Now I wash only her feet. I wash off the dirt, the dead, her husband.

'Mother — the woods,' she persists, as I fill a bowl with water.

12

'It's just some fuss about a road.' I test the water with my hand, lift the bowl. I'm not as steady as I used to be and water sloshes over the edge, darkening the flagstones. I glance up, but Persephone is gazing out the window. I could tip the whole bowl out before she'd notice.

'It won't happen,' I tell her. I stand again to fill the kettle, then stoop to wash her. 'Your feet are freezing.'

'But the trees are all in nets.'

'To stop the birds from nesting. They can't fell the trees if the birds are in them.'

I pat her feet dry with a towel. Such pale skin. So fine-boned. I pour the water from the bowl, refill it, set it on the table for her hands.

'Fell the trees? Your trees?' she says.

The kettle boils. I make her tea, set it down next to the vase of dog violets I picked this morning. I sit down too and take her hand. For years, I wanted Persephone to care, or at least show interest. Now here she is doing both, and here I am wishing she would not. She pulls her hand away, frowns — she still looks like a child when she frowns. She puts her hands in the bowl, trails them there, stares into the water. I look at her, grey-eyed, fair-haired. I want to take her in my arms again.

'It'll be fine. You know I can deal with things,' I say, 'if I have to.'

She glances up, lifts her hands, starts to flick the water from them. I pass her the towel.

'My headache's starting.'

'I'll take your tea up for you.'

'No, I can do it.'

'Well, the attic's ready.'

She stands. I kiss her. Either she is growing, or I am

shrinking. I have to tilt my head back to reach her cheek.

'It's lovely to have you home.'

She smiles, blinks, nods, carries her tea out of the kitchen. I listen to her climb the stairs, then go down the hall to the back door to let the apple know that it can bloom.

2

PERSEPHONE

The attic is barely a room, a triangle of space between the top floor and the roof, but it is the least cluttered part of the house. My mother never saw the sense in storing anything but food, so for years the attic held only grass and grain. Now nothing is stored up here but me, a bed, a little table, a few books. My mother added a skylight forty years ago. It gives me a lawn of sky to lie in, the bed right under it.

For the first two days, I do not stir. I've read about jet lag. I've seen the machines, more like fishes than birds, swim through the sky. I understand how the body holds on to the pattern of light and dark from the land of departure, struggles to adjust to the land of arrival. Time up here is second-sharp — it throbs and stabs. My head pounds and the hunger pains are the worst I can remember — a clawing that begins in my stomach, then digs into my back. I have learnt to take the eating slow but this year the pain persists, as if food is not the remedy. I wonder if water is. Not to drink, to bathe in. But the bath does not feel deep enough to match the pain — I will have to try the pond.

The pond is at the end of the back garden. It's where the well was once. I first met Hades there. When I was very small, I thought the dark lived down the well, that it rose up at night, flooding the earth and sky. My mother laughed at me, but she used to fear I would fall down it, and it was she who had it covered over later, after I had gone missing. She filled it clod

15

by clod, leaving a great dip in the earth beneath where the chestnut now stands. She hollowed the dip out more, packed it with stones and then tipped in bucket after bucket from the river behind the house. She put bunches of barley in the water to keep the algae out, so the pond would be clear right down to its stony bottom. No hint of the deep, dark hole that was our well. I like the pond. It is one of the few places I feel I am nobody's. On no one's land. I look forward to the cool, indifferent water.

It is early morning, a week after my arrival, when I make it downstairs, in a long T-shirt, with a towel.

I am already past the apple tree when I see her. My mother. Laid out. Naked. It should be no surprise — she has never worn a swimming costume — but I am taken aback. By her body, by her lying unguarded, eyes closed to the day. Beside her is a pile of black horse chestnut leaves she must have pulled up from the pond, to ready it for me. One black leaf is stuck, like a plaster, to her right forearm. I see the grey of winter in her face, her hair. She is smiling slightly. I like the smile least — the idea that she should be enjoying lying down, awake, but doing nothing. I stand, clutching my towel, as if I am the one exposed, then turn and walk quickly to the house. So that she need not know I saw her, so that I can pretend I never did.

I make it upstairs to the bathroom, shaken, annoyed — the ache in my middle now feels unfair, as if my mother were to blame for it. I sit to pee and feel something else slide out of me. I turn. There, in the yellow water, a dark drop. It sinks, hits the white enamel of the loo, and blossoms into red. I stand amid my mother's handmade lotions and stare. I have not bled for years. I barely bled, even as a girl — my starving soon put a stop to it, and then I went underground where nothing new can grow. When I first returned up here, I remember my body tried its

16

best. In the early years, by midsummer, my breasts would be tender, there might be a thin trickle, a sad attempt at coming back to life. But then I would have to leave again, so even these efforts stopped. What was the point? I did not miss it.

But now, this. Sudden. Gory. Bright red. Such a dangerous colour.

It lasts three days. It pulls down in the centre of me, silent, vivid, like a kind of grief, though I do not know what I have lost. I had forgotten that the underground of my body holds not only bone, but blood. It reminds me of the flooded river, far below, flowing out of nowhere, of how it made me hungry, cajoled me into saying something reckless. And then I think of my husband, left behind, angry, bereft.

But it is my rule not to think of him now I am here.

This is how I have survived — not to think of the other place, in either place. In the dark, it is easier. In the light, where there are horizons, hills, it is harder. The dead press on with surprising confidence and certainty — the living look back. Most years, I work hard not to look. My mother believes I spend too long with my nose buried in a book, as if it were a lazy choice, not a matter of necessity. This year, however, I have already looked and seen too much — a man up in the sky, my mother naked on the earth, and now this — red between my legs.

I do not tell my mother. I am too appalled, too frightened. When she is in the village, I descend, hunt out some old napkins to catch the flow, hope she will not notice, will not smell the blood when she brings my food up to the attic. I can smell it. I hide under the covers, arms wrapped tight about the pain, as if it were something precious.

Why now? After all these years. What does my body know that I do not?

Demeter

A mild day, white sky — there were days like this in January, and the blackbird started nesting — I had to tell him to hold off. Now is the time to be busy. I go down early to the kitchen, water the beetroot seedlings by the windowsill, fetch the flour. The letterbox clicks, but my hands are already thick with dough — the post can wait.

Even when I am down in the kitchen and my daughter is in the attic, I can feel her. She is quiet, but her presence is huge. I do not think she has ever understood this.

I birthed her right here, on the kitchen floor, cursing the day I lay with Zeus as his thunder rolled across my back. She slithered out at last, bloody, wrinkled, red.

As I make the bread, I think back to her babyhood — even then she had a presence that could not be ignored. Maybe it was my doing, maybe I gave her too much too early, but I was determined she should have everything I never had. I laid her under the apple tree, where the light poured through the leaves. I took her to the riverbank, to watch sun flicker on the water. I gave her all the light that I had lacked. So much she seemed to glow, lit up from the inside, so I could see the blue threads that ran across her temples.

My nipples were the stems she ripened on. I fed her from my breasts and then I fed her from my fields. I loved to watch her brand-new mouth, open like a question, ready for each answer that I offered her — a pea, a grape, a salty olive. At first her mouth, more than her eyes, was how she learnt of life. She ate the world. It brought me joy. And then it hurt as much when she began to starve — the worst thing she could have done to

18

me. At least I thought it was, until she left.

She loved to be held against my shoulder. I would stand here by the sink and rock her, wondering what she saw behind my back. I never was a seer. I was too full of today's feast to think further than the next glass of wine, loaf of bread. I could never have foreseen how things would go.

I should have — disappearing was her favourite game. She would wind herself in the bedclothes, then unravel into the light, dazzled by her own reappearance. In the back garden, she hid behind the fruit bushes. As she grew older, she vanished into the corn stalks in the fields out the front, and my looking became part of the game. I followed the script of loss years before I knew it would be real: 'Where's Persephone? She's gone. I can't find her anywhere!' as loud as day, mock gestures of despair, as I looked in every place where she was not. At last, she would step into view, proud as a miracle: 'Oh, there you are!' and then she would be gone again. She was rehearsing both of us.

She never liked to be the seeker, the one left looking. She said it was too hard, 'You are good at finding things, Mama, everything comes to you. It's different for me.'

It was true I loved being the host — the one to issue the invite, the gatherer of guests and goodness. I teased the grain from the ground, the fruit from the flower. I thought Persephone would be the same.

As soon as she was old enough to use a trowel, I cleared a plot for her at the far end of the vegetables, near the well. We planted a cherry sapling together and a row of sunflower seedlings. She watered them too often or not at all.

'Look at your garden!' I scolded her one morning as she sat dreaming, back to the well. She did not look at it but at me, and I realised I was more disappointed than she at the lack of flowers and cherries. Everyone else wanted to learn from me, why not her? She began to cry. I softened. 'Come here.'

I sat her on my lap, thumbed the tears from her face.

'Don't worry. We can plant something else.'

Each year, I reassured myself.

'What shall we grow next?'

Her answers, once sure and clear, grew slower.

I gave her light, warmth, water, nourishment. Why did she not grow towards me? I did not know how to love a life that did not turn and open to me, simple and warm. It was not from a lack of love, but a lack of knowing how to love that I fell short. I fear I drove her into hiding, for she had begun to go missing long before she left.

I finish kneading the bread, set it to rise near the stove. I clean the dough off my hands, fetch the post. Some charity wanting money from me to help save the world, and yet another letter asking me to leave the house, on account of the road. They both go in the kindling.

Persephone

The gate creaks open. Someone is in my mother's garden.

I climb down the attic ladder, go into the study, look out. No moon, only a thin starlight, by which I can see the garden gate is shut. But there, by the wall, something, someone, skirting the edge of the first field. A fox? A man? Maybe one of the road people, as my mother calls those trying to stop the road from being built. She told me she has watched them from this window, walking past the house to reach the village.

I perch for a moment on the edge of my mother's chair.

I don't usually come in here, both because this is my mother's room and because it was once mine. My bed was by this window.

I would lie and hear things in the fields. At bedtime, my mother told me the story of the corn. She made me a necklace of corn kernels. She said I was her precious corn child, that I too would grow tall and true. One night I asked her how she knew.

'Because everything grows up towards the light,' she said. She stroked my hair.

'Mama, is light inside dark or dark inside light?' I asked.

'What do you mean, you funny girl?'

'Does day swallow night or night swallow day? Which is inside which? Did light grow in the tummy of the dark like I grew inside you?'

'They are evenly matched, day and night, turning round one another. Part of the great pattern of things, which you are part of too. Light and shade need each other as you need sleep. Go to sleep, now.'

She kissed my eyes shut. I listened to her stride out onto the landing, then down the stairs, two at a time.

I looked into the dark behind my eyes. It had loops left in it from the light and other shapes: tiny specks and grains of different darks pressed against each other. I opened my eyes back onto the dark within the room — it had swallowed the chair, my corn dolls. Under the blanket, it had taken my legs, arms, stomach. When I held my breath, I could hear it breathing. One day I feared the dark would take me and never give me back. My mother said night and day were equal, but night seemed to me the greater.

I remember the day I decided to find out how much my mother knew. I hid her soup ladle in the cellar. I slid my hand down between the wine barrels, left it there against the cold mud floor. It was dark in the cellar. The dark went down into the earth. It stretched far over me at night. It was inside me. The dark was older, deeper, higher than the light. When the sun went down, the truth came out: dark never receded, day simply obscured it. My mother never found the ladle.

But I did follow the corn up, tall and true — she was right about that. My body changed. Breasts budded, hips curved, limbs lengthened. It felt like a spell of growth my mother had cast on me. Best of your father and your mother, people said. His hair and height. Her eyes and mouth. The boys admired me. I felt afraid — my mother had taught me to mistrust men. 'They can eat you alive,' she would say. 'But don't worry. I won't let anyone eat you.'

I remember a feast, not long before my first blood came, when my father paid us a visit. We heard his voice from fields away. The mighty Zeus, gracing us as a guest. My mother rolled her eyes, made light of it, but I could tell she was tense. The air was thick, the heat heavy.

My father sat beside the fire in the front garden, legs stretched out, thick as tree trunks. I felt his eyes on me. His big sky-blue eyes that I used to worry were following me from above. But in that moment, I understood that he had never watched me, that this was the first time he had noticed me. He called me to him, lifting a golden arm, and when I hesitated — 'There's nothing to fear,' he boomed.

I went, obedient. I stood before him and he slid his hand

22

under my chin, lifted my face. I remember the weight of his thumb across my cheek, the prickling heat of my skin, reddening under it. He smiled. 'Good girl,' he said. He stroked my hair, that was like his, then let me go. As I turned away, I saw my mother at the front door, scowling.

A storm broke that night. I was already in bed, watching the lightning out of the window, when my mother came to me. She sat by me, here in the dark, as she used to do when I was small.

'You awake?'

'Yes.'

'I want you to promise me something.'

She slid down and knelt beside me so that she was level with my face.

'If your father ever touches you, you come straight to me and tell me. You understand?'

I nodded.

'Good girl,' she said, kissed my eyes that were like hers, and left the room. I lay, listening to the rain.

I stand, shake off the memory. There is no one in the field now. I go back to the attic.

But I cannot sleep. As soon as I shut my eyes, in the dark behind them, I sense my husband. He will not stay buried this year. I try to think up, not down, imagining the sky man, but that takes me to the woods, and there, my husband is waiting for me once again. So I think back instead to when I did not know him, to when he was a story only. Of all the men I was meant to fear, he was the most terrible.

He was a part of every childhood, the man, god, monster under the earth who would come and catch us if we misbehaved. He

23

was the King of the Dead and the richest man alive for he owned everything beneath us: not only root, worm, dirt, but gold, silver, diamond. They said he wore neither wool nor cotton, nothing grown under the sun, but rather jewel-encrusted armour, thick with crystals. His strength must be immense, we thought, if he was clad in clothes of stone.

My friends and I would lie by the tall, green stalks on the edge of the fields and picture Hades reclining in his palace on a throne far under us, while the dead mined the earth, building a shore of precious pebbles at his feet. We wondered what he dined on. We knew the rules — eat the food of the dead and you were as good as dead, stuck down there forever. Hellen thought he ate grubs and worms. Zoe said he ate jewels. Phoebe, my best friend, thought if it was jewels, he would like diamonds most. But I thought he'd feast on rubies. My mother had a pair of ruby earrings that she kept in a box in her bedroom, shiny red teardrops. Once they must have lain on Hades' shore — by right they should be his. I was afraid he might come looking for them. My mother laughed when I warned her and hung them from her ears, ready for the evening's guests. But she did not like to speak of him.

I found a pigeon in the back garden one day, headless, flies buzzing in and out of its red, open neck. Grey feathers lay scattered on the grass beside the apple tree. 'Fox got it,' my mother said. She dug a grave for it behind the well, under the pine tree that stood there then. My mother eased the body onto her spade, lowered it into the earth. I squatted beside the hole.

'Will it go to Hades? Will it be able to fly again? How will it fly under the earth?'

'It will find a way,' my mother said.

It was strange to see how still the pigeon was as the earth fell on it. I tried to imagine it swooping through the sky. The air was filled with fluffy white seeds, floating upwards in the heat. I wondered if the dead drifted in the darkness underground like the seeds did in the light.

'Mama, will I die?'

She finished filling in the hole, patted the ground flat, so no one would know we had hidden a bird there. She lifted me onto her lap.

'No. You come from an immortal line.'

'But I was born. You told me. I came out of you.' I touched her tummy. 'Doesn't that mean I could die?'

She frowned. I liked it when she frowned. I ran my fingers along the brown, bumpy lines that crossed her forehead.

'There'll never be a time when you won't exist again.'

'Why not?'

'I won't allow it,' she said, smiling. I rested my head against her chest, watched the white seeds float across the well, over the wall, into the meadow.

'But will I grow old?'

'Yes — over a long, long time. Mortals age fast — the gods do so much more slowly.'

'What about you? Could you die?'

'No,' she said, impatient suddenly.

She put me back onto the earth, took hold of the spade, stood up.

'We've given the bird to the ground. Now, you leave the dead alone.' She strode up the garden. I ran after, daring one more question.

'What's Hades like?'

My mother frowned again. She swept her hand over the

garden, made the seeds swirl in the air. 'I wouldn't give a grain of what I have up here for what he has. Now come, we've the living to look after — there's a pile of corn to grind in the kitchen.'

But still I wondered. Phoebe and I would go down to the river's edge behind the house and look for special stones, pretend we had found treasures washed up there. The wet stones glistened like real riches, but by the time I had carried my hoard home they were dried out and dull. I was disappointed but glad too. I had taken nothing of Hades'. There was no reason he should come up to take me. And he didn't.

In the end it was I who went to look for him.

3

PERSEPHONE

'Want to come?' my mother asks, from the doorway.

I am sat at the kitchen table with a book. I look up at her. We both know I will say no. I hibernate all spring and summer long.

'No, thanks.' I go back to my book — a murder mystery I found in the bathroom.

'Well, have a lovely afternoon then.'

I watch her through the front window, as if she were someone else's mother. She looks smaller than the mother I know. The hem of her skirt snags on one of the rose bushes and she has to stop, bend, disentangle it. She waves back at me. A bright smile. Then off she goes, left across the fields towards Whitecross Green Wood. The wild garlic is starting to come up, and it is best to pick it early. Usually, she would go to Prattle Woods, but she wants to avoid the road people.

I try to read. The house's smell, my mother's — dried lavender, yeast, sweat, sadness — seems to intensify now that she has left. On the table the vase of primroses, the stacked lunch plates, watch me, as if they had been set to guard me while she's out. I put the book down, go along the hall to the front door.

The bleeding and the cramps are gone, but they have left me feeling empty, light, and I am restless. Slowly, I fetch my coat. I pause.

Birdsong. Distant traffic. The quiet house. My heart. Hunger. Not for wild garlic. Not for food. I cannot sit and read all afternoon.

I go out of the door, through the front garden, open the gate. I do what I never do now. I step outside my mother's home. I go straight over the first field towards Prattle Woods.

I walk this way each autumn. I walked this way when I came to look for Hades. I had no idea who he was. I had found a strange man near the well at one of my mother's parties. Today I simply need air, and to feel myself in motion, to feel even this much simple capability.

I step into the woods. I half expect there to be no one about, because the sky man seems like an image from a dream and because, if my mother is right, the road and road people are a lot of fuss about nothing. Nonsense, best ignored. I look ahead at the netted trees. The woods are eerie without birdsong. But then, from nowhere, a song starts up. Not birds. Voices.

> Sumer is icumen in
> Lhude sing cuccu!
> Groweþ sed
> And bloweþ med
> And sprinþ þe wode nu
> Sing cuccu!

There they are, through the trees — the road people. There must be about thirty of them. They are gathered round a fire. I stop, hand to the trunk of a young oak, breath held.

They are a strange mix: some look like the walkers I watch from the house, crossing the fields, in waterproofs and stout boots. Others could be in their living room, lounging about in sweatshirts and leggings, still others might have stepped off a city street, with jeans and jackets, one man in a waistcoat. They are different ages too — many are young, but there are some older ones. Children. A small woman with a baby.

I walk one tree closer.

Together they sing of summer coming in, but there are other seasons and moods among them. Many seem sad or exhausted, slumped by the fire, resting chins on knees. Around them, high up in the trees, are their nests — the odd shelters I saw before. Beyond them are the netted trees. Between these, startling amid the quiet colours of the wood, men in bright yellow jackets and red hats stand on guard.

I keep measuring my way in trees. Another tree nearer. Then another.

A tall woman with purple hair and ears full of silver is blowing on a whistle — she is wearing a harness, clips hanging from it that clink as she moves. Another woman, in a cap, is sitting up on a log, holding an instrument shaped like the lutes people used to play when I was a girl.

Next to the lute woman, I see the sky man. He is kneeling on the ground, a drum between his knees, hands flying fast to pull the song along. Even in kneeling he is tall.

I am terrified and transfixed, as I was years before when I came to look for Hades. I should leave, as I should have done back then. I am about to go when one of the children runs around the group — the sky man looks up, out, and sees me. He sends one long arm up, missing a beat to beckon me over.

My heart sounds loud as the drum and faster, as I walk towards him and sit down on a plank around the fire.

> Sing cuccu nu. Sing cuccu.
> Sing cuccu. Sing cuccu nu!

The cuckoo song ends and a new one starts up, led by the

woman with the lute, a song about the road, the greed of it, the speed of it, the trees they are felling and the lies they are telling about where this new road will lead. Next to me the sky man taps out the beat quietly.

There is nothing of sky about him. He has thick legs and long arms, and drawings of branches snaking up his neck, leaves crowding round his collar bones. He has a big wiry beard, but his head is bald. His eyes are hazel. From each of his ears hangs a black ring. The holes from which they hang are stretched so that I can see a scrap of light through them — a spyhole in each ear. He wears a long brown coat, big walking boots, and a harness like the woman with the whistle. He stops drumming, stretches out a boot to push the charred edge of a log further into the fire.

Looking at him, I think of a much smaller animal — a field mouse — how it trembles, how it cannot hold life inside itself without quivering. He does not quiver, but the life seems to pour off him. I see it in all of them — life pouring off them as simply as heat and light pour off the fire. They take it for granted. They have come here to save a wood, but they do not seem to notice that they are like a forest themselves — complex, upright, undeniable.

A blackened kettle on a stand starts to steam. The man in the waistcoat takes it off. He kneels and pours out teas which are passed round. A woman on my left with henna-ed hair and an eyebrow ring passes me a mug. They go on with their song, their tea-drinking, fire-watching. My mother used to have fires like this in her front garden. Across the circle one woman is lying with her head in the lap of another — I remember Phoebe and me lying like that. I remember the crackle and hiss of flame on wet wood, the smell of smoke, the sting in my eyes. And

I think again of the night I left the fire, went round the back, saw a man beside the well, and how I slipped back to the fire later, with a hammering heart and a white flower made of bone hidden in one hand.

The road song comes to an end and people cheer, clap. I clap too. The sky man turns to me.

'So, you here for the protest or the party?' he asks me. 'Got anyone who can vouch for you?' His voice is deep, gentle, and angry.

'Give it a break!' the henna-ed woman says. 'Ignore him, he needs to chill out,' she tells me.

'How can I? Look at them!' He tips his head back so that he can point with his beard over at the bright-yellow men between the trees, 'Even on a flippin' Sunday!'

'Roll him a spliff,' someone calls from across the fire.

'Fuck off!'

I hold on to my hot mug. The sky man covers his bald head with both of his big hands, looks down. I don't know what to say. I am out of practice with talking to anyone but my mother, or my husband. Protest or party? My mother is the one who holds the parties.

'I'm here for the protest,' I tell him.

'Yeah, me too. But I'm tired of being watched. Even at night. There's CCTV cameras tucked into those nets. And someone was poking about the camp at two a.m. — a pig, I reckon.'

'Let's get on,' the henna-ed woman says, standing up. She turns to the group, 'Who's coming tweeting?'

'I will, but my phone and binoculars are at the back of the bender,' a thin man in waterproofs says. He gets up and steps along a plank that leads from behind the fire to a large shelter on the ground.

'You coming?' the woman asks the sky man. He shakes his head.

'I want to sort the walkway between us and Big Ben's — it's too slack.'

'Okay. Do you want to come?' and I realise that she is asking me.

'No thanks,' I say, because I do not know what going tweeting means.

'Right. See you later.' The henna-ed woman and the others go.

The sky man is standing now, tightening his harness, ready to move on.

'Which is your tree house?' I ask him, though I think I know.

'That one,' he says, pointing to the oak near which I saw him two weeks ago.

'Is everyone here living in the trees?'

'Nope — only ten of us.'

'What about the others?'

'Day visitors. People here to help — and, at the weekend, to party. We get all sorts. Every kind of nutter.' He is looking down at his harness as he talks, unscrewing a clip, snapping it open. 'And you? Where you from?'

'My mother lives in a house about four fields away, past Noke, on the way to Islip.'

He looks up. 'What, the big old one, on its own, near the river?'

I nod.

He shakes his head, 'You're still there?!'

'In spring and summer.'

'No, I mean they haven't turfed you out?'

'Why would they?'

'You're right on the route. Look,' he says, taking out his phone, squatting down beside me. He presses it to life. On the screen is an image of a bird caught in a net. It is a song thrush, upside down, each thin pink claw splayed, tangled in white threads, its small sharp beak stretched open, its wings fanned out in an effort to fly away.

'That's what Nonny's off to do,' he says. 'It's like Newbury in the nineties, only now we're tweeting more than the birds. Hashtag "nests not nets" and "free the trees" — search and you'll see …'

I feel sick. And thrilled. To be sitting here, to have this big man with tree branches growing up his neck and daylight showing through his ears be talking to me. Not because I am Persephone, the daughter of Demeter, bringer of spring. Not even because I am beautiful, which is why, over the years, most men have talked to me — even the workman who came to install electricity at my mother's house struck up a conversation because he liked my looks, was hopeful, hungry. This man is not hungry, or not for me anyway. He is more angry than hungry. More sad than hopeful. He has followed these things — his rage, his grief — and they have led him, not down, but up, out here to these woods. My woods. I have never cared much for this world — that's been my mother's job — but this is my place of arriving, of leaving. This is the way I have walked for years, with only these trees to watch.

'Look,' the man is saying. 'Here.' He has pulled a map up on his phone. His finger points to a thick red line that runs from Pennywell Wood, through Woodeaton Woods to Prattle Woods, then on across the fields. 'Your house is there, right?' he says, stopping on the red line, near the river.

'Yes.'

'I'm amazed they haven't evicted you already.'

'My mother will never leave.'

'Wish it worked like that.'

'What do you mean?'

'Compulsory purchase orders.'

'What?'

'They'll force you out. Pull down your house to build a thousand more in estates along the route. That's their plan, anyway.'

'They can't force my mother out.'

He scrunches up the left side of his face, half shuts his eye, as if in pain.

'Sorry. Not much to be done. And lots to be done — so far, we've delayed them by two months and cost them a couple of million.'

I nod.

'Come and help out,' he says. 'There's shitloads needs doing.'

I nod again. I hold still, because I don't want this conversation to be over and I don't want the things I am hearing in it to be true.

'Not sure I asked your name …' he says.

I hate saying my name, but I am not good at lying.

'Persephone.'

'Snow,' he says, putting his phone back in his pocket and offering a hand. I am glad to take it — I want to thank him for having a name at least as strange as mine. I like this odd formality, shaking hands under the trees. I can feel the callouses on his palm.

'Snow?'

'Simon White — nicknamed Snow White, seeing as I'm clearly the fairest of them all.' He tugs at his beard, raises his eyebrows.

'I'd best get on, or rather up,' he says.

'Thanks for showing me the map.'

He nods, 'See you again, then.'

He turns, walks off towards his tree. I walk away from the fire, towards the fields, then stop, lean against a birch trunk, look back. I watch the sky man called Snow climb up his tree. He is clipped on to a knot on a thin rope, with a separate loop attached for his foot. He slides the knot on the rope up as high as he can reach while his weight is on his foot, transfers his weight to the line, dangling for a moment, hoists the foot strap higher, steps into it, slides the knot up, over and over. Up he goes, twisting slowly as he rises. Not flying, not nimble, but graceful somehow, all six feet of him, long limbs hanging and spinning, creaking up and away from the earth into air, until at last, he is level with his platform in the oak. A gangly astronaut of earth, not trying to escape it but to protect it. Nothing like my husband, who is small, quick, full of hard-edged detail. And as I walk back out of the woods, I break my rule again and think of him.

On the night when I met him, I thought he was a boy at first.

I had finished offering the tender meats to my mother's guests. I had filled up their cups. I had eaten nothing, drunk nothing, and was proud of this. I left the fire at the front, wandered round the house to the back and saw a pale shape, flickering to and fro across the path, like a moth attracted by the lanterns placed along it. Now it was beneath the pine tree. Now by the well. I saw it stoop to look into the water, then up to the house, to me. A slight figure — it must be a child.

It was no one I recognised. I turned to fetch my mother, ask her about the gatecrasher, the troublemaker. But as if I were the moth and he the light, I felt the pull of him across the dark. So I walked down the garden, towards the well, found him beneath the apple tree.

He was not a boy. He was a man. Like none I knew. The field labourers were big, broad-backed men. My father too was huge. Then there were the skinny village boys who had grown too fast, lanky-legged, little heads on long bodies. But this man was short, wiry. He sat cross-legged, head bent, hands busy. He wore a tattered leather tunic, no shirt or shoes, trousers made of furs.

It felt like coming upon a deer within the woods — I did not want to startle him. I dropped down onto my hands and knees and, quiet as I could, crawled under the apple leaves. I drew close enough to see his breathing — fast, like a baby's. Close enough to see the skin on his arms, smeared with earth yet underneath, white as a root. He had an animal stench. He never looked up. I crouched, still as stone, my heart sprinting.

I knew he should not be here. Nor should I.

He was making something in a little hollow in the earth. His fingers were deft and agile, his hands fine and delicate, like a woman's but not like my mother's. She had wide palms, thick fingers. I studied him: he used his hands like eyes and made me use my eyes like hands, feeling for the shape of him, the ridge of his jaw, the ledge of his shoulders. He was odd, angular. But I wanted to touch him.

Then he lifted his head, stared straight at me, as if he had known I was there all along, so that I was the startled one. His eyes were small, barely open, his face jagged, his left cheekbone higher than the right. I looked down, saw what he was making. He had taken the bones from the meats my mother had prepared, fitted them together, bound them with grasses to form little sculptures. He lifted one for me to see — a star, made from a cluster of wishbones. He picked up another bone, drew out a knife, began to whittle. White fragments flew from his blade. I watched, barely breathing.

I loved his care, his artistry, so different from my mother's extravagant generosity. He wasted nothing. I wanted to be lifted like that, studied like that, crafted by those hands. I fell for him.

'Here,' he said, and his voice was crackly as dried corn husks. 'For you.' He balanced it on his hand — a vertebra shaped like a flower. I stretched out and took it up. The bone dug into my palm.

I did not know falling in love would feel so much like falling. Phoebe had talked about it more like flying, something free and light. But what I felt was a dropping with nothing to hold on to. In that moment, I wanted to die. I wanted this man so keenly that dying seemed the only thing I could name big enough to hold the want.

Before anyone could stop me, I leant forward, and I kissed him. He tasted metallic, like the cool water in the iron spring beyond the village, where the water ran red with rust. He looked so sharp-edged I was surprised how soft his lips were, and I thought of how the hard wood in the fire could turn to silky ash. He reached out, gripped my wrist.

'Persephone!'

My mother was calling from the back steps. I pulled away, wanting to protect him, my discovery of him. But he was faster than my fear. He had let me go, was already by the well. I watched him slide onto the wall of it, swing his legs over, disappear.

37

I ran over. Far down something shone in the dark — his eyes? The water? Could he swim from the river underground to the one behind the house? Or would he hide in the well shaft and climb out when my mother and the other guests had gone?

My mother was behind me. She slipped her hand over my shoulder. For a moment we stood together, looking down the well.

'What are you doing?'

I shrugged, gripped the bone flower hidden in my hand, said nothing.

'Come on. Phoebe asked me where you were. Come back to the fire and have something to eat.'

She led me up to the house, her arm around me, her body beside mine, sure of herself as ever.

The next morning, I went searching for him.

I went and peered over the well's edge, let the bucket down, imagined him dropping too. I pulled up water, clear, innocent, but it must know where he had gone. I dipped in my hand and drank.

As my mother lifted platters, left from the feast, out of the long grass, I sat on the doorstep, the bone flower in my hand. I had found a length of leather in my mother's mending basket. I threaded it through the bone and hung it round my neck, under the string of corn kernels, under the wreath of roses and poppies my mother had made for me that morning. The bone flower swung beneath my dress, against my sternum, bone against bone, light and hard. I felt alive and dangerous. I knew nothing would ever be the same again. I wanted the morning to go on forever, a forever in which everything was always on the point of change.

I went to the river. I felt like I was solving a crime, though nothing had yet been taken, and no one had yet died. I looked among the reeds along the bank. No sign. The bone flower pressed against me. It burned. My bones burned. For whom? What was his name? This no-man man. The first I had wanted. The small, ugly stranger with beautiful hands. Who was he? Nymph? Animal? Artist? God? Someone different. Someone true.

I searched all day. The sun was setting when at last I came to the woods. The last of the light had left the ground and was turning the treetops gold. I doubted that I would ever find him now. I came to a young yew in the centre of the woods. I stopped, listened, waited.

He was not there. I leant against the yew and thought of how I used to lean against my mother's body while she was busy talking. I looked down at mine, dressed in poppies and roses, a little girl. I felt ashamed. The woods went cold. Best go back home. I turned to go, and the earth split open at my feet.

4

DEMETER

I carry the beetroot seedlings out into the back garden. The broad beans are in the pocket of my apron. The sky is a blank blue, as if it has never thought or seen anything bad in all its time of arching over us. It doesn't fool me, but I'm glad of the dry weather. I never used to start the beetroot indoors, but these days they don't stand a chance, otherwise. It's not the late frosts anymore but the relentless rain — they get washed away. So I seed them by the kitchen sink. But they're ready for the deep, wide world now. Two little green leaves, one ruby red stem — a clue to the fat purple root to come. 'Early Wonder,' this kind is called — they give them some daft names, but I like this one.

I kneel down, like I'm in prayer, but I'm not sending anything up into that too-blue sky — I send my wishes down. I don't need a radio — I bury my feet in the veg patch to hear my news. But I never dig down as far as my daughter goes. I listen to the roots, but at a certain depth they stop. They travel for miles sideways but not down, which is why I was frantic when she first went missing, for I could hear no news of her.

I scoop out hollows, slide the seedlings in, fold the earth back round them so they look like they have always been there, small and proud, red and green. Next to them I do a row of beans. My fingers aren't green — they're grey. Earth in the lines on my palm — my future looks black, yet fertile. At the end of the row, the blackbird finds a worm, pulls it up, eyes me at an angle, then he is off to the nest in the honeysuckle. I heard his alarm call before dawn. I was worried there might be a fox after the hens. I'll check on them once I've got these in the ground. I cover the beans, ready for their secret change. The blackbird chirrups loud and sharp, and I look up.

Persephone is standing at the end of the row. I've not seen her yet this morning. This is our rhythm once she's back — I get up at dawn, make the bread, coffee, start on the garden. She appears when she likes, nine, ten, maybe even midday. I kneel up — impossible not to be glad to see her, my girl in jeans and a yellow blouse. She's frowning.

'Morning, love.'

'Morning,' she says.

'You going in?' I ask, nodding down the garden to the pond.

'Not now.'

I wait. She looks at the seedlings.

'Watering can's right behind you.'

She turns, picks it up, goes to the tap by the back door, returns, one arm long and shuddering with the weight. She never was a strong girl, except in will. She sets down the can.

'Thanks.' I start to slosh the water out, darkening the earth along the row of beets. She watches, puffing hairs out of her face that are barely there.

'What's troubling you?'

'The road.'

'Thought I told you not to worry about that.'

'But —'

'But what? I said I can manage things,' I straighten up. The empty can swings in my hand. 'If I must.'

I pass Persephone the can. She takes it, does not move. I look at her, rest the backs of my hands on my hips, shake my head, vexed by her, by the scolding mother she can still make me become.

'Listen, love, men — and it's always the men — have been building roads and houses round here for years. If I got involved in every one of their mad plans, I'd never have time for my beans. I'd never have time for you.'

'But this is different.'

'And why's that?'

'You've got eviction letters in your kindling basket.'

'Best place for them.'

'You can't just burn them away.'

The skin on her neck is reddening like the stems of the beets. She hated her blushes as a child and that only ever made them worse. Now the redness irritates me too — shame has no place here, in my garden.

'I am not moving from this house. From this spot!' I point to the earth, between the beans and beets, 'And no one is going to make me. Understand?'

She looks young, afraid. I feel old, impatient. I take the can back from her and go fill it myself. I turn the tap on full and the water hits the metal bottom of the can so hard that it sprays up on my forehead. I cross back, dripping. Persephone stands at the end of the row in my way. I push past her, start on the beans.

'I went to the woods yesterday,' she says.

'Did you?' I pull up. Every summer, I try to persuade her to go out. I should be pleased. I am not. 'So that's what this is about. Those crackpots living in the trees, filling you with woe and worry.'

'I saw a map of the route — it goes right through here. They're trying to stop it — you should help them.'

'I'm busy.' I tip the can, watch the arc of water spill onto the earth.

'They're going to fell the trees, ruin the fields. Don't you care anymore?'

'And since when did you care so much?' I straighten up again, look over at the corner of the plot, remembering the seedlings and the sapling that she failed to tend. 'Anyway, you know I gave up farming seventy, eighty years back, when the machines arrived, when they started drilling the fields. Drilling, as if seeds were screws!'

Persephone is staring past my shoulder, like she did as a child. It always bothered me.

'I thought you loved the land,' she says, still staring.

I glance behind me, towards the hens — there's nothing there.

'Look at me,' I tell her, and she does. 'I do love the land. But I love you more. As long as I have you, whatever nonsense they decide to build, spring will come, we'll go on.' I empty out the last of the water. Look back at her. 'I'd risk the world for you — I did before.'

'Maybe you shouldn't,' she says, the red spreading up into her face, her hands curling into fists. 'Maybe you never should have.'

I stare at my sullen, stubborn girl on the edge of my veg patch. It's just like the old times, but not the good times. The times that turned us both cruel. The skin around the edges of her eyes, near her temples, looks taut — a sign only a mother could spot. I think of the vacuum cleaner that a door-to-door salesman showed me this winter — press a little button and its electric lead whipped inside, sucked in at speed. Told him I'd stick to my dustpan. But she can pull herself inside like that. I

43

hate it. Because however fast she goes, it takes an age to reel her out again. Years.

She juts her jaw forward.

'I think you're losing touch,' she says.

I should leave it. But I can't. I never could.

'And I think that you have no idea. You don't live here. You only visit for the summer months, and then you leave!'

'But it's real!' Her voice is turning shrill. 'You've got to do something! The road is real!'

'So are all the other bloody roads they've built. So are all the extra shops, the houses they put beside them. All real! Grand! Super! And who do you think is going to last longer? Who do you believe in more? The road? Or me?'

Now I've done it.

Made her cry.

I did not mean to shout at her — I never did before either. But something about her drawing in, jutting out, made me snap, made me remember a time that still hurts, when I could have snapped her. Her wrists, ankles.

She has her face in her hands, at the other end of the beans.

I walk along the track of darkened earth towards her. I take her fine fingers in my grubby ones.

'I'm sorry,' I say. 'It's not your fault — the world being such a mess.'

Her hands are cold — they're always colder than mine.

'It's okay,' she says, her eyelids sliding down, blinking me away.

But it isn't. She has gone limp, instead of taut. I don't know which is worse.

She pulls her hands away and turns, walks down the garden to the pond.

44

Best give her time. Though this is my time with her, and I am jealous of every moment of it that is taken from me.

We used to argue. We rowed often in those months before her disappearance, when she was no longer a girl, but barely yet a woman. We rowed at her full moon feast, after her bleeding came. I could not find her as the guests arrived — she should have been there to greet them. I wanted to show her off, my best harvest yet. I was not worried then but furious.

I found her in the end, hiding in the cellar, down between the barrels. 'I don't feel like feasting,' was the only reason that she gave. It was not long after that she began to starve herself.

And now, this pulling away from me again. A row over a foolish road.

I should check on the hens. I take the watering can back to the tap near the steps and swap it for the egg basket. I walk along the path to the right of the veg patch, down to their enclosure. I can hear them chucking as I approach so I know all is well. They run towards me as I round the bend by the fruit bushes, desperate for their seed, pecking through the wire by the gate.

My hand is already on the latch when I see the fox. Laid in the grass on its side. Sharp face and ears. Red fur, white belly, ruffled by the breeze. Dead. I kneel. It's a cub — no more than a month old. It should still be with its mother, underground. The hens keep pecking at the gate, no idea of danger near. I've had a fox get the hens before, and they're savage. Blood, guts, and feathers across the coop. I'm glad they are untouched, but what got the fox?

The roadwork? Have they started digging?

Or was the creature chased up by something already underground?

It is unmarked. Not killed by another animal.

And how did it get here?

I go still as the fox, thinking of the answer.

But — if it is Hades — what does he mean by this?

To frighten me? To threaten? To tell me death is at my door? Whose?

It is a cub — is this about my young? Has he come for her? Now? In spring?

I look towards the fields, where the corn once grew, to the woods, where the road people are, where Hades may be again.

5

DEMETER

This is not the first time that men have come to fell the trees near here. Not by a long way.

Hundreds of years before Persephone was born, the woodlands were vast, and I had a sacred grove behind the house. The villagers from near and far would bring offerings to lay beneath the trees. One in particular — a great oak, thick-girthed, bark running like muscle in a swerving pattern from the ground — became my tree. People climbed it to tie coloured cloths to its branches as thanks for my kindness and my care of them and in the hope that I might bless their harvests again. I liked to walk in its shade, to look up at the mosaic of leaves pressed into the sky, to give a kind of thanks and prayer myself for the wonder of it all.

I was coming back from the fields, carrying sacks of corn, when I heard the blows and then the shouting from behind the house. The voices sounded hard, and the blows were rhythmic. I left the grain, spilling from the sacks, and ran. Kicked off my sandals to cover the ground faster, feet flying over the field, up the garden path, down the flagstones in the hall, out into the long grass of the back garden, fear in my belly, my hands forming into fists. Past the well I flew, out through the gate, and stopped.

The trees were felled. All but my oak. The sky had never looked ugly until then, an eyesore above the trees, lying how they never should, their canopies at my level, which only that morning had swayed high.

Years upon years it had taken them to grow that tall. We take our motion for granted — running hither and thither over the land — but for a tree to go somewhere they have to grow there. With more patience and persistence than any man or woman these trees had budded, flowered, fruited, thickened, to make their way down through the earth and up through the air, marking their passage in their bodies, from the seed of their departure to the point of their arrival at the sharp, bright edges of their leaves. Now a few blows had brought them down.

The men stood where the trees had, axes in their hands. One in their midst was shouting at them to fell the final tree — the oak, thick as ten men, tall as twenty, festooned with its offerings to me. The others shook their heads. No, they would not fell that tree. They were frightened by its size, its majesty, its meaning, and by me. They saw me now, one by one, as I stood staring at what they had done to my woods without my permission. But the man in charge — Erysichthon was his name — he did not care. The sight of me enraged him. Everyone loved me. Everything loved me — grain, flower, bird. Someone was bound to resent it, to hate instead of love. I had yet to learn how far that hate could go, how deep. For now, this seemed to me its limit. Erysichthon snatched an axe from the nearest man and set it to the oak. I asked him to stay his hand. He did not. Like a mad man he struck at that oak. He was already eaten up with greed.

'I am building a palace,' he cried as the axe flew. 'Inside my palace I will have feasts. Every day!' The axe cut into the trunk. 'I shall live like a king!'

I looked up at the horrible emptiness of sky that he had made behind my house, and I placed it in his stomach. It only took a moment. No one even noticed. I slid a little disc of aching air inside him that he would never fill.

'I will want for nothing,' he called out, hacking at the huge oak.

'You will want everything, and it will be for nothing,' I replied. And then I turned away from that terrible scene, though I see it still behind my eyes.

'Bring me some bread and drink!' I heard him scream.

That was just the start. I never saw him again, but I heard how it went. How he demanded feast upon feast but still was hungry. How he sold everything he had — even his daughter — to fill the emptiness inside him, and how each meal only made it worse. He ate himself in the end, gnawing at each limb, till there was nothing left.

I thought of Erysichthon when Persephone began to starve herself — how he had eaten everything and yet was never full, and how my girl ate nothing and seemed well satisfied by this.

Nothing has never satisfied me. I want to be able to hold what I believe in — I'm a god with little faith. 'You've got to do something,' Persephone said over the beans. If Hades is here again, then she is right — my stubborn ways will not be enough to keep us safe — from him, his greed, from the men with their encroaching road. Hades may even have come up here to help them. He would be glad to see me forced out of my home, as that poor fox has been from its. Well, if I am to do something, I best go now.

I bury the fox cub beneath the chestnut, then leave the house at once. I do not plan. Power is not planned. It comes, it rises like sap, steam, smoke. I never planned to bring winter on the world, nor emptiness into Erysichthon's belly. I never planned to turn that boy into a lizard.

Out of the front gate. Across the first field. Over the stile. Three more fields. Over the road through Noke and on past the netted trees of Prattle Woods. He was called Abas, that lizard boy — the little brother of Persephone's best friend. He was insolent to me, opened his hard eyes wide, stuck out his tongue. I saw his tongue sharpen to a point — that was all it took. The change caught like fire, flickering through his face and down his arms. Had I been less hungry, less tired, had my child not been lost, it might not have happened. I walk on.

At last, I come out of Woodmoor Copse and start up Drun's Hill. I hear them before I see them. It's no dawn chorus, rather a midday cacophony: chanting, shouting, a bell clanging, a shrill tune on a whistle, the whine of chainsaws drowning out the rest. And then the creak, crack, and thump of wood breaking, trees falling. I think of sprinting, but I am too old, too tired now for running up a hill.

I reach the edge of Woodeaton Woods at last. I had hoped I would never see this scene again. The trees lie like captured giants. Even within the nets their branches are grand and graceful. A bulldozer, with its heavy metal blade, pushes them to one side. Beyond are the trees, still standing, netted, and between them, on the ground, is the thick, dark-green growth of where the bluebells will be out in another week, if they're allowed.

Men in yellow jackets, white hats, with 'security' spelled out in blue across their backs are trying to clear the woods, not of trees, but people. Others, in red hard hats with visors, carrying chainsaws, are waiting to resume work. A straggling line of road people sit, arms linked, in front of a spinny of silver birches and two big beeches in nets. Up one of the beech trees is a man with a beard, no hair on his head, slashing at the net. A woman with purple hair jigs about with a penny whistle. Another young lad is dressed as Death — or his idea of it —

in long black robes, black hood, carrying a wooden scythe, walking round the site with a bell, calling out like a town crier: 'You are killing the earth and all life on it!'

They're mad — the whole lot of them. But then, I've done all these things before: laid down the law, cleared land, protected and protested. That was what the gods did once.

A young woman in a green raincoat, wide-eyed, earnest, approaches one of the police officers round the edge. 'There's a badger sett over there — work should stop. It should never have started!'

'Appropriate measures have been taken to relocate protected wildlife.' The officer sounds tense, irritated.

'And where are you rehousing a badger family whose sett is a hundred years old — getting them a nice house on the route are you? One of the millions of new homes? Think they'll like that?'

There's another woman — the one with purple hair — being pulled by the security over to the police. The police officer breaks away from the badger woman to step in.

'Get off me! Get your fucking hands off me!'

'Okay, young lady.'

'Don't "young lady" me. Get them to take their hands off me.'

He hangs his helmeted head, delivers his speech, chin down: 'If you continue to obstruct the work, you will be arrested for aggravated trespass and could be charged. If so, bail conditions will be placed on you to prevent you returning to the site.' The woman glares at him, shakes the security man loose, 'Look, I've a right ...' The chainsaws interrupt her.

'What the hell are you doing? You can't start felling now — it isn't clear!' the man up the beech tree shouts down. The

51

chainsaw and security men ignore him. Death stands on the edge and shakes his scythe, records the scene with his phone. 'Security! My arse! There's nothing safe about you. You should have "Danger" written on your backs!'

I look at them, on whatever side, in whatever outfit, standing, sitting, shouting, like trees without roots. None of them belong here. They have the curse of Erysichthon already. I feel the emptiness in them, the exhaustion. I feel worn out, too.

Then a single, slender silver birch tree falls. It narrowly misses the beech with the man in it. I see the silent shock move through the men and women. It is like a wave. It has the same rhythm as the falling tree, sweeping through the air, smashing on the ground. A second birch tips over, thuds down, and in the second of silence after the scream of the saw snaps off, while the shock of the felling still trembles in the air, I stand on the orange stump of an oak, and call out:

'Halt!'

I have a big voice. Everyone turns. The chainsaw men, the security, police, the protesting people, the trees.

'Set down your tools. Take off your helmets. Jackets. Costumes. Go from this wood now. For if you stay, then you will never leave it.'

No one moves. Time thickens. Pools. Begins to set. The security men loosen their grip on the road people. The road people let go of one another and of the trees. A police officer takes off his helmet and holds it, as if at a funeral, waiting for the change to take him. And already, they are changing.

They hesitate, sway. I see their skin start to tighten, harden, their torsos twisting to trunks. Slowly they raise their arms, as if at gunpoint, in confusion and dismay, and as they lift them, they are breaking open, splitting into many arms, odd-angled, new-jointed, fine-fingered. Knuckles swell to buds. They open their mouths to call for help and leaves push out, crowding their faces. A wind whispers through them.

My arms lift too. 'You are arrested,' I cry. 'And you will never leave, for you are wood.'

Suddenly, a badger, blind with terror, tears through the birches, and away between the felled trees.

I stare after it. Another animal from underground. Up here in broad daylight. Is Hades near? Now?

'Fucking hell!'

The bearded man up the tree is shouting, pointing the way the badger went. The other men's arms are down too, and maybe they were never up. I feel suddenly confused. Frightened as the badger. Exposed. As if I am the one who should not be here. I, not belong? On this land? But the men are still men, unchanged. As if their view, their version of things is now stronger than mine. I feel a lurch as though I had missed a step — a drop that I did not see coming.

And now the security men run at the protesting lot, who are running for each other, the trees, the badger. The police are piling in to block their way. And the security men catch and kick the road people because they can. They shove them to the ground, drag them through the mud. They tread on their hands as they try to struggle up.

'Thanks, dear, you just made our job easier!' one of the security men shouts over to me.

'Hear what the old lady said? You're not going anywhere,' another security man tells the woman in the green raincoat as she tries to pull free. There is blood on her face.

'Assault! It's assault,' Death screams, running up to the

police, pointing with his scythe but the police are laughing. Everyone is either crying or laughing. They laugh horribly. Hard enough to shake the fear out of them. They cry hysterically. They are back under their own curse — the one they call the real world.

I stay unmoving in the midst of it, as if the change that I had meant to bring on them I have brought upon myself. Like a felled tree, I feel cut off from everything I know. You are losing touch, Persephone had said. Now I fear she may be right. It could be the world, or it could be me? One of us is turning too fast, tilting too much, the ground rearing up, the sky rushing down. Everything starts spinning.

'Think you've caused enough trouble for one day, grandma.'

A tall security man has his hand under my arm, 'Let's get you off site.'

He drags me from the stump. 'I'd leave the protesting to the young next time, eh?'

'Let me go.' I say it quietly. He does, but then I need to lean against a tree to balance, and there are none — they've all been felled — so I sit right down on the cleared ground.

'Dear me. Where do you live, lady?' the man asks, bending over me. He is pushing his face up to mine, speaking too loud, too slow, as if I am deaf or daft. I stare at him, say nothing.

'Come on. Let's find out where you live, shall we?'

'Leave me,' I hiss at him. I get to my feet — my anger steadies me. 'I can make my own way home.'

He looks me up and down, decides he has done enough, and goes, glad to be rid of me.

And then another man is coming. The bearded one, who was up the beech, the one who swore when the badger ran.

He is quiet and full of care. 'You okay?'

I look at his bald head, do not answer.

'I think I've met your daughter — is your house in the fields over there?'

I want him to leave me too. I want every one of them out of these woods. Off this land. Away from me and my daughter. How dare he claim to know her!

'Shall I walk you back?'

'Be gone,' I spit. I shoo him off, like I shooed off the boys that gathered round Persephone when she was young. I flap my arms as if I were a crow. Let them think I am mad. A mad old lady. As long as they leave us alone. As long as everything that's underground stays there. As long as badgers do not bolt into the day, and Hades never climbs up here again.

6

DEMETER

'Where did you go?'

Persephone is on the front doorstep, wrapped in a towel, angry, anxious.

'Just the village,' I say and smile. It is not hard to smile at her — the smile is not a lie. She nods.

'You going in the pond?' I ask.

She nods again, moves away into the house, towards the back door, but leaves the front one open.

Now that I am home, the dizziness has gone, the shakes too, though they have left a new thing, under my ribs, lower than my heart, a seed of something I don't want to grow — doubt.

Perhaps it was there, quietly growing already. Pernicious as bindweed, thriving in dark and damp conditions. The problem is my power never flashed from my hands like her father's bolts of fire, designed for everyone to see. My power came up from my feet. It was simple, like breathing, nothing that needed effort. And because of this, because it unfolded like the leaves, it is hard now to understand that it might be gone.

But perhaps things have changed — the changing has changed. Boy to lizard, woman to reed, men into trees. Such changes are considered childish now, the domain of fairy tales. After the cold came, the clay of people hardened. Dreams are as fluid as they ever were, but the things men and women have agreed upon as real have set hard, like the pavements they brought to the village sixty years ago, the tarmac they use to build their roads. Nothing can transform in such conditions. People's dreams are trapped like fish under the ice in winter. 'Reinventing yourself' is the word used nowadays, instead of change. It means change your clothes, your hair, your look, which is to say how the world looks at you, not how you look at the world, not who you are. A lady from the village shop passed on her old TV to us. Persephone said I should have it and I agreed, to please her. Its workings seem stranger to me by far than a woman changing to a reed — a tangible thing instead of these high, fast flickerings: words and pictures flung invisibly across the earth, turned into an image caught in glass. People gather round the TV as once they sat around a fire. Now that the heat is in the walls, they do not need a hearth, but still they long to be close to a changing light and to have stories told to them. I see them behind their thin curtains in the village. Persephone likes the shifting pictures, the news. I still prefer the fire. I shiver now. It is warm out, but I feel cold. I take up the latest lot of letters from the council, twist them, stack them in the stove. With my flint, I strike a spark — a little line of household lightning. It is enough. The white pages turn red, then black. I fear that paper to ash is the only transformation I can now perform.

No, flour to bread — that is another. Nettles to soup. Egg whites to meringues. Over the next hour, I do these. Bring out a jar of berries from last year. The meal is ready.

'Supper time,' I call up the stairs. And Persephone comes down.

'How was the pond?'

'Warm,' she says. No more word about the road.

We eat. I still love to watch her eat. She has a big appetite once it comes back — one of those people that finish up great

57

platefuls and yet still be a slip of a thing. Not like me.

I put off going out to shut up the hens. I like the well-fed silence — bigger than both Persephone and me, kind enough to cover up scrutiny, my doubt, our differences. But then I think of the foxes, and rise from the table.

'Just shutting up the hens.'

She nods.

In the house the windows darken quicker than the day. Outside the sky is still deep blue, and the moon is rising, waxing crescent, over the river.

I go down the back path that leads to the hens. I enter their enclosure, look inside the coop. They are roosting, pressed against each other in the dark. I feel in the straw below — take up one egg, laid late in the day, cold now. I lower their wooden door, swivel round the metal hook that keeps them safe from foxes. I think of the cub I found this morning. As I go back out the gate, I glance down to where it lay and freeze.

Like a rock within the dark, crouched low, is a man.

Mud in his hair, on his clothes. Grey skin. His eyes are small slits in his hard face. He opens his mouth and something between a sigh and a groan slips out.

It has been nine thousand years, but I know him. Hades moves an arm to pat the ground beside him.

'You got my gift?' he whispers, his voice, hoarse, crackly, unused to use.

I grip the gate post and my other hand wraps round the egg inside my pocket.

'Go! Now!'

'I've come to take what's mine.'

'I have nothing of yours.'

'Your daughter —'

'Is not yours.'

'My wife —'

'You stole her.'

'She came to me.'

'Get back where you belong.' I speak low and steady, as I would to a stray dog come begging at my door.

'Not without Persephone.'

Even to hear him name her feels like a theft.

I stare down at his hunched body. It is hard to believe he is here, in my garden. I have hated him through a thousand winters. I have made every effort to forget him, yet he has sat, like a toad, a cold, ugly thing under our lives. I am not afraid of dirt or blood. I am not squeamish. But he repels me, makes me faint. And I am never faint. I am firm. I am steady. Till today. Till I grew dizzy in the woods. I lean into the gatepost.

'How dare you come here now!'

'The river under the earth is rising.'

'What business is that of mine?'

'It has flooded. The water is so wide, so swift, I thought Persephone would be unable to cross over to the other shore. And when she did, I feared that she might not return. So, I crossed too. I followed her. And I found that far from losing her, the time has come for her to stay with me for good. Because I know now what is happening up here to flood the world below.' He smiles.

I do not want to know.

'The winters are warming,' he whispers.

I want rid of him.

'You have lost control.'

I hiss at him like a wild cat, but he goes on crouching, goes on whispering.

'You can weep all year long and the buds will still swell. You can rage at the ground and the grain will still grow, or if it does not, it will not be your doing. Fires, floods, storms, droughts, are coming to your precious earth, and your blessings cannot save it. Everyone must flee to me, under the ground.'

Thin and grubby in the darkening garden, this scrawny son-in-law of mine has come to tell me everything I have begun to fear. I would take hold of him, wrestle him, but the thought of touching him sickens me, so I clap him away, as I did the man in the woods today. Quick as a lizard he darts under the fruit bushes, further up the path, and I understand that he too is afraid. In this upper land, even by night, he feels exposed, like a creature that lives under a stone and panics at the awful emptiness when it is lifted.

I start up the path. He is on my veg patch. I come near to him, look down.

'You have been buried too long, brother.' I speak quietly, not wanting Persephone to hear us in the house. 'You cannot surface now, kill a fox, and tell me that you know the world.'

He looks up at me. His crackly voice is soft, 'I know what happened in the woods today.'

I feel cold and hot at once.

'It was you, then — I knew it — sending that poor badger up into the day!'

'The whining saws disturbed me.'

'Too scared to come into the light yourself.'

'I did nothing. I only watched you fail.'

Dizziness turns through me again. To ground myself, I have to stoop and press my hands into the earth beside him. I look into his eyes. His pupils are tight dots, as if after many dark years they have given up on any hope of light and are no longer able to dilate. His irises are blue — same as his brothers, only they won the kingdoms to match that blue, the good prizes. Hades pulled the short straw — Zeus made it so. He was wronged, but long ago and not by me.

As I stare at him, I remember other wrongs as well, other times when things went wrong. I look away, up, as if for help, and see the evening star in the west, above the apple tree. I remember its hard, white light on the night my daughter first went missing. I remember scanning the garden, fields, hoping she was hiding, seeing her nowhere. I remember sitting on the front step, feeling as young as she once was, not understanding how she could not be there. The men waded through the corn, beating it apart, calling her name. And then, when they returned with no news, I saw her everywhere. That night and every night thereafter I saw my daughter in the tangle of the garden roses, the stones of the wall, in the edges of the hawthorn at the field's end.

As I kneel, held fast in the horror of the memory, Hades crawls out from the bushes, and moves up the path. I realise with a start that he is going to the house, to take my daughter now, to leave tonight.

'Stay!' I lift my hand, and though he has come to scorn me, he hesitates, like the men in the woods stayed and swayed at first. I stand, run, level with him. I look into his broken eyes.

'If you break the deal, you will lose any right to her you have.'

'She ate my food.'

'And she has eaten mine in every summer since.'

A light comes on upstairs — Persephone, heading to bed. For a moment we both look up to where she is. He takes another step up the path. He is beside my apple tree, under the sky, exposed again.

'My love for her will outlast this earth.' He speaks softly, and I do not know if he is talking to me, himself or to the night.

'There are no seasons where I am. Every time she leaves, it is as if she goes forever. The river, dead, dark — nothing shows me that she will return. And without her ...' He stops, and now, although he still looks up, his voice hardens and I am sure he speaks to me.

'Without her, the only outlines that I feel are those of rocks. Without her, nothing I touch touches back. Nothing holds me when I hold it, but her. You think you need her. You do not. Spring can come without her. But no life comes to the dark when she is not within it. I have more need of her than you. She is my wife, muse, queen, lover. She is just your child. You should have let her go before. And now you must.'

I am shaken anew. I hate his claim of suffering a greater loss than mine. I do not want to hear his loneliness. I draw close to him again and speak with quiet fury.

'You have no idea what it is to mother. You can understand nothing of tending, caring, growing. You cannot know what would happen to the earth without my blessing.' I no longer know either, but right now, I do not care.

Hades turns away from me, as if to walk towards the house, but he is tense, uncertain — I know whom I must name.

'And what of Zeus?'

He stiffens.

'The deal was his idea. Have you asked him if it can be undone?'

He looks back at me. His face is slow to show anything, but his hands lift, fingers stretched as if to ward off ill. He hates his

62

sky-bright younger brother almost as much as he hates me. And he fears him. For a second, he is lost. A lost, scared boy, the king of gold and dead and dread.

'Prove you have power still,' he says slowly, 'Stop the road, as you failed to do today.'

'I will.'

'And if you cannot — then she is mine.'

'Give me three moons.'

'So long?' He mocks me, but he is trembling.

'By midsummer, I will have stopped the road.'

He gazes up at the lit windows.

'I have waited nine thousand years. I can wait three more little moons,' he tells my daughter, hidden in the house. He looks back at me with angry joy.

Then he turns, sprints over the veg patch, across the garden beyond, light as a pond skater over water, barely bending the grass. He vaults over the wall into the empty fields and I watch him, fast as a fox, as he heads to the hedgerows for cover and is gone.

I stand very still on the dark path. The other night, the night I lost her, is here too, under this one, and every night I have been without her since.

I cannot lose her now, forever. I do not feel dizzy anymore. Nothing is reeling. Everything is sharp and stark. Not because I am calm. Or strong. I feel a terrible fear. White as the moon. Keen as my grief when my girl was gone. What can I do?

I think of Zeus. I used his name — should I call on him? No. I went to him before, when she was missing. I will never forgive him for what he said to me that day.

I cannot ask Persephone. She must not see her mother's fear. And, catching in my throat, there is another fear, one from which I have long hidden, but tonight it must be named: I fear she would be glad to leave me.

I walk onto the veg patch and drop down on my knees for the second time today.

I have been the strong one for so long. The helpless, hungry, sick came to me, queued across my fields. It is horrible now to be the one in need.

I look across at the white blossoms of the apple tree, just opened. They keep on blooming, even in the night. And I must do the same.

I was never worshipped like Zeus, for my tricks, or dramatic transformations. It was a deeper, slower change for which they followed me. I could turn a seed into a meal, put food on tables, fill bellies, sustain lives. And in return the people gave me their allegiance, tied ribbons to my trees. I taught them how to farm — it is my fields that fed their growth, that changed their villages to towns, their towns to cities. Perhaps I can no longer turn a man into a tree, but I can at least remind him of his roots. People still need to eat, no matter how the world is changing. I feel the slight weight of the egg in my pocket. The beets look up at me, orderly, proud. I start to feel more angry than afraid. I bare my teeth, roll up my sleeves. I do not know if it will help, but I must do something, and right now it is the only thing that I can do — what I always did before, what I vowed to do when I fell out from my father's mouth: to feed.

7

PERSEPHONE

'Help me carry these bags to the woods, will you?' my mother calls up the stairs the next morning.

She is standing in the kitchen with four bulging Sainsbury's bags for life and a rucksack.

'What's in them?' I ask, as I come downstairs.

'Flapjacks.'

'Flapjacks?'

'They must be getting hungry out there, working in this wet.'

'Who?'

'Everyone. On the road.'

'What? You're not making flapjacks for the men cutting down the trees?!'

'Why not? It's hungry work.'

'You should be helping the protestors.'

'I've made enough for them as well,' she says, pulling on her raincoat.

'Mother, how does this help?'

'Feeding people is what I do,' she says, smiling, angry. 'Never underestimate the power of a gift of food. Well, don't just stand there. Grab your coat. I can't manage this lot on my own.'

She speaks to me like a little girl. I fetch my coat.

It rained heavily in the night, but it has thinned to a fine drizzle, light against my face as we trudge over the fields with our bags. We come up Drun's Hill to what was Woodeaton

Woods. There is a huge pile of felled trees waiting to be burnt. Road workers in yellow jackets. Two bulldozers. Churned mud, the smell of sawdust, diesel. Bright-orange stumps across the site, an empty sky. I want to scream.

I look for Snow.

He is easy to spot because of his height and his big beard — he stands in a line of protestors, arms linked, pressed against a big oak. I am relieved to see him, as if his presence proves something I need affirmed, is evidence.

'Come on then,' my mother says. She is holding out an old tin of Quality Street sweets. She takes off the lid — inside are golden flapjacks.

She points me towards a security man, as she used to direct me to her party guests.

I go up to the man in his high-vis jacket, clutching the tin. He is standing, bored, wet. I feel shy, ridiculous.

'My mother thought you might be hungry,' I say.

'Oh, thanks,' he says, surprised. 'I was thinking it must be nearly time for a break. Don't mind if I do.'

The security man next to him sees, so I go to him, and he takes one too. I work my way down the line and soon the tin is empty. I go back to my mother for more. She has taken her rucksack off her back. Out of it come Thermos flasks, from which she is pouring cups of tea, setting them on tree stumps. I go back with more flapjacks. Word spreads across the site, the foreman calls a halt to work, and the chainsaws cease their whining.

'Hey, these are good!' one of the security men calls out, back to a bulldozer.

The protestors relax their arms, sit down by the trees. I hand the flapjacks round them too.

'Hi,' says Snow. 'What you doing handing food out to

them?' He nods over at the huddle of security men.

'My mother's idea,' I say, reddening.

'Really?' he says, raising his eyebrows, but he takes a flapjack from the tin.

I go back to my mother who is passing round the tea.

'Need more?' she asks.

'I think everyone's got one.'

'Well, they might want seconds,' she says, bringing out another tin. Then she stands, hands on hips, surveys the site. Everyone is sitting or standing, propped against a tree, or a machine, drinking, eating, talking.

'There now,' she says. 'That's better.'

'But they'll start work again in a minute!'

'And they'll be different when they do,' she says, nodding.

She makes me pass round seconds. I remember how it was from this — handing out her food — that my secret hungering began. I would get up, move round the feast, play the dutiful daughter, fill cups, fetch loaves, and somehow forget to feed myself. Hunger was a strange new emptiness inside me, a space that I could call my own.

For the next fortnight my mother bakes almost every day. When she is done, we go out to Woodeaton Woods, what is left of them, and hand round her goods — tins of cakes, breads, biscuits. They come to expect us. They stop work as soon as we arrive. Progress is slow, because of the protestors, the wet, making everything more dangerous, and because of my mother and her tea breaks which are long and convivial. But everyone goes back to their roles afterwards: felling, protesting, arresting.

'They're still cutting down trees!' I tell her.

'And we are still feeding them.'

'But —'

'Patience!'

'There's no time for patience.'

'There is always time for patience.' But she sounds brisk, dangerous. Not patient. She hands me her latest bag of goods.

'Off we go.'

She has always seemed unquestionably capable. I walk with her, longing, as when I was a child, both to prove her wrong and to discover she is right. If she is right, I will be the wrong one yet again, but it would be a relief — back to our usual roles. If she is wrong? I do not want to think of it, so I feel, instead, annoyed as I follow her, that she should even have given me this worry. I remember her lying, exposed, by the pond in March, resting. At least now she is upright, at least she seems to have a plan, although I do not understand it.

But I am glad to leave the house, go to the woods. I am glad to see the protestors. I talk to them a little, day by day. There is Nonny, Snow's sister, with a piercing in her eyebrow and henna in her hair. Big Ben, a kind man who is even taller than Snow. A little woman called Nut with a baby called Berry. And then there is Jane with purple hair. Maggie, Sue, and Ash. I hand out food to them and they welcome it.

'You get tired of lentil slop after a while,' Snow tells me, 'And everything tastes of wood smoke anyway.' I am pleased that he stays serious, that the tea breaks do not make him as cheerful as my mother. He never drops his intent, rarely shifts away from whichever tree he is defending, even when work has stopped.

Once I am done handing round the food, I sit and watch Snow and his friends. They sing, stamp, shout, and wait — mostly wait. I watch them flex their fingers in the wet woods, listen to their banter. They call themselves activists. As if it were a job, as if resisting the world were one way to be in it. I know about obedience to the men who make the laws. My mother has fought such men, but she has her own beliefs of how the world should work and what is due to her. She is not, at heart, rebellious. I envy Snow and his friends for their bright convictions, their lack of shame.

'There's a big gathering coming up,' Snow tells me one afternoon, as I pass out my mother's gingerbread. 'May morning. It'll be more than just us,' he nods down the line of regular protestors.

'Who else?'

'Other activists, the XR lot, locals against the road, people from Oxford that usually celebrate May morning in town.'

'A party?'

'Crack of dawn we're gonna walk the route of the road, out from the A40 by Marston, ending at our camp. It's a party but it's also more than that — we need to gather support for when they reach Prattle Woods and the eviction comes.'

I nod.

'Come, if you like,' he says, pulling at his beard, looking over at the pyre of felled trees.

An invitation to a party — not one of my mother's. Heart loud and high near my collarbones, my stomach tightening, as if from hunger.

'Thanks,' I say. 'I will.'

I am elated to be allowed to join them, even for one morning. I have been lonely for a long time, though admitting this feels like a betrayal, because I always have company — my mother's, my husband's. I am the lucky one — the one who does the leaving, never the one left behind.

69

I carry on handing out gingerbread.

'Here, you have one.' my mother says when I get back to her.

'No thanks,' I say and smile. She frowns, says nothing.

Walking home behind her, I remember, for the first time in many years, the morning when she first confronted me about my starving — there was no going back after that.

She had stopped me in the doorway as I went to leave, led me back to the table, sat beside me.

'I saw you. You ate nothing. Again. You will eat your meal now.'

She had a wooden spoon in her hand. With the other hand she held the back of my neck. She dipped the spoon in the polenta on the table. She tried to feed me as if I were a baby. I was not a baby — my breasts had been sore for days. 'Eat,' she said. I shook my head, locked my jaw. I did not dare to speak because that would mean opening my mouth and if I did, my mother would push the yellow food inside me.

I liked the new hardness of my body. I liked the way I could feel my ribs, hip bones, spine. I liked the sharp corners, sure edges. I liked the hollow ache inside. It was better than the dull heaviness of meals. It was better than the sunny days in which I wanted to cry without reason, because I was the fairest of girls with the best of mothers. I wanted instead this change I had discovered I could make, this taut, light body, this power. I would not let the spoon in, however hungry I was. My mother had a wild look. It gladdened and frightened me. 'Eat,' she said again. I shook my head, and that was when she hit me.

She took her hand from my neck and slapped my cheek so hard it stung. When I gasped, she moved fast, pushing the spoon into my mouth. I tried to spit the cornmeal out, but she covered my mouth with her hot hand: 'Swallow'. I shook my head again. The yellow polenta was grainy against my teeth and tongue. I wanted it and I hated it. The tears came then, I swallowed, and the food went into me. I tried to cough it up but now I was crying — my body was pulling in air, so my mouth opened again, only a little way, but enough for another spoon. I pleaded, 'No more,' but there was more. I tried to stand, to run — my mother gripped me by the wrist. She jerked me hard, my knees buckled, and I fell. She knelt over me, pulled my teeth apart and pushed the food in.

She fed me a field, a whole field. There were tears, snot, cornmeal, spit all over my face. And all the while, outside the window, the corn was whispering in the summer breeze. And all the while the crows were calling, and the field labourers were singing a song about my mother and her generous bounty, a prayer for her blessing. And all the while she forced the polenta into me, pulled my jaw open, hit me to loosen it. I wanted the hunger because it was mine. The food was hers. I hated that she was stuffing more of her corn, her goodness, herself into me. And I wanted her. I longed for her to hold me like she used to do when I was small. But this I could not say.

DEMETER

Usually, I love this time of year. Everything at last in bloom or about to be so. The apple blossom is still out — white and lovely. The horse chestnut will be in candle soon, a thousand more of its flowers reflected in the pond. Celandine, sweet cicely, red campion, under the garden wall. The elderflowers ready for picking in a few weeks' time.

There used to be a point around now, at the end of April, when Persephone was back and settled, and her leaving was still far enough away not to feel a threat, when I could almost pretend that this was how it would always be again. This year she will not settle though — she wants to go to the woods to celebrate the May with the road people. I don't like her going off to the woods alone. Meanwhile, the hot days, in between the rainy ones, are record-breaking — they say so on the TV, which Persephone turns on after supper. Cold keeps. It freezes and preserves. With this new weather — the wet, mild winters, boiling skies — memories come loose, floating free. They make me giddy. But worse, however busy I keep, fast I bake, I feel Hades lurking near, waiting for me to fall, to fail.

He was around in the weeks before my daughter first went missing. I know it now. When I stood at the edge of the field at night, there would come a whisper in the corn that was not the wind. That was him, waiting. And all the while she was starving, as if in readiness for him.

It made me mad when she began to starve. There we were, in a never-ending summer, harvest after harvest, and she sat, shivering, empty, as if she were inventing winter, her wrists so thin I could have snapped them. She would squat, down by the well, still as a cold-blooded creature, conserving energy. I had taught the people how to farm and feast. Now here was my daughter, too mean to move, making a mockery of my gift.

She tried to hide it with flowers. She threaded daisies into chains that she wrapped about her ribs as they began to show. I called her my flower child, as if it were an innocent game, her dressing herself up like a pretty fairy or a woodland nymph.

But I guessed soon enough at what those flowers were burying.

I tried compassion. I spoke to her in a soft voice, asked her why, told her she was good, beautiful, must not do this to herself or me. She shook her head, shrugged her shoulders, locked her jaw, as if letting the words out was as dangerous as letting the food in. She was starved of sense. Mad girl. My girl. Whom I had fed from my body. My land. There was one morning I had nothing but fury left. It was an easier place to be than in the fear. It suited me better, though had I any idea of the destruction it would bring I would have tried to stay with terror longer.

After that she refused even to meet my eyes. Daisy-chained, and under the petals this brittle, stubborn thing. It was awful, the way her skeleton pushed through as her soft body slipped away. In the end, I could bear it no longer — I joined in hiding her.

It became our ritual together. It was a relief after the warfare of a meal, and a way to keep an eye on her. If I had won and she had eaten, then I dared not leave her. I caught her once, behind the well, fingers down her throat, her recent food spattered on the earth.

We did not say much. I would sit on the back doorstep. She would wander through the garden picking flowers or grasses. She brought them back to me and I would weave them into a wreath to sit like feathers round her neck. I threaded poppies into long loops of fluttering red that I could coil down her arms or wove plaits of grasses to hang about her dress, so as to hide how it hung, limp and loose.

It was a desperate game, but I was desperate. I did not want the world to see her starving. I felt shame, anger, even disgust, and that hurt more — to be disgusted by the daughter whom I loved above all else. I hoped the flowers would do more than

73

hide, that they might be a kind of medicine, remind her of who she was. Some days she looked so fragile I believed the blooms were holding her together.

I saw such a strange mix of arrogance and self-loathing in her. She longed for me to notice her and hated it when I did. I could do nothing right. Apart from the flowers. They were the only thing that she would let me do for her. It was a way to be together, to wrap buttercups about her shrinking waist. And when I had finished, I felt a painful pride, for she looked beautiful.

The more she starved the more ornate were the displays in which I bedecked her. Every day, she looked dressed for a festival, fine as a May queen. Sometimes, after she had picked the flowers, she would rest her head on my knee while I threaded them together. I lived for those times. To feel the weight of her again. Her willing touch. Not the hardness of the rigid girl over her bread. I could feel her breathing. In those moments the picture held. Mother and daughter, goddess of the harvests and her child, surrounded by flowers. I could believe again that this was who we were, that the endless glory of the summer would last.

8

PERSEPHONE

It is like breaking something, walking out into the day before it has begun, as if there is a scarcely visible lace left by the retreating dark.

I am wearing the patchwork dress, a garment my mother sewed one winter and presented to me in the spring. It is made from old tablecloths and sheets, diamonds of stripes and solid colours, bird and flower patterns, white, green, blue, and yellow. I pulled it out of the trunk at the bed's end this morning. When I thought of the many-styled clothes of the protestors, I decided that it would do for a May morning party, over jeans and a vest.

As I reach the hawthorn at the field's edge, I snap off a sprig of may and stick it in my hair, thinking of the time I walked this way, looking for Hades, wearing roses, poppies.

At the edge of the woods, a group of tired security men, at the end of their night watch, trudge past, heading towards the Woodeaton road. I walk the other way, into the woods, thick with bluebells now, a startling sweep of colour in between the trees. New security men are stationed under them, though with the woods empty of protestors, it looks as if they are on guard in case the trees themselves decide to rise up in revolt, attempt to run before they are felled.

I reach the camp. It is deserted. There is a neat stack of wood by the fire pit. They must be on their way, walking the route of the road. I go to the edge of the camp to watch for them. I stand between the yew and the oak in which Snow lives.

The yew's trunk rises only a little way before it splits into branches that twist and lurch, athletic, but with the speed of a tree that thinks in thousands. The oak is taller than the yew, though younger. It goes up to the full height of the yew before it forks. Snow's treehouse is higher still, lashed between three branches near the top. I cross over to touch the bark, peer up, feel the exhilaration of the tree's height.

From here, under the oak, I look back at the yew — the life and death tree, by which I once stood hungering for Hades. I wait and the sun rises — day hardens into certainty. Still no sign of anyone. I stand in my patchwork dress, hawthorn in my hair, waiting. I feel foolish, as I did when I could not find Hades.

I look down, remembering again how the ground split.

I have read since that they call them sinkholes. They occur in karstic land where there is water, where there is limestone — but I knew none of that back then. I knew only what I saw — that the earth had broken open.

It was a thin crack. No wider than my foot. I had become light from lack of food but that evening I felt suddenly too heavy for the earth to bear. I gazed through the crack, into the underside of everything, and saw a man within the earth.

It was him. The one I had been seeking.

He looked up at me, and as his small, sharp face peered out I thought he must be young after all. A strange, wild boy.

I knelt, rocked forwards and reached inside, offered a hand, as if to rescue him. He did not take my hand but reached past it for my wrist. I braced myself, ready for his weight. He made no effort to climb out of the hollow. Only slowly did I realise that he was expecting me to come to him. I had thought to pull him out — he meant to help me in.

At last, I reached out my other hand, and he raised his, held me under my shoulders as I tipped forwards and he lifted me into the earth.

He set me next to him. There was only room enough to sit, hunched, side by side, like birds in a buried nest. I could feel the shape of him beside me, his breathing, quick and shallow. Beyond him the cleft narrowed and sloped down into the dark.

'Who are you?' I whispered it, as if the trees were spies.

'I can't tell you,' he said in his cracked voice.

'Why not?'

He looked down.

'First promise you will come with me.'

'Where?'

'Promise, and I'll tell you.'

His hands unlooped the flowers my mother had laid around my shoulders and in my hair. He ran one finger down my neck, vertebra by vertebra. I felt his desire for me then — it frightened me, but I was glad of it. I wanted to drop out of myself, out of the world. I would go anywhere with him.

'Yes.' I said. 'I'll come with you.' I kissed him, the earth pressing us together. He slipped his lips from my mouth. He breathed into my ear, held my wrist.

'My name,' he said, 'is Hades.'

The jewel-clad giant, the commander of dead slaves, the god of dark, the richest man alive. I stared at his thin, grubby hands. I had promised to run away with Hades — it was the most terrible thing that I could do. I was appalled. And thrilled.

'Where will we go?' I whispered, though I knew.

'Down,' he said, and for a moment I still believed that he might have a diamond studded palace waiting. 'Come on,' he said.

77

I took a last look at the leaves against the sky. As I tilted my head upwards, I heard a call from the fields. I paused, listening.

'You promised to come,' Hades hissed.

'I'm coming!' Already I was reassuring him. It felt absurd. I had only ever been the child, needing comfort or refusing it. I had never been the one to give it. I thought of my mother and felt something different for her then, too new to name. Not love. Not hate. This man, this god, was everything she wasn't — she never hid anything, never doubted anyone's allegiance. He trusted no one, and his feelings, I would learn, were like underground streams, impossible to see until a sudden surfacing.

More voices drifted over from the fields.

'We need to go,' Hades said, urgent.

'Wait — first, we need to cover this.' I pointed at the gash above us in the ground, amazed at my new certainty, 'or my mother will follow us.'

Hades tunnelled down, then returned, rolling a pale boulder which he pushed up into place. I packed earth and smaller stones around it, buried the world.

I was under everything with Hades. All day I had looked for him and found nothing — now there was nothing but him. No light but instead his hand in mine, pulling me down, bent double, my back scraping the rock. I tried to imagine it — the habit of sight still strong, translating everything into terms I would soon learn to forget — colour, distance, shape. I shut my eyes — more likely to find light inside than out and better to be within a dark of my own making.

In the world above it would soon be night. I felt a jolt, for when I thought of night I thought of home. Fire in the front garden. Moon at my window. My mother, moving somewhere in the house. But I had blocked her way to me with stones. The King of the Dead was leading me down into the earth, and I was glad because at last I felt alive.

A high, single-reed song, calling through the woods, brings me back to now, May morning, and this upper land. There, at some distance, people walking this way, a piper at their front. I stay, still as the trees, and watch them come.

They are many. Far more than I imagined. I have got used to the regulars, the ten committed protestors from the camp. Here come a hundred more. They wear leaves, wreaths of ivy and may blossom in their hair. Paint on their faces, bells, sticks and whistles in their hands. Costumes of green and white. Coloured ribbons tied to them, feathers too. One wears a set of antlers. One is painted black and white like a magpie. And underneath they have on jerseys, jeans, phones in their pockets.

They are not bold, brazen, angry, as I have seen them when defending trees by day. They are not protesting. Rather they have something of the reverence I felt earlier walking the fields here, breaking the skin of the day. It is not clear whether they are gathering to celebrate the May or mourn it, as if this were the last spring that the earth will see. A final flowering of hawthorn, leafing of oak. They are being people, not protestors, doing what people have always done to cope with change: dressing and painting themselves, becoming other things — trees and beasts and birds.

One figure is taller than the rest, in a great coat of green rags, with a structure of wire and wood resting on his shoulders, covered with leaves. As they approach, I see the figure has a beard — it's Snow. Snow, with nothing white about him. All green. He smiles at me as he passes, and the whole green rustling head of

79

him nods. I am scared and glad, as if a real tree had turned to talk to me. Next to him walks Nonny, in army green, with a green face, grinning. I follow them, join the line of people as they wend their way behind the piper into the camp around the fire.

They form a circle. The fire is lit while the pipes play on. Then a woman, also in green, stands up on a log, ready to conduct the crowd. Others with instruments draw round her, and they begin to sing:

> Hal-an-tow, jolly rumbelow
> We were up, long before the day-o
> To welcome in the summertime
> To welcome in the May
> For summer is a-coming in
> And winter's gone away-o

A great cheer goes up at the end, a whooping and a clapping, and then another small woman with black hair stands and leads a song, a chant this time. A chant of tall trees, warm fires, strong winds, deep waters, and then of earth: 'Mother, I feel you under my feet. Mother, I hear your heartbeat.'

They sing of Mother Earth, of Gaia. I know her daughter — she'll be up by now baking bread, glad of a dry day because she has been fussing about her beetroot seedlings. I feel fury at my mother's stubborn ways and sorry that she could have come to this, because she was glorious once. Gorgeous enough to make the corn reach out the ground to draw near her, branches finger further into air. I resented her then for all her loveliness and power, and I resent her now for having lost it.

At the front, near the fire, the sky man, tree man, Snow, is sitting drumming, free of his head dress now. I push my way through the crowd and find a place on the ground nearby. I feel nervous of him but also safer near him. Two big kettles are on the fire. They are coming to the boil and the day is breaking fully now. After two weeks of rain the sky has wrung itself out, so it hangs blue and empty in between the trees. A sense of renewal, in spite of everything.

Tea is going round and now the cans of beer appear as well. Someone brings out a music machine — that's what my mother calls them — and it takes over from the singing. Big blaring beats. The excited, tired crowd who have traipsed from Oxford are ready for this now — jumping, shouting, shaking hips, fists, feet. Glad and furious that they are alive, that it is May, that they have spirit and legs enough to dance in this condemned wood.

'Up with the May!'

'Fuck the road and all who drive on it!'

'Long live the trees!'

I sit and watch as I did at my mother's parties. I do not want to dance. I want to hold still and take it in. I want to be near Snow, who is also sat amid the wild dancing. As long as I am near him, the hunger, close to panic, that has been there ever since the hidden river flooded, ever since my husband said I had to stay down in the dark, is eased.

Then he gets up. Snow goes over to the sound system, balanced on a log and turns it down.

'Hey man, what you doing?' a young lad calls from the dancing crowd.

'Let's not give them a bloody excuse to kick us out,' Snow says, grim-faced.

'It's May morning, for Christ's sake!' The lad steps forward and turns the volume back up, louder than it was before. Snow glares, fists coming out of his leafy arms, but Nonny is beside him.

'Leave it, Si. Just let them be. It'll be okay.'

He looks down.

'I'm not in the mood,' he says and turns, walks off towards his oak. I feel the panic rising as he goes. I get up, run after him.

'Wait!'

He pauses, looks back.

'Can I come with you? Up the tree?'

I hear myself say this, as if I am the girl beside the yew, staring back at the woman I have become, shocked, embarrassed at my asking. Snow looks embarrassed too. He frowns. Slowly, thickly, through his beard he answers, 'No.'

I feel myself reddening. I wish the earth would split again and take me.

'No,' he says, but gently now, 'You need a harness.'

Nonny has come up beside him and already her hands are on her harness, unbuckling it.

'She can borrow mine.'

Snow shakes his head, puts a hand on Nonny's arm to stop her.

'C'mon, Si.'

'I don't trust them. I've no reason to trust them.'

'Well, trust me instead. There's not going to be a frickin' eviction this morning. I don't need this right now,' she says as she steps out of her harness. He looks at her. His eyes look sad enough to cry, though his face does not make any of the shapes that go with crying.

'Really,' Nonny says.

'Okay,' Snow says, 'Okay.'

'Plus, the more people who learn how to climb the better — you've told me that a million times. More of us to defend the place when the time comes!' Nonny marches off towards the oak, beside the yew. I follow.

'Right, your jeans look fine for climbing, but you okay to take your dress off? It'll be easier—' Nonny says. 'It's an amazing dress by the way.' I hesitate. 'Do you want my jacket? I've got a spare in the back of the bender.'

'Thanks.'

Nonny takes off her jacket, an old khaki army one. I take off my dress, lay it down on the ground, and slip the jacket on. Now I smell of wood smoke too.

'Here,' Nonny says, holding out the harness for me to step inside. She tightens the straps around my thighs and waist.

'There. You're all set. I share that treehouse with Si, so it's already got two lines rigged up from it. You're in good hands. Have fun!' She turns back to the fire and the dancing, leaving Snow and me standing at the bottom of the tree.

'What do I do?' I ask.

'Right,' Snow says, practical now, pointing me with his beard towards a thin blue rope, which he unties from the oak's trunk. It comes free, hanging down from a branch high over us. It has two loops knotted within it.

'They slide,' he says, showing me how the knots can be pushed upwards. He clips me on to the higher loop. 'The lower one is for your foot. Prusiking. It's dead simple — basically a series of leg ups that you give yourself. Just do what I do.'

Snow goes across to another rope, on the other side of the oak.

I put my foot into the loose loop hanging from the blue line. I look up the line to the branch far above where it is lashed. I do not understand how it will hold me or how I can climb it. I am terrified. I have not felt like this since that evening when

83

Hades led me down into the earth. No knots then, except the knot of our hands, Hades' tight around mine, pulling me on.

'If it'll hold me, it'll hold you,' Snow calls over. 'Slide up the top knot.'

I push the knot that links to my harness as high as I can. I am on my tiptoes, barely holding to the earth.

'Slide up the foot loop. Weight on the foot, slide up the top knot,' calls Snow. I step up, leave the ground and start to swing. It is hard to push the top knot up now that there is nothing solid to steady myself against. 'Weight off the foot and into your harness.'

I am hanging, inches from the earth, legs dangling. Across the way, around the fire, thumping music, stamping feet. I cannot stamp now, only revolve slowly, looking down at my patchwork dress left lying under me.

'Now, the foot loop up,' says Snow. I am amazed how taut the line has become now that I am on it. The line that was slack and spindly, is rigid, proof of my weight. I remember, as I first travelled down into the earth, how easily Hades lifted me over rock and root, how fast he had been able to pull me, slithering down passages, how appalled I was to feel how light I had become.

'And repeat,' calls Snow.

Foot in loop, give myself a leg up, slide up the line that leads like a baby's cord to the middle of me, sit back, dangle, slide up the foot loop, step into it. I continue to spin. I cannot control which way I am facing: trunk, Snow, yew, fire, dancers, the way towards my mother's house, the way to Oxford — I turn between them. Slowly I climb higher. I am level with the yew now. I have never been this high before without a floor beneath me. I can look down on the heads of the people as they whoop and leap below. I am leaving them behind. I remember climbing down into the split in the earth, how the call from the fields seemed both near and a million miles away.

'You're doing well,' Snow says.

Then suddenly I am not doing well. The knot sticks. The harness cuts into my legs and waist. My hands feel red and raw, slippery with sweat. I want to hold something to stop the spinning, but I am still climbing in parallel to the trunk, too far from it to reach and there are no branches near. My arms are weak, my legs dangling, helpless. I look down — the earth looks distant, too far to fall, and nothing else to hold, if the rope snapped, clips broke, harness came undone. I try to look up instead, but the sky is sickening and vast. Fear sweeps through me. I look across at the yew, remember my terror as I went down into the earth, the moment when I would have given anything to turn back, when I faltered in the pitch black. 'What's wrong?' Hades had hissed, but I had nothing to say, so he lifted me onto his back and, like a mother carrying a child, he bore me down into the deeper dark.

'Keep going,' Snow calls, 'You're halfway there.'

I pull myself back up out of the dark of then, into the bright air of now, this May morning, this thin, blue line, this oak.

I try to look only at the rope, the tiny fibres in it.

'Slide up the knot. Foot in. Step up,' Snow calls over.

Finally, I reach the branches. They are huge and strong. It is exciting to be near them. I am close to the platform of the treehouse now. Snow has reached it already and crosses over to help me. I come up onto the platform on hands and knees, relieved, shaky.

'Well done,' says Snow. 'Come on in.' He is lifting up the edge of the dark-green covering of the treehouse for me to crawl inside.

It is small, simple. Like a cave, but in the sky. Two sleeping bags. Big blankets. Cardboard on the floor. A makeshift stove made from an old gas canister. Some kindling and wood. Two packets of digestive biscuits. A water bottle. It is not big enough for Snow to stand full height inside.

'The best bit is the view,' he says, lifting up the green covering on the other side of the shelter, walking out to sit on the edge of the platform. I follow, crawling, too scared to stand. I want to hold on to Snow for safety but do not. I squat at the entrance of the shelter, not by the platform edge. I look out. I am on a level with the highest branches. I can look down on the dark green of the yew. To the left I can see through the trees to the fields, the houses of Noke. There is a light wind and I feel the tree around and under us shift.

'It moves,' Snow says. 'It's going to be hard to be back in a house.'

I am amazed by this sense of the tree under us. I did not expect being up high to give me a keener sense of down, of the unseen forest of roots that I must push through to reach my husband.

'I don't want it to go,' Snow says.

'No. Me neither.'

Then I am brave. I go to sit beside him on the platform with my feet hanging down. It's like being a child again, before my legs were long enough to touch the ground. I feel high on the high of it. Of having climbed up here, to where the branches break into thinner arms, then creak into twigs, usher into leaves. I look up at the blue between the branches, think of my father, feel for the first time what he might feel, living up in sky. The giddiness. The grandness. But I will not let the blue go to my head — instead, it fills my body. Below us, the party is thumping and bumping. I am at another kind of party, drunk on light, leaf, breeze. I want to hold on to Snow as I fear now that I may fling myself off the platform because I am in love with air. I grip its edge. I ask, 'What's it like, living in a tree?'

'It's like living in a living thing,' Snow says.

'What do you want?' I ask, because being up here I feel I can.

'I want the trees to live. I don't care too much about the people anymore, if I'm honest.'

'Why?'

'I think we deserve whatever's coming to us. Sorry if that sounds brutal. It's where I'm at right now. What do you want?'

We are not looking at each other. It feels good to sit beside him and look out at the same sky. I think down again into the earth. How I thought I had found the truth of everything down there, when Hades held me and felt along my bones. His hands, articulate and deft, followed the curve of each rib, the point of my shoulder blades, the furrows between each knuckle of my hands. His hands felt my skull, as if, like a baby's, the bones were still soft and must be pushed together. He pressed my cheekbones to my face. He thumbed my teeth, my jaw. Lying in total darkness I had felt seen for the first time in my life. He showed me the parts of us that will endure. But now, up here, up high, looking down on bluebells that will stop flowering in a week, in a wood that may be gone in a month, I feel a different truth, the one of things that do not last. I turn to look at Snow, looking out. I see specks of sky through the stretched holes in his ears. I look at the tattooed black branches snaking up his neck.

'What do you want?' he says again.

'I want to see the rest of your tattoo,' I say.

He turns his head sharply, then points his beard skywards as he breaks into a laugh.

'Fair enough.'

He pulls his legs up off the edge of the platform, takes off his coat of green tatters, his T-shirt under that.

A whole tree is on him. Black branches, black leaves, as if it were in silhouette.

The trunk grows up his belly, then splits where his ribs begin, the branches spreading across his chest.

'Summer on my front. Winter on my back,' he says, swivelling to show me the stark outline of a bare tree, following straight up the length of his spine, sweeping out over his shoulders in elegant, curving lines. I think of the thin, tight line of rope that held me on the way up here. I think of the loops of the line when my weight left it, as soon as I arrived onto the platform. I see both these things in the black tattoo, feel them in me, in the tree, in Snow, how taut we are, how slack, how soft. I want to run my fingers along the ink sunk in his skin.

I am a married woman. I have not touched, not been touched by, any man but Hades. My husband too has been faithful all these years. He is the opposite of my father, philandering across the skies. My mother rolls her eyes, clicks her tongue — 'Men! They're all the same,' she says, and I do not bother to correct her, because she would not want to hear which man disproves her theory.

'Tell me there is no one else for you,' Hades says, each year. 'There is no one else,' I recite into the bone behind his ear. But now, before me, is another man — one I want to touch.

Snow swivels round.

'Like it?'

I nod. 'What makes it permanent?' I ask, calm as I can.

'The ink goes down into the second layer of skin and stays there.'

I stare at him, at his tattoo, amazed that even skin has depth.

And then I ask, 'Can I touch it?'

He frowns, puts his head to one side.

'Suppose so,' he says, hesitant. 'Summer? Winter?' He half twists his body round again, to show the other tree.

'Winter,' I say at once, because then he will not see me doing it. And afterwards, he can put his T-shirt on again, teach me how to climb down, and it will be over.

He turns his back to me.

With one finger, as if the tattoo were an ancient painting, I trace the trunk up his lower back.

I look only at the dark line of ink.

I try to pretend it is not a picture painted on a man.

But I can feel the point of touch, between the tip of my finger and the ink-tree through my whole body. I can feel the whole of Snow's body, tense, tired, listening. And I feel my own skin come alive, as if it too were inked over with symbols, messages.

Then Snow is turning round. Slowly, through his beard, he says, 'Do you want to go inside?'

And I nod, yes.

We go into the shelter. It is dark green, like the inside of the yew. Snow takes his harness off. He shows me how to loosen the buckles on mine, just enough to step out of it, how to set the harness down so it is laid out, ready.

'You've gotta be prepared,' he says, serious.

And then he is unzipping the sleeping bags, laying them out over the cardboard on the floor so that they overlap. He is calm, practical, as if he were making up the fire for the camp. I am panicking. I would run if I could, but I am on a tiny platform, high in the air — there is nowhere I can go.

Snow lies down, props himself up on his elbows so that the tree on his chest is visible. He looks at me.

'Sumer is icumen in,' he says, with a sad smile.

I do not move. I stay kneeling beside the harnesses. Full of fear. Longing.

'Promise I won't bite,' he says.

I crouch beside Snow. I draw my fingers over the summer tree, that grows up his belly, across his sternum, chest. I look at the ink, buried under his skin, the pattern of the skin itself, the fine hairs and thicker hairs growing there, the tiny pores, a landscape of their own.

I wish this was not happening.

But my desire to touch him is a wish too. And though the guilt is terrible, the wishing feels innocent, like the wish of a child for magic, the wish of the May morning revellers to transform themselves, the same longing to change, be changed into something new. I think of my father again and how many of his betrayals involved just such change, and I wonder if he felt this innocent, every time he made love with another woman who was not his wife.

Then Snow is lifting up his hand.

'Can I?' he asks.

I frown, afraid, confused. His palm is turned towards me, with its ridge of callouses.

'Sorry,' he says. 'I thought…'

And then I understand. I am shocked. No one has ever asked before whether they can touch me. Not my mother, father. Not Hades, or any other man or boy.

'No,' I say. 'I mean — yes. You can.'

He laughs to shake off the embarrassment.

And then as I touch the branches and leaves on his chest, he touches my arms, the muscles there that I did not know I had until this morning.

His hands are strange. Big, cautious, clumsy. As if he is still checking, asking. So different to my husband's — certain, deft, precise.

'It's been a while,' he says, apologising.

'It's fine,' I say, thinking of Hades, of how this is not fine at all.

I tell myself none of it counts, because we are high, away from earth. But I know the opposite is true, because being up here I feel the downward motion of the oak, how great, how intimate is its grip on the ground. And it is this that makes me want to go on touching, this feeling of depth and height, of how far both can go, in the tree, in us.

I close my eyes, but in the dark behind them I find, again, Hades, waiting near, curled in the roots, sleeping like a baby. And despite myself I remember the first time he made love to me — how, after he had accounted for every part of me, he came inside me, and his body tensed, arched, no longer counting, accountable and I heard him weep. I sat up, felt for his head, his face. I rocked him, suddenly calm, 'All is well,' I whispered, as if I were his mother.

I open my eyes. I keep them open. Because I want to be here, not there. I want to be wide awake to everything. To the cracks of blue above, to the rattle of branches, to the silent surge upwards of the oak, to the reach of its roots, to the thump of the party, to the coming in of May, to my hands touching Snow, to his touching me, in this cave to which I climbed, up in the sky.

9

DEMETER

I listen to her shifts of weight in the attic above. She went to the woods for the May party today. But she came back. Most evenings I go out like a light, yet tonight I feel such fear of losing her again, I cannot sleep. Tonight, the moon is new — it will wax only twice more before midsummer, when Hades comes to claim her.

I roll over onto my side, away from the fields, the woods, the road work. The robin in the back garden is wide awake too. The only other times I could not sleep were when Persephone first came, and then when she first left.

The night after her birth I nodded off, then jerked awake in shock, as if remembering a recent death, but realising instead she had arrived — her tiny body beside mine, breathing, already bravely taking in her share of life. But soon, even on the second and third night, I could not imagine that the world could ever be without her. So when she went missing it was an old idea — long forgotten.

It comes back keenly now, how I lay in this bed in the days that followed her disappearance. I looked stupidly at things: the bedside table; a pile of folded clothes; a jug of water, and I resented them, that they were here, vivid as ever. My arms longed for her. An ache in my chest, in my stomach, womb, thighs, ankles, in the soles of my feet. Everything hurt, was both hard and too sensitive to touch. I made crazed deals in my head: if I offered up the house, cut off my hair, my hands, I'd get her back.

I told the field labourers to stop all other work and only look for her. I ordered my fields to be scorched, my hedgerows cut. I wanted them to strip my land, to make it bare, burnt, as empty as I felt, till there was nowhere left for her to hide. I sat at the end of each long day, waiting for news. None came.

One night I started up from bed in simple disbelief. It was six days since she had gone. I had been afraid to enter her room. I made myself go in. I leant out of her window into the vicious rain and screamed her name into the night.

'Persephone! Come home! Come home!'

I went to her bed and sat where I had a thousand times. I gathered up the bedclothes. The scent of her was in them — hot grass, dried roses, still the smell of a child. I pressed them to my stomach, and an awful howling came from me.

After that night I tried to stand where she, of late at least, had not been, and I did not expect her: in the veg patch, by my dressing table over there by the garden window. But it was worse. My sense of her came sharp as a knife. Because then I missed the back of her, strange as it sounds. I missed her head tipped forwards, looking down the well; or cocked, staring out over the wall. Or, a younger shape, when she laid on elaborate banquets by the apple tree: she stooped and offered seeds to her dolls — her small spine rounded in concern. Only then did I understand that in all our days together, I had seen more of her back than of her face because she had never been one to stand, chest open, head up. Always she was turning away, spiralling into or out of my arms, but near.

Now she was nowhere. I was terrified. After the fights we had had. The times she had hidden from me before a meal or after, the times I had been unkind, impatient or worse. She was only a girl, now more in need of care than ever. I remembered

Erysichthon, how he ate himself with hunger. Could she have faded so fast? She had been here, thin, but not as thin as leaves, not so close to nothing.

I thought of asking Zeus for help. But I did not trust him. He was more likely to take her from me than to bring her home. She was mine to find. When my last field had been scorched, and nothing found, I set out searching.

And now? If she went missing? I do not have the energy I did back then to search the world. But this time, I would know where she was. The question would be only whether I could summon up the strength to go down there again and make it back. I grip the bedclothes, close my eyes, see a tiny light rocking in the dark, hear the river underground.

I watch the tilting of the light, feeling hazy now, on the edge of dreaming.

'I must keep her here,' I tell the house. I keep my eyes closed, focus on the little light. It is leaf-shaped. And as I watch, I realise it is one of the yellowing chestnut leaves, falling to the pond. I need to put it back up on the tree — it is not autumn yet. My daughter is still here.

I look up. I see it is not the only leaf to turn early. Others are colouring too. And not only yellow. Orange. And red.

Red?

The chestnut leaves never turned red before.

And they are not falling down, but up, little flakes of them drifting into air. The tree is tall. Like a spear into the sky, covered with sharp, shimmering red leaves.

It doesn't look autumnal.

And then, with a start, I understand — they are not leaves — they're flames.

And it isn't the chestnut. It's the pine.

The pine that stood here long ago. The evergreen. Not green now. Ablaze with colour. The tree that lit my way down into the dark when I went to fetch my daughter back. I can smell its resin, hear its hiss and crackle, feeding the fire. Its diagonal branches are stark against the sky, which is red too, as if the air itself had turned to flame.

Did I start this?

With my pine torch?

Could I have set the whole tree burning? I know a tiny spark can turn into a terrible conflagration, and this fire is terrible — fierce, wild, spreading. It could reach the house. The fields. The woods.

I watch, appalled, as the flames lick along the pine's trunk, as the whole tree blooms, bright-orange now, and smoke pours from it. It starts to shake. Its branches snap, crack, and then, above the fire's roar, I hear screaming.

Persephone?

With horror I realise I no longer know what season we are in — is she in the house? Or underground? I cannot see her through the smoke. The heat is unbearable, like a summer gone wrong, the sun too near the earth. And, as I look around, desperate, the tree collapses — tumbling out of the red sky to the burnt ground with an almighty crash.

I start up. Breathing. Sweating.

It was a dream. A nightmare.

But the crash wasn't.

The crash came from above.

What was it? My daughter never makes a din. I am out of bed already, calling up the ladder, a horrible dread upon me.

PERSEPHONE

'It was just a party,' I told my mother when I got back.

'Yes, but how was it?'

'It was fine.'

'Good. Don't bring the may in the house!'

'Why not?'

'Brings bad luck — and we don't need any more of that.'

But I liked my sprig of may, did not like my mother's superstitions, so I brought the blossoms up here, put them in a jug beside the lampshade on my bedside table.

Just some blossoms. Just a party. A man. A tree. One morning. Just another infidelity. It happens every day. I envy the ease with which my father shrugged his off, went on to the next. He never felt remorse.

I do. Part of me wishes I could undo it, go back in time. Never leave the house. Stay with my mother. Go to my husband. Tell him, again, 'There's no one else.'

Or I wish I could lie. He seduced me. I was defenceless. All the ways to tell the story circle me. As they have done for many years about Hades. How he abducted me. Raped me. Tricked me into eating the pomegranate seeds. The stories my mother told, that others took up, that I have come to think must be the truth of it. I was so young. I was so ill afterwards. 'You were out of your mind,' my mother tells me. She likes that part of the story, where she nursed me back from my delirium.

But tonight, my body is singing with a different story altogether. And I feel such fiercely different things, I do not know what to believe. The guilt? The happiness? The shocking freedom? One tips so fast into the other. And suddenly, it seems imperative that I remember right. That to understand this morning, when I climbed a tree, held a man, I must understand what happened nine thousand years ago, when I went underground.

The myths have grown over the memories like thickened skin. I think of the callouses on Snow's hands from where the rope runs through them. I think of his tattoo, and of my skin coming alive as I traced over his.

I sit straight up in bed, in the dark attic, as if waking from a dream.

But it is not a dream.

I know I did not dream it.

I refused the pomegranate when Hades first offered it to me.

'Now let us eat,' he said, after we had made love.

I am not sure what I thought would happen next, but I did not expect a meal. I was already imagining being back home. I wanted to lie in a known place, my bed, by the window. To feel, not only the bone flower that still hung about my neck, but my whole body — every bone in it — a souvenir of him. Of us. I had a lover. Not any lover. Hades. I wanted to tell Phoebe. I was excited, elated, and I wanted to take these things away with me, like the stone treasures I carried as a child from the river. But Hades had other treasures to show me, and food to share.

He took my hand and led me to a place where the dark grew warm. I felt him kneel — the dark flowered open, glowed red as he raked over it. He blew into the glow, set a torch to it, lifted a flame.

We were stood beside a large rock with a flat top, like an

97

anvil. Tools lay scattered on the ground beside it: hammers, chisels, tongs. The floor was strewn with rock, metal, slabs of clay. I saw silver, gold, diamonds: the stuff of which his palace should have been built, but they were crude hunks of jagged stone — nothing like the glittering things in my girlish dreams. Beside them lay a hundred finished and half-finished things, worked from the raw stone: emerald apples, nuts of copper and bronze, fish with moonstone scales. His mimicry was brilliant and disturbing. This was closer to what Phoebe and my other friends had dreamt of — a feast of jewels. Nothing I could eat.

'I will make you a harvest more beautiful than anything above,' he whispered to me. He set the torch down, came behind me. I felt his hands about my neck, fingering the necklaces I wore, the corn one my mother made and the thread which carried the bone flower. He snapped the first — the kernels fell away into the dark. I felt a pang — my mother would notice it was gone — but it was a childish thing. Then he broke the cord that held the flower.

'No,' I said. 'You gave me that. I want it.'

He laughed, ran the back of his hand along my jaw. He threw the bone down, stooped to pick up something else.

'I can give you better things,' he said, laying something new about my neck.

I glanced down — saw, in the torchlight, another corn necklace, but this was made of gold.

I wanted the bone flower back — I had loved how hard and light it was. The gold was heavy and cold.

'Now follow me,' he said, taking up the torch.

He led me to an archway at the back of the cave, where a thin stream ran under us. He brushed my hand along the arch.

'Limestone,' he whispered. 'Made from the first dead. The tiny skeletons of swimming things.'

Then he bid me crawl through after him.

The dark took a cold, slow leap into a vast space. Hades lifted the light: black lines of flow twisted above us. He lowered it and I saw the same dark snaking shapes in the rock under our feet. He pulled me over the sinuous, uneven surface.

At last the light, striking out before us, showed the dark ahead tighten, grow dense, solid. It was a pillar, wide as a house. Hades led me to it, lifted my hand to touch it. It had deep grooves within it.

'What stone is this?' I asked.

'Wood,' Hades whispered.

I stood, still stupid.

'This is a tree, my love.'

My love — my mother called me that. A tree under the earth, or this man's love — which was more unlikely?

Hades took me in his arms and held me.

'Older than any of us. It will outlive the gods. The greatest thing alive and the best hidden.' He ran his hand along the bark, then down my spine, went on.

'My brothers got the sky and sea, I got the underneath of everything. From the dark belly of our father, I came into the belly of the earth. When I first arrived, there was no one else. There was the river. Rocks. Caves. Passageways. I thought I was the only one with any kind of thought, will, life, down here, until I found the tree. I leant against its trunk, envying my brothers in the light. It was under this tree that I first dreamt of a queen.'

He was breathing hard, holding me harder. His story thrilled and frightened me.

'I went looking for you at night. From cracks within the ground, I spied my brothers, chasing whichever women glittered, shone, took their fancy. I wanted someone different. I searched the shadows — dark woods, quiet caves, secret streams. I could not find you. At last, I dared to stray into the fields, where I least expected you to be — in the middle of the feast. And there you were. Waiting. Hungry. But not for your mother's grain. For something else.'

He tilted the flare to the ground. Amid the massive roots were dark spheres, round and smooth. He lifted one between us, balanced it on his palm: a fruit, red, its skin hard, its stem like a crown.

'A pomegranate.' His voice was the most tender I had heard it. 'A many-seeded apple.'

Here, in his hand, was food.

He led me back over the black roots of the cavern, to the close heat of his workshop. There he planted the torch between rocks. He took the fruit, picked up a knife, cut it open. He showed it to me, as proud as if he had made it — he might have for it was crammed with jewels. Bright red. Inside each, a fleck of white, like a shard of bone.

Hades whittled out the jewels.

'For you.' He spoke as if he loved me. He opened my hand, laid the shining seeds there, one by one.

'Eat,' he said.

I felt the heat behind my eyes. I felt Hades' longing, his loneliness. I play-ate, like once I had made my dolls do, like I had done at my mother's table, lifting the food to my lips, moving my mouth but not letting anything inside. I smiled trying to include Hades in the game.

'Don't be afraid,' he said.

He bit into the pomegranate half he held to show me how. It was then that I realised the rules of the dead are no different to the living's, no different to my mother's rules of hospitality. I knew well the obligations of the guest: better not to come at all than enter and refuse, and yet any gift of food accepted binds guest to host, creates a debt. If I ate, I'd have to stay.

'I'm sorry. I cannot.'

Hades' hand was on my hand. He forced the fruit to my mouth. I shut my lips. The seeds smashed, their juice ran down my chin. He pulled my hand away and now it was his tongue pushing at my lips, my body wanting him still, letting him in, the sharp taste of the juice on him, as he pressed seeds from his mouth into mine. I held them against my teeth. He pulled away, smiling. I smiled too, turned and spat into the dark.

When I turned back Hades' face had changed. It looked broken, with the finality of glass, as if he could never be made whole again.

Too late, I understood that when he'd asked me, back up in the woods, if I would come with him, he had already meant forever. I wanted to take him in my arms, to rock him, but his hands were furious: he had me by the wrist. He took up the torch, pulled me to the stream that cut along the cave edge. He plunged the torch into the water as if it were a sword and he a murderer, killing light.

Pomegranate, gems, tools, Hades' face — gone. Dark. Only his hand again in mine. He pulled me after him. I felt the ceiling slope down, the narrow opening, the cold air over us, the walls widening into the cave where the tree grew. He halted, brought his hands to my hips, lifted me through another opening in the rock, set me down. Freezing water round my feet. Another cave. Then another. This one seemed large again, the sound of water disappeared. Hades dragged me forwards. Stopped. Turned me round.

He stroked my hair, hands moving down my back, clasping together, holding me close. We were both breathing hard. He was kissing me, tender again. He kissed me until our bodies slowed. He started to turn me, turn us round.

The dark revolved around me. Hades touched his lips to my head, like kissing a child goodnight. His hands were on my shoulders, light as moths. He spun me and let go. I turned in the dark alone, unsteady. I turned again, again, trusting another revolution would bring him to me. Fear closed on me like a fist.

'Hades?'

There was no answer. He was gone.

I curl up on my side in bed, press my eyes into my knees. In the dark of the attic I remember the denser dark of underground, of the days — was it days? I had no way of knowing — that I spent lost under the earth.

I did not know whether Hades had left me in the dark to throw me away, or to keep me safe, like buried treasure — I had his jewels on me. I remember I stood, shaking in my summer dress, then pulled the gold from round my neck, heard the metal seeds scatter on the rock.

I tried to find my way back to the river. I followed thin threads of water until they vanished into cracks or ended in freezing pools I dared not enter, not knowing their depth or width. Once the ground grew soft, boggy, and I hoped I had climbed near the surface, but then it dried and hardened once again. The passageways narrowed, yawned open, tightened into dead ends.

Over and over through that lost time, I felt Hades near.

When I stopped — scrabbling, sobbing, dragging myself through the dark — I could hear breathing. Mine? I could not see my body so my breath seemed like another's. I held my breath. I had played the same game as a child, hiding under the covers, listening to the wind in the corn and anything that might be breathing in the dark. It was too faint ever to be sure I did not dream it — that there was someone else there, taking in air, letting it out. But he did not help me, did not speak, or touch me, so I cannot know that he was near. I struggled on, alone.

I tried to escape. I wanted to return.

Today is not the first time I have betrayed my husband. He felt betrayed already then when I would not eat his food and tried to leave. He felt betrayed this year, beside the flooded river, when I told him I had no choice but to return. He is a man who thinks in absolutes: never, always, nothing, everything. It is why he hates the deal with such vehemence because it forces him to live a life of sometimes. He is older than me, but I cradle him, hold him still, after we make love, and, despite his certain, hard-edges, I have a fleeting sense of his being lost, irretrievably, in some even deeper dark than I can reach.

A light rain patters on the skylight. I smell the may blossom on the bedside table, the damp earth, the petrichor outside. I try to come back to only here, only now. I feel afraid by what I have done, and by what I have remembered. Everything seems to draw near. I made love to another man, and it has brought my husband to me, my keenest memory of him yet.

I lie very still, hear — think I can hear — the squeak of someone stealing up the stairs. I hear — think I can hear — the twist of a hand on the attic ladder. I think I can smell sweat — not mine. I want to call out to my mother, like a girl, afraid of what is coming for me in the dark.

I roll onto my side. I need to sleep.

Another creak. In the attic now.

An inbreath. Out. Not in time with my breath.

It is nothing.

A ghost my guilt has conjured.

I lengthen, open out onto my back.

And something lowers down onto my bed.

A hand cups over my mouth to stop my scream.

I open my eyes. In the faint starlight, through the attic window, I see the outline of a man.

My hand goes to his hand, across my mouth. I feel his knuckles under my palm. By these I know him. With his free hand, he takes my other hand. This is how every winter starts. Hand in hand.

But it is May.

We are in the attic of my mother's house.

His presence here, now, feels almost as great a violation as my infidelity.

I prise his palm from my lips.

'What are you —'

'Shhhh.' He squeezes my hand.

'— doing?'

I push up. He presses me down.

'Shhh,'

'But you —'

'Don't worry, love.'

The familiar quiet of his voice. When we speak, if we speak, one of us consoles the other. One of us must be the child. Right now, it is me. I cannot understand that he is here — I fear I made this happen — I summoned him.

'Why?'

He sighs.

'I came to tell you —'

'What?'

He bends to me.

'The deal is over.'

'Over?' I feel blank, as after an awful accident.

'Your mother cannot control the seasons anymore.' He whispers it into my neck.

'But spring is here!'

'It would have come without her. Without you.'

'No!'

'The world is dying,' he whispers. 'But this time it is not your mother's doing.'

'What do you mean?'

'People are killing it. Killing themselves. The seas are rising, lands sinking. The forests are burning, crops failing, animals dying. There is not long left, my love. But I will give you shelter, under the earth.'

He is quivering — I have not felt him this exultant since the first time we made love. He sits up, strokes my hair.

'You need not climb here anymore.'

'But —'

'Aren't you glad?'

'My mother —'

'Cannot even stop a road being built through her home.'

He takes both my hands again — for once his excitement is greater than his hurt.

'That's different to —'

'If the road keeps coming — when it comes — at midsummer, I will fetch you.'

'But —'

'Shhh.'

He presses me down again.

The world dying? My mother powerless?

The deal, over.

The deal that has been more than set in stone. Stones shift over millennia — the deal has not. It has defined my life, and I have hated it because I never chose it, but now I hate that it could be undone, suddenly, as if it had been a flimsy arrangement all along.

Everything — my breath, heart, thoughts — is going too fast. At the same time, Hades' hands, slow, precise start to move down my spine. This is our ritual — after the hands — his inventory of me. Like a doctor performing a medical inspection, like an artist checking his work, his hands move over me, as they did when he first made love to me. He checks, reclaims, re-makes, each bone, joint. And, each year, I lie and let him do it.

But not here, not now. I reach up, catch his forearm. This is against the rules. He shushes me, undoes my fingers, goes on, down my vertebrae. From there he will feel my collar bones, ribs, scapula, and then my arms. It is in my arms I feel most the ache of climbing, of wanting to touch another man. I do not want Hades to find this feeling there or take it from me.

'Not here,' I say. I break another rule.

'Why not?'

I cannot answer this, cannot say any of the answers.

'My mother.'

'Is sleeping,' he says. He has reached my shoulder blades.

Quiet, quick as I can, I stretch out my right arm. Touch the bedside table. Find the lamp, the square of plastic under the bulb.

I press — it clicks: the light goes on.

My husband's body spasms in the glare. His arms flail out, swinging at the lamp, striking it away. Lamp, bulb, vase, blossoms fly, smash under the eaves.

Dark as sudden as the light.

Hades' knees, clamped either side of my body. He is panting.

The light is like a knife I drew on him. It is worse than the breaking of a rule. The dark is where we live, where we love. The dark is our togetherness.

He presses me down hard, his fist on my chest.

'Persephone!'

My mother, calling from below.

The landing light comes on.

'Persephone! What's wrong?'

I reach for Hades' fist.

'Nothing,' I call down. 'I just knocked over the lamp. Sorry to wake you.'

He lets me take it.

'Oh, I'm glad it's nothing else. I'll go get the dustpan and brush and a candle,'

I uncurl his hand.

'No, don't! Don't worry.'

I interlace my fingers with his.

'It's fine,' my mother calls up. 'It won't take me long.'

We listen — Hades and I — as she goes down the stairs. And for these moments, we are back where we began — he is a strange boy who should not be on my mother's property. I am hiding him. And, incredibly, this old, simple story is enough to override all others, all the rules and rituals that this day has broken. There is no question that he would stay and face my mother. There is no question that I would reveal him to her. We both know how this story goes.

I sit up. I kiss him.

'Wait there,' I say.

I go down the attic ladder and turn off the landing light. As soon as it is dark, Hades joins me, and I lead him into my mother's study. I pull up my old bedroom window. It is stiff but shudders upwards. Hades is already sliding out onto the ledge.

'At midsummer,' he says, 'I'll come for you.'

He squeezes my hand. I squeeze his back. And then he is climbing down into the night.

Afterwards, a candle on the table, everything swept up, my mother again in bed, I climb back into mine.

But when I close my eyes, I see my husband's face in that electric second of light — an agony of uncertainty upon it, as if he was about to gain or lose everything he ever wanted. I have never seen his face in such a light. Only in shadow. Maybe he has looked that way for years, ever since the deal was made, and I never knew.

But now, he says, it's over.

There was another time when I thought it might come undone. When the astronomers arrived. Their science. Explaining away what the gods did once. But we carried on. Because summer still meant happiness. Winter was still sorrow. And my mother's moods could be felt a field away, or more.

And now?

A road is coming through our home. The world is changing, irrevocably. What's left to trust?

My husband would say stones and bones. My mother would grab a clod of earth, reveal a seed — seeds last as long, she says, as stones.

But I am not sure I believe either of them anymore. Tonight, the most real thing I know is a tree I climbed. The feel

108

of ink sunk in a layer of skin, under my hand — a slight raised edge. Things that are already gone or will be soon.

10

DEMETER

It doesn't take much — bake them a few buns and within a week they are calling me a goddess again.

'Here she comes,' the road workers say, 'The goddess of the goods!'

There are many of them now — plenty of mouths to feed. Alongside the chainsaw operators and bulldozer drivers, there is a ring of security round Woodmoor Copse. Then there are the police, the tree experts, badger experts too — conservationists — though how anything can be conserved while it is being wrecked, I don't know. There's a new lot too, people from the papers. More people, from the villages and beyond, come to watch. So I am kept busy, which is good.

I will never tire of seeing the great and simple change a meal can bring. Seeing how well-fed bodies slacken, loosen, lean, weight resting, digesting. That is when the stories start. When names are exchanged, roles slip, and before you know it one of the security, the toughest-looking one, has fallen for the woman with the shaved head who is living in the trees, and he has swapped sides. No thunder bolts or magic arrows, no love potions — just a bit of lunch did that. It is not only wine that loosens the tongue. Elderflower cordial and a good loaf of bread will do the job as well.

Slowly, as the May moon waxes to full, then wanes, they start to talk to one another, and they talk to me. The tall, wiry police officer is called Moses. He's been in the force for thirty years and he shakes his head and says it's not what it was. Then there's Will, a younger lad in the security line. He had a job filling shelves in Tesco, got depression, was put on drugs, says this job is the best he's had because there's no strip lighting. There are the stony ones, grim-faced, lock-kneed. But in the end even they accept a sandwich and once that's done, I know I've got them. They start to tell me who they are, why they are here, what they think, what they wish the world was like. People always have. Everyone, that is, except my daughter.

'You got a magic porridge pot?' Moses calls out to me when I arrive with my bags of biscuit tins, as I do every day now.

'No, just big mixing bowls and strong arms,' I say, smiling.

'You're gonna need more than that to keep up with the numbers coming in now.'

He is right. Two hundred security men arrive in coaches on the Woodeaton road to form a human fence around Woodmoor Copse and Prattle Woods. The road people are growing in numbers too, in the trees, on the ground, in among the last of the bluebells. Not just the purple-haired and the big-bearded ones I saw before. New ones turn up with bright banners, placards. One lad wears a badger costume, spends the day talking to the kids from the villages who have come to hang out too, to watch the fight and the fun. The weather is erratic. Too hot one day, a downpour the next. But they carry on, nonetheless. It is like a festival in among the netted trees. Music. Dancing. Crazy costumes alongside bright yellow uniforms. People filming, taking photos. I provide the food.

What with the wild weather, the tea breaks, the sheer numbers now in the woods, slowly the work loses momentum. There are mutterings. It is costing huge sums to keep the tremendous machinery of it going. It takes a ruthless confidence to organise this many men to come and cut down this many trees, to press the vision of a road onto the land. I know this. It is the same angry certainty it takes to change a boy into a lizard. You have to hold the vision steady. No room for doubt. It used to come to me easily — now I am only sure of two things in that whole-bodied way: that I am glad when my daughter comes, sad when she leaves.

They came here to change a wood into a road, but they are wavering. The netted trees are headline news. And then there is the photo of a cuckoo, its head and beak, tangled in the white nylon of a net, near the base of a tree. 'The Cuckoo that Cannot Call' it says over the picture in the papers. That does it. That and my tea breaks.

'Word's come down from on high, we're clearing out,' Moses tells me. It is the last Monday in May. 'Tomorrow they're to start taking the nets off.' I smile, offer him a swig of elderflower cordial.

'Thought you'd be pleased. Only postponed it mind you. They'll be back as soon as nesting season's over.'

'That's a few months away yet.'

'September, October. Still, that lot will be whooping,' he says, pointing over to a huddle of the road people, my daughter among them.

'Yes,' I say, 'they will.'

The next day Persephone and I take sandwiches to Prattle Woods and watch the nets come off the trees. Moses is not there. There are far fewer security and police, since they know there'll be no protest. Under a wide blue sky, everyone works together for once to unveil the trees. Two cherry pickers drive in from the Woodeaton road. Men on the picker's platform cut the white threads up one side of a tree and then a long line of workers and road people pull from the ground, until at last the branches, that were bent under the strain of the net, fly up free. They look glorious. Oak, ash, beech, birch, elm. Like new inventions. Elegant, complex structures, aimed straight at the sky. A cheer goes up with each new tree released. Everyone looks easier — the workers too, as if they had been granted an unexpected holiday.

I open up my bags of goods and hand out sandwiches — egg mayonnaise in some, blackcurrant jam in others. The men help themselves. They stand back and admire their handiwork, taking big, glad mouthfuls.

Persephone has moved over to be near the group of road people — the original lot, led by the man with the big beard. While I have been befriending the security, workers, police, Persephone has spent her time with them. When she is done handing round the food, she goes and sits next to the big-bearded one. I wish she wouldn't. I was always unhappy about her friends when she was a girl, the boys at least. None of them were good enough for her, and then afterwards I would have swapped any one of them for the man she married.

I look over at her. She has pulled away from the bearded man now. She is crouched down, her back to a beech tree. She is smiling, watching the nets coming off, but she looks white. It reminds me of how she was before she left, when she was with me but missing already, barely there. There is one egg sandwich left in the tin I am holding. I go over to her, offer it. She shakes her head.

'Go on, love. You didn't have any breakfast.'

She hesitates, takes it. I stand back behind her, pretend to watch the work, watch her. She sniffs at the egg like an animal, nibbles at one edge of the bread. Then suddenly, she is hunching

113

forwards, head thrust down. I run over.

'You all right?'

She is retching, mouth wide open, nothing coming out. Then she hides her head between her knees, sets the sandwich down on the ground, wraps her arms around her legs.

I put my hand on her back, rub her shoulders. I remember feeling the bones of her before. I remember how sick she was when I first brought her up from underground. How she could not keep her food down. I think of how pale she is still, and slow to eat, whenever she first arrives. But that is in March. Not May. Not now.

'What's up?' I ask.

She shakes her head, keeps looking down.

'Just a bit under the weather,' she says, and even her voice is thin. Under the bright, blue weather. I keep my hand on her back but look down with her, think down. Hades is under us, waiting, ready to take her. I look back up at the freed trees, spiky with life, patterning the sky. But he can stay away. There will be no road here by midsummer. This wood will still be wood. My girl will still be mine.

11

PERSEPHONE

I wake, feeling queasy again.

Hunger can make you sick. You can be so hungry that you cannot eat. My mother has never understood this.

From the attic I smell dust, blankets, the house under me, my mother in the kitchen, the raw dough in her hands. I sense it — puffy, wet, claggy — and I gag.

The only thing that helps the sickness, curbs the worry, is the woods. Though I am sure it makes it worse as well, feeds the hunger. Still, I go whenever I can. I climb the tree. I lie with Snow. I abseil down. And the climbing and the sailing are part of it. To feel my hands, pulling up the tree. My weight on the line. Then his hands on me, bringing me up. Mine on him. These things steady me. Up in the oak there's volumes of air and I can breathe without retching.

I need it. The need is unbearably physical. I wish it wasn't. I wish I was in love. But I feel it in my stomach. In my thighs. On the inside of my elbows. In my palms, teeth, throat.

No, I tell my mother, I can't manage flapjacks. Or sandwiches.

I want Snow to touch me. I want to touch him.

He looks surprised when I show up.

'Can I visit?' I ask. I try not to sound desperate.

He rubs his bald head, tugs his beard. 'Just so you know, I'm not looking for a relationship right now.'

'Me neither.'

He laughs.

'Well, in that case ...' He shrugs, smiles.

Nonny lends me her harness.

I am like a stray animal who has discovered someone who will feed it. I feel pathetic, but I cannot stop. I tell myself that if Hades had not come to me, not told me the deal was over, I would not be doing this. But he did. So I do not have long before I will never feel these things again. I do not share my mother's optimism about the road, even though the nets are down. It is over a month now since Hades came. Only a couple of weeks until midsummer when he said he would be back.

I roll onto my side. Slowly, I slide one foot off the bed onto the floor. I drop down onto all fours and crawl through the dust to the top of the attic ladder.

In the bathroom, sun is streaming through the open window. I sit on the loo. The room is full of more smells that I can taste — lavender, bicarb, peppermint. I pee, stand, look at the white loo roll, remember the shock of red that slid from me in March. I feel sick again, throw the tissue in the water, lean over the loo.

I retch.

I bled a second time in April.

It is now June.

I did not bleed in May.

Not since I lay with Snow.

I retch again.

I try to stand, lean against the bathtub. I am shaking.

I feel stupid. Stunned.

Bathtub. Door. Edge of ladder. I have to hang on to things, — the names of things. I look at my hands on the rungs as if they belong to someone else, another woman I have never met. I hear my mother go out to the garden down below.

I make it to my bed. I stare at the dust motes. I remember when I first began to starve, I had a hollow centre that was only mine. Now I have another secret. One I can scarcely believe. Not nothing. Something. Someone. Life starts in hiding.

'Found you,' I say, and the words make the dust whirl.

I count it out. My life has been measured in sixes. Six moons here, six there. This will take nine. Would take nine. My heart thumps and my mind leaps to terrible futures: Hades taking his inventory of me, discovering the swelling, striking me, killing it. Or could it live? Could I hide a child in the dark? But it would not survive down there. It has a mortal father. I imagine lying bleeding in the dark as this new life leaves me. Or maybe, before I go underground, I will miscarry. This, I realise with disappointment and relief, is the most likely course. Because I was never strong, could never carry much. My mother bore the sacks of corn, always gave me the lightest load. Yet despite the certainty that it will die, I cannot stop the sudden joy. I am sick, hot, shaking. But I am amazed that I can do this, can mother someone, however small, for however brief a time. I want to hug something — the bedding, dust, my body. The sky. Snow.

I need air. I stand on the bed and lever up the window as far as it will go. Hot sky on my face. The smell of wild oats, barley, rye, in flower — the grasses my mother tamed. A wind blows from the south and the trees in the back garden surge. Birdsong. And a shout. A voice the wind caught up and flung across the fields from the woods. I will walk out that way.

I get up, dress, go downstairs. My mother is washing potatoes in a big bowl of water, lining up the clean ones like pebbles on the table.

'First ones of the year,' she says, nodding at them.

117

'I'm just walking out to the woods,' I say.

'Have some breakfast first.' She points to the rolls, just baked, on the board beside the open window.

'Thanks,' I say. I take one up and I bite into it in front of her. It is easier to eat now I understand the sickness. She nods.

'You'll be back for lunch.' It is half a question, half a statement.

'Yes. I won't be long.'

I smile and go.

I am halfway across the field when I hear another sound cutting the air, a whine I have come to know: chainsaws. Then sirens. I reach the stile, climb it, see blue lights flashing along the Woodeaton road. I stumble on towards Noke. More whining. More shouting. I am nauseous again. I throw my breakfast roll into the grass, cross the last fields to the woods.

It is only three days since they took the nets away. The protestors had a celebration round the fire. They had the summer at least, Snow said. A temporary victory. But now, as I approach, I see police among the trees, the usual kind and others too, wearing helmets with visors. A blue-and-white tape flutters round the camp. A digger is breaking branches off the trees and a cherry picker extends its long-jointed arm between them.

I reach the site, look up — a big man is standing in the sky. Snow. As I first saw him. On the walkway between his oak and Big Ben's. The cherry picker is at his tree, two men in its bucket. Another man, in climbing gear, is on the treehouse platform, with a knife.

'Last warning!' he shouts.

'You can't,' Snow shouts back.

'I bloody will.'

'Snow! Move! Now! For fuck's sake,' Big Ben calls up from the ground. Snow starts to inch along the walkway.

I spy Nonny in the corner of the site, hunched over, handcuffed, behind a line of police. I run round the cordon to be near her, squat down. I want to reach her but am scared to touch her. There is shock, grief, rage in her body.

'Nonny!' She turns.

'What happened?' I mouth it.

'We all relaxed, didn't we? They attacked — bastards.'

'But the birds?'

'What the fuck do they care? No one's watching now.'

It is true. There are no spectators but me. No cameras. No phones filming. No one expected this.

'What'll happen?'

'Taken in. Charged. Released on bail I expect.'

'Where will you go?'

'Nut says we can stay at her folks' in Islip.'

She is looking up as she talks. I do the same.

Snow is the only one left in the trees. He has clambered onto the walkway's upper rope, and from there into the highest branches of his oak. He clings to a slender branch. The cherry picker manoeuvres its long arm up. The hard-hatted men lean across and haul him off the branch into the picker's bucket. He has leaves clutched in his hands. They lower the bucket to the ground.

They bring Snow out of the cherry picker, handcuff him. I stand. I want to go to him, but there is the blue-and-white tape in front of me, police either side of him. He spots me, looks away, as if he does not want to be seen. As they start to lead him off, he pulls back, swears. The policemen yank him forwards.

The other protestors are dragged off after him, through the trees.

I stare after them, him. Because I am always the one to leave, I have never felt this tearing away before, that I feel now with Snow — my whole body crying out for him, for his, across a distance.

I came here for one morning of elation. To climb an oak. To hold the father of my child. To feel these words in my mouth with their astonishing new meanings. Father has always meant Zeus. Child has always meant me. I wanted this morning to soar, like the woods, now in early summer leaf.

I turn back to the camp. The oak is trembling. A man is already at its base, pressing a chainsaw into it. I have climbed that tree. My arms know its height. It is in that tree that the baby began. I cannot believe there is a life inside me. I cannot believe the tree will fall.

It tips. Its topmost branches, to which Snow was holding only minutes ago, judder sideways. They swing down, describing a huge arc. As it lands, I feel the thud in my feet. It lies stretched out, beside the yew. Snow's shelter, smashed.

I am shaking. I go up to a police officer standing by the cordon.

'What about the nesting season?' I ask.

'The camp scared away the birds. No nests here, so they can come down.'

He is wrong. There is a bird, a tiny one, a coal tit. It is flitting from one branch of the fallen oak to another, not understanding how the tree can be at this angle to the earth.

I feel as confused as the bird. And I feel a new thing — outrage. Because the tree should not have fallen. The road should not run here. The baby should stand a chance.

They fell more trees. The beech. Ash. Pine. Thunk. Thunk. Thunk. As if it were nothing. The men with the saws, with their protective headphones, seem neither to hear, nor to notice what they are doing.

Only the yew is left. Ten thousand years old. No one has built a house in it because its many branches with their million needles are too dense to prise apart. This tree, surely, can defend itself. Its needles are dark, except at its edges, where they are light green with this year's growth. There are knots along its scaly branches, like joints but also like thoughts, stories, spells. I spy slivers of sky through its needles, as if the sky and it fit together, part of one fabric, so that if the tree were felled the sky too would fall. No one could harm this tree without being harmed themselves.

But here they come. Even they feel it — they lower their visors, redo the velcro on their bright yellow jackets. They go inside the tree, because it is like that — a tree that you must enter, a dark green room. I know. I know the tree with my eyes closed, from underneath it. I have crouched within its roots, year after year. I will never see the men again. The yew will kill them, the earth swallow them. I hear the whining from within. The needles quiver.

It does not take long. Ten thousand years of growth, over in minutes. But the tree hardly shifts. It does not perform the dramatic arcing of the oaks, because it is not tall and spacious but wide and thick, so it only tilts, rests on its huge outer branches and is done. The sky holds. And out come the men, unharmed.

My entrance to the underworld — gone. Am I stranded with the living? I imagine, for the first time, being trapped here, not there, imagine having a life up in the light beyond the summer. No. There are many ways down, other passages, hollows, tunnels. Yet it's as if I've glimpsed something extraordinary, a rare sight — a golden eagle over the woods, already flown, but it leaves a sense of awe. And fear. And hope. Though, right now, sharper than any of these is grief.

I stare at the life and death tree, on its huge green side. It is like losing something I did not know it was possible to lose. Until this year I have been careful. I have not grown close to anyone or anything up here, so that I can leave lightly when the autumn comes. The yew was how I left. The first and last life that I passed. Like a grandmother — a mother without the difficulty of her longing. The yew has let me come. It let me go. Now it is gone.

The digger comes for it. It hauls the yew aside. It breaks its branches.

I hold on to the thin blue-and-white plastic tape because there is nothing else to hold.

What feels terrible is the lack of proof that there will be. They will take all traces of this tree and of the others. I think of the life inside me, the youngest possible, too small to see, as I watch the smashing of the oldest thing I know, besides my mother, besides the only other tree that could match this one, the pomegranate, far below. A baby, conceived in a tree. It is evidence, proof that this wood was.

I do not understand it, but I know the child changes everything. Until now, part of me has always felt I was to blame. I left. I ate the seeds. I did not choose the deal, but I believed that I deserved it.

But the trees did not deserve to fall. The child too has done nothing wrong. Its only guilt is growing.

The road is coming. My mother cannot stop it. Hades will find a new way up here to take me, us, down. I stand and watch them drag the trees aside. Standing and watching is all that I have ever done. I turn and hurry from the woods, towards my mother's house. It may be too late, but I must try. After nine thousand years of walking this way with even steps, I break into a run.

12

DEMETER

She is late for lunch.

We do not eat every meal together. Not breakfast, but most lunches, every supper. Until this year, once she had arrived, she never left but stayed within the garden walls. I am not used to waiting for her now, in June.

She only went for a walk in the woods. Yet she has not been well. There comes the old fear in my chest, like a cuckoo's egg hidden in the pipit's nest, a feeling that has no rightful place in me. Only a walk. Only the woods. That was all it took the first time. But the woods are safe now, and it is summer. My season. Out of the front window, above the sink, I can see dog roses and beyond them, poppies. Little rags of red. Not a tidy flower. They stayed wild, even once the corn was growing in neat rows.

There is sweat on the nape of my neck — I feel it when the wind blows, and it cools on my skin. It was a day this brilliant when she went. A south wind then too. I listen. Birds. Grasshoppers. Cars. Somewhere, a siren and a shout. Everything sounds far away. I wonder if I am growing deaf or if it is only that there is less and less I want to hear these days. I begin to wonder what my place is here. If I have one. But I am still a mother. Not to the corn. To Persephone — I am her place in the world.

And she is still not back.

I get up, go down the hall to the front door. I consider walking out to find her. That is what I did before. I do not want to think of what I found instead, but this afternoon I cannot resist it, like being unable to turn away from a dreadful accident. There is horror hanging in the air today, as well as pollen.

I stare out towards the woods — that was where I went first, took hold of every tree, shook it for answers, as though she might come tumbling down. The trees shivered, shrugged their leafy shoulders. 'Not here,' they said. She had been, though. She had passed that way. But now the woods were quiet, ordinary. I left.

I waded through rivers, crossed grasslands, beating back the growth. I climbed mountains. I lifted every rock, scrabbled through the scree. When I reached the mountaintops, I screamed her name. I spat at the wide land, crawling with life, not hers. The horizon was a shining line of silver. If she was nowhere on the land, I would have to search the sea.

I stumbled across beaches, slippery with seaweed, picking up empty shells, their smooth insides twisting into secrets. I looked out into the endless rolling blue-black water. Not my realm. I listened for her sighs amid the slap and swell of sea. I stood on the sands, waiting, and the waters drew near, crept over my feet, calves, covered my knees, thighs, circled my hips, lifted my skirts.

For a moment my heart boomed with hope — someone was coming. In a great spray of white foam, my second brother rose out of the water. The last of us to be swallowed. Poseidon.

'Have you seen my daughter?' I called out.

'No,' he bellowed back, 'But I have seen her mother who is just as fair.'

I turned in disappointment and disgust, to wade back to the shore. Behind me I felt the waves rising, leaning into me, tasted their salt. I heard him coming after. I felt my own wave of rage lift me and I began to run. Something of the sea, its foam-edged crests, came into me. My running became faster, my feet harder, my face grew more urgent, my hair wilder, teeth tighter. I galloped at last out of the sea, hooves beating, mane flying, straining up the shore. But Poseidon followed my change. He caught up with me, mounted me as a stallion, pinning me to the ground.

After that I could not speak. That was when the drought began.

I would have drained the ocean, but the waves rolled on. I walked back home, not as horse but woman, with no tears left. And no child. It did not rain again. Even as I followed it, the river slowed, grew thick with mud and weed.

Everything began to shrivel. The leaves aged a hundred years. The grain was parched. I did not care. I had no care left in me but for one thing.

I do not want to remember any more. I turn, go back into the kitchen. I go to wash the strawberries, sitting in the sieve beside the sink. Glossy red but for the pale tip of one that must have had a shadow over it and missed the sun. I run the tap, hold my hand under the stream to feel for the cold, gaze out the window. The water pours over my hand. It is icy-cold now. It keeps pouring, I keep looking, for there, climbing the stile, is my daughter. Either the news is terrible, or wonderful, or both, for she comes as I have not seen her since she was a girl. She comes running.

I leave tap, water, strawberries, rush to the front door. She looks white as she comes in through the gate.

'Love, what is it?'

Someone has hurt her. One of the road people. That bearded one. She sprints up the path, pushes past me, runs down the hall. I glance over the fields to check no man is following.

Not the road man. Not Hades. I turn, hurry after her.

When I come into the kitchen she is standing, hands on the back of her chair. She is staring at the lunch, laid on the table, breathing hard, hunched over, as if she might be sick. I turn off the tap, go to her.

'Sit down, love. Catch your breath.'

She shakes her head, presses her eyes shut. I put a hand between her shoulder blades. She flinches at my touch, shrugs me off.

'You can't stop a road with lunch,' she says, pointing at the bowl of salad on the table.

'What do you mean?'

'They came back. The trees are down.' She holds the chair again and her voice wavers high and small. 'The yew.'

I remember my shock and rage when Erysichthon cut down the grove behind the house. I feel only a dull ache now. It is too late for more. I lift my hand to my daughter's back again. She lets it stay.

'But they said ...'

'I know, but they came for the camp. They've evicted it. The road is coming.'

I shiver in the heat of the day. But Hades is not here. Not now. Not yet.

'Listen.'

'No.'

'Just sit. I'll get you some water.'

I go back to the tap, run the water cold again, fill her a glass. Her hand is shaking as she lifts it, drinks. I pick up the glass, go to refill it.

'Hades will take me now.'

I freeze to hear her name him. I turn.

'Has he come to you?'

'You cannot stop him.'

'Has he? What did he say?'

'And it isn't just me.' She sounds hard, angry.

'What?'

'You'll lose your daughter,' she looks down and her voice lifts high and small again, like a tiny song. 'And your grandchild.'

'My?'

She looks up.

'I'm pregnant.'

Something deep rises in me, like water drawn from a hidden well. My child, with a child. The chance to be, not the mother, but the grandmother, to watch as life unspools, not mine to tend, only to love. Something I never allowed myself to want. I would weep, but here is my girl, pulling all the breath she can into her slight body, because it is shaking out of her in horrible shudders now, so I go to her, set down the empty glass, and there is nothing I can do but hold her.

A cuckoo calls in the back garden. A mayfly comes in from the pond, alive for a day. I did not know the seasons could come so fast on one another — such gladness, such sadness. If only I could stop the turning year, hold her here forever in this early June with the green of everything outside. If only some greater god than me could petrify us now. I hold still in case my stillness can still everything. Already she is slipping from me. She pulls away, red-eyed.

'Love,' I say. She says nothing. And then, though I know it is the wrong thing to say, she looks so pale and weak I cannot help myself.

'Just have some lunch, and then —'

'No!' She reddens.

'I'll not let you be taken.'

'You've failed.'

'I promise —'

'I'll have to do it. I'll join those actually taking action,' she shouts. And then she walks out of the kitchen.

I listen for her storming up the stairs but hear the back door instead. She'll go to the pond. I should leave her, give her time, but I cannot. Not now. Not with this news. I follow, out the door, down the garden path, stop at the apple tree.

She is not by the pond. She is by the gate in the back wall, one I barely use anymore. The path is overgrown with ground elder, brambles. She cannot get to the gate. She is going for the wall. It is dry stone — I built it. There are foot holds enough but it is not steady.

'No! Persephone!'

She does not turn. She straddles the wall, swings over her other leg, pushes, and jumps down. She walks out into the meadow.

I do not move, cannot move. It seems I can no longer command myself. Let alone the harvest. Let alone the seasons. Let alone my daughter, disappearing now, towards the river.

'Persephone!' I call again, not to order her. I want her help. She ran away from home in secret the first time. Here I am watching her go again, doing nothing — she could outrun me now. But she is not going down to the dead — this I know. And she is carrying a life. The father will be that tall one with the beard. It will be him to whom she runs. But I know men — he'll care more for his cause than her. And his actions, the ones she so admires, will never stop the road. All their displays of protest, their slogans, and their banners — they'll never be enough to keep her safe.

I think little of her plan of running to the father, but I fear that I must do the same. I vowed I never would again, but for Persephone I will. I'll go to Zeus.

13

PERSEPHONE

A Lucozade bottle and a can of beer lie on the bank. I lean against a willow tree, worn out from making it across a meadow. The river is bright green with duckweed — it looks as if I could walk over it. I stare at the ground, as if it too were a trick, might split again and take me — the baby too.

The baby, quiet as the water, growing inside me. A swan comes out of the reeds, hisses at me. It is only trying to protect its young. I want to hiss too. Keep away. Keep off. Keep us safe.

I have to find Nut's house — that is where Nonny said they would go. The swan drifts through the green weed, leaving a wake of black behind it. I follow it, along the river towards Islip.

I cannot remember the last time I was down here. My mother says this is where I was conceived. It frightens me: the dark water, green weeds, willows, swan, the memories lurking in the reeds along with the swan's nest. The river joins the woods to here, the living to the dead, things that happened thousands of years ago to now. It joins me to Phoebe. My best friend. Red-headed, freckled, sharp-eyed, faster than me. She had a baby too.

Before my mother made the pond, the river is where we came to bathe. Phoebe and I used to wade in, feel the mud between our toes, then stand, backs to the current, watching the 'V's we made as the river pushed against us. We let the water run through our fingers, then lifted them, flicking droplets upwards, making split-second jewels that rained down round us.

It was here that Phoebe first told me her news. We were lounging on the bank, watching the coots, and she lifted up her smock, put my hand on her tummy.

'What are you doing?'

'Feel anything?'

'What?'

She laughed.

'Phoebe!' She looked the same, but I understood that she had changed.

She had the baby while I was still missing. I saw them again once, by the other river, underground.

I cross out of my mother's meadow into the neighbouring one, better tended, where the grass is shorter. On the opposite bank is a field of rape, a pungent yellow under the blue sky. I keep walking, keep remembering — the river underground, the view across it, Phoebe.

After leaving me lost in the dark, Hades reclaimed me at last. Out of nowhere, I felt him. I should have been furious, but I was too grateful for his body, holding mine, too afraid that he might leave again. I clung to him, and I could feel how glad he was as well. We were like children, hugging in the night.

'I have something to show you,' he said.

I thought it would be more jewels. I feared it would be food. But it was neither. It was worse.

He led me to the river, where, at that time, phosphorescence glowed in its depths like sunken stars, filling the chamber with an earie silver light.

'Look,' he said, pointing across the water, as if I should be pleased.

Men, women, children were gathered on the far shore,

wasted, filthy, crying out for passage. The crowd stretched back as far as I could see. A mass migration underground. The air stank of urine, faeces, fear.

Then Hades pointed to the river. Willow leaves floated on its surface, yellow, brown, and black. I had never seen leaves that were not green.

'The world is not well,' he said, gently. 'See how the people run to me, to us, for refuge from their suffering.' He took me by the hand, pulled me beside him. 'Your place is here now, as my wife.'

I stood, horrified. The ferry boat was pulling in, further down the shore. I broke from Hades, ran to it. I would get in and cross back over.

'Persephone!' Hades ran after me. 'No! You must stay! I need you here!'

But I had eaten none of his food then. He could not stop me.

As I drew near the boat, the people disembarked. They were thinner even than I had been before I left. Their legs and arms were sticks, their faces hollow. They staggered up the bank, gave themselves over to the dark. I felt shaken by the sight of them, afraid of what could have caused such famine. I came closer, ready to climb in. One last woman stood in the boat, carrying a bundle in her arms. I looked into her face and froze.

'Phoebe!'

She frowned and shook her head, the bundle tight against her chest. Her baby. She had only just begun to swell before I left — I had no idea I had been gone so long. I offered a hand to help her out, but she did not look at me. She bowed her head to the bundle, stepped onto the shore, dropped to her knees. I crouched down by her.

'Phoebe. What happened?' I whispered. She did not move. I leant in, saw the brand-new face of her child, eyes closed. It looked empty and full at the same time. In that moment I understood that it is the places we are not that give us life, the gaps inside us that allow air, blood, sound and thought to flow. The baby had none — it looked solid as stone.

I lifted Phoebe. It was like cradling a shadow — she was unbearably light. I carried them — her in my arms, the baby still in hers — further up the shore, away from the river. I set them down on a flat rock.

'You will be safe here.'

Phoebe lay hunched around her baby, breathless, quiet, dead. I stood as if I could protect them from what had already happened.

I stop again now by the next stile, newly appalled. Here I am by another river, with another baby. Mine. It too does not deserve to die. It is buried in me now, expecting life. Conceived in a tree. It must be dreaming of the wind, the leaves, and light.

I pull myself up over the stile. Another grassy field — some cows in the far corner. From here I can see Islip bridge. I keep walking, close to the river. Today the sun is as hot, maybe hotter even than when I was a child in the days of endless summer. I remember the hushed ravings of the dead that I heard as I stood by Phoebe. They spoke of unimaginable things — the sun struggling to rise, sky turning white, water turning hard, crops failing, trees stripped bare. And they spoke my name, my mother's name; they said the world had turned ill from the day I left.

I had thought the earth would carry on, my friends straggling in the fields, my mother in the kitchen baking bread. I had thought the sky would stay blue, the trees green, the corn gold. I was a fool.

Hades was standing, watching, waiting for me. At last, I left Phoebe and her baby, and went to him.

'What's happened?'

He slid his hand around my ribs and drew me to him.

'The world can't live without you. It is following you down. It is your dowry to me,' he whispered.

He kissed my neck.

'But, my mother —'

He kissed my mouth.

'Shhh, how can the grain grow with you gone? But don't worry — you belong here now.' He kept on kissing me.

A thousand deaths — my doing. Phoebe's. Her baby's. I wanted to die, too. I thought the shame and horror of it should be enough to kill me. I still do.

I reach Islip bridge. I hold on to the railings near the road. I am sweating. I look at the river. The duckweed is less dense here, but the water is a tangle of lilies and reeds. For a moment I dream of slipping inside it, under it, of drowning. But it is barely deep enough, and though I have hated myself for years, I do not want to disappear. Not anymore. In truth, I did not even want it then. When Hades took my hand and began to lead me back into the dark, I pulled away.

I would have walked back to the shore. I would have stepped aboard the boat and crossed. I would have climbed up to the woods. I would have gone home over the fields. I would have done what I could to make amends for what had happened.

But as I turned away from Hades to the river, I heard a voice. It came from over the water, from the passages beyond. It carried above the cries of the crowds gathered there. It echoed down the tunnels of the earth and made them tremble.

'Persephone!'

I stopped.

'Persephone!'

My mother had found me out.

'Persephone!'

She had come to fetch me back.

I heard, even from that distance, the grief in her voice. The need. And I could not bear it. I could, I would, have faced the anguish of the earth, its peoples. I could not face hers.

I turned. I took hold of Hades' hand and went with him into the dark.

I climb over the railings, onto the Woodeaton road. I cross the bridge into Islip, keeping close to the wall. I leave the bridge. There is a pub called The Swan opposite, and a woman is outside clearing glasses from the tables in the front. I cross the road, stand by the pub wall.

'Excuse me.'

'Yes dear?' She looks up, five glasses gripped in one hand.

'Do you know where Nut lives?'

'Nut?'

'Dark-haired, small. She has a baby called Berry.'

'Oh, Natalie — one of the Caseys' daughters? Yes, on Middle Road. Up the hill, first right, then first left — it's the one on the corner, tulips out front.'

'Thanks.'

I walk up the narrow street ahead. It is a hundred years at least since I have been into the village. I should be nervous, but I am furious.

The grain could have grown without me. Phoebe and her baby could have lived. It was my mother's doing, not mine. She killed them. And she is doing nothing now to save us. Me.

The woods. This baby. My baby.

I climb the hill to Nut's house.

I sit in Nut's parents' living room, a plate of baked beans and toast balanced on my knee. A thick, pink fitted carpet under my feet. A huge TV on the wall opposite, above a gas fire — neither of them turned on. The room smells of air freshener, of flowers canned and sprayed. A radio is on in the kitchen, next door. Nut's little boy is pushing himself to standing using the glass coffee table in the middle of the room.

'He's only just started doing that,' Nut tells me.

She is on the armchair. I am on the sofa. A big, brown leather-looking one that squeaks when I shift on it. I am glad to eat and nod and not say much. I hadn't realised how hungry I was. Back down the little hall, out of the front door with its leaf pattern pressed into the glass, past the neat tulips, down the hill, over the bridge, along the river, through the meadow, is my mother, in my mother's house.

'You all right?' Nut asks.

'Bit shaken.'

'Yeah, I'm sure. I had to get Berry off-site as soon as the sheriff showed up — I didn't want him there.'

Berry has made it to the far corner of the coffee table. He grins back at his mother. Her phone, lying near her at the other corner, buzzes.

'It's Nonny. They're not going to be kept in overnight.' She bends over the phone, 'I'll tell them to come straight here.'

I finish up my toast.

'Put the plate on the side in the kitchen — I'll load the dishwasher in a bit.'

I get up and go into the small kitchen on the left. The

surface by the sink is a smooth, mottled white and grey. The dishwasher is white. The floor is white. My mother's house is not dirty, but it is full. Full of objects — lost, found, made, mended, gifted. Full of surfaces that are full of stories — every stone, beam, table, doorway, window. And in between the solid things, drifts dust. A million flakes of other times hang in the air. It is a relief to be in this clear, white house.

'Nut,' I say, coming back into the living room, 'can I stay the night?'

She looks at me, head to one side, Berry on her knee.

'Need some space from your mum?'

I nod.

'Tell me about it. Luckily, mine still works. She'll be back about six. And my dad at seven.'

'Don't worry if it's difficult.'

'No, they're all right. Do you mind kipping on the floor?'

'No.'

'We've only one spare room — my sister's — and Nonny and Snow will need it. But we could grab the cushions off the sofa.'

'I'll be fine on the floor.'

So I stay. I spend the afternoon in Nut's sitting room, on the wide, squeaky sofa. I mind Berry while Nut loads the dishwasher. He goes back and forth along the coffee table like a tightrope walker practising his act. He turns and smiles at me like everything is simple and fine, and I want to believe him because he has no doubt in his little body. I look out the window to the square of lawn, edged with tulips. I dream of hiding here in this dust-free house, of changing into an ordinary woman, pregnant, like Nut was. Going to have a baby with clear eyes, tottering legs and no doubt.

Nut's phone buzzes again. She picks it up.

'They'll be here in a minute.'

And then the doorbell goes.

Nut goes to the door with the leafy glass, and I follow, holding Berry on my hip as if he were mine. She opens the door, and there are Nonny and Snow. They smile but look worn out. My heart goes faster, because of seeing them again for the first time since the eviction, and because Snow is the father of whoever is inside me. Nonny is the aunt.

We pile into the living room. Berry goes back to his coffee-table trick, and I hug Nonny, then Snow — his whole body, tight, knotted. It is strange to see him in a house — I remember when I first went up the oak, how he said he'd find it hard to be back inside. He sits beside me on the sofa and the room looks cramped now he is in it. Nonny sits on the armchair. I am grateful that neither of them questions my being here.

'So?' Nut asks from the doorway.

'Released under investigation,' Snow says.

'No charge then.'

'Thank fuck.'

'That's something. What were they like?'

'Like coppers. I don't really want to talk about it.'

I know that feeling. Snow has his head in his hands. He runs one hand to the skin and muscle of his neck, rubbing them. He looks up.

'We need to go back and rescue whatever they've left of our tat.'

Nonny groans. 'Not now!'

'They could burn the lot — they might have done it already. I've got a bloody good sleeping bag in that treehouse.'

'I'll go,' I say, heart thudding.

'Thanks.' Snow puts a hand on my back.

'I can take you in the car as soon as mum gets back,' Nut says, 'It'll still be light.'

'Got any painkillers?' Nonny asks.

'Sure. Pers, can you flick the kettle on?' Nut calls out, heading up the stairs, 'It's just on the right by the cooker.'

I help make tea for everyone.

Nut's mum comes back. She is a small, brown-haired woman, like Nut, smartly dressed. She looks surprised to find so many people in her living room, but not cross.

'Hi, Mum. Did you get my texts? You know Snow and Nonny. This is Persephone — they're all staying in the spare room.'

'Yes, I got them,' she says, sitting on the sofa, weary.

'And we need to rescue our stuff from the woods. Will you babysit Berry? And can I borrow the car?'

'Give me a chance, dear!' She takes up the baby, smiles at him. 'Okay, Natalie. Go on then.'

Nonny goes up to bed. Snow, Nut and I go out to the car. Nut drives us back to the woods. We park on the Woodeaton road, where the police cars lined up this morning.

The evening light is beautiful as we enter the woods, see the trees lying, long and silent. A digger has gauged out the yew's roots, but little has been done to clear the camp.

Snow climbs through the branches of his oak, over them, under them. He ducks inside what is left of the treehouse, comes out with two sleeping bags and a water bottle. He spends half an hour going round the shelters, the bender, pulling out saucepans, bedding, cursing over the tools that have been confiscated. Nut and I carry all that he finds through the woods and load it into the back of her mum's red car.

'Where have the others gone?' I ask Snow.

'Crashing at mates' in Oxford, or home,' he says, carrying the camp kettle and its rack from the fire pit. 'That's everything I can find. Thanks for your help.'

We are quiet in the car on the way back. Quiet having another round of toast in front of the TV.

Nonny is already asleep on the bed in the spare room. On the floor, Snow lays out one of the sleeping bags that he fetched back from the woods.

'Don't want to disturb her,' he says, nodding at his sister. 'Anyway, I don't think I can handle a bed yet. Here, do you want Nonny's?' he offers me the other sleeping bag.

'Thanks.'

He lays it down on the grey carpet next to his, between the bed and the window.

We both climb into our sleeping bags. I watch Snow, staring up at the white ceiling in the darkening room. He looks like one of the felled trees, lying in grief, but quiet as wood. I think of the baby, in me, in the sleeping bag. I want to tell him. I do not.

Instead, I slip my hands out of my bag and reach across to him. I brush his face, his beard. He closes his eyes. I roll towards him and hold him though it feels awkward. He throws one long arm round me. I think back to the start of the day, to waking to sunlight and sickness in the attic. The carpet under us smells of cleaning powder. Snow still smells of the woods and the smoke from the fire.

'You're not giving up yet, are you?' I whisper to him.

'No.'

'I want to help.' His arm tightens round me.

'It will get hardcore.'

141

'How?'

'Now we've nowhere to live on site, it'll be all about the actions.'

'Like?'

'Lying down in front of diggers, locking onto them. Scaling the bloody great fence they'll build in the fields. Have I put you off yet?'

'No.'

'You're hired.' He kisses me on the cheek. 'The more the merrier, though it may not be very merry.' He lets me go. We roll apart.

'Night,' he says.

'Good night.'

Out of the window the sky is dark blue. There is a fingernail moon, newly risen, a sideways silver smile. I dare not trust its hopefulness. In this neat house, my life is a story no one would believe. I think down, through the bedroom floor, through the tidy living room under us, to the layers of concrete, down through the earth, into the old dark that is more constant than anything up here, and I know it is real enough. After that slender moon grows full, midsummer will come, and Hades will be here.

14

DEMETER

She did not come back last night. I couldn't sleep. The silence
was too loud. Not that she usually makes a great clatter. I do
that. She makes little sounds — a puff of breath to clear the
hair from her eyes. The creak of the attic ladder, the pad of her
feet to the bathroom. The noise of none of this kept me awake.
There were only the owls. Foxes in the fields. A zealous robin
in the early hours.

Today, I will set off to find her father. I boil a kettle. My
fingers feel clumsy, cramped. I must have been holding nothing
tight all night. I take a mug of hot water out to the back door,
pick some mint leaves from near the top of the path and let them
darken in the water. I do this most mornings in the summer,
when she is here.

I sit on the back step, look out past the growing beets and
beans, the apple, the pond, to the meadow. There are two of
them now, out there. My child and my child's child. I know,
for now, that she is still up in this world. I do not feel the ache I
have when she is gone from it. That is something — or, rather,
everything.

I watch the robin, the same one that started the
morning songs, who feeds not only her brood but some thrushes
too. I am envious. It is all I want to do — to feed my young. The
day will be hot again. I should be picking redcurrants, planting
out the leeks. I sit, look at the water in my mug, now pale green,
the drowned mint leaves at the bottom.

If Hades is right, the earth now has no need of me. The robin will keep feeding, the currant bushes fruiting, whatever happens to us next. It is horrible to be frightened in the summer, to be out of step, out of season.

Where did she spend the night? I asked this every night when she first went missing. Her absence was most awful then. I used to dread the sunset. I would have held up the sun if I could, not wanting to have darkness come without her safe within the house. And then, once I had realised where she was, I wished the sun would sink as soon as it had risen, hoped it would never make it higher than the trees.

It was out here, in the back garden, that I finally understood.

I had searched the earth, the sea, for her. I had come home to search the sky.

All day and night I sat on my back doorstep, in the withering garden, and looked up at the realm of looking. Midday, the sky looked back at me with its unblinking blue. No clouds. Only unrelenting sun and empty air. I hauled up a bucket of water from the well and the birds flew down in their hundreds. Not only songbirds, but the big birds too — buzzards, eagles, hawks. The ones who could fly highest, see furthest. I asked every one of them — have you seen her? They dipped their beaks in the bucket, tipped back their heads, shook themselves, looked at me sideways, no, they said, nothing. At night I asked the owls. Their answer was the same.

I stared dry-eyed at the stars. Could she be lost among that multitude? I looked for any trace of her — the grey of her eyes, the ribbon of blue that runs across her temples. I looked for these tiny things and for the vast — I feared I might see her placed up there as a new constellation, a glinting picture for her father's gazing pleasure. She would not have been the first, pinned aloft forever.

The moon waned, then waxed. The night that it came full its light swept every corner clear. The sun blinded me, but the moon was studied in her light, forensic. If Persephone is in the sky, I will see her there tonight, I thought.

I sat where I am now and searched every crevice, every inch of air. I searched until the night itself grew tired and grey.

As day came, my mind was blank as morning. No thoughts, only a terrible thirst. I got up and walked along the garden path, past the leafless apple, its fruits shrivelled on the branch. I reached the well.

Our well was deep. I picked up the bucket. It banged against the walls, swinging as it jolted down. Persephone used to marvel at how long it took before she heard the splash of water. At last, the bucket hit the hidden river. I let it settle, sink, fill. I started to raise it, hand over hand, heavy as life. The taut rope cut into my palms. Was a bucket of water too much for me to bear? Had I grown so weak? It felt as though I were pulling up all the sorrows of the world.

Halfway, I paused for breath. The bucket hung, the rope pulled. I sat on the wall of the well and looked down. I felt the damp and cold come up from the depths, as heat comes from a fire. The well glowed with dark. The horror of it took my breath away, the memory of sliding down my father's throat. My grip slackened, the rope ran through my hands, ripping my skin raw, the bucket fell and crashed into the water. At last I understood.

My daughter was not on the earth. Not in the sea. Not in the sky. There was only one place left I had not looked — the only place I could not go. Down.

I realised I had known it from the start but refused to let it be the answer. Even then, when I had searched everywhere but there, I wanted to deny it. I could not find her in that dark and, worse, I would lose myself while looking. My eldest brother, the one nearest me inside my father, held that realm. Hades.

Persephone thought the night lived down our well. I used to laugh, would haul up clear water as if to prove her wrong. I never told her that a far worse dark than night dwelt there.

I had wanted to find her on my own. But if she was down with the dead, I would need more than a bucket and rope to fetch her back. I would need help.

This morning, I must again fetch help. There is less than two weeks before the third moon grows full, and then midsummer comes. I get up off the doorstep and go back into the kitchen. I pack bread and cheese, a bottle of elderflower, into a battered blue rucksack that some walkers once left lying on the garden wall. I leave the potato salad, yesterday's lunch, in the fridge. I write a note, in the hope that Persephone returns before I do: 'Welcome home. I've gone to get help. Food in the fridge. Water the garden if you can. Feed the hens. I may be gone a few days, but I won't be long, I promise. x x x'

I go down to the hens, fill their feeder with grain and top up their water bowl. Then I set off. I go the way she went, down the garden path to the overgrown back gate. I pull the nettles, brambles, and ground elder up so that the gate swings open easily. Best to clear it. I don't like the idea of Persephone climbing over the crumbling wall again if she comes back.

I can see the way she walked through the meadow yesterday, where the grass lies flatter, parted like long hair. The earth under the willow is scuffed. I follow the signs of her into the village. I head over the bridge and left, then up Church Lane to the little shop, at the end of the village hall — the place I go for my groceries and gossip. I want news of my daughter, before I set out after Zeus.

Sure enough, two women are leant over the shop counter, talking. They straighten up as I come in. I recognise them but do not know their names. Few people in the village know me now. I have been many things to many people over the years — goddess, witch, sage, midwife — but nowadays I'm just the crazy old lady from the fields. The women nod and smile, nervous. They have glossy well-cut hair, neat earrings, good clothes. I know what I look like — wild grey hair, bramble-pricked arms, a blue dress made from a pile of old jeans, dusty sandals. I pretend to look around the shop. The women close back to their talk.

'The police came early.'

'I know, I saw the cars on the Woodeaton road.'

'It's a shame.'

'Well, it was never going to last, was it?'

'I suppose not.'

'Were they arrested?'

'I think so.'

'Four of them came in here earlier,'

'Really?'

'Natalie Casey and her little boy and three others.'

'What were the others like?' I ask. The women look round, startled.

'There was a tall man with a beard and two women,' the lady behind the counter tells me.

'A fair-haired one? Silvery-fair?'

'Yes,' she says, frowning. 'You looking for someone?'

'Just checking she's safe.'

'They took Nat's little boy to the playground opposite. Might still be there.'

147

'Thanks.' I buy a packet of digestive biscuits and a local newspaper. I leave the women to their talk and sit outside the shop on a bench. I can see the playground from here. They are not there. I have a moment of wondering how it might have been if Persephone had lived up here, separate, but near. But it is thousands of years too late for that.

As I thought, she has run to the father of the child. The tall one. And now I'm to do the same — go find the father of my child.

I stare up at the sky. It is years since I have seen Zeus, but every now and then I have caught a glimpse of him, whipping up a storm, swaggering in the background of a photo in a newspaper with other men of power. I have heard stories of him too from the young women and men whom he has taken as his lovers and then left. For all I know, he could have vanished into that brilliant blue, or be living on a mountain, far away. But I do not think so. He is a god that needs to be worshipped. It was why he agreed to the deal in the first place, so that there would still be people left alive who could adore him.

I open up the newspaper. There are headlines about the road. Predicted heat waves. A possible storm — Zeus may be near. I skip to the adverts at the back and the listings of local and national events. One near Leicester catches my eye — Download Festival — the premier rock festival in the country. That will do. I will head that way. I could catch a train, but I prefer to walk. I will have a better chance of finding him. He could be in any summer field, lying with his latest love. That is where I found him last time I went looking.

I used to be good at finding things. I hope this is a power I still have. Zeus was never good at hiding — I do not imagine this is a power he will have gained. My younger sister, Hera, his jealous wife, always found him out.

I put the paper in my rucksack, the rucksack on my back and walk down the hill towards the river. I walk to the end of Mill Street, over the weir where the River Ray meets the Cherwell and on into the fields. The Cherwell will take me towards Oxford, then onto Banbury, from there I will have to trek cross-country. Distance does not concern me, and I have a good sense of direction, as long as there is light — sun or stars — to guide me.

I am glad to be moving. The idea that I could lose Persephone, and forever, comes and goes under the bright sun. It is hard to hold. I was not built for fear. I am better at hope, but this is a desperate kind of hope, to be seeking Zeus out, to be hoping he will have a power I have lost, to be hoping he will even want to help when last time he did nothing. Worse than nothing. But still, he is Zeus. He used to be the king of everything.

I catch a flash of blue, a kingfisher diving from reed to river. Blue wings. Green reeds. I must keep alert. Zeus could be anywhere, anyone, any colour. Last time I did not recognise him at first. I walk, and as I do, I remember how it went, and sometimes I wonder which time I am walking through.

I had followed the river's course then too. It led to the foothills of Olympus. It was no more than a dirty trickle by then. Fish, dead and rotting, lay on the drying mud. The willow trees had turned skeletal.

I walked all day across the barren fields. My feet and skirts grew grey with dust. The dry stalks of the grasses snapped and crackled underfoot. The ground had become hard. I stared at it — my daughter was down there.

I remember some cattle lying at the edge of a field, their flanks lifting and dropping in the heat, dry-uddered, too weak to stand. A few farm labourers were out, desperate to harvest whatever grain they could. Once I saw a rat, scrabbling amid the brittle stems, searching for a seed. But, for the most part, the fields were empty.

It had been late afternoon when I neared the foothills. I was about to leave the river to turn to them and start the climb. I glanced up at the sky. An eagle soared and circled overhead, looking for food. Good luck to it, I thought — there was nothing for it here. But then it ceased its circling. It hovered in the blue. I looked ahead for what it might have spied. The river curved round to the south and a dry scrub of hawthorn blocked my view.

Suddenly, the bird dived, like a dark arrow pointing down towards the river, and at the same time I heard a woman's cry. I broke into a run, reached the scrub, pushed through. I came out into the clear, rounded the river's curve, and saw them.

A swan was fleeing from the eagle in a whirr of fierce, white feathers. It rushed into the arms of a young woman, dark-haired, not much older than my daughter, who was standing on the riverbank. The eagle swooped low, then dived as fast again upwards, back into the blue. The woman held the swan, or was held by it — I could not tell. Its great wings spread around her like a cloak, its neck wrapped about her neck, its beak against her breast. She called out again, in shock or fear, and fell back onto the bank.

I drew close, clapping my hands, to usher the swan away. I remember vividly how the swan slid its neck from the woman, turned and hissed as if it were protecting her, as if I were the threat. It half-raised its wings, like pointed elbows, stretching forwards. As it hissed, I saw the jagged ridges along its orange beak, its dark, narrow tongue. I looked into its small black eyes and in the blackness saw a tiny image dancing there, not myself reflected back, but someone else — my brother.

I stepped back, startled. The swan swung round again towards the woman who sat, unmoving, terrified. It stroked its neck against hers. It lifted its wide wings in a shudder of feathers, then softened, lying quiet along her body.

At last she moved. Slowly, trembling, she eased herself out from underneath the swan, struggled to standing, then turned and ran along the riverbank.

The swan watched her go, stretching its long neck after her. As it did, the neck began to bulge and swell, its beak to split, its ridges spiked to teeth. A ribbon of blood ran from its mouth. The wing-bones cracked and splintered, the white feathers wrapped around themselves, grew fibrous, muscular, and knitted into skin. The webbed feet and thin legs ripped apart and lengthened. The hairy head of Zeus thrust its way out of the swan's slender body. At last, there he stood, King of the Gods, a scatter of feathers and blood at his feet as if marking the site of where some smaller bird had lost its life in a skirmish with the eagle. His changing was brutal, not a shifting and a merging, but a murdering of one form to make way for the other.

He was not as elegant as the swan, but he shared some of its long-necked arrogance, its wide-winged power. And those intense black points in his eyes were the same. My younger brother. The only one of us to grow up in the light, and he forever had the glow of sun about him. I felt his heat as we stood beside the parched river. Above him the eagle circled in the blue.

He still looked the way the woman had run.

'You frightened her away,' he said.

'It was not from me she fled.'

'You look a sight. Enough to startle any young woman.'

I glanced down at my torn skirt, my arms and legs, scratched and dirty, the hair on my shoulders, matted and tangled.

'You should take care,' he said.

I swallowed my anger. 'Our daughter is with the dead.'

'Indeed.'

'You knew?'

'Yes.'

'And you did nothing?'

'Why should I?'

'Nothing to save her? Nothing to tell me?'

He stood, gleaming, golden, composed. I wanted to hit him. But I needed his help.

'You must fetch her back.'

'Hades is a great god. It is an honour that he chooses our child as his bride.'

'I do not feel honoured.'

'Why not?'

'He stole her.'

'Did he? Did she go against her will?'

'Yes.'

'Are you sure?' He narrowed his sky-blue eyes.

No, I was not sure. But it did not help to think this.

'You should be glad she is well loved,' he said.

'Her place is not down there.' I stamped on the hard earth. 'It is up here. With me.'

He sighed, went to the river's edge, sat on the bank and looked at the water left in the drying bed. He patted the dusty earth beside him. I did not move.

'Come here,' he said, his voice softer. People did what he said. Even me. I sat down on the bank.

'Children leave home,' he said. 'Girls grow into women. They yearn for more than their mothers can give. They want their fun, their freedom, just as you did when you first came to the earth — remember?' He put one of his mighty arms about my shoulders. I stiffened. 'You are too fond. She needs a man.'

'Not that man. Not there.'

'You have to let her go.'

'I came to get her back.'

He frowned with his great, thick eyebrows. 'She may already have eaten his food.' He lifted his arm from me, pointed to the dried mud of the riverbed. 'Then what could I do? She would have to stay.'

I stared at the earth.

'You do not understand.'

Zeus swung his arms back, rested on them, watched the eagle circle. Evening was coming on.

'I'd best get home,' he said. 'Hera will be wondering where I am.' He smiled, trying to make me his conspirator. I looked away.

'Go home,' he said. 'Think it over. Change your clothes, brush your hair. Perhaps you too have yearnings.' I was still staring at the mud, when I felt his hand slide down my thigh.

'No,' I said, hissing like the swan.

He shrugged again, unruffled. Stood up. He gestured to the dried land, clicked his tongue, 'And restore your blessing to the earth.'

'Not with our daughter gone from it.'

He looked at me with those blue-black eyes. 'Do not make

others bear your grief,' he said. He turned and began to walk away, back up to Mount Olympus, in long easy strides.

I crouched, close to the dry, cracked earth. I wanted to thrust my fingers into the cracks, to widen them, to reach down between them to my daughter. I had no blessings in me. Only curses, dry and dusty.

It muddled in my mind — my fury at my brother, the swan, the white of its feathers, the young woman running, the loss of my daughter, the fear that Zeus was right, that she had wanted to leave me. I did as he said. I went home and thought it over, and that was when cold came to the world.

I do not remember clearly the walk back to the house, nor the days that followed, when the first winter began. I remember only how I watched at the window as the world changed. The sky grew white as the swan, the earth black as its eyes. The water in the kettle, dew on the ground, the clouds — all froze, hard as its beak.

I hated Zeus' certainty. I had seen the swan molest the woman. I had seen her fear. He had told me that it was I who frightened her away. He had told me that my daughter wanted Hades. I would not believe him. That was his story, not mine. Yet his words chilled me. Fear crept into me, but not the kind to make me run. Instead, it made me shuffle about the empty house. 'He's wrong,' I'd say out loud, my breath like a ghost, hanging on my every word, haunting me. I wrapped myself inside a blanket and sat for hours at my daughter's bedroom window. I would spend every winter waiting by that window, but I did not know that then.

In the end I had to ask the question: what if Zeus were right? What then? What use was I? I, who had always felt full of purpose. I, upon whom so many depended. Somehow it meant nothing if my child had no need of me.

'You need to let her go,' Zeus said. How could I? Not to the dead. Not where I would never see her. I longed for her. Still I saw her everywhere — as a young girl running across the field, as a child digging in the earth for worms, as a baby, suckling by the window in my arms. All times and ages came to me. How could I let her go when she was part of me? How did any mother ever do so?

I slept and woke where I was. Day ran into night. Night into day. She had asked me once which was the greater — day or night — I had told her they were even. Now I no longer knew which was which and did not care. I did not change my clothes or brush my hair. I sat, and the cold deepened its grip on me.

I had no guests. Everyone stayed hunched inside their homes. People had given up trying to scratch food from the ground — there was none. The search was over. I knew where my daughter was. There was nothing to be done but sit and watch the world grow white. I willed it to grow colder still. I was not cold enough, not numb enough. I still had a horrible ache. I would get flickers of it easing — a moment of looking out at how the frost edged the hawthorn, at how the brief light shone inside the icicles that hung along the eaves. But then it would come again, like the eagle diving from the sky, an awful plunging. How cold would it have to be for me to feel nothing?

One morning, as if in answer to my question, it began to snow. The first snow there had ever been. I did not know what was happening. I thought the sky was cracking, crumbling, a million pieces of it falling to the earth, hiding any colour that was left. I went down to the front door and held out my hand. The sky-pieces were icy-cold but soft. Like ash. Like feathers.

I was surprised and moved. It was the first soft thing that I had felt in weeks.

The snow settled on grass, wall, branch, stile. It covered everything and showed the truth of it — its barren beauty. Here was another stage of grief. Not hard and angry. Not howling. A grief close to a caress. It made me want to lie down, be covered by the swirling flakes, never get up again.

But not everything gave up. Though I saw no one, the snow told me I was not alone. I saw tracks — the splayed three-fingered feet of birds along the wall. The paw marks of a fox, printed across the field. Were it not for them, I would not have made it through that winter.

Then one day, as I sat by the window, there came a knocking at the door. I started up. Had she come back? Had someone news of her? I staggered down the stairs. Could it be Zeus? Come to help me after all?

I opened the front door. It was not Zeus. No god at all. There stood a woman, small, hollow-cheeked, thin. Her skirts were dirty, torn as mine. She was frail but could not have been old — her hair was ruddy-brown, not grey. She steadied herself on the door lintel.

'Forgive me,' she said, and I wondered for what — for her presence on my threshold? Her frailty? Her ragged dress? I felt sorry for her, and it was a relief to feel something that was not hate or hurt.

'Come in,' I said.

I sat her at the kitchen table. Our breaths rose together in the frozen room.

I looked at the woman, huddled where so many had sat feasting. For days, cold had been the stiffness in my bones, the white land out the window. But now here was cold close up, in another, in how this woman held her arms pinned against her sides. I felt a flicker of pride — no guest of mine should sit here suffering.

I went to the fireplace, knelt, cleared the ashes from the grate. I reached for the wood and grass, still stacked beside the hearth. I took up my flint and iron-stone and struck a spark. The dry grass caught, threads of brown turned gold, snaked into life. The fire grew. It was strange to see orange again, to hear its hiss and snap. I had not noticed how silent the world had become, as well as white. Now here again was colour, sound, motion — the fire changed the room. I knew why I had not lit it before — its bright hope was hard to bear.

'Here.' I invited the woman to draw her chair closer to the fire. I fetched the well bucket, which stood by the back door. It had frozen solid. I took it up and set it by the fire to let the water thaw so I could give some to my guest.

'Thank you,' she said, smiling, and for a moment it was as if we were both remembering another time.

'Have you come far?' I asked.

'You do not recognise me?'

I looked into her small worn face. I saw the sadness in her eyes, the dark around them.

'Yes, but I'm sorry, I can't remember ...'

The woman tried to smile. 'It's Misme. Your tenant from across the river.'

I was shocked I had not known her. But she had changed. It was one of her sons, Abas, that I had turned into a lizard in my rage at his insolence. Her daughter was a friend of Persephone's. I looked down in shame.

'What can I do for you?' I asked.

'Our stores of grain are gone. And with this cold, nothing

157

will grow. I'm sorry to ask ...' she trailed off.

'I am sure there is something I can give you. There's only me here. I do not need much. I would be glad to help.'

'Oh, thank you.' She dropped onto her knees as if in prayer and praise. I knew she owed me nothing.

'Please. There is no need ...' I gestured to her to rise. She sat back at my table.

'Any sign of your daughter?' she asked.

'No.'

'I'm sorry.'

'And how is yours? How's Phoebe?'

Her eyes filled with tears.

'She's gone. Her baby too.'

'Oh, I'm so sorry. When?'

'Only three days ago.'

I reached across the table, held her hand. She rested her head in her other hand while she cried.

'Sorry,' she said.

'I understand.'

'I miss her so much.'

'Yes.'

'I'd do anything to get her back.'

'I know.'

'I'd go down there, to the dead, and fetch her if I could. I would not mind the horror.'

I stared at her, at her tired face, her thin body. Her life was simple, brief and hard. She was a farmer. One of my many tenants. And yet she had more strength than me. I stood.

'Help yourself to any food that you can find within the house.'

'Thank you. We are very grateful.'

'It is I that must thank you.' I was already at the door. She stood, confused. 'No, stay. Help yourself. I'm sorry, but I have to go now.' I turned and walked into the back garden.

My feet crunched on the snow. I reached the well. My daughter was with the dead. If Zeus refused to help me bring her back, I would go myself.

I looked down into the icy black. I had sworn I would never go into the dark again. If I were to go down there, I would need a light.

I went to the back door, took up my best knife, my leather pouch, turned again, walked past the well, down to the pine tree by the back wall. It was the only tree stubborn enough to have stayed green despite my grief, to have kept its sharp leaves. I had scowled at it before, resented its defiant growth, had even struck it with my knife, but now I was glad, both of its life and of the wound that I had given it. Resin, thick, sticky, and fragrant, clumped over the gash within its trunk. I scraped it off, gathered all I could. I collected twelve pine cones from the ground, frost-covered but intact. I smeared each with resin, then cut a branch, thick as my wrist, that was still green with life. I stripped it of its needles, slashed it at one end to make a slit, pressed two pine cones into it. I stashed the rest of the cones inside my pouch, strode back up to the house.

Misme was standing within the larder where I kept the grain.

'Oh,' she cried out, as if I had caught her at a theft.

'Help yourself.' I waved my hand towards the corn.

'Thank you,' she said, near tears again. I turned away, not having time to comfort her or receive any more thanks. I knelt, set my pine torch to the smouldering logs. It caught. I stood, flame in hand, and hurried from the house.

I came again to the well, looked over with the torch held high. Far down in the dark a small light shone — the flame's reflection in the river. It was enough.

I climbed over the edge, braced myself against the cold, damp stones, and slithered down into the dark.

I stop walking and I stop remembering. I am not ready to remember more, not the descent, not now. It is strange enough to think of that moment in the snow, the bitter cold, while the sun beats down. I have reached Banbury.

I stand for a moment on the towpath by the River Cherwell. There are a few ducks and swans out, sliding magically along the water. But their magic is their own. Today these swans are swans. Zeus is not here. I must go on.

15

PERSEPHONE

'I think you should just watch,' Snow says. 'It's dangerous.'

'It's safer than doing nothing.'

He laughs at that, kisses me.

'True, in the long term. Not now. They call it non-violent, direct action, but I've got to be honest — it can get violent.'

'I've told you — I want to do it.'

We are on the edge of the woods, scrunched up under an elm, eating digestive biscuits. Snow, Nonny, and I got up before sunrise, met Maggie and Ash by Islip Bridge, traipsed on the footpath out towards the new road site. The work has moved to the fields near my mother's house. I half expected to see her out searching for me, clawing at the earth, but there was no sign.

At dawn, after the night security left, Snow loosened the bolts in one of the panels of the fencing round the site. Then off we went to the woods to wait and eat biscuits. I reach for another — it eases the sickness.

My heart is thudding, but it seems to do that all the time these days — be loud and dramatic, like my mother. It sounds as if I am on the run. In a way, I am. It must be working hard too because of that other heart, under it, stammering to life. I have not yet spoken to Snow about the baby. My mother is the one who is generous with her gossip. I do not give news — never say anything new. In anger, I told my mother, but now, with Snow, I do not know how to tell it. Every time I think of it, it feels too new, this news. Too fragile. As if in sharing it, I might lose it.

I do not know what to say, and I do not know what Snow will say. I know how my husband would respond, not what any other man — this man — would do. I am afraid he will not want it. Afraid he will not let me join the actions — it has, anyway, been hard to persuade him to let me come. So, I stay quiet, and my heart stays loud.

Nonny has brought two loaves of bread. 'From the reduced section in Sainsbury's,' she says. 'Not for eating. For stuffing up exhaust pipes.'

'Right,' Snow says. 'I'll take the bread. You lot climb up the machines, high as you can, and tangle yourself in their hydraulics. Then hold on. No locking on today — we don't want the police out if we can help it. Not so soon after the last arrest. We just want to let them know we haven't given up.'

That is our briefing.

I am in Nut's jeans, too short in the leg, too big at the waist, and Nonny's army jacket, also too baggy, and her old trainers. 'No sun dresses and sandals on an action,' Snow said. 'You need your elbows and knees covered and your feet and hands able to grip.'

Snow is unfolding now from squatting. His height is like a trick that he performs.

'C'mon. They'll be breaking soon.'

And we are off.

'Where's everyone else?' I ask.

'Working. No one pays us to do this shit. The opposite — they charge us if they can.'

We are close now. Staying by the edge of the field, crouching near a ditch full of nettles. I can smell the hot metal of the fence, the diggers — there are two of them and a bulldozer visible through the bars of the fence. The machines are vivid yellow against the blue heat of the sky.

The nearest digger judders to a stop — its clawed bucket resting on the ground. The man inside it tips his hard hat back, gets out his phone.

'Pers and Nonny take the first digger,' Snow says. 'Maggie and I will take the other. Ash, film the lot.'

The driver has climbed down, gone off towards a white cabin in the corner of the site.

'Go.'

We walk up to the fence. Snow undoes the bolt he loosened earlier, pockets it, slides the metal pole out of its concrete block, props it on the ground, creating a narrow opening into the site. He gestures to us, half bows,

'After you.'

I step inside. For now, the digger is hiding us from view. I feel like a thief. I've never stolen anything, except my mother's ladle, and myself. What am I trying to steal now? The land? A digger? Myself again?

As soon as we are all inside, Snow stuffs one of the Sainsbury's loaves up the exhaust pipe of the first digger, disappears around the side.

I draw near the machine. It is strange how much it feels alive. Nonny climbs up onto its caterpillar tracks. I follow over the thick, bumpy rubber.

Nonny is hoisting herself up from the cabin onto the roof. I copy her. The edge of the cabin digs into my stomach. My hands squeak on the hot metal.

I'm up. A shot of pride to be at the top. To be where I shouldn't. To see the whole field, the men below.

'Oi!' We've been spotted. Or Snow has. He is running, a loaf under one arm. I have never seen him run. He is like a bird, long-legged, tilting back as he sprints forwards. I imagine any

163

minute he might kick off from the earth, escape the security men by taking flight. He reaches the digger, crams the loaf in the exhaust, starts climbing.

Nonny is shunting herself out along the arm of our digger, up to the joint. I follow. There are thick black wires running up the digger arm, under me. Halfway along, a silver pole juts out, linking to the section of the arm that hinges down to the bucket resting on the ground.

'The hydraulics,' Nonny twists and mouths to me, pointing at the pole. I lie down, cheek against the pole, arms wrapped round it, legs gripping about the thicker arm beneath. From here I can see the rest of the site. The road workers are by the cabin in the corner, swigging cans of Coca-Cola. One wolf-whistles us. Lunchtime entertainment. Meanwhile the security men, in their high-vis jackets, white hats, have pulled Snow down — one on each arm. He has gone limp, playing dead, so that they are struggling to drag him out the way. A smaller man climbs up after Maggie who is on the digger's arm. She and Ash both get pulled off, hauled out of sight.

My hands are growing sweaty. The metal hurts to touch.

'Come on ladies.' The small man who pulled Maggie off walks up to our machine. He has no top on underneath his sleeveless jacket. His arms are orange-brown from working in the sun. He reminds me of my husband, but his face is more symmetrical. He squints up at Nonny and me.

'You coming down? Or do I have to come up?'

We do not move.

'Last warning, ladies.'

The man starts to climb. He has a small silver ring in one ear. I think this is a good sign, but even as I hope this, I know that it means nothing. As he climbs, his yellow jacket shifts and I can see the lines of his tan, the paler skin inside, the dark hairs under his arms. I am scared. And disappointed that this is it. That it is going to be over so fast, after waiting the whole morning. I had hoped it would take longer, that they might even give up for the day, expecting a grand reaction to my small action, as my mother might. But it does not work like that — Snow told me — 'We have to chip away,' he had said, 'It's all we can do.'

The man is on the cabin roof now. His hands are on my shoulders.

'Come on dear, game's up.'

I bunch in, hold tighter. Nonny is sitting up, watching.

'Well, maybe let's deal with you first.'

And now his hands have left me, but his sudden full weight is on my back. He is using me to reach Nonny. As I am pressed into the metal, I think of the baby, of its doll-sized heart. His weight lifts. Nonny is shouting at him to go easy. I put my chin on the pole to look ahead to her.

She is downclimbing the digger arm. The man, after her already, is kicking at her hands. She is near the ground when he slides down low enough to shove her hard in the stomach so that she cries out and falls the final foot. She smacks against the ground, curls up in a ball.

'Nonny!' I hear Snow's shout from behind us — he must be being held over by the fence where we came in. Another security man, slower, bulkier, comes over, pulls Nonny up to stand, leads her off, bent double.

The security man with the earring is climbing back up, for me. I imagine being kicked like Nonny. I imagine falling. I want my mother to come out of her house. I want her to be strong as a digger, to scoop me up, change the men to poppies. Or even my father — I wish he would swoop down from that too-blue sky and carry me away.

I think all this before the man has reached me because it does not take long to imagine a hundred horrors and have another hundred hopes. So, I have already imagined it when I feel his foot jam into my forearm.

'Don't say I didn't warn you.'

Then he does something I did not expect. He swivels me round, so that I am hanging, upside down, my upper body against the main arm of the digger, clinging on to it with my legs, my arms still on the hydraulics. And now the man is undoing my legs, so that in a moment I will be holding on with only my hands and they are sweaty.

I feel the blood draining from my head. I could faint. I will fall. The ground will punch through me, slam me, the baby. My legs are off. All my weight is in my arms. My hands are slipping.

'No!' I cry.

The man is sitting above me smiling.

'Help me!' I shout at him.

He leans in, 'Why?' he whispers. 'Why should I?'

'Because I'm pregnant!'

I scream it.

The man grabs my jacket, is hauling me back up, till I am straddling the digger again. He takes my wrist, tugs me to him.

'Either you're a lying bitch, or a selfish cunt — risking a child's life. Get down.'

He keeps hold of my wrist, part punishment, part a display of protection to the others watching, and I know they are watching. He brings me down, leads me to the fence where they are waiting. He pushes me towards Snow and Ash.

'Don't know which of you two gentlemen got this one up

the duff, but please don't let her climb any more diggers.' He tenses his face into a smile. 'Now, fuck off the site before I call the police!'

We walk over the fields. Behind us the machines start up. No one speaks. No one is looking at me but the sky, which stares down hot and blue. We walk the way I would walk in spring. We reach the stile in the hawthorn hedge. Maggie and Ash climb over first, then Nonny. She turns back.

'We should probably give you two some space,' she says. She looks at me, then Snow.

'Where you going?' Snow says, as if he would rather go with her.

'Back to Nut's. Though I might sit by the river on the way. Recover.'

'Text me where you are.' He sits down on the top of the stile.

'Sure.' Nonny and the others walk away, over the first field, down to the river, past my mother's.

'I'm sorry,' I say to Snow's back. He does not move.

I climb the stile, brush Snow, the edge of my arm against his, as I pass over. I sit below him on the stile's step.

'I'm sorry,' I say again.

He is staring at the empty earth — the stuff my mother ate when I was in her.

'Why the hell didn't you tell me?'

'I was scared.'

'Of?'

'I didn't know what you'd say.'

'Any idea when you were planning to find out?'

'I thought you might stop me joining in the actions.'

'Too fucking right I'd have stopped you.'

He looks at me for the first time since we left the site.

'That security man was right — it's fucking stupid. On every level.'

I look down. I feel sick. Sick with shame, with fear, sick with a baby. I need to hold on to something. I run my hands along the hem of Nonny's army jacket, which I am still wearing. I feel a hard object in the right-hand pocket, pull out a packet of polo mints. I unfold the green and silver wrapper, take out a white mint, spy the grass under me through the hole in the middle, think of the stretched holes in Snow's ears. I offer Snow a mint. Whether he takes it or not seems of the utmost importance. He does.

'I was trying to save the child,' I tell him.

'By climbing up a bloody digger?!'

'By helping stop the road.'

'What the hell do you mean?'

I have never told anyone my story. Other versions of it — my mother's, my father's — have been passed down through the years. Not mine. But if anyone is going to believe me, it will be a tall, bald, bearded man called Snow White who has trees growing on his skin — a man who is himself strange as a story, so there is a chance he might accept mine. At least, this is what I tell myself, because I know that now I have to tell it.

I have dreaded this. I have lived my summers up here as a recluse so that I would neither have to tell the truth nor lie. My mother loves the melodrama of the tale. I would rather keep it buried. That is one thing I like about the dead — they never ask me anything. I feel the familiar tightening that I have endured for years on the far side of the river, waiting for the boat — the resistance to return, the pull against the steep climb up. I could let Hades take me. Let the world go on up here without me. Let the baby die. It would be simpler. I look down.

Snow's boot is beside me on the stile. I remember it inside the climbing loop, his single foot bearing his weight as he hoisted himself up the rope to his treehouse, spinning. I remember following, prusiking up the thin line, the thrill of my arms pulling skywards — the sheer unlikeliness of it.

'I'll try to explain, but it's going to sound crazy,' I say.

'Can't be any madder than going on a bloody action when you're pregnant.'

'I've never told anyone this.' I offer him another mint. He takes it.

'Go on then.'

'Well, my mother is a goddess.'

'So was mine,' he says.

I stare at him.

He shrugs. 'She died last year.'

'I'm sorry.'

'It's how Nonny and I can afford to be here, on a protest — we're living off the sale of her flat. Anyway, you were saying about yours ...'

'I'm sorry,' I say again.

And then I do it. I tell him. I tell him how my mother made the field in front of us, how the summer was endless. I tell him of how, in the midst of plenty, I went hungry, of how I hungered for something my mother could not grow. I tell him about Hades. I tell him that he might have heard my mother's version, that I was raped and wronged — and I tell him the truth. I tell him about the dark, the dead, and then of how cold came because I'd gone. And all the while Snow sits on the stile and listens. Every time I am not sure whether I should go on, I offer him another mint, and when he accepts it, I take it as a sign to tell him more. And so I tell him the whole story, until there is one last mint left in the packet, and when I hold it out to him, and he takes that, I tell him about the deal.

While my mother called for me, under the earth, I lay with Hades amid the roots of the pomegranate tree, willing the dark to fill me.

But I did not disappear. Instead, Hades made love to me again, and the ground grew harder as did his body and mine — rigid muscles, tense, insistent hearts — and my mother's voice, getting louder, closer: 'Persephone!'

'I want you here forever,' Hades whispered. 'No one but you.'

'Persephone!'

My mother was coming.

Her cries echoed along the tunnels of the earth so that the living and the dead, the animals, grasses, rocks, rivers, every worm and dumb seed heard my name.

I wanted to run to her, beat against her, hold her. I wanted her to have the power she once had to make amends for any grazed knee, torn dress, broken plate. There was a time when I had no question that she could heal any shattering. I hated her for having lost this power, though no one had taken it from her but me.

'Persephone!'

Hades was inside me, tense with pleasure. He too cried out my name, and above his call I heard my mother shout for passage over the river. I wished I were a child again. I wished I were a different child, the one she wanted: simple, open, running to her. I shut my eyes on the dark and saw white. Milky white.

I saw my mother standing in the kitchen, over the fire,

beating milk in a pan, and then pouring it out into a cup, setting it down for me on the table, white and warm. But instead of drinking it I let it cool. And as it cooled its surface wrinkled, and the wrinkles held. A thin skin. Thin but firm enough for me to touch without it breaking.

'Persephone!'

At last, Hades arched, his hard face cracked open, and the ground shook as my mother set foot on the shore.

I tried to bury myself in Hades, but he lay now soft beside me.

'Persephone!'

My mother's cries were closer still. I thought of the warm milk, the kitchen, home. I had not eaten since I had last seen her, had felt no need for food down there. Now suddenly hunger came — a clawing ache that began in my belly but filled my whole body. It scratched its way down my arms, and up inside my face. I felt how thin I was. I put my fist to my mouth, pressed teeth into knuckles, to try to stop the wanting. I wanted bread. I wanted milk. My stomach clenched. I curled up, took my fist out, and retched, my body taut with trying to rid itself of everything that wasn't there.

'Persephone!'

I retched again. I sat up and pulled myself from Hades.

'Yes,' I told my mother, 'I am here.'

My mother carried a torch when she came for me under the earth. Its light flickered among the branches of the pomegranate tree. Tall shadows trembled on the cave walls. My mother's hair was loose and wild. She had bare feet, her skirt was drenched and torn, her face dirty and strange.

'Persephone,' she said, not how she had called it through the earth, but as she might across the kitchen. She opened her

171

arms, and all I had to do was go to her.

It was ten steps. No more.

I had come down here to find something of mine. I had found darkness, death, desire, and a man who wanted me as his. I had wanted my mother. Now here she was, and I could not move. Like the cooling milk I felt the skin of me setting. There was nothing I could do to stop it. I did not feel stubborn, but helpless. In that moment hunger was the surest thing I had — the only thing I knew was mine.

Hades sat beside me. He reached over a root for a pomegranate. He took up the dark fruit, bit into it, scooped out the bright red seeds. He set six of them upon his hand.

I knew the rules. When I had been alone, I had refused his food because I wanted to return. Now my mother was here, the choice seemed different. I was a child again. I was hungry. I lifted his hand and brought it to my mouth. The seeds were wet and sweet, the white pips, hard and woody. I looked at my mother as I ate. Look, this is what you taught me to do, I said to her, without speaking. If I was under any spell in that moment, it was hers, ours.

The shadows in the cave shook, a hundred arms waved a hundred flames as my mother quaked in disbelief and rage. She bent double on the rock. I thought she might be dying. But she shuddered, stretched tall again and came at me. She thrust her fingers into my mouth, trying to find the seeds, to pull them out. Her fingers were pushing down my throat when Hades gripped my wrist and dragged me from her.

'Leave us. She belongs here now,' he told my mother.

'She does not!' She took hold of my other wrist and wrenched me back.

She began to run, pulling me across the cave. Hades

sprinted past us and stood, blocking the way. He held the half-eaten pomegranate, lifted it towards us.

'You tricked her — you bewitched her!' my mother screamed.

'Give her to me —'

'Get out of our way!'

'— And I will let you pass.'

'You shall never have her.'

They stood, staring, hating.

All this time I had said nothing. Now, I began.

'Stop,' I said, although no one was moving. 'Listen.'

But I got no further, because then my father came.

We felt his approach, like thunder rolling through the rock.

The air grew heavy, as if the whole sky were trying to push itself into this cave far under the earth. Through the narrow entrance in the stone he came. The structure of the rock made everyone bow, lowered everyone's dignity, even his. He straightened up once inside, shook himself out. Father Sky. King of the Gods. In one hand he held his thunderbolt, a hard, jagged thing — a deadly weapon.

He was dressed for summer, bare-chested, a cloth draped loosely about him — he was never far from naked, not feeling the need to be robed in anything but his own power. He stood, surveying us. He throbbed with heat. My mother pulled me to her, held me, her arm across my chest.

'So, there you are,' my father said. 'I came searching for you. I went to your home, but you were gone.'

My mother's arm tightened, and I understood it was to her, not me, that he was speaking.

'Even Olympus has grown cold. There is snow banking up around my throne. You did not follow my advice.' He furrowed his brow to demonstrate his displeasure. 'The sacrificial fires have gone out. The festivals are not observed. The temples are deserted. The world is dying,' my father said, taking a step forward.

'When our daughter returns up to the light, the earth will be restored,' my mother said, low and quiet.

Zeus turned to Hades. It was strange to see them side by side — the tall golden god, the crouching, pale one.

'Brother, I know well the need for love. You need a queen — I'll find you another, but you must let my daughter go.'

Hades held the pomegranate up into the light.

'I will have no other. She belongs to me.'

Zeus looked at the shining fruit. Hard red evidence of Hades' right to me. My father frowned. He turned back to my mother.

'Then it is you who must let her go.'

'Never.' My mother's hold on me grew even fiercer.

'There is no doubt that she belongs to you, brother.'

'Then the earth dies,' my mother said. 'And all the peoples on it.'

The father of the heavens sighed. The air in the cave felt closer still. The sky was resting on our heads. I could feel my mother, behind me, shaking with anger. She hated his slow deliberation. She hated that he should have the power to do this, that it should be he who could decide.

'Come on,' she said, turning me around, as if we could leave through another hidden passage.

'There is no other way,' Hades said from the opening in the rock by which he sat hunched. My mother hesitated. My father beckoned me to him.

'No,' my mother said.

Zeus raised his thunderbolt. My mother's arm slackened. My father stretched his out. I felt small, unsteady, as if I were much younger, taking early steps, walking from my mother's to my father's arms. No distance, but it seemed miles. When at last I reached my father, he held me by the shoulders. He bent down, so that he was level with my face. He put his hand under my chin.

'You are well loved, my dear,' he said softly. 'The Goddess of the Harvests and the King of the Dead — both cannot bear to be without you. For a little thing you have made a great deal of trouble. What are we to do?' He raised his eyebrows. I opened my mouth as if to answer but he was not asking me.

'How much did she eat?' he asked.

'Six seeds,' Hades answered.

My father nodded. 'Six seeds,' he repeated. He frowned again.

And then he smiled. He puffed out a little gust of air. It was almost a laugh. 'Share her,' he said, and his tone was casual, careless. He paused, as if expecting some applause. That was when the light went out.

I do not know if my mother put it out, or if the torch ran out of fuel, but everything went dark — that was all the applause my father got for his ingenious idea. Everyone disappeared. I heard my father push out his breath in annoyance. He went on though, as if nothing had happened.

'Six moons down here,'

'No!' my mother said, out of the dark.

'Six moons up on the earth,'

'But she is mine!' Hades said.

'There is no other way,' my father said.

Silence, thick as the dark.

175

'She comes with me now,' my mother said.

I heard Zeus sigh, but more with satisfaction at the brilliance of his plan than with regret. He stroked my hair. I felt my mother's hand brush, then grip my shoulder. Zeus let her take me back.

He must have turned to Hades, for I heard him whisper, though loud enough for my mother and I to hear every word, 'In six moons, I will bring her to you.' I imagined my father's smile, Hades' scowl, my mother's mouth downturned. But nothing could be done — the King of the Gods had spoken.

No one was happy with the arrangement but my father. No one considered how it would be, what it would mean. No one asked me what I wanted. It was clear that it was for the best: my mother could have her daughter; Hades could have his wife; the earth could live.

The way back up to earth was long and hard. My mother and I picked our way in silence over rocks, boulders, clambered uphill along the channels made by streams, water worn. Both of us weak, both of us hurting, both of us fumbling in the dark. We came to a ledge of rock, felt different paths twisting upwards from it.

'This one,' I said, as if I knew the way, had always known the way back up to the world from deep within it.

At the end we had to dig our way back out. My mother moved the stone that Hades had pushed into place to prevent her finding us and following. A dim, grey dawn seeped into the little hollow left. Even that faint light hurt after my months of dark. My sickness started then, but the fever did not take hold until we reached the house.

My mother pulled herself out into the woods first, beside the yew, then turned to lift me from the ground, to brush the soil from me.

I did not recognise the place I saw. The earth had changed. There was frost round every brown leaf, every blade of grass, as if the world's hair had turned white with worry while I had been away. I stood for a moment, amazed. I watched my breath rise from me like smoke for the first time. I turned to my mother under the winter sun, pale as a moon.

She had changed too. I had not seen it in the dark below, only felt her jubilance at having found me. Now, up here, she looked smaller, older — or had she always been this size? Was it that after looking into darkness for so long, the edges in the light now seemed so sharp as to diminish even her? Her eyes looked red and tired, her mouth tight as if she was unsure of what to say.

She held out her hand. I took it and we tramped on through the woods, over frosty fields together. The bare, blind trees reached out to me as we walked by, as if I were a miracle worker and they, sick with winter, believed that I could heal them. The grasses began to murmur with rumours of my return. A daffodil opened its yellow mouth to call out I had been found. A blackbird picked up the news: soon the sky was crowded with song, loud enough for the whole world to hear. Even the glaciers far North, the mountains in the South, creaked as we approached: ice and rock relaxed and trembled, sighing in streams that slithered down their sides and told the valleys I was home.

But it was my mother's heart opening beside me that made life come again, the earth lighten enough for leaves to grow. Over the years, she and the world have come to behave as if I were the spring-bringer. But I never had that power, nor any like it. Simply by her sighs, the softening of her face, brightening of her eyes, summer was made inevitable again.

Summer then. Summer now. Nine thousand years later, some things have stayed the same. I point to a poppy near the stile, its floppy red petals shiny with heat, as if this little flower is evidence of everything that I have shared, which, for me, it is. The summer has always been this — overwhelming proof of my mother's love for me. A butterfly — a painted lady — zigzags up and down, in front of us, lands on a grass near my foot, blinks its orange-black wings open. It also confirms everything.

But the empty field in front of us, the rumbling machines behind, the heat, are evidence of other powers, not my mother's.

'This year,' I say to Snow, 'Hades followed me up. He came to the house to tell me that the deal is over, that my mother has lost control of the seasons, cannot even halt a road, that I would be his forever now. He said he would come for me at midsummer, if the road had not been stopped. That is why to save the baby, I have to ...' I peter out.

Snow is looking down at the butterfly.

'Do you believe me?'

Snow puts his face in his hands, opens them again, as if he were playing hide-and-seek with a young child, except he looks in pain.

'Look,' he says. He sounds tired but I can hear he is trying to be kind. This makes it worse.

'I've heard some crazy shit in my time — probably too much. A big veggie slop of divinity goes round the eco-activist scene — all sorts get invoked: Gaia, Pan, Shakti, Woden. There's some I've met who'd fucking love listening to you — they'd be all over you.'

He pauses. I slide off the stile step, crouch in the grass. I feel the redness up my neck, heat behind my eyes, try to lick the tears away as fast as they come.

178

'Thing is I'm just a bloke who hates cars, likes trees, likes living outside, hates the messed-up state of the world, can't sit on my arse while we trash the planet and crap over the rest of life on it. But I decided long ago that if there are any gods then either they don't give a shit, or they think we deserve everything that we've got coming. But really — I think we're on our own. I'm sorry — I really am — but you picked the wrong guy.'

I can feel the woman I am to him now, the one he does believe in — lost, alone, mental health issues, stuck at home with her mother too long. I can feel how he is repelled by me, by the fact that he was once attracted. I wish Snow's version of me — a mad, sad girl — were true.

Suddenly I miss my mother. She is only a field away, but it feels further. She has always seemed both too close and out of reach. Her version of divinity is so down to earth — cups of tea, meals on the table, weeds to pull up. I could try to explain this. That she and Snow would get on well. That she too hates nonsense, dreams. She too likes being outside, hates cars. I could invite him back. Maybe he would believe her. People like my mother. They always have.

'Okay,' Snow says. 'You asked me a hard question. Your turn for one now. Do you want to keep it? The baby?'

I wipe snot and tears off my face on the back of my hand, wipe my hand in the hot grass.

'Wanting it is not the hard part.'

'What is?'

'Keeping it.'

'Why?'

'I told you — but you didn't believe me.'

Snow has his face back in his hands.

'Jesus Christ — don't worry, I don't believe in Him, either.

179

At least you know it's not personal.'

He gets up off the stile, kneels in the grass beside me. The butterfly takes flight. I look at his hands resting on his knees.

'Look, I've got to be brutally honest. I can't promise to be the best of fathers.'

I shake my head. 'I don't expect much of fathers,' I say.

'I have fuck-all money. Just enough to be here for now. Not enough to support anyone else. And besides that, I don't want to bring anyone into the world. Not with it in this state. I don't think it's fair.'

I look up, through the little hole above the black ring in his left ear.

'I understand.'

'I'm not saying you can't keep it. It's your body. Your life. But I need you to know I can't promise to be there for you, or the child. I'm sorry.'

I nod. It is strange and wonderful to hear him because he talks as if the baby will be born. As if there is no doubt about this. As if the problems ahead of me will be to do with it being here, alive, in the world, and with my struggle to look after it alone. For a moment I feel dangerous, giddy with hope. I look out across the field and furiously unravel a future for me and the child. I imagine summers, winters — every season.

'Oh, and we can't stop the road,' Snow says. 'Not unless you can pull off some kind of goddess magic. It's a longer fight than that. They want this one to happen. We can cost them time and a shitload of money, but they'll build this one. And absolutely no more actions. Okay? It's not good for the protest and it's not good for you, if you want the baby. Got it?'

I want to howl. Instead I nod.

'Right. I need some food.'

He gets out his phone, presses it to life, thumbs a message to his sister.

'I'm gonna head off and meet the others. Do you need me to help you back home?'

He is not inviting me along. He does not want me with them now. I shake my head. I can walk across a field.

'I'll stay here, thanks. I need a moment.'

'Sure. Look ...' he combs the grass with his big hands, 'I'll see you around. Take care.' He pats my knee, gets up and strides away.

I have told my story, and it made me sound mad, as I feared it would. The road cannot be stopped. My mother has lost her power. The deal is over. Hades will be here soon. I do not know how long I have. Probably only days. A few days left to live among the living.

I am hunched in the grass by the stile. In the past I would have told myself that I wanted to die. Now I understand too late that all I ever wanted was to live. When I starved, when I left with Hades, year after year when I wanted to stay down with the dead, I was hoping, doubting that I could earn my right to be up here. But now that I am a mother, for however brief a time, I understand that I did not need to earn it. It was already given. Not how my mother gives. There was no bond of reciprocity. Life is a wild, reckless gift with no heed paid to what is given back.

I start to cry again. Now Snow is not here I do not hide it. And there is no redness. No shame. I do not hate myself. I am not sorry for myself. I cry as simply and steadily as water falls out of the sky. I open my hand as I might to check the rain — its weight, temperature. It is heavy and warm.

I cry for all the winters I have missed. I cry for Phoebe and her baby and all those that died in that first winter and in every winter since. I cry for the baby in me that I will never meet. For the future seasons I will never see. I cry for the long list of things I never knew I loved up here and for the years of never knowing.

I feel sad and this feels strange. Sad is not something I have felt for many years. I have stuck to anger, resentment, shame, guilt, indifference. I have left all the grieving to my mother, while I did all the leaving. Sad, along with the grain and the growth, has been her province. She made a winter from her sorrow. I learnt to fear sadness because it killed. It starved, froze, withered. But now, suddenly, sad is possible, and I am amazed and saddened further because I realise that, if only I had my mother's power, my grief would not bring winter. I could weep woodlands into being. My sadness could make summer.

I will miss summer. I will miss its colours. I will miss light.

It sounds so obvious now — I love the light. The way it rushes headlong to the earth. The many ways it moves — flickering, sliding, leaping. I feared darkness as a child, but I realise now I also feared the light. Lightning was my father's weapon. Like him, light looked — it touched without consent, made love to everyone. Light was an ingredient of my mother's. It made everything grow big, extravagant. I think I ran underground into the dark, in part, because it seemed the safest course.

I cry because at last I can admit to loving light, to being, after all, my parents' child. But I do not love light as they did — not because of any powers it bestows. I love how it tears ahead of me, and then towards. I love how it creates difference, distance — everything the dark undoes.

Finally, I cry for my mother, only a field away. For how

hard it is for me to close the distance between us, when that is all she ever wanted.

I do nine thousand years of crying, and afterwards, as after any storm, the world looks washed clean and I see it, startling and vivid — so that it makes me want to cry again. I feel envious of my mother. She had only one person to grieve. Everything else was still here for her. She had the world but would not notice it for missing me. I will miss the world.

I watch a wasp on a blade of grass near me, cleaning its legs, rubbing one against the other. I can see the throb of its abdomen, the stripes of yellow and black that make up its body. I shift my leg and see the white indentations that the grass has left across my calf, a brief memory of the field pressed on me. On the stones at the base of the stile are orange lichen, like maps of other worlds. Everywhere I look is patterned. I will miss this too — the mottled-ness of this land, which I had barely noticed until now.

My mother used to talk to me about the pattern of things. The light of it. The dark. She comes from a time famous for fate. Nowadays, she says, free will is more fashionable.

'It's your body,' Snow said. As if it were a simple choice. But I have never had a simple choice.

Maybe my mother is right — there is a greater pattern at play. Maybe things have unravelled in the only way they could have.

There are stories of men, my grandfather Cronus among them, who tried to thwart their fate, did desperate things — ate their children, abandoned them — but always their actions brought the destiny they dreaded down upon their heads.

My mother speaks of free will as if it were a modern invention, like a mobile phone, a plastic device men cradle in their hands to make believe they are all-powerful, possess unlimited calls, instead of being only a tiny speck in a vast pattern they cannot control or understand. And for once, as I look at the pattern of the field pressed on my leg, I feel a quiet respect for her, not irritation.

I get up. I walk, tired, hungry, across the first field, as if I were returning, bringing spring. I am calm and clear. I will leave this world for good. The baby will not live. It was never up to me. Maybe, now I understand this, I will be able to meet my mother's eyes.

I go through the garden gate. The front door does not open. I have never had to knock.

I go around the house. The garden is empty. The back door is unlocked. I go inside, stand in the hallway.

My mother is not here.

16

DEMETER

It has taken me six days to reach Download Festival, but as soon as I arrive, I'm glad I came. They call it a rock and heavy metal festival on the posters pinned up on the fence, as if in tribute to everything beneath us, but I do not believe they are in love with Hades. Even if they dress like death, they do not want it. I look at the band names on the posters: Iron Maiden; The Offspring; Hot Milk — these people long for life.

I am too old for climbing fences but do not have the money for a ticket, so I make my way to the 'Press and Guest' entrance — tell the lad on the door I am Iron Maiden's backstage shaman. He looks afraid, nods me in.

I walk into a great, long grassy arena with four huge stages at each corner. The warm-up acts are on. I pass fire jugglers; hoop dancers; a sword swallower in sequins, sliding blades down her throat up to the hilt. People sit on the grass, drinking, or stand, queuing for their hot dogs. They wear silver, gold, black, red. They have painted their faces, dyed their hair. Once the gods were worshipped at festivals like this, not stuck in cold, stone buildings. I'm glad to smell sweat, make-up, the yeast of beer, to be amid people ready for dance and song so ecstatic it makes their hair stand on end. I did not know how much I had missed this.

I wander through the crowds, and I wonder where Zeus is. I am nervous, like a young girl, as if Zeus were my new man, instead of being a brother I have long resented, a lover I never

185

meant to take. I feel more hopeful than I have done in weeks, maybe years. As day darkens, the people's priests appear — musicians, shown large on lighted screens either side of every stage. The beats begin and the crowds turn into oceans that crash against the stages.

I cannot see Zeus, but there are signs of him — in the lights that wheel across the sky, in the stature of the musicians, in their thunderous drums, in the way everyone is lusty, glad of having arms to hold, hips to swing. It was the people stopping their dance and song that bothered Zeus when winter came — not the cold or hunger. Surely he will be here somewhere. He would be up on a stage if he could; I like to be among people, he likes to be above them. If he is not on a stage, he will be somewhere set apart.

It is night now, but there is light aplenty — electricity pumped across the site. I walk away from the crowds through a few pine trees, past the loos, a water point, the beer tents, off into a camping field. I look among the many tents. He is not there.

Suddenly, away from the festival's euphoria, I feel foolish. There must be a thousand other music festivals around the world — why did I think to find Zeus here, at this one? Or he could be somewhere else entirely — on the top floor of a luxury Manhattan skyscraper. Or back where he grew up, with a woman tending to his every need, in a mossy cave upon Mount Ida. I shiver in the summer night. I fear I have lost my knack of finding things as well as changing them.

I wander, aimless, back to the main site, between beer tents. I walk around the back of the hot-dog van, and there he is.

I recognise him at once, though he has changed. My god, he has changed. Our god, the god of the gods, sprawled on the grass, a woman either side of him — that much is the same. His golden locks are black, limp threads. He has shaved off his beard. His body hair is grey. He is covered in tattoos: an eagle spreads its wings across his chest, a thunderbolt zig zags over his white, soft stomach, ending above tight leather trousers. He has a jungle of imagery along each arm — an ant and a bee on his right bicep, a swan and a cuckoo on his left. I understand these pictures — each commemorates a lover, the forms he took to trick, seduce, screw them all. They are scrawled over his skin lest he forget, lest the world forgets, who he is, was.

He has grown bigger, put on weight, and it makes him look smaller. I cannot see his actual thunderbolt, only the sign for it on his belly. He is sweaty, but not from running — he has been lolling here for a while, judging by the beer cans round the three of them. I recognise the lady on his left as the sword swallower I passed before. She has blonde hair, a blue-sequin leotard, long, fishnet legs. I never shared his taste. The other lady has a skull drawn on her — a dead face on her living one, skulls too on her breasts, silver spikes studded around them on her bra. He is kissing death, dolled up, while his free hand clutches at the sequins of Ms Sword.

He has not seen me. I stand for a moment in the warm night. The lights from the hot dog van and beer tent streak the grass. Music pumps off the main stages, the crowds roar, like a mythical creature, come to life. Meanwhile, this mythic man lies, drunk behind the hot dogs, near enough to the loos for the stink of them to reach him — the shit but also the chemicals they use to hide the shit. And still I am not ready to give up on him, on the hope I felt from having found this festival, on the pride I feel for having tracked him down — it must come to something.

'Zeus,' I say.

He does not respond, merely swaps over, starts groping Lady Death and kissing Ms Sword, his tongue far down where the swords went. He is not fit anymore, so he soon comes up for air. I can see he is both more and less of who he was — more of the bluster, less of the power. There are mortal men who can play at being king better than he, these days — he no longer wields a deadly weapon, but there are those that do.

'Zeus,' I say again.

'Go away. I'm busy!'

The women take a good look at me — he doesn't bother to do more than glance, then buries himself in Lady Death's skull-tits. Why are they with him, these women? Has he paid them? Or does he still have a whiff of thunder and lightning about him? That does it for some, though it never did anything for me.

'Zeus, it's me. Your sister.'

'Who?' He stops, turns at last and I see that his pupils are swollen — the sky-blue irises for which he was once famous are pale rims around the fat, black centres of each eye.

He is staring at me, new beads of sweat breaking out on his forehead. Suddenly, he releases the women, sits up, clasps his hands together.

'Please,' he says, 'Please don't tell her.'

'Tell who? What?' I ask, though I have guessed.

'There's damn spies everywhere.' He looks round wildly at the hot dog van, beer tent, loos, the pine trees.

'It wasn't your wife who sent me.'

He gazes at me. He seems to have forgotten how long it is since we last saw each other. I don't know how I thought our reunion might go. I had not rehearsed it in my mind, only focused on finding him. But I had not expected this. I want to laugh. To cry. To scream.

'Look, I'll do a deal with you,' he says.

'I came about our deal,' I say.

'But we haven't made it yet.'

'Do you remember nothing?'

He looks worried — I can see remembering is not his strong point, the all-seeing, all-knowing Zeus does not know very much. A white skein of snot hangs from his nose. I scour his body, his tattoos for any record of me. There is none. He did not have to turn into an animal to have his way with me.

'We have a daughter, you and I.'

'We do?' He frowns, still scared of Hera, of what else he might have done.

'Persephone.'

At her name he smiles. For a moment I am moved — I allow myself even now to believe he might be the father that he never was, the one I never had.

'Yes,' he says softly, 'I remember. She was lovely, coming over the corn, sitting by the fire.'

'She still is.'

'I'll get a poppy done for her,' he says, pointing to a small space on his forearm, not yet tattooed. He rests back, dreamy, brings the hand of Ms Sword across between his leathered legs, holds it there, starts to rub. I want to hit him. I don't. Not yet.

'She's pregnant.'

'Ah, good girl — is that what you came to tell me?'

'Not with Hades.'

'She's been having a good time with another man, eh?' He grins, grinds harder.

'Hades doesn't know. He wants her down with him forever.'

'I've got it!' He sits up again, jerky, fat-eyed. 'Here's the deal. I won't tell Hades about Persephone's new man — you don't tell Hera you've seen me here. How about it?' He winks, gloats, rests back. The women take him in their arms again. He must have paid them.

'I came about the other deal. The one we made to share Persephone. Your idea. Hades claims the deal is over. He wants her only for himself.'

But Zeus is gone — his tongue is being swallowed by Ms Sword. Lady Death has her hand down the leather trousers.

'I came here for your help!' Now I am shouting. I draw near, pull off Ms Sword and Lady Death. They look at me with hatred.

'Brother!' I hold Zeus' head in my hands, force him to look at me. 'Don't you care? What if our daughter disappears forever? What if the earth dies? Is dying?'

He stares up with his swollen eyes.

'I won't tell Hades. You don't tell Hera — that's our deal,' he whispers. I can smell the drink on him. I can see the white powder on the inside of his nostrils. I spit in his face. I let go of his head, lurch back, shaking.

'Why did I think there was any point in coming to you?'

He is already rubbing himself, while Ms Sword and Lady Death stroke his thunderbolt belly. I shudder with rage, disgust.

'I'll tell Hera everything!' I scream.

'Oh, never mind,' he moans, wanking harder, 'It will be worth it.'

I spit again. I am shaking as hard now as I did when I went to get my daughter back. When I watched her eat the seeds. When Zeus said that she belonged to Hades. I will not waste another moment here.

17

DEMETER

Out of the festival. Out along roads, through towns and villages whose names I do not recognise: Coalville, Birdingbury, Long Itchington. I walk through the night over this land called England to which I never moved, but where I've always lived.

On the way to the festival, looking for Zeus, I picked my way across fields, through woodlands, past a reservoir. Now Zeus is found, a lost cause, I want to be back as fast as I can, so I follow the roads. I cross the M6, walk along the A423. They have made so many roads now that they name them with numbers that tell nothing of where you've been, or where you might arrive. I remember as I walk how much I used to walk, how far — to Sicily and back — thinking nothing of it. The land was still new enough to feel revelatory, a dazzling emergence from a world that had been only ocean. The clay of the world, of its one continent, was soft. We made our paths by walking them. I remember the names of the places I walked then: Enna, Arcadia, Attica, Olympus. The land was wood, mountain, river, and when I made them, fields.

Now I walk over stones crushed into powder, mixed with sand and water to make a grey paste that hardens so that the earth is buried under it. The fields — where the soil is still allowed to breathe — are exhausted. The next road is never far away. The stars too have been covered over with a wash of orange light, flung upward by the posts that march beside the roads. The night would be light enough without a single lamp

— the moon is nearly full. The wind is picking up, blowing moonlit clouds across the sky in shocking shapes, big as ships. The night feels terrible and urgent. After this midsummer moon Hades will come again and I believe him now — the world is no longer listening. It has been changed but not by me.

The last time I went walking was when I was searching for Persephone. I have walked out less and less since then. Less far. Less often. When she is at home, I do not want to leave her. When she is not, I want to be there lest she returns, and anyway I do not have the heart to walk the world, knowing she is not in it. And if she goes from it for good? What would I do then? Walk forever, or never take another step? And what would the world do? Freeze? Burn? Or go on just the same?

I walk all night, rest only when day comes and it grows too hot to walk. I lie down in the shade of a hedge outside a town called Southam. Two young women stop to offer me a drink, one of their sandwiches. I take them, thank them. I, who invented homes, mistaken for a tramp without one. But I understand now that this is what's become of us. The old gods are the waifs and strays, the mad, the drunk, the drugged of this changed world. I sleep, fitful as my father hounded by the Furies. I dream of him, of his huge mouth, and I dream of, or remember — I do not know which — what I have worked hard to forget these last nine thousand years. My descent into the dark.

The water underground was so cold, it was like being stabbed. The dark and freezing stream confused me. I knew only that I had to follow the water, that it would lead me down, and that I had to keep the light alive. I remember the hiss of the resin as the flame struggled, the smell of it. Fumbling with numb hands for another pine cone, pushing it into the top of the torch, scorching my fingers that were already burnt with cold. The redness of my hands in the torch light. The black water. The pale-grey limestone. Then at a certain point, as the tunnel dropped, and I felt myself go further down inside the earth, I know I began to call my daughter's name.

'Persephone!' I cried, as if she could save me, when it was I who had come to rescue her.

'Persephone!'

I was looking for my daughter, but I wanted my mother. I wanted to be back in that one brilliant moment at my birth when my mother held me, before my father swallowed me. Many times I thought I would turn back but, when I called out for Persephone, my breath fed the flame and it flared up, grew brighter, fiercer. I kept on.

At last, I came to the great river that borders with the kingdom of the dead, stepped onto the black sands of its shore. In the world above I had been alone for days. Now, suddenly, I stood among a crowd. Men, women, children, ragged, wretched and weeping, filled the bank. As I pushed through them to the water's edge, I saw each clutched an object — a cup, a spoon, a doll — the last of whatever they held dear. When I reached the shoreline, it was strewn with these things, lying among blackened leaves.

I cried out for the boat to come, to carry me across. I made the waters quiver, calling my daughter's name.

The boat slid into the shallows. An old woman, in mourning dress, sat at the oars. Her dark skirts billowed out onto the seat on either side of her and trailed in the bottom of the boat. Her eyes, black as the water, had sunk deep into her skull. Tears stood in them, too far back to fall. She scanned the shore.

The crowd surged forwards, like a flock of crows, calling in hoarse voices to be taken. Each held out their offering to

193

the woman, their coins, beads, trinkets. A boy beside me had a single corn kernel cupped in his palm. The woman gave a nod to him, a slight incline of her head. She steadied the boat with an oar upon the sand as he climbed in. Others whom she invited followed, too. Though I was standing at the front and centre of the crowd, she gave no nod to me. I waded into the water, gripped the boat, went to climb aboard. With surprising strength and speed the old woman swung her free oar across, jabbed it at me.

'What have you got to give?' she said. Her voice creaked like the boat. Her face was like a map covered in contour lines of a land I did not know. 'You must pay for your crossing.'

'Not me.'

'Everyone pays.'

'What is the price?' I asked.

'Whatever you least wish to give away.'

'I have nothing to give.'

'Then you cannot cross.'

I felt a rush of rage, that I should have laboured down into the dark, fighting horror the whole way, only to be refused passage here.

'Everything I have of value is on the other shore,' I hissed at her, pointing over the water.

'You have a torch,' she said, eyeing the flame.

'I cannot give the light.'

'Light is not needed here.'

'I need it! To find what I have lost!'

The woman looked away then, across the crowd, as if searching for someone. Not finding them, she went to push off from the shore, to leave without me. I lunged and gripped her oar, tried to pull it from her, but she held it fast.

'Take me to my daughter,' I said, quiet and fierce.

'If I do, then next time you will have to pay a higher price,' the woman croaked.

'I will never come down here again.'

'Next time,' she said, 'You must come without that light, in darkness.'

'I'm an immortal!'

'I know who you are,' she said, unperturbed, 'and I have set my price.'

I stared. Her eyes shone with their un-falling tears. I saw myself, tiny, double, in the black of them. What did she know? Insolent old woman, threatening me with death. I would never come down here, like a mortal, in the dark. I would never cross and not come back. But her words stayed with me, tucked themselves into my body, in the tender places between bones — at my knees, elbows — places that, when struck, make me tingle with a nervous pain that herbs won't soothe, and I remember, try to forget, the ferrywoman's price.

Back then, I waved my arm, dismissed her, clutched the boat, cursed the splinter that it gave me, heaved my sodden legs on board. The others moved to the bottom of the boat, to make space for me on the narrow seat. I sat, furious, shaken, while the woman tipped back and forth, rowing us over the river to the dead.

And so I made it to the cave that held the tree, still with the torch in my hand, and Persephone was there — impossibly pale and thin, but it was my child, alive. I started to tremble with joy. I opened my arms. And then she ate the seeds.

Why did she do it?

I never got an answer from her I could understand. I asked her when she was still sick, after I fetched her home. I would take her in my arms, as if she were a child again — she was long-limbed now, but nearly as light. Hot and limp, I carried her through the house. 'You stole the summer, it is raging in you, give it back now,' I would whisper. And then, 'Why did you go? Did he force you? Why did you eat the seeds?' I did not expect an answer then, and I got none — only a faint moan, or a twisting of her head. I asked her again once she grew stronger, as she and the corn recovered together, while we walked the edge of the field.

'Why did you eat the seeds?'

'I don't know,' she said, staring down to where the stems sprung from the ground.

'I was hungry,' she said another time, as we sat on the back doorstep admiring the apple in bloom again. As if it were that simple. Another time, late at night, I asked, and she did not answer, rolled away from me as if already asleep, but as I went to kiss her, I felt her face and pillow, wet.

In other years, I asked in other ways.

'How was your winter? Did your husband treat you well?' But her answers — always halting — told me nothing. She never told me what I longed to hear — that she never meant to go, never meant to stay. She never told me she was glad to be back home.

'It's good to have you here,' I would say. She smiled, nodded. Nothing more. In the end I decided to take matters into my own hands, where they felt safest. I sealed up the well, dug out the pond, cut down the pine tree, gave away the wood so I would not have to smell it burn. I put it about she had been tricked. Over time I came to believe it myself, certainly that she had been deceived by Hades, had no idea of what would grow from those seeds inside her mouth.

I told the tale to the village children who would marvel at my daughter's reappearance with the buds each year, and they in turn told their children, and so it went on. Children are mythical creatures — too young for memory. I saw the truth of my tale reflected back inside their eager eyes — my child had been raped and wronged. It was so much easier to feel fury at my brothers than dismay at her.

And now, in a ditch on the edge of Southam, on a hot June afternoon, I again take refuge in my rage. It is better than despair, which I cannot afford. I bury the question, 'Why?', wrap it up, stow it away, for it can wait. 'Why?' has waited years. It is not important now. What matters is that I save her, and my grandchild. That I find a way to keep them in this world.

As soon as the heat lessens, I set off again. Evening comes. A bat clicks close to my face, and whirs away. The rooks settle on the elms beside the road. All the while the cars keep coming, an endless stream of them, their white eyes fixed on forward progress, leaving me and the road behind in red.

As I walk, I remember the Furies, older than any of us, who pursued my father. I never saw them, but I heard different stories of their fearsome form — that they were snake-haired, had bloodshot eyes, bat wings. But in every tale, they were women. Of course they were. What else can we do but sprout wings, grow snakes? What else can we do but scratch and screech, in the face of the greed of gods and men? They call it madness, but I'm not mad. I've not lost my reason — I can count them, my reasons: my father ate me; my first brother stole my child; my second raped me; my third refused to help. Meanwhile the men on earth cut down my trees and built their roads across my land, and now they want to drive me from my home. And, after tonight, Hades

197

will come to take my child again. My grandchild too.

So when the evening of the third day comes, when I reach the River Cherwell, follow it back to where the weir joins it to the Ray, when I draw near my house, see the lights, hear the engine in the fields, I am ready to do whatever must be done.

I arrive at the first field beside the house, only to find I am too late – the road works have already reached the house. The hawthorn hedge, that ran along the edge of the first field, is down. Only a single tree still stands beside the stile. The space is horrible. Around the emptiness, as if it needed protection, runs a fence — it stretches across the second field, diggers parked in the far corner. On the outside of the fence is a low red, rectangular machine on wheels, monotonous in its noise — they had ones like it at the festival. It has a long neck, four lights atop it that glare over the field. Beside the machine sits a man in a lurid yellow jacket.

I walk over to the stile, to the one hawthorn left, as the moon rises above the house. It is full at last. Strong enough to feel close. Close enough to show its craters, pits, pockmarks, its whole creased and battered face. The night is clear. The stars too are out in force. The sky challenges the earth, and all of us upon it, to a staring match. I am the first to look away. I look back up, find the wings and eye of Cygnus, the body of the bear called Ursa Major, the reclining sequence of stars called Cassiopeia. The old gods named the stars, storied the sky — our history hangs there still, despite how far we may have fallen now.

I stand up on the stile and feel everything move through me. Chug, chug goes the red machine, against the quiet booming of the moon. A robin sings into the night from my front garden. A car drones past on the Woodeaton road. I listen harder and hear fainter sounds — my daughter's heart, thumping in the attic of the house, a field away. She is frightened. And under hers, my grandchild's, the faster, lighter beat of a boy — tonight I am sure of this. He is excited. I think of Persephone standing where I am now, up on the stile, her first appearance to me in the spring, her last before she leaves in autumn. I think of when I knelt in this field and ate the earth when she was in me. I think of the corn, green then gold, then cut, then green again. I think of the roads, riddling the land, linking to other roads in other lands, for heavy lorries, for a billion cars. I think of the rivers, running long before the roads ran anywhere. Sleek black lines — the Ray behind the house, flowing to the Cherwell, to the Thames, to the sea, where life began, rolling, restless, heaved upwards by the moon tonight. I sense the stream that runs under these fields, that cuts down to that river below, where all life ends. I think of the festival-goers, imagine them in these fields now, pumping music, jumping bodies. I look at the single security man on his camping chair. I look down at the poppies by the stile, silvered by the moon. All these things — memory, sensation, thought — draw together like a pattern of stars, a trillion miles apart and yet they make a shape. It is a constellation of wonder and of wrath — 'How can this be?' is the question that they share. I feel untold fury and I am calm as the moon. I want to tear down the fence, upturn the diggers. I want to run to my house, hold my daughter, and never let her go.

I get down from the stile and walk over to the man on the chair in front of the fence. As I draw near, I recognise him — it is Will, one of those I befriended out in the woods, the one who was glad to have escaped working in Tesco, a nice lad. Last time I saw him I was bringing biscuits. He stands, smiles when I come up, as if I might again have flapjacks.

'You need to leave,' I tell him.

'What?'

'Now.'

'Why?'

'If you want to survive.'

'What the hell?'

I go up to the chugging machine, find its switch, flick it off. The lights go out.

'Hey, what are you doing?'

I need the silence. And the moonlight. I turn to him.

'I'll tell you why you must go.'

I make my tale swift. I tell him about the boy I turned into a lizard, the man I cursed who ate himself with greed. I tell him about the way I starved the world and turned it white. He laughs at first. And then he doesn't. Then he starts swearing, sweating, reaching for his phone. I pick up his bag.

'Oi, give that back!'

'I'm giving you this chance,' I say.

'I don't believe you.'

'Then you're a fool.' He is standing now, trying to get at his bag. I come up close, stare in his eyes.

'Just give me the bag, and I'll clear off, okay?'

'Good lad.'

'C'mon.'

'You must never speak of this.'

'They'd call me a bleeding crackpot if I did.'

'Tell no one what I have told you.'

'Just give me my frickin' stuff.'

I hold it out. He grabs his bag and runs across the field to the Woodeaton road.

He does not look back.

I am alone. And not alone — it is hard for anything to play dead tonight, under this moon: stars, roads, rivers, robin, house, breathe with me. I sit in the chair for a moment, look out over the field, feel the fury in me, the wings at my back, snakes in my hair. I stand, slip through the gap in the fence that the chair was set to guard. I walk onto the road site as if I were a builder, going to work. I know what I must build tonight — it will not be a road. I look about the site — at the shabby white cabin in the corner, the chemical loos. Their sickening smell reminds me of Zeus. But in front of the cabin is something beautiful — two diggers and a bulldozer. Quiet. Waiting. Once, a long time ago, I filled in the well, buried the river that runs beneath the house. Tonight, I must again draw water from the deep.

I walk up to one of the diggers, climb on its hard-ridged wheels. I try the door to the driver's cab — locked. I climb back down. In the opposite corner of the site lies the debris from the hawthorn hedge. I cross to it. It was an old hedge, the kind that can't be built but that grows, fairy tale-like, over a hundred years. These old hedges are worlds unto themselves, thickets of knotty life. Not only hawthorn lies in the pile of broken branches — I see field maple, hazel, blackthorn, even holly. But it is a thick branch of hawthorn I take up — a twisted one that shows the cunning of the tree, growing to scavenge for light through the tangle of the hedge.

It only takes three blows to smash the glass in the digger door. It is a stunning shattering, spreading through the glass like sudden frost. The shards, once they explode within the cabin are gorgeous too — silver and blue, and, when I pound them, they make a turquoise powder on the floor. I break every door and window in each machine. I smash the worker's white cabin open too, a locked box inside that, and find a stash of keys. Then I come out and gently, using the hawthorn branch again, I sweep the smashed glass off the seat of one of the diggers, climb in, sit down.

From here, within this digger, I face my house, the moon above it. My daughter is inside it. My grandchild is inside her. Wonder and wrath. Love and fury. They are not far apart. I cannot remember the last time I told my daughter that I love her. She used not to like to hear it, but I want to tell her now. I look around for how to start up the machine. Eighty years ago, when the tractors first arrived, Old Mr Cely on Manor Farm let me take a turn, but this machine has different levers. I press one red handle down, on my right, it makes a satisfying click, but nothing happens. Behind it I spy the place to slot a key. I slide one in, from those I've found. It fits. I turn it. Under me, the machine judders to life. On either side of the seat are further levers. I push the one on the right forwards — the great arm of the digger jerks, lifts, like a neck, almost graceful, up into the sky. I try the lever on the left — it stretches the arm out from its hinge, halfway along it, so that it can reach higher still. The levers do not only move forwards and back — they go from side to side too, and when they do the bucket on the end opens up to the night, as if trying to dig for stars, and the whole cabin swings. I make the neck-arm dance, lift it, lower it, make the bucket, the mouth of the thing, reach and retract. I make it take a single bite of earth. This is what it has been built to do. It is an earth eater. I am a road worker. I feel the power of the machine and I feel the power in me, and I recognise it of old. I understand the desire behind the builders to have been, all along, the same as mine — the wish to shape the world around you. I have wanted this. I have wanted tree, grass, flower, fruit to like me and be like me. They want this too. To be in charge of change. I marvel at this as I make the metal arm lift into the night, lower it down, set its teeth to the ground, and start to dig.

18

PERSEPHONE

They are working even at night, hurrying to get the job done. I lie in the attic, listening to the revving engine, the scoop and slap of earth. The calm acceptance of my fate that I felt before has gone. My chest feels swollen as the moon in the skylight over me, though I am nothing like as steady or serene. At midsummer, soon after this moon, Hades will come for me. It is hard to imagine never being here again.

The baby is six weeks old inside me, but I am only one week old. When my mother is here — and she has always been here until now — the house and garden are like extensions of her body which I float inside. I am not hopeful that she will return with help. Without her here I have been like a newborn, keeping odd hours, sleeping in the day, crying in the night, not getting dressed, eating every hour, or not at all. It is shocking how loud her absence is. It makes simple things seem like a lie — walking downstairs, going to the bathroom, making tea, are feeble pretences at being ordinary.

Perhaps, at last, I understand how different it is to be the one left behind. The constancy of everything is a betrayal, not a comfort. I have watered the garden, fed the hens, sat at the study window, waiting, watching. I have felt her loneliness.

I watched them take down the hawthorn hedge, watched Snow, Nonny, and Nut try to stop them, watched them get hauled off. I went into the front garden, waved them over. They came, and I handed back the clothes that they had lent me. I asked them in, but Snow said he was too tired. He is afraid of me now — pregnant and mad. That was yesterday, I think. Time is starting to behave as oddly up here as it does under the ground. Today I have spent hours curled up under the bedcovers, as if I could hide from Hades there. I have wondered whether I should leave the house, if there is any village, town, wood, valley, to which I might escape. Even if there were, I feel too sick to travel. So, I have spent my last week on earth, my first alone, eating baked beans on toast and watching daytime TV, dozing on the sofa, having baths in which I stay until the skin on my fingers puckers.

Sleep will not happen tonight. I want to be awake — soon I can sleep all I like. I get up, climb down the attic ladder, descend the stairs into the kitchen. I stand barefoot on the cool floor, watch the silver fish slip across the flagstones. In the moonlit kitchen, listening to the machine in the fields, I feel something of my mother's spirit stir in me — not her loneliness, but instead her reckless certainty.

'No more actions,' Snow had said. Soon there will be no more of anything but dark, rock, river, and my husband's hands. I have nothing to lose that I will not lose, anyway. I think of the baby, of the security man's eyes when he told me how selfish I was to risk my child's life. I listen to the road-building machine. I listen to my heart, loud as its engine. I turn. I walk down the hall, put on my walking boots, the ones I wear to leave each autumn. Then, in my nightdress, I step out into the moonlight, ready to lie down before a digger.

I cross the front garden, field, come to the stile that still stands despite the emptiness beside it, like a door in a ruined house whose walls have gone. Over the top of the fence, I can see the digger working — its arm lifting up a bucketful of earth, spilling grains, swivelling, dropping the load, turning back for more. I am mesmerised by the dance of it. I feel terrified and euphoric, as I did when I went to look for Hades, when I first entered the earth with him. I feel like I am falling in love, though I do not know with whom. Not with Hades. Not with Snow. I wonder if this is what people feel before they die. If this is why unhappy people kill themselves, for this one hit of joy that comes with choosing to act, even if that act ends everything.

I am going to slide myself into the earth where that digger is digging. I am going to let it lift me. I am going to grip on to its arm — no one will pull me off. I cross to the fence. It is unguarded — an empty chair before a gap. I slip through, stand, and stare.

There is a deep cleft before me in the ground. What are they doing? Laying down power lines? Suddenly, I fear Hades is already here. I search the opened ground for any sign of him. I look up — the digger's arm has stopped, raised, clutching its latest load of earth. Could he be in the digger?

And then I see. Not Hades. My mother.

She is seated in the driver's cabin as if it were a throne, made of shattered glass and moonlight. I feel her eyes on me. I feel the space between us. The many times and ways there has been space between us. Across the kitchen table, the veg patch, the pond. Between our bedrooms. Over fields. Across a cave. And now this distance — a gash in the ground apart.

She does not speak, does not even say my name, and I am glad. Only the digger engine talks, with its rhythmic grunt. Tonight, speaking would undo us. Maybe it always has. She motions me to come to her. She is holding something out, in her hand. I move around the cleft, climb up on the digger's tracks to reach her.

206

It is a key. A small silver one with a black head. She looks at me with pride as she hands it to me and for once I do not mind. She nods to the corner of the site, to where the other digger sits. I understand her. If we dig deep enough, we might manage to flood these fields — could this be enough to stop the road? I do not know, but if there is a chance, it must be done.

I go to the other digger, climb on its tracks, up through the broken glass of its door, sit down. I learnt to climb a tree. Now I will learn to drive a digger. I find the slot for the ignition key, turn the huge machine on. One by one I try the levers, find which one controls the metal arm, the cabin, the tracks, and how to make them move. Slowly, I roll the machine forwards so that I am beside my mother, before the hole in the earth. My arms shake but I push the levers. It is strange and frightening to feel such power. To be like a god. Like a man.

As the stars wheel over us, and the moon crosses the sky, my mother and I dig. We pile earth beside our hole. The mound grows higher. The hole grows deeper, and wider. It becomes a crater, a pit. It reaches to the fence that guards the site. We knock over the fence, flatten it, keep digging. We drive the machines down into the pit, eating mouthful after mouthful, as if making a new passage down to the dead. We pile the earth up, as if building a new mountain to the sky. As night begins to pale, we strike stone. Limestone. Bedrock.

But we do not stop. We retract our digger buckets so they make metal fists, tucked tight, and with these we pound the rock. We smash it into a powder, soft and grey, like grinding grain to flour. It fissures, crumbles, puffs into the air. And at last, something black shows, seeps, trickles, rushes — water. We have unearthed the stream that runs under the fields, that fed the well, that flows down to the deeper river underground. But now we stop its flow. The limestone falls into the water. We push it there. We take scoops of the earth we have piled beside the pit and we press them into place, so that the water cannot reach the woods. We keep pressing, pushing crushed rock and earth into the left side of the pit, building a dam. We smooth the surface, seal it with layer on layer of compacted earth, and slowly the stream starts to pool, to fill our pit.

As day dawns, we drive the diggers up out of the pit and switch them off. I climb down. My mother too. She looks young, girlish even. She smiles and offers me her hand, as she did years ago when we first surfaced into winter. I take it. We stand and look at the hollow and the hill that we have made.

The hill is as wide and almost as high as the house — it could be an ancient burial site, or a monument to a deity even older than my mother.

The hollow looks as if a meteor had landed here. It fills half the field. Water wells up from its base. As the sun rises, the growing lake shows the sky back to itself and both blush pink.

Hand in hand, my mother and I turn and walk across the first field to the house.

19

DEMETER

Look at them — the world and his wife come to gaze and gawp, slack-jawed, round-mouthed, holding up their phones to photo or film our work in the middle of the fields. Our little lake. Our young mountain.

There is nothing like a stretch of water to make people stand and stare. It brings them to a stop. Since they cannot walk across it, they look over it with longing. They go on holiday for this.

From the study window, I watch them watch the water. Not just road workers. Villagers, and the wild lot who were living in the woods. I went for a little lie-down and when I got up, there they were, stood about in little groups, like some sudden overnight blooming as occurs in desert lands. I feel excited, like a child, nose-pressed to the window. People used to travel from far to admire my lands. Now here they are again.

It is still growing, our lake. Slowly, because it has not rained for over two weeks, so the water level is low, but it has almost reached the top of the pit now. I want to shout up to Persephone to come and see, but she is resting. I am glad to let her rest. Glad, above all, to be able to protect her again. The doubt that has been growing in my chest for weeks is gone. It's one thing no longer to be in charge of grain but another to be unable to keep my child safe.

Police sirens sound along the Woodeaton road. What will they do? Arrest the river? Question the earth? If they were wise, they would ask the birds. I can hear them now — the robin, the blackbird, agitated. The sky too is looking tense, no longer blue-eyed. Clogged with clouds like slow explosions. I gaze up, hear a bang below. Police in the front garden, at the door. I run down the stairs, two at a time, my heart light as a lark.

And so begins a day of visitors. Three police officers first — two men and one woman. Big black uniforms, shiny silver buttons. Important and awkward round my kitchen table. Kettle on, while they ask me what I heard or saw in the night. I tell them how I've been putting wax in my ears so the machines don't wake me in the morning, so I slept right through, but my daughter heard them, thought it was the workmen making up for time lost in the woods. Can they speak to her? Then I am flying up the stairs, sad to disturb her but, even now, all too ready to show her off. Flustered, shy, crumpled from sleep she comes downstairs. Still beautiful.

She confirms what I told them. Yes, she knows some of the protestors a little, no, they never spoke to her of any plan such as this. So, they are pushing their chairs back, thanking me for the tea.

Next come curious villagers. Three of them. More tea. The biscuit tin comes out. Then they go and four of the wild road lot turn up — the tall bearded one, his sister, another long-haired lad, a little skinny girl with a baby bouncing on her knee, then crying the house down, till I take a turn with him, soothe the little man while the others chat. The bearded one was rounded up, taken in for questioning at the police station in Oxford, let go again. Persephone, beside me, is nervous, unsettled as the birds who are still wheeling, landing, taking off again about my house. Did we know anything? Play any part in this incredible action? They lean in. Well, we might, is as much as I say, winking at the baby. They grow less wild after that, more tame. They drink their tea, clutch their mugs, don't know whether to nod or shake their heads. The little boy in my arms — Berry he's called, plump and rosy as a real one — is doing both, nodding, shaking, laughing and laughing. I could get used to having a baby about again.

This goes on all week. We have many visitors — not one of them is Hades. I keep the kettle on. The sun rises and sets, the days are long, the nights short. The clouds huddle, confer, but no rain falls.

The people gather as they might around a terrible accident. They gather as they would around a site of beauty. Appalled and awed, they come and go. The lake stays. No road work happens. No one seems to know what to do. But I do. I know what to do.

A week after the full moon, I take Persephone by the hand and lead her out towards our lake. The air is warm and thick enough to wade through. The sky has shivered with a few drops of reluctant rain, but no more than that. Its clouds to the west, over Otmoor, are flushed with sinking sun. The one hawthorn left by the stile looks scared. There's nothing to fear, I tell it, as we pass. Persephone too is anxious. I lead her to the water's edge.

We stand. I want her to admire it anew, to see that while the road builders have done nothing, others have been busy. Life moves in fast, given half a chance. Small circles appear everywhere across the water's surface as if it were raining from the inside — fish, coming up for an evening meal of midges. They have swum in underground from the river behind the house. I peer in — grayling, dace, and minnow, slips of silver hanging in the dark.

Dusk happens over us, the whole hushed army of crepuscular birds, beetles, and moths starts to stir. Persephone breaks from my hand to wander round the water's edge. A crow, who thinks he owns this patch, is on the side of the earth-mountain. Another, a contender, perches on the seat of one of the machines. With their glass gone, even the diggers, resting on the far side of the lake, are easing into the landscape. In front of them a heron arrives, turns stone-still, sharp-eyed. I feel crepuscular myself, not ready for sleep.

I am gazing at the heron when Persephone cries out.

She points to something grey at the edge of the water. For a moment I think it is a seal, somehow swum this far inland. But as I walk closer, I see its hair is thick, glimpse one side of its face, under the surface, a white strip, a black one, a beady eye buried in the fur — a badger, bloated, rolling in the water like a log. Death as well as life arriving at our lake.

'We haven't done enough,' Persephone says, in a whisper, as if Hades is already by the hawthorn.

I go to her, put my hand on her thin back.

'Don't worry. If he comes, I can face him now. I know what to do.'

20

PERSEPHONE

We're going to have a party, my mother tells me.

It has been a hundred years at least since she held a party, but it seems to be her answer to everything, even now.

'When?' I ask.

'Saturday,' she says, on Thursday morning. 'A solstice celebration.'

As if midsummer, this year of all years, is something to celebrate. Hades is near, I am sure. A party did nothing to deter him before. But my mother is as irrepressible as summer.

'Why? How will it help?'

'We have stopped the road — now we must mark what we have done.'

'But —'

'No buts,' she says, beaming, already rolling up her sleeves.

I am to pick strawberries, pod peas. I hide in these tasks, study the hundred seeds sunk into the sides of the berries. I feel sick, tired, slow with worry. Everything takes ages. My mother meanwhile scrubs floors, chops wood, mixes punch, bakes shortbread, rushes to the village for sausages, butter, more flour. On Friday she goes out early, returns with a record player in her arms, a speaker on her back, a bag of records hanging from each shoulder. Every time someone arrives in the field, to take stock of the damage we have done — villagers, road-workers, police, protestors — she hurries out, invites them to the party. I watch her from the kitchen, the bowl of peas beside me.

Friday afternoon, she heads to the river, returns with bundles of willow, heaps the green wands on the kitchen table. 'Your turn,' she says, and so I have to walk out, looking for flowers. I fear Hades but see no one and the earth does not open. Instead, the sky closes, clouds gather — pale and voluminous. My mother weaves the foxgloves I find into graceful garlands, lays them on the smashed-up diggers. The house too is bedecked, dog roses and sweet briar over every doorway, vases in each room. Saturday morning, she plants white candles in jam jars, sets them up the path, across the field. She crowds the kitchen table with food. She heaves a huge silver pot up from the cellar to fill with elderflower punch.

'Look what else I found!' she says, triumphant, as she comes back into the kitchen. She is brandishing a large, blackened, long-handled spoon.

It's the ladle — the one I hid long ago.

'I'd given up on ever finding this. No idea what it was doing down there.' She beams at me. I shrug, say nothing. I am sullen, as if I have lost a bet that I had thought I'd won. I want her to know it is too late — she should have found that ladle years ago. But I cannot help wondering if it's a sign — perhaps my mother and her party will prevail.

Early evening, she runs up the stairs, returns in her favourite smock, poppy-red. 'You'd best change too!' She tells me. I search the clothes trunk, find a thin, light-blue cotton dress, something from a village jumble sale. 'Ready?' she says, as I come down, but before I can answer, the first guests are arriving through the garden gate.

A great queue of people forms across the field, as if my mother's house is the ark, and tonight the floods are coming. Teenage girls in tight skirts, boys on mountain bikes, with baggy jeans and slicked-back hair. Young parents with toddlers, Nut and Berry among them. Maggie, Ash, Nonny, and Snow. Other protestors. Road workers and security men but without their yellow jackets and hard hats. I recognise the short one, with the earring, who came for me and Nonny — smart now, a belt, a shirt, a shave.

My mother has timed it well — people are in the mood for a party, though I doubt any share her reasoning, her wish to celebrate and seal our victory over the road. They come because they fancy a dance, some free food, to pick up a date, a weekend adventure. They come because it is light till late, because they are nosy, because the vandalism in the fields has broken something open and they want to talk, drink, to step out of their ordinary lives.

My mother stands by the gate and welcomes them all, including the police. 'Just came to keep an eye,' one of the officers tells her. She shakes his hand, radiant, as everyone arrives.

I feel queasy, not just because of the baby — I am nervous of the numbers my mother has invited, nervous of who may come, uninvited. I would rather be curled in bed, or crouching in the cellar, as I did long ago, but I play my part, pour punch into glasses in the kitchen. The guests spill into the back. They sip, eat, plates held in one hand or balanced on their knees. They marvel at my mother, her food and flowers, the odd old house. I listen to their chat, remember as a child how I would stop hearing the guests' words — the voices emptying of meaning, sounding instead like rapid water sliding over stones.

An hour in, my mother calls a toast. She stands up on a log in the front garden, glass in hand.

'To the summer!' she says.

215

Everyone cheers, drinks.

'To the land!' Another cheer.

'And to my daughter!' She lifts her glass towards me — a third cheer goes up. And I want to hide again, or head for the woods. Instead, I provide another round of drinks. My mother lights the fire in the front garden.

The polite talk peters out and one of the protestors starts strumming a guitar. Slowly bodies unravel, backs lean into walls, arms relax enough to find their way onto other people's knees. Someone has brought an extension cable and I help unwind the wire, make it snake through the front garden, out into the fields, where my mother places the record player with pride.

At last, the sun goes down on the longest day, dark rises and the party proper begins. Popular hits, strong beats, fill the field. Teenagers stand on the garden wall, punch the air, jump off with screams of joy. Whoops from the children, excited to be up late, playing hide-and-seek. Splashes and shouts from the back garden when the pond is found and the night swimming begins. Couples slink into corners for a kiss. In the front garden the red of the fire deepens.

Nauseous still, I gather up plates that have slid into the grass, carry them in. My mother is in the kitchen, tears of laughter rolling down her cheeks, a policeman and Nut's mother round the table laughing with her. She beckons me over, hugs me, bids me fill another jug of wine, as if I were a girl again. As if there had been no interruption, no other season but the summer, as if the feasting had never stopped.

When I wander out to the back garden, I find she is not alone in this charade — the other gods have joined her. Down by the pond, my uncle, Poseidon, is lounging — worn as driftwood, smelling of fish. By the fruit bushes, I pass Aphrodite, long hair trailing down her back, lips pouting, mascaraed eyes shifting across the path. I walk back round the house, to the fire at the front. By the front garden wall, a heavy man is busy pressing himself up against a young blonde girl. He glances over his shoulder at my approach and fear flashes through me. My father turns back to his business with the girl. Even Zeus is here.

Everyone except my husband. Every moment, I expect him. I see him nowhere and everywhere, in the jewellery worn by the richest women from the villages, in the shifting shapes of the dancers in the field. He is genie-like, curled up in the dark of the jug I have set down by my feet. We are meant to celebrate my mother's triumph over him. Not for the first time, I am envious of her certainty, of her idea that the never-ending summer could be restored so simply, with a night of digging and a party. I stare into the fire, see my husband there too, think of his buried forge.

I start up. Someone is watching me. Not Hades. Snow. He crosses over to sit on the log beside me, rests his arms on his long thighs, looks into the fire.

'How you feeling?' he says. He is asking about the baby.

'Sick.'

He nods. This is as close as he will come to telling me I am, perhaps, not mad, or at least that he admires what my mother and I did. He says no more but stays. I am glad to have him near, quiet, solid. Not believing in anything but kindness, righteous anger, and trees, while the party grows wilder and the old gods shuffle in. Everything else — fire, music, drink, guests, gods — pulls back. Only Snow and the baby keep me here.

And now my father, hands on his hips, swaggers up to the fire. It is strange to see him. He is changed — older, beardless, overweight — but still I tense at his approach. I have always feared him — a dull resentment has been the extent of my rebellion. His gaze passes over me. He must have lost count of his children long ago.

'I'm thirsty!' he announces. He seizes the jug beside me, finds it empty, tosses it aside — it breaks against a stone around the fire. People shift position, sit up. One couple decides it's time to go.

'Come on. A drink!' My father paces round the fire, accusing us. Nonny stands.

'Here,' she says, offering a can of beer. He eyes her, her dark hair, eyebrow ring, big boots, combat trousers. He takes the can, cracks it open, tips it back, crushes it. His eyes roll back to her.

'Finally, a woman who knows what a man needs!' he says. 'Where've you been all these years?' He reaches out an arm, slides his hand around her back. She pulls away.

'No thanks,' she says.

Snow crosses to Nonny. My father lifts his arms.

'Do you know who I am?' he cries. He jabs a fat finger at Nonny. 'I'm the king. I'm the fucking king!'

The other guests in the garden stop kissing, dancing. My father takes up a log from the pile, stacked ready for the fire, wields it in both hands, as if it were his thunderbolt.

'No one denies the king!' He strides to Nonny, stops before her, holding his log. Snow tugs at her to move away, but she stays, not prepared to run screaming as my father expects, wants.

'I like vigour in a woman, but you have to be careful, girlie, whom you take on.' He throws the log down in front of her, it thuds, rolls away. He lunges forwards, grabs her. 'But maybe we can make it up?' He strokes her breast with his free hand.

'Get off!'

'Maybe I'll give you another chance?'

Snow is struggling to pull Nonny free, but Zeus thrusts him away. I am flimsy, less strong than Nonny or Snow, but this is my father. I feel terror but also shame. I can no longer sit, watch, do nothing. This year I have climbed a tree, driven a digger, slept with another man. But more than any of these things, I have had moments in which I have imagined what it might be like to be him, Zeus, the king of light, and it is this that gets me to my feet and, trembling, I face him. I try to hold my voice steady.

'Leave. Her. Alone.'

He turns his head, slow with drink and drama. He stares at me, lets Nonny go. Red veins, like rivulets, run across the whites of his eyes. Suddenly, he reaches out and grips my face in his hands.

'It's you,' he breathes, as if he has been searching for me all these years. He turns me round, pulls me against him.

'Look who I found! Know who this is?'

A crowd of guests has gathered — he has an audience.

'This, ladies and gentlemen, is my long-lost daughter! Queen of the Dead!'

My mother is on the doorstep, looking murderous. Snow is standing near, protecting Nonny. Zeus turns to him.

'Did you know that? Queen of the Dead! Did you?'

Snow tenses, hesitates. 'Yes,' he says, 'I did.'

I want to thank him, do not dare.

My father nods back. 'My little girl — a queen. And I'm the king! The fucking king of kings, d'you hear? Anyone have a problem with that?'

He lets me go, lifting his arms to the sky, palms up, tips back his head, as if he could command the clouds.

'King of the skies!' he roars.

And then, it starts to rain.

A drop at first, as if someone had touched me lightly on the shoulder. I half turn, but there is only the dark, people standing, appalled, enthralled by my father crowing at the sky.

Another speck. On my arm. I lift my face. Others do the same. Quiet as we wait for it — the miracle of something falling out of nothing.

Here it comes, pattering as it hits leaf, roof, earth. The candles in the jars across the garden stutter out. The fire smokes, blackens. My father finds a wine bottle, holds it high, lets wine and rain fall into him. He takes the bottle by its neck swings it in wide circles. People panic, because of the deeper dark, the rain, the drunk man shouting at the sky. They scrabble to find each other, coats, bags. Wet hair plastered to faces. Water running down the backs of necks. Children crying. Guests fleeing over the fields. Someone rushing the record player indoors. Rain drumming down, heavier now on heads, house, garden. Wind picking up.

Lightning.

A flash within the clouds that turns us all to split-second criminals, caught in the act of living, then plunges us back into the pouring dark. Thunder, like a heavy rock being rolled back from a cave, and yet it comes from nothing solid — the clash of air, water, light.

'See!' my father screams. 'See the might of the king!'

Another flash, cloud to earth, a vivid vein of light over the fields.

Soon the garden is empty, but for my father. The guests have either gone or huddled indoors in the kitchen, damp, dazed.

Snow is here. Nonny too, and a few of the other protestors. The people who have stayed are those who do not have comfortable homes to which to run. I stand with Snow and

Nonny in the little room that was once my mother's pantry. Now we have the TV in here. There is a small window onto the back garden, and I can see across the kitchen, to the front too. We do not talk, but listen to the rain, wind, my father waltzing with the raging sky, arms stretched wide. The sound of the rain hardens into hail. Ice bounces off the windows like gunfire. Lightning again, out front, startling each time, white threads, huge and intricate across the night, like a hidden map, suddenly revealed. Thunder, closer, louder, deep booms, high crackles — the storm is almost overhead.

I feel like a child again, as if I have spent my whole life here — thousands of years near this window, with my father flashing and thundering outside. The chestnut and the apple trees are wild with wind. The storm seems vast, alive, the biggest I can remember. I crouch down, wanting to protect the tiny life inside me. My father is striking at the front door.

'Let the king in!'

My mother stands, rigid, by the kitchen table. My father moves around the house.

'Beware! Beware!' He hammers on the back door.

My mother hurries down the hall. I stay, staring out the pantry window onto the back garden, dark with rain.

Suddenly, a flash. A fierce white line. Close enough to feel its heat. The apple tree is lit for one brief, awful moment. An enormous crash and cracking of sky and wood, and then, as if the tree were a bag of sticks, its branches and bark fly across the garden, the window shatters, the lights go out. Night invades the house.

The only light left is a red glow within the tree.

I move into the hall. My mother has taken down a torch that hangs on a hook by the back door and is walking out into the storm. I follow her. She heads to the apple tree, moves the torchlight over it. One huge branch is down. A deep gash runs the length of its trunk. It is white — a ghost tree, burning from inside, where the lightning passed through it.

My mother swings the torch round to find my father, slumped against the wall of the house, as if blasted there. He winces at the light, looks up at my mother.

'You're done for,' he tells her, through the pouring rain.

Another flash of lightning, pinning us in place. My father sees me, lifts his arms.

'Come to your Daddy!'

I do not move.

'How dare you — lay claim — to our daughter!' My mother's voice has breaks in it. The light shakes in her hand. 'After all you've done. Not done.'

My father drops his arms, closes his eyes, leans back.

'How dare you destroy our celebration! Bring a storm! Tonight!'

'He didn't.'

Fear creeps through me.

'The storm is not his doing.'

Not white or hot, but old and cold.

I turn to see who spoke, though I already know. There, beside the burning tree, a man is standing. I know him by touch, scent, sound. My mother has turned too, swung the torch round. A noise, small and strangled, comes from her.

Hades steps out from the burning tree, in his tattered tunic. With his hard face. Fine hands. Infinitely familiar, utterly strange.

He is here. Not in secret, as before. In full view. Come to fetch me away forever.

My husband takes a step towards my mother. My mother sways, stares, steps to him. It is the first time I have seen them together since she came to claim me back, under the earth. It repels me, to see them close. I feel ashamed, as if keeping them apart has been my task, and the consequence of failing at it will be terrible. They are fixed on one another, ready to pick up where they left off, to argue over me, like a bitter, broken couple, except now my father is in no state to arbitrate between them. He is leaning over the back step.

'Look.' My husband points.

My father vomits.

'Behold, the god of thunder.'

Zeus' head lolls to one side. He slips into the pool of sick. His eyes close.

'He has no more power than you,' Hades tells my mother — his voice, almost gentle. 'You don't control the seasons. He does not command the sky. Poseidon no longer rules the seas. Death alone remains unchanged. The deal is over. Persephone is mine.'

I feel disembodied, as if I were lightning, looking down on us. I see a woman near an apple tree. A stricken mother. A drunken father. And a hard thin man, part mineral, part animal. I do not know what to do, so I do nothing, again.

My mother is pointing to the fields. She speaks one word at a time, each an effort, like throwing stones out into water, watching them disappear.

'I. Stopped. The. Road.'

'You dug a hole,' my husband says. 'It will delay the road by a few weeks. No more. She comes with me tonight.'

He reaches for me. My mother runs to block his way.

'If the deal is over, my daughter stays with me,' she cries, 'where she belongs!'

Hades flinches in her torchlight, dives out of the beam, close by her side.

'She belongs with me,' he says, with quiet hate. 'All these years you have only ever borrowed her.'

They stare at one another as if they are in love. I turn, run to the pond, crouch down like a child, as though the matter is nothing to do with me, is someone else's life.

But Hades is coming after me, lithe in the darkness. My mother stumbles after him.

'I will not — let her — GO!'

She bellows it out and up into the dark, as if telling not only Hades but the storm, the burning apple, the chestnut, the hidden moon. As if the world were listening to her still. A shout of anguish, as when she called my name under the earth.

Another light, a tight bright bead, blinks on.

'What the hell's going on?' Snow's voice, coming down the garden.

The light finds me. From the back of his phone.

'What are you doing?' He addresses only me. 'Are you going somewhere?'

'I don't know,' I say quickly.

'Well, what do you want to do?'

My mother and Hades turn.

I wait for their outrage. Dismissal. Who is this man? What right does he have to intervene?

But they say nothing. They are looking down at me. Waiting. For what I have say.

As if it were up to me. At last.

After all these years of no one asking what I wanted, someone has, and I am mute. I stare up at Snow's phone, my mother's torch, the rain falling through the bands of light. I try to fight my way up, as if from a long way down, try to surface. I force myself to stand.

'I ... want ...'

My husband takes my hand, his fingers, sliding into mine.

Desperate, I search for the words. Find nothing. So I do what I have always done. I look to my mother. To her mouth. For my words. And they are coming.

'Bella ta maaa,' she says.

But they don't sound like words.

'Mother?'

'Peeersavaneeeer!'

It slurs, slides from her before she has had a chance to form the sound. As if she has drunk more than my father.

Snow's light flicks to her. Her mouth is twisted into an expression I have never seen. The right side, dragging down, the left twisting up. Her contorted mouth is opening again. She is reaching for me with her left hand.

'Ta ma.'

Everyone — even Hades — is staring at her, as if watching an accident in slow motion no one knows how to stop.

Her torchlight shudders violently. It goes to the chestnut, the pond, me, then drops, shining on dead leaves on the ground.

'Peerseervaneer!'

She staggers forwards, clutches my shoulder.

But her grip is weak, her body heavy. She leans against me. I cannot hold her up.

'Ta ma,' she cries, sliding down me. She crumples to the sodden earth. In the dark. By the pond. My husband stands over her, holding my hand.

'Come on,' he says. 'Let's go.'

21

PERSEPHONE

'Wait,'

'Why?'

'My mother.'

I kneel. I do not understand what has happened to her. Her eyes are closed, her breathing heavy.

I try to raise her, to set her upright, as if this could cure her of whatever malady has brought her down. I cannot do it. Her head rolls in my hands. The right side of her mouth still droops down to her chin. The loosestrife by the pond strains in the wind towards her.

'Mother!'

'Persephone!'

Not her. Hades.

He draws me up, pulls me into him, holds me. I lean into his hard, known body. I am crying.

.'Her time is over. You can come with me now.'

I am shaking with shock, fright. He trembles too, with hope, desire.

'Let's go,' he says again.

'I can't.'

This is true. I cannot move. I feel like a tree with sudden roots. Hades stiffens.

'There's no fucking signal even for nine-nine-nine!' Snow says, out of the dark. 'I'm going round the front. You stay with your mother.'

He goes at a run. Helplessly, I watch the dot of his phone light as it dances across the garden, disappears.

'Is there someone else?' My husband's voice is urgent, hushed. 'Is that why you will not come? Is that why you wanted to return here in the spring?'

Almost without thinking, I lift my hand to feel for his face. I find his jawline. His grip on me eases enough for me to free my other hand, take it to the back of his neck. The rain falls. I feel the pattern of him under me. This is my autumn and winter — his body, wanting mine, in the dark. I remember being grateful for his heat under the ground, remember how easily desire mixes, confuses with something even older, even younger — the need for safety, shelter.

'No,' I tell my husband. 'There is no one else.'

In this moment I learn to lie, a skill my mother always had that I never did. I realise it is simple — I have only to believe myself, to think this is the truth: right now, and in the end, there is no one but him. I smell the burning apple, remember crawling under the old apple on a warm night long ago, finding this man there, and kissing him. I kiss him now. And the discovery that I can lie lifts me from the horrible panic of my mother's fall. I feel astonished, as when I first climbed the oak, and capable, and clear. I know what I must do.

I cannot leave my mother now. Tonight. I owe her this much. Yet my husband could drag me away, under the earth, and there would be nothing I could do to stop him.

But he does not. Not yet.

Because he wants me to come, as I did before, willingly.

Refusing him is dangerous. I know this. It is why he left me in the dark when I would not eat the seeds; it is why, this year, he followed me up here — because I did not tell him I was his, beside the flooded river. I must make what I need now — time to tend my mother — not a denial of his right to me, but proof of it — a thing that he alone can give.

How much time would he give me? A day? A week? A month? It was Hades' precision that I fell for when I met him first, not his extravagance. A request for too much will enrage him, and he will force me down with him tonight. Instinctively, I think I know the most that I dare ask of him.

We have so many known exchanges. Our rituals of touch are like a dance, developed over years, like mating birds. I start with these.

My fingers feel for his spine, between his shoulder blades.

'Do you love me?'

'More than you know,' he says, his hands mirroring mine.

'If you love me, will you give me something?' My hands stay familiar, tracing down his back, as my words change.

'If it is in my power to give.'

'It is.'

'Tell me.'

'It will be hard.'

I lay my fingers along the curve of his ribs — again, his hands follow mine.

'What is it?'

'It may be too hard.'

'I have given you the hardest stones.'

'It will be harder.'

'What could be?'

I lean into him, my mouth against his ear: 'One final summer here.'

His hands, around my ribs, press my breath out.

'Why?'

'To tend to her. To say goodbye. Then I will come to you. With autumn. On the harvest moon. The time I always come.'

'And then you'll stay?'

'Yes.'

'Forever.'

'Yes.'

His head drops to my collar bone.

'How can I wait?' he asks, as if helpless, but there is danger in him still. 'I need you with me.'

My hands run round his shoulders, along his arms, to his hands, for which I loved him first. I open his palms. Our fingers interlace. The rain falls inside the cup of our hands.

I look up across the dark garden, and the apple tree gives me the answer.

'While you wait, make me a summer underground so I need never long for this up here. You promised it to me long ago.'

He shudders, moans. I kiss him again, feel desire quicken in him, the keen ache which is close to, may be the same as, his hurt, his deep and endless need to make up for ruling only dead and stone.

'Do you promise to come to me at harvest moon?' he whispers.

'I promise.'

'No later?'

'No.'

He lets go my hands.

'You shall have one last summer,' he says, soft and slow. 'And I will make another, unending summer for you in the dark.'

Then he holds me, in the way he does, tight enough that we can both feel every bone within us, all our buried structure.

'I love you,' I say, and I believe it. Back up his spine my hands go. I barely dare breathe, lest he retract what he has now agreed. But I need not fear this — he hates hesitation. Now it is decided, he lifts my hands from his shoulders, presses them. I return the pressure. We both let go. And he is gone.

My calm and clarity go with him.

For a moment I stand, dazed by what I have just done, then drop down to my mother. Terrified, I feel round the wet ground, find the torch. It still works. I shine it on her. Her heavy face, weathered skin, closed eyes. I look down at her legs, sticking out of the bottom of her party smock, at her sandals, sliding off her feet. I have never seen her like this. I remember as a child coming in on her in bed, feeling the shock of her abandoned body. But then she could be woken, would take me in her arms. Now neither I, nor rain, nor wind can rouse her.

Only hours ago, she seemed back at her most capable. Hauling the cauldron up from the cellar. Standing at the front gate, as everyone arrived. Now her chest rises, drops, every breath an effort, as if she herself were hills and valleys she must cross.

And I am doing nothing to help, have no idea what I should do.

I shine the torch up the garden. The lights are out in the house, but I hear voices.

'Snow! Nonny!'

'We did it!' Snow's voice, not far away. 'Had to go all the way to the bloody stile to get a signal.' They come out of the dark. Kneel by me.

'She should be on her side,' Snow says. We roll her, like a huge log.

'The ambulance will be here soon,' Nonny says.

'You'll have to meet it on the Woodeaton road,' he says. 'Open the gate into the field near Islip bridge — see how far the driver can get.'

'Right,' Nonny says and goes.

'Stay here. I'll go to the house — find a blanket and a pillow.' Snow runs, is quickly back. We lay the cover from the downstairs sofa over her. I lift her head, slide the cushion under it that Snow has brought. He hands me his fleece jacket.

'You're soaked. Take this. What happened to that man? Was he your husband?'

'He left.'

'Good.' He shakes his head. 'You okay here on your own?'

'Yes.'

'I'll go help Nonny guide the ambulance.'

He goes, and my thoughts grow simple. I am here with my mother. The rain is soft now, the wind still strong. I switch off the torch. I do not want to look at her. The chestnut tree thrashes its branches for her, the loosestrife strains towards her, though if my husband is right, neither tree nor flower care. But I have witnessed the world listening to her — to her moods, gestures, thoughts — for so long, I cannot suddenly believe in its indifference now.

At last, I hear the siren, see the blue light, in the distance. Snow's voice comes round the corner of the house: 'This way.'

And then they are here, larger than life, two men with head torches in dark-green uniforms with reflective yellow jackets, like the road workers, but they have on proper coats, not vests, and they are coming down the garden path.

'What's going on?'

'My mother fell.'

Kneeling, checking her breathing, her pulse.

'Explain what happened.'

I tell them about her slurring words, her falling arms, her body coming down on me.

'When was this?'

'I'm not sure.'

'About forty minutes ago,' Snow says.

'Right. Let's get her in.'

They are rolling her onto a stretcher, strapping her in. I think stupid thoughts, like how I am sorry she is unconscious because she would enjoy the attention, would like these men, would want to make them cups of tea before they carry her off to hospital. They are walking, almost running with her now, but she is heavy. We are following, a strange procession in the dark. My mother is lying like a queen, like a goddess, like a dead woman, being carried through her garden, across her meadow, behind the house. The ambulance is near the river, one full field away, its blue light pulsing in the dark. Everybody does what they must do, as if this were a performance we had rehearsed, and of course for these men, it is something they have done many times. This is just another old woman needing medical attention, fast.

Snow walks beside me, lights the way with the torch on his phone. The fields have turned to mud.

'You going in with her?' he asks.

'Yes.' Though I had not even thought that far ahead.

'Shall we clear up from the party?'

'No need.'

'We'd be glad to.'

We reach the ambulance. They are opening the doors, carrying my mother inside. Snow is still talking.

'To be honest, Mrs Casey — Nut's mum — might have had enough of us …'

They are securing the stretcher on which my mother lies to a tall stand.

'So, could we look after the house — just for now?'

'Sure.' Right now, I do not care about the house.

'Thanks.' Snow fumbles in his pocket, pulls out a pen, a scrap of paper, scribbles on it. 'Here's my and Nonny's numbers. Call us. Let us know if there's anything you need.'

I nod. I start to take off his fleece jacket.

'Keep it,' he says. 'And the tenner in the pocket.'

'Thanks.'

They let me go in with my mother. We are shut in, like goods to be delivered. The men climb into the front and we are off, bumping through two fields, before we reach the road, then speeding along, the siren wailing, telling the night, and anyone listening, to make way for my mother.

22

PERSEPHONE

The bed has white metal railings, cold to the touch. The nurse led me from the waiting room, past other beds, other people, to this one.

'Here,' he said. 'The doctor will be round shortly.'

I have never been inside a hospital before. When I was young, the sick came to our house and my mother healed them with her herbs and with her hands. This does not feel like a house of healing. A huge, square building, into which my mother was wheeled along corridors, with swinging doors.

My husband says the world is dying. In here, it feels as if it is already over. The smells I know are gone. Only a disinfected one remains. I was asked to put a transparent liquid on my hands to strip them of any trace of what or who I've touched. I am in an Intensive Care Unit in the John Radcliffe Hospital, Oxford, level two, bay five. But I could be anywhere. I have never felt more lonely or more lost.

When Hades abandoned me beneath the earth, though I was lost, I understood the map. I knew that somewhere above me were fields, home, my mother. Here, now, I do not even understand the map. There are no windows — I cannot tell in what direction the house lies. I do not know what season we are in. I do not know where my mother has gone, though she is in the bed before me.

Hades said her time was up — what did he mean?

They took her away when we arrived, 'to have a CT scan,'

the lady behind the desk told me, as if I would know what that was. I had to sit and fill out forms containting questions to which I did not know the answers: my mother's date of birth, full name, doctor's surgery, medical history. I made it up. Ms Demeter Corn. Born on June twenty-first, nineteen fifty-five. At the end, I had to sign and state my relationship to the patient. It seems the only thing I know about the woman in the bed before me is that I am her daughter. Beyond that, I know little else — nothing for certain.

She is lying on her side, in white, under white sheets, head and chest propped up by pillows, like a boat hauled high onto the shore, lest it slip out to sea. Her right arm is resting over the covers, a plastic tag about her wrist. Her fingers are curled in tight, though her palm is empty, as if she had lost something yet holds still onto the memory of holding it. On the inside of her elbow, two tubes slide into her. Clear fluid coils down the tubes from pouches strung up on a stand beside the bed. Small patches on her chest link her to a machine.

She is still breathing hard — shuddering, gasping. I am afraid to look at her. I feel repelled by her and then ashamed of this. The slackness of her skin, the spittle at the corners of her lips, the dark tunnel of her mouth. It reminds me of turning over stones in the back garden as a child, near the well, the sudden exposure of a hidden world to light — the white roots, the delineated, flattened earth, the woodlice curling into balls, worms squirming away. I do not want to see my mother like this, upturned, unearthed. I never thought I would.

I told Hades I wanted time to tend her. Now, I feel a childish resentment that she has let this happen, this sudden, stark reversal in our roles. I want her to sit up, bundle us out of here, walk us home through the stormy night, without ever looking back.

I hold on to the railings of the bed, wait for someone I have never met to come and tell me what has happened to my mother.

The doctor arrives at last. The nurse too. Both men. Name badges clipped on to their pockets: Dr Kapoor and Mr Scott. Mr Scott swishes a blue curtain about the bed. He turns on a light, attached to the machine.

'Good morning,' Dr Kapoor says. 'You are Ms Corn's daughter?'

'Yes.'

'We're going to check her level of responsiveness.'

They speak to her, press her nail, pull up her eyelids, check her pupils. I wait. My mother sighs.

'Right,' Dr Kapoor says. He picks up his notes that he had set down on the machine.

'Good news, bad news. We'll do the bad first. Your mother has suffered a stroke — ischaemic — caused by a blood clot — very common, but in your mother's case it was a particularly large one.'

Of course — my mother never does anything in moderation.

'Primarily, the left-side of her brain has been affected, resulting in paralysis on the right.'

I nod, wait.

'The good news is that you got her here fast, within time for us to administer this.' He points to one of the sacks of fluid, curling into her. 'I am hopeful your mother will regain consciousness in the next twenty-four hours. Unfortunately, it's very difficult at this stage to know the extent of the damage done — I'm sorry.'

I look at the sheets, say nothing.

'Any questions?'

I shake my head — I do not want to hear any more answers.

'Okay, we'll be round later. I would just add, there is a huge variation in the extent of recovery — a good deal is down to the motivation of the patient and to the quality of care that they receive.' He pauses, both frowning and smiling at me. 'You can make a difference,' he says.

The nurse pulls back the curtain, clicks off the light. They go, and I am left in the bright night of the hospital ward, with my mother in my care.

I sit back by the metal bars. My mother heaves and sighs. I feel young, confused. I want my mother. My mother is in the bed. When did she change and how? From a goddess with veins like rivers, hands as broad as fields, heart as steady as the sun, to an old lady with narrow arteries and clotting blood?

I move the chair further down the bed to where the metal bars stop, so that I can reach in and take hold of her left hand, the one that lies open, limp. It is ridiculous that this requires courage, but it does. I am shy to touch her. Even as a child, when I wanted to be held, my mother was the one to do the holding, the giving of her arms, of herself. She touched me. I did not touch her.

Her hand is warm. It is odd to hold it and not to have her hold mine back. My mother breathes out.

'Uuuuh,' — a thin thread of sound. She looks so old and tired, I look away, close my eyes. As soon as I do, I feel better. I feel her hand, hear her breath, her thin voice. I know this place, of hands and sounds and darkness. I spend half my life down here.

I begin to breathe in time with my mother. I squeeze her hand with every inbreath. Grip. Release. Over and over. I do not know how long I sit there doing this — an hour, maybe

237

two. And then, as I press her hand, I start to feel my mother's fingers pressing back. The movement is so slight at first, I think I am imagining it. I keep on dreaming it until, at last, it's certain. A returned pressure. She grips my hand as if she has just found me or been found.

Years ago, whenever I returned home in the spring, my mother would tell me stories of the winter I had missed, of snow and ice, of cold and loss. She liked to repeat the story of the first winter, of how far she had gone to look for me, how terrible it was to have lost me. She wanted me in turn to tell her of my months away. She wanted to hear how unhappy I had been down with my husband underground. I could not tell her what she wanted to hear, so I never told her anything. I was too sick in those first days of my return to explain, and then, once I had recovered, it seemed best to look to the summer ahead, sweep winter away. So, I never told her of the dark. I never talked about the textures of the rock, the grit of limestone, slippery flowstone, crumbling chalk. I never told her of my husband. Of the rituals we have, of being lost and found. Because when we let go in the dark and move apart, even a short way, we could be at a great distance. During the first winters some part of us touched always — shoulder to shoulder, his head in my lap, his raised knee against my side. Then, slowly, he allowed, grew to want, the thrill of coming out of contact, losing touch. Finding me again. It became our game. Hiding. Seeking. Meeting. Holding. Except when he was working. Then he placed me as he wished, reclining on the rock. I would lie and listen to the striking, scraping, chipping. He returned to touch me, check my shape, went back to work. Until at last, he would take my hand and lead me to feel what he had made. I felt the contours of my body in the stone, like a mirror without light.

I never told my mother this.

But now, at last, I sit, holding her hand, and start to speak. I speak only on her out-breaths. I tell her how I survive the dark. I tell her how I have learnt to follow sound, how I know the distance to the walls by calling out, the size of a chamber from the hum of water flowing through it. I tell her how space and time change underground, fold into one another. How you can be more alone than anywhere with light, and yet less separate, because the dark joins you to everything. I tell her how startling and vivid are the dreams that blossom in that dark, but that she need not fear them. And slowly, her hand, gripping mine, softens but holds still. Her breathing eases. She no longer sighs. She listens. So, I tell on. I retrace my steps, back through the dark, the years, till I am right back at the beginning, and I tell her why I starved and why I left.

The corn was yours, I say. I wanted something of my own. I tell her I meant to go, but I never meant to stay. I tell her how I refused the pomegranate when she was not there. That I ate it when she came, not out of spite, but longing.

And all the while my mother lies, listens, holds my hand.

I tell her things I could never say if she were awake. I do not know what she hears, but I feel closer to her than I have for years. Perhaps as close as I have ever been. I tell it all in a whisper — the others on the ward must think I am muttering prayers over my mother. Maybe I am.

I love you, I say.

I'm sorry, I say.

I ask her to come back. I tell her that I do not want to be left up here, alone. I do not think I am ready for it, or that I ever will be.

At last, the light behind my eyes reddens. They have turned

on the ceiling strip lights in the ward to signal it is morning. We are meant to wake up now. I open my eyes. My mother is asleep. She looks peaceful.

I feel exhausted. I want to crawl into the bed and for her to climb out and sit beside me. I rest my head on the metal bars and feel a wave of nausea. I did not ask Hades for nine moons, only three. He would never have given me nine. I have enough time, I hope, to take care of my mother. Not enough for the child. But it was never going to live. My mother, though, is meant to live forever.

23

PERSEPHONE

I ring Snow and he comes. He brings a change of clothes. Food. I am relieved to see him. He is proof that the rest of the world still exists. I sit in a pink chair, with metal arms, while he paces the little waiting room.

'How's your mother?' he asks.

'She hasn't come round yet. The nurse promised to fetch me if she wakes.'

He nods.

'Is everything okay in the house? The lights back on?'

'Nope. No light — but we've cleared up. The lake in the fields out front is huge from the storm. And the river has flooded the meadow behind the house too. We fed ducks and swans this morning, standing on the back garden wall.'

I nod.

Opposite me, set high, at an angle looking down on the room is a TV, switched on but with the sound off. Words appear as captions at the bottom of the screen. I watch a silent couple look at old houses which they hope to turn into white apartments with double-basin bathrooms.

'Hey, I don't know what you'll think of this.' Snow stops pacing, stands in front of me, 'But —'

He squats down, looks at me.

'We'd be wasting a chance not to stage a protest from the house.'

I am tired. I have not slept. I avoid his eyes, look at his beard.

'What do you mean?'

'Just be good to make it a bit harder for them to turf you out.' He puts his big hands on the metal arms of the chair.

I look now at the tree branches on his neck.

'The fact is they'll evict you soon,' he says, quietly, 'and then demolish the lot.'

I stare back up at the TV, where the couple are viewing a bedroom.

All this time, however much I may have told my mother she was wrong, that the road is real, the world changed, deep down I still believed she was in charge, would win out in the end. She always has, except once, and that was my doing. I knew this was coming. But I am shocked. To hear they will knock down the house. Somehow this news is worse than anything the doctor told me. Because I cannot separate my mother from her home. Every image that I hold of her, but one, is in that house, or garden, on her land. Right now, the fact that it will be taken is proof she could be too.

I keep watching the TV. The young couple buy the property. I feel Snow's hand on my knee — I press my eyes shut, but it's too late.

He puts an arm about my shoulders. I let myself lean into him. He has not touched me since I told him about the baby. More tears come at this thought. He passes me a tissue from a box on a little table by the chair.

'I'm sorry,' I say.

'No need.'

'I'm worried about her.'

'I know. Been there — I told you — I lost my mum last year.'

I pull away from him.

'How do you cope?' I ask. I want to know.

'Well, you don't, for a bit. And then ...' He shrugs. 'Nonny says I'm still in denial, that I should stop and grieve. But to be honest, I don't see the point. I don't want to sit round feeling miserable. I'd rather be busy.'

He half-smiles, stands, as if uncomfortable to have admitted this much. I know he is telling the truth. For the brief time I have known him, this is who he has been — busy, and sad.

'But, I dunno, I reckon your mum might pull through — she seems pretty tough.'

Footsteps. The door of the ward swings open. I tighten my hands on the chair arms, ready to stand. The steps pass on down the corridor.

'How long?' I ask, 'Till they come? For the house?'

He smiles, relieved to be back onto this.

'End of July I think. A month at most.'

'And what would it mean? The protest?'

'Well, ideally, we'd empty it. Barricade the windows. Take out the stairs.' He stops. I am crying again.

'I'm sorry. I'm a dickhead. I shouldn't have brought it up.'

I stare back at the TV, watch renovations underway.

'And if it's not okay for us to stay there —'

'It's fine.' This, I know. Visitors. Guests. People to fuss over. People to muck in. She has missed this. 'Just wait before you start doing anything else.'

'Of course,' he says. 'And thanks for letting us stay. That's brilliant.'

'Look, I'd better get back. I need to be there when she wakes. Thanks for coming, and bringing supplies.'

'No worries.'

He pulls me up to him. Holds me. His arms are so different

to my mother's, or my husband's, solid, undemanding, holding on, letting go. I am more grateful for this hug, already over, than anything else he has brought me today.

'Call, okay? Let me know what's happening,' he says.

'I will.'

'I hope your mum's okay.'

Then he goes, almost running, off to meet Nut and Berry who are playing in the hospital car park, off to dream of staging a protest from my mother's house.

The ward is different by day. Crowded with details I did not see at night: a pouch of dark-yellow urine, hanging at the foot of the bed; sick bowls of grey, wrinkly cardboard on the bedside cabinet; white circular lights in the ceiling, like fake moons.

I sit by my mother. She is still asleep. I feel afraid of her waking, afraid of her not.

'She's doing well,' Dr Kapoor said, when he came round before lunch, 'Making good progress,' as if my mother were a student. Studying what? The flow of blood? Breath? She is good at life, even now. I am not. 'She's stable,' the doctor said. I feel anything but stable — my body is brittle from no sleep. I hang on to the metal bars, look at my mother's left arm, the paleness of her skin on the inside of her elbow, her veins showing through, as if age were making her slowly more translucent. I look away, spot her poppy-coloured smock stowed in a plastic bag, beneath the bed.

I glance back at my mother and my heart leaps — she is looking at me. Her eyes are only half open, as if the light hurts. She looks like a child.

I feel relief, and almost as fast a frightened irritation. But she is already closing her eyes, going again.

'Mother.'

Her eyes blink open. As she gazes at the ceiling, at its fake moons, her face changes slowly, like something monstrous coming back to life. Her nostrils flare, lines score her forehead. She turns her head to me, wincing. She looks at my mouth, opens hers — nothing comes out. She shuts and opens it again, as if she expects the words to fall out from the simple act of making space between her lips. She grins, not a smile but an effort of muscles.

'Di,' she says — more breath than word — 'Di.'

I am afraid to speak to her. 'You've had a stroke,' I say.

She shakes her head, opens her mouth, this time pushing it down,

'Ma.' She freezes, listening to herself, as to a bird's song she does not recognise.

Her right hand is still curled, holding nothing, but now, with her left, she starts to push the covers off, to lever herself up, swing her legs out of the bed. Her right leg will not move.

'No.' I lay my hand on her left leg, now exposed. She grabs my hand.

'Ma,' she whispers.

'You need to rest.'

The nurse is coming, running — it is the man, Mr Scott, the one who was on duty when we first arrived. My mother struggles to move her right leg, gripping my hand tight.

'You're not well,' I tell her.

She snorts, her eyes wild like an animal's ready to attack.

'Ms Corn, you can't get up yet!' says Mr Scott.

The weight of her torso is against me, her left leg is out and down, ready for walking, leaving.

'Mother, stop!'

245

That horrible look at my mouth again. She draws her lips together, as if the world tastes sour, then lets them go.

'Wa. Waaaa.'

Another nurse comes, swishes the blue curtain round us. My mother's panic grows. She bares her teeth, sees, for the first time, the tubes in her right arm, cries out, lets go of me to try to rip them off. The nurses pin her arms and shoulders down, but even in her weakened state, my mother is strong. Another nurse appears through the curtain with a needle and syringe.

My mother glares at me. 'Waaaa!' She is breathy, urgent.

I stand, miserable, doing nothing.

'This will ease her distress,' the nurse says.

'Waaaa,' my mother cries out.

'Wait!' I tell the nurse with the syringe. 'Just a moment.'

I sit on the end of the bed, take my mother's left hand.

'You fell, by the pond.'

She shakes her head.

'I had to bring you here, to hospital.'

She frowns, drops her head in frustration, lifts it, parts her lips.

'Ba. Ba. Baby.' She presses forward.

I do not know if she means herself, or me, or her grandchild, or none of these.

'Baby. Baby!'

'What about the baby?'

She lets go my hand, starts to struggle against the nurses again.

'Mother,' I am shouting now. 'Listen!'

She hesitates.

'You had a party. Remember?'

'Baby.'

'Last night.'

'Baby.'

'There was a storm.'

She looks down.

'My husband came.' Her head jerks up. She grimaces.

'I stayed with you.'

'Ma,' she says. She softens, rests back onto the pillows, stares at me. 'Ma, ma.'

She feels for my hand. I take it. She closes her eyes. The right side of her mouth twitches. I nod to the nurses that they can let her go.

I do not tell her that the protestors want to take over her house. I do not tell her that I promised my husband I would leave.

'I'm here,' is all I say.

24

DEMETER

Snow's coming, she says.

Snow?

Out the window. No snow. Sun.

Don't care — snow or sun — she's here.

She wasn't before.

Went wandering the world to look for her.

Woods black. Burnt.

No birds.

Corn flattened.

Rivers dry.

Earth cracked. Split like dead skin.

No sign of her.

Thought he had her.

Then I felt her hand.

Still afraid he was near. About to take her.

But then —

I stayed, she said.

Happiness hurts.

Everything's sore.

Head.

Heart.

You had a stroke, she told me.

A stroke?

I stroked her when she was young. In bed. Her hair.

Try to rock your right leg for me, they say. Gently does it.

Rock, gently? But I know rock. It's hard. Unbending. Heavy.

My leg is rock. Arm too.

Here's a stick, my daughter says. To help the rock.

A stick? A grey metal thing. Plastic at the top.

A man comes up to me. Hair on his face, not his head. Takes the stick. Gives me a hand.

Man on my rock side. Daughter on the other.

We're going to take you home, she says.

About time. I left the hob on — the milk will have boiled over, the pan will be black, or worse, the house burnt to the ground.

Others, in blue, get in our way.

They talk. Discharge forms. Rehab appointments.

Too tired to listen. I babble with the baby. He understands. We go at last.

The rock leg hurts to lean on. Feels like winter.

Good leg, rock leg. Over and over. This is walking.

We go through doors. The doors hear us coming — they open as we near, like the mouth of someone huge, lying on their side.

They tested my mouth. My swallowing. I can swallow. I can take in. Take it all in all right. But out is hard. The words stick in the rock.

One more door, my daughter says.

It opens wide.

Air, blue and green.

I remember this.

Coming out of my mother.

I take a step on the rock.

Remember my father too.

This way, the man says.

Steady now, my daughter says.

But I'm in a hurry — I need to get back, turn the hob off, rescue the pan, the house. The man leads me over hard, grey ground to a red metal room.

Let's get you in the car, he says.

They strap me in, as if I would try to leave. My daughter sits beside me. The man in front. The seats face the same way, as if we are expecting something to appear, or happen.

Then we move, without moving. I watch the world running away — all the colours.

I hold my daughter's hand. For years, she has been the missing thing, the ache. Now she is here, but other things are aching and are lost.

Bump. Bump. Bumpety-bump we go. The baby likes it, too. Off the smooth, hard, grey, on to the bumpety-brown.

Can't get any closer, says the man. Ground's too soft. We'd never get the car out.

This'll do, my daughter says.

Ho-o-ob eeerff, I say. The words like dry soil in my mouth. Hob erf.

Actually, I told them to put the kettle on, says the man, smiling.

I feel afraid, but when they let me out onto the brown, I see the house. Not burnt. I'm glad. Then sad, because the feeling has not gone. There must be something else, left on, not done.

I look around. Everything is changed.

A season I don't know. The ground is water.

I want to know how deep. Walking already feels like wading. But they steer me away, towards the house.

I walk between man and daughter, piggy in the middle.

Step step warm cold light dark summer winter. Years pass.

I stop. I smell something green, spiky. Nettle. The word stings. They stand — each with one good green leg, like me.

I'm tired. I cannot think how tired. Tired as mountains. Another step. Another. The rock leg follows me, heavy as a question.

Uuurrr.

That was me. Head hanging. Hands shaking.

It's okay, my daughter says. It's early days.

Early days? I don't think so. I want to cry. I look up.

The kitchen is walking out to meet me. Not the room. The things inside it — over the bumpety ground, things I know like-the-back-of-my-hand — words in strings, come easy like songs. The table, set down in grass. I reach it — it reaches me.

There you go, someone says.

Chairs arrive.

Take a seat, they say.

I do. Stroke my table.

My daughter says hello to a woman, a little boy, another woman full of rings, two men. She told me she had friends to stay. We did this once, long ago. Had people over. Ate out. Under the blue. They bring me warm water — leaves in it.

Welcome home, my daughter says.

Everyone smiles. Like I'm the guest.

They introduce themselves — odd names — Ash, Nut, Berry, Big Ben, Nonny, Snow. Not her husband. He would not dare. Not in this light.

Pee wi peeee wi, sings a bird.

Bumpety-bump, sings my grandson.

I am full of bumps. Knarly, knotty, clumpy. Alive with threads of things. You have lost control of the seasons, he said.

The world is not listening to you now, he said. Maybe, but I am listening to the world.

Part of me, the dark, rocky part, wants the storm to rage still. I want to roll in the grub. Piss in the pond. The hospital was too white, too clean — bad for my health.

But for them, my daughter, her baby, I must be good. Must remember the thing that isn't the hob, the hurry. I am annoyed to have forgotten it. I start to push up.

What is it? my daughter asks.

Hob eerff.

It is off.

I'll go double-check for you, the Snow man says before I can stop him. He is back quick.

Yup, it's fine. All off.

I sigh and sulk. I knew that. But there is still a thing to be done. Near. Even my rock leg can feel it. Tingles with it. I swallow the leaf in the cup. Spit out a word.

Whaat too dooo? I ask my daughter.

She listens, head to one side.

A thing. Too doo. Thee thingg. Theere. I lift my green arm to the house.

I think my mother wants to know what the plan is, she says to the Snow man.

Sure, he says, sitting on top of my table.

We want to prepare, he says, for when they come to kick us out.

He talks about the people who want to build the road. He wants to hold them off. To defend the earth. We have to clear the house, barricade it, he says.

I nod. I do not care about the road. If they want to build it, they will — I told my daughter that before. But I am happy to

252

turn the house out. A spring clean. Should have done it years ago. It is the only way I will find the thing that is not the hob, to turn it off, or on.

And to get things ready, for when her husband comes again. Because he will.

Sooner-the-better, I say. Like-the-back-of-my-hand. Barricave the house.

Against him. Do it now.

Great, he says. We'll get going.

25

PERSEPHONE

July.

I feel sick and irritable. My mother is sick but happy. She has many guests, and she must think that I am staying for good — she behaves, for all the world, as if winter will never come again.

She sits in her study chair, now out on her veg patch, with a stick cut from an apple-tree branch, saved from the storm. She smiles as sofas and armchairs are carried out into the fields, as pots and pans are stacked beside the fire pit in the front garden. When Snow and Big Ben carry her bed downstairs, my mother points her stick towards the chestnut tree, beside the pond. 'You can't have your bed outside! What if it rains?' But she waves me away. They follow her orders and place her bed beneath the tree.

She sits and smiles as the study window is boarded up, and every other window too, with thick planks, reinforced with joists nailed to the floor. She smiles as the stairs are smashed. When they were in the woods, the protestors riled her. Now they are in her house, taking it apart, she loves them. I want them to remember it is her house, not theirs. I do not understand why she seems so unconcerned at its dismantling. Perhaps because she saw it go up. She built it. I did not. I never knew the world without it.

For years, grieving has been my mother's job. Now, suddenly, it is left to me. I burst into tears, seeing a vase balanced on the apple stump that once stood on the kitchen table; a bedroom rug laid out upon the grass. I want the stairs to blunt Snow's saw, the furniture prove impossible to move. But, as with the yew, it seems that thousands of years of life can be undone in a day. This summer I have seen things end which I thought couldn't. It frightens me.

They told me in the hospital it would take time for my mother to recover, but I don't have much time. I watch the first moon since the storm come full. Two more and then I go. She is still weak. Often dozing. Stilted in her speech and in her steps. Her face looks smaller than before, more wrinkled, like one of the beans she stores over winter to seed when I return. I want her better now.

And I wish that she would feel worse.

I am envious of her smiling, envious of how Snow, and the others, behave as if loving her is easy. I remember this as a child. This precise feeling of not being part of the ease. It's why I left.

Meanwhile, Snow is friendly to me, but, mostly, he is exultant that this is happening, after the disappointment of the woods, and busy, working every day, mixing concrete, to make 'lock-ons' inside the barrels that once held my mother's wines. 'Stick your arm down the drainpipe in the middle of the cement,' he explains, 'handcuff yourself to the bar at the bottom. When the bailiffs come, they have to angle grind, hammer and hack their way to your wrist — hours of fun.' The eviction, he claims, is only weeks away.

Snow never asks about the baby. I never mention it. I still daily expect, hope for, dread, seeing blood. I did my own deal, bartered for a final summer, have been granted a short reprieve from my fate — but it does not change it. I cannot expect that.

I help the protestors out a little, but protecting the house is not why I am here. I stayed to tend my mother.

I have to feed her.

In the evening, I help her from her chair on the veg patch to the pond. She eases herself onto her bed. I lift her right leg, swivel her round, get her under the covers — there are leaves and a few early conkers in green cases on the bedspread.

She leans back, closes her eyes.

'I'll fetch supper.'

'Thanks.'

I head up the garden, round to the fire at the front. The electricity never came back on after the storm, but the protestors use the fire and some camping stoves to cook — they have a rota. I return with a bowl of curry.

A heron has landed across the other side of the pond. My mother is sitting up, matching its stillness. It is the most alert I have seen her all day. The heron moves first, lifting its huge grey wings, flapping itself clear of the garden wall. My mother slumps back.

'It was hoping dinner,' she says.

Her speech is better, but sometimes she misses out words, at other times she adds them.

'Here's yours.' I offer her the bowl, put a spoon into her good left hand. 'Curry, care of your garden.'

'Put it down,' she waves the spoon at the stool beside her bed, 'while it cools.'

'That's what you said at lunch, and then you forgot about it.'

'Forget me not now,' she says, smiling.

I sit with her. She gazes at the midges dancing above the pond. She does not touch the food. The spoon falls from her hand. I take it up, dip it in the stew.

'Open up,' I say, and, to my dismay, she does. Parts her lips as if to object but then leaves them that way, saying nothing, lets me slide the spoon into her. It feels like a game, like my pretending to feed my corn dollies, her going along with it to humour me. But it is not a game. I do not like the wet, vulnerable inside of her mouth, the effort she has to make to swallow. Worse is the way her eyes follow me, as if it is a thing of great wonder that I can sit here, lift a spoon, hold a bowl.

I chat, to make it ordinary, to hide my discomfort.

'A police officer visited today, while you were dozing. Didn't arrest anyone.'

She smiles, but more at me than at what I have said. She is so busy watching me that she forgets to open her mouth.

'Come on,' I say, playing as parents do, that the spoon is a bird, flying in. 'Open up.' Her lips part, enough for breath. 'Bit more.' A little of the soup spills from her mouth, down her chin. I have a cloth — one of her old tea towels. As I wipe her chin, go to swap cloth for spoon, she catches my hand.

'I'm glad you stayed,' she says.

I look down, find the spoon.

I want to disappear forever.

I want never to leave her side.

'Open up,' I say. 'You're nearly done.'

'Nearly done,' she repeats.

I have still not told her that, when summer ends, I have to leave. I am waiting till she is strong enough to hear it.

DEMETER

Web beside bed.

Spider in it like a brooch.

Tree humming.

Grandson singing.

Sun, grandson, spider, tree — no one else up.

The thing to turn off, turn on, was not in the house. They emptied the lot — every last pan out. Nothing but dust.

Shhhhhh, grandson said.

Listen, heron said.

Spider said nothing but sat still, for hours.

I was tired.

Thousands of years of telling the world what to do — maybe it's time I was told.

So, I listen.

Things I hear make my eyes run.

Birdsong. Plop of frogs. Silk slide out of spider.

Bubbles of air pop inside chestnut leaves.

I love those leaves — how they fan out like feathers.

A green-lipped case grins down at me, its mouth full of conker.

Should have brought the bed down here years ago — so many wasted nights indoors.

I wanted them to bring it here, by the pond, to where I fell. To pick up where I left off. I shut my eyes, try to remember that night. The dark is red and I remember, not storm, but stomach. Hades was there then too — in my father — holding on to stone. This from thousands of years ago comes back easy. Storm, from a few weeks past, is vague.

Ragged sense of rain and wind.

Terrible headache. Only had one glass of punch.

Beat of blood in my head.

Blow to apple tree.

Her father, stupid with drink.

Hades.

His hard, pale face, hands reaching for her.

My arms, filled with stones, sinking as I fought to lift them.

And then the Snow man, coming out of rain, asking my daughter what she wanted.

Open eyes, look at pond, quiet and bright, black and green. I cannot remember what she replied, if she replied. She is here — that should be enough. Still, I would give up all the other words — hand the whole lot in — to know those she used in answer.

But no matter — I know this much — her husband will not have given up his claim to her.

He will be back.

I must prepare.

When will he come?

I need to think.

Close eyes on morning sun.

I keep odd hours, and the hours are odd. Some gone in seconds. Others stretch out like centuries.

I dream.

I can change into whatever I wish, and nothing hurts.

I am apple tree, whole again.

I am pine, needle-sharp, evergreen.

I am oak, the one Erysichthon cut down. I feel what it is to live on light, the loveliness of leaves instead of lungs. No boom, boom, boom, breathe in, breathe out, but the longer beat of being tree.

I am eloquent beyond words — perform a slow soliloquy.

At summer's end I bow, rustle my own applause, retreat, rehearse lines underground.

Sun high when I wake. Bowl of porridge by the bed. Gone cold. I missed her.

But she's not missing.

Not taken.

Not yet.

He won't come now.

Not in this heat, not in these days of growth.

He'll come only as they end.

The time, in other years, when she has left.

At summer's end — I dreamt it.

I feel it. Even my rock arm, rock leg can feel it — it is the only thing they can feel. They needle with it.

How will he come? From where?

Not through the woods. The yew is gone. And he won't travel far to try to find another opening. He hates the surface, even at night. The open sky.

Close eyes.

Think, dream, again.

Now I am everything that moves.

I am heron, great wings, long legs.

I am robin, plucky, tight-chested.

I am blackbird, sweet-songed, smart boy, spy a worm. I go tug it up, but it slips down and I slip with it, and then I am worm, bunching my way through earth, all squirm and wriggle, muscle and mouth, eating my way down, tunnelling, naked.

Wake once more, without knowing I had slept.

Scent of honeysuckle, whir of bats — it's late.

I have dozed the day away.

I give myself a good talking to — stay leaf-sharp, spider-ready, bat-quick, conker-hard, worm-deep, I say.

I lie in the gathering dark, thinking of worms.

Of tunnels.

Of the way that he will come.

26

Persephone

August arrives.

Incredibly, we are still here.

Word comes that they are concentrating their efforts on land near Bern Wood, further along the route. Maybe we have a bit longer, Snow says, cautious, still making lock-ons.

My mother is getting stronger — feeding herself — but I worry about her still, especially at night, sleeping by the pond, alone. I watch her in the mornings, a little figure in bed, under the chestnut tree, a vast, deep-green against the sky, and, slowly, an idea grows in me. I feel shy about it, but one afternoon, I ask.

'Would it be possible,' I say to Snow, 'to build a treehouse in the chestnut?'

He stops stirring sand and stone, looks up at me, grins.

'Yes,' he says, 'It would.'

And so we do.

Snow finds me a harness I can use, and we spend two days in among joists, pallets, hauling them high into the tree, strapping them in place. We cut willow branches from the river, bend them into a roof, drag a tarpaulin up to cover them. Years ago, my mother gave me a corner of the garden to make my own, but I never did. This shelter, hidden under leaves, at last feels like mine. Mine and Snow's.

We sit, swinging our legs off the platform edge. We do not talk — the leaves do that for us — but it is obvious that, being up here, we will touch again. It is different than it was in May, because we are less awkward and because this is our treehouse. I spend my first night in a tree.

I love the waking moment, looking out at light and leaves, and one morning, I realise, with surprise, that I do not feel sick. I am hungry and it feels good — not a tightening of my stomach but a simple wish for food. And my wish to lie with Snow feels simple too. I am less stricken with guilt than I was before. My husband gave me one last summer, to tend to my mother and to say goodbye. Every time I climb the tree, every time I lie with Snow, I say goodbye.

More people show up: XR activists, old-timers, newcomers. And when they do, they learn about Snow's and Persephone's treehouse. Snow puts his arm around me by the fire and suddenly, we are a couple. It is strange — everything I have with Hades is unseen, even by us. But now I have a lover in the light. It will not last — it is the fact of being part of something bigger — other people, this joint-effort — which makes up my togetherness with Snow.

The next three weeks pretend they will go on forever. It is the summer which my mother has been trying to recover for nine thousand years. And, for the first time, I understand why. For the first time, I love the summer too. It is hot, busy, full of food and fires, and of people making things together. A new couple — Dave and Ruben — paint murals across the house. A man called Pete, with a dog called Bear, starts building up the garden wall with corrugated iron and barbed wire. New plans form around the fire at night — we decide to build a tower and a tunnel.

'They can make an eviction last days longer,' Snow explains, excited. 'They need to be safe but wonky. Safe enough for you and me, not safe enough for bailiffs.' Turns out that means making them the way my mother has always made things

— with oddments, scraps, the materials to hand.

We set to work.

The tunnel starts in the middle of the veg patch, to one side of the beans. My mother lets Ash and Nonny uproot her spinach to clear a stretch of earth. They dig straight down, then sideways, in twists and turns, shoring the passage up with wood as they go. They put in doors to slow the bailiffs down. They call it 'Big Mama Two', in honour of the tunnel at Fairmile in the nineties, and in honour of my mother. She takes a keen interest in it, but I will not go down it. No need to go underground until I must. Right now, I am greedy for the sky. Snow and I work on the tower.

The tower is lashed between the chimney stacks up on the roof. It feels illicit, rebellious, to be on the house, instead of in it. We build the tower one scaff bar at a time, not using right angles, but diagonals — we want it to be hard to climb. We reach high enough that the land starts to look like a map of itself, the fields a pattern of green, the river, a swerve of black. Houses hunch together and church steeples salute us. I am growing strong — the climbing ache in my arms feels like a good kind of longing. I never thought I could make anything. Now, I have made a treehouse and a tower.

Dave and Ruben design a banner to hang from our tower top — 'Defending Mother Earth', it reads. It is a beacon, seen for miles. Taken altogether, I realise, we have made my mother's house into a kind of temple. Standing in the hall, I can see up to the roof. It is quite dark — the only light allowed slides in between the tiles. The only way in is through a hatch in the back door — those that enter must come on bended knee. The house, which has been slowly crumbling for years, is impressive once again. If only my mother now would match it. Because she is still up and down, better one day, dozing the next. I want proof that she will never fall again.

One morning, I wake early. Next to me, Snow sleeps. I roll over so I can look down at my mother in the bed below. I like to spy on her, a shape under the covers.

But the covers are pulled back. Her bed is empty.

Immediately I fear the worst.

I am scrabbling out of my sleeping bag, pulling on the harness, reaching for the line, clipping on, sliding off the platform, lowering myself. She must have got out of bed on her own. Have fallen, never made it back.

I reach a gap between branches, hang and stare.

My mother is by the pond. Not down. Up. Standing. Without her stick. Her stick is behind her, driven into the ground, like a pole. She is in her nightdress, barefooted. She stands very still. Intent, like the heron. Like a child, rapt in play. She has the charisma of these things too, so the morning garden seems to revolve around her. I watch her. She looks beautiful. Somehow, hanging a few feet in the air, I am free of everything that stands between us on the ground. She starts to walk. Not shuffling. She strides. One step. Two. three. Stops by the air pipe that extends from the tunnel's end. She turns. Strides back. Like she walked when I was young, with such purpose I could not keep up. I am overjoyed to see her move with such confidence again. I descend and go to her.

'Mother, you walked! Without your stick!'

She looks startled to see me, but then glad — always glad.

'Had to. I needed the stick for something else.'

'What? What are you doing?'

'Never you mind,' she says, smiling, 'Making my own preparations.'

265

Already I am irritated. By how she talks to me like a child when I have tended her for weeks. By how my relief at her being strong again can have vanished so fast. The guilt is back. Dread too. Because now I have to tell her — the moon has waxed to its second fullness since the storm. When it comes full again, I have to go.

DEMETER

I have worked it out.

In the fields, they have undone our dam, drained our lake. The water flows under the earth again between river, house, and woods. I know that way. I used it once myself. Afterwards, I tried to block it up, to fill the well. But I hurried the job, and over the years, the earth I packed into the well has washed away. There is a hollow under that rise in the ground, across the pond from my bed. It runs close by the tunnel end.

Hades, like a rat, prefers familiar routes. He will stick to what he knows as far as he is able. On the night of the storm, he must have used our lake — swum up into it, run through the rain.

But now, with the lake gone, the yew gone, there is only one way: to follow the water under the fields, to the well-hollow beside the pond, and dig up to the tunnel.

When summer ends, I will wait for Hades there.

I do not tell my daughter. I don't want to frighten her.

My grandson knows. I can keep nothing from him. That boy is to be born in winter. A new life, in the midst of cold.

But he'll survive. He is a little fighter, already practicing his punches.

And I must practise mine.

I have spent my life gathering. Corn. Potatoes. Eggs. Guests. Now I must gather strength.

I think again of the oak that Erysichthon struck down, of how it was festooned with prayers to me, in ribbons. Now I do the praying: I ask each thing in the garden — loosestrife, nettles, chestnut — for a little ribbon of life, because I see how they are streaming with it. They each give what they can. And I lie, quite still, like spider, and draw it in.

It is hard because it is so close to dreaming, this kind of gathering, so close to letting go. And part of me is tired. Goodness knows how tired. And I begin to crave a strange thing — shade.

I could never have enough of sun before.

But now, I doze the hot hours away, preferring the cooler ones — dusk, dawn, night.

Sun starts to bore me. One baking day after another.

I am done with baking.

Never thought I'd hear myself say that.

They use my wine barrels to make lock-ons. I'd like to be stowed in one. To be steeped in a barrel in the cellar. Darkening. Maturing.

If I didn't know better, if I didn't know that Hades will arrive with autumn, I'd think I was looking forward to a colder, darker season.

But I must not dream yet, must not stray from my intent. I have a task — to squirrel away strength.

Soon enough, I'll rest.

Lying here, by the pond, has brought back to me the time

before the house, when I slept out every night. I walked the land with the first mothers, their babies on their backs, my hands skimming through the wild grasses, their silver seeds sticking in my palms — that was what gave me the idea to plant them. Not my best idea. I think I have a better one.

Yet for now, I prepare.

My grandson keeps me on my toes. At midday, I jerk awake — he's singing to me, from the roof, that he's king of the castle. That makes me a dirty rascal. I squint up.

'Don't fall!' I want to cry.

But my girl does not look like she will slip. I know what fright looks like on her, how she wears it, how it wears her. Her shoulders are broad, head up, arms long and loose. She is happy. Whoever would have thought it — my daughter has a head for heights.

I am glad she is up there, as far from Hades as she can be. Less chance of him grabbing her and her boy, if he does pop out of that hole in the ground.

Not if.

When.

27

PERSEPHONE

Time's up mate.

A text on Snow's phone, from a friend who has a brother in the police force. We are sitting round the fire in the evening when his phone pings.

Mon 8 Sept. They're coming for you.

'We have a date,' Snow announces.

Everyone tightens. With excitement. Fear. Sadness. Determination. It feels harsh to have this hard, stubby little number intrude into our circle round the fire. No one has bothered much, through August, with dates or days, with knowing whether it is a Sunday or a Monday. But from now on, it will matter. The moon is dark. I look up at the empty sky, count out the waxing phase against the numbered days. I hope that I have counted wrong. Around the fire, they are discussing plans.

'When's the next full moon?' I ask, in a pause.

'Hang on — I've an app for that,' Nut says, pulling out her phone, her little boy asleep on her lap.

'Sunday 7 September. Hey, man, there's a lunar eclipse. That's the night before they come. How's that for mental timing? We'll all be high and howling!'

Others exclaim — I stay quiet. My husband tracks the moons, even underground. The river beneath the earth links to every other river and to sea, and so is tidal too. I promised Hades I would come on the night of the harvest moon. This year, 7 September.

I feel distraught. To have to leave the night before the eviction starts. Not to be there for it, for Snow, the house, my mother. Not to know how it unfolds after a whole summer of preparation.

Snow, beside me, is marking the box of 8 September in the grey grid of his phone's calendar. Today is Saturday 23 August. I have fifteen days left. So does the house. Everyone else must prepare to stay — to fight to do so. I must prepare to leave.

In other years, I made no preparations. My mother was the one to grow busy as autumn neared. The jars came out — my mother lined them up, newly scrubbed, across the kitchen table, ready for jams, chutneys, syrups. The acrid smell of stewing fruit filled the house, the sum of summer, simmered and preserved. Look at all that has been grown, the jars said, in quiet accusation. The air around my mother cooled.

But this year, for the first time, I have things to line up too. Not jars of jam.

I start listing them — the things I have to leave. Small things first.

My harness, I have come to love. How it holds, affirms, my weight. The clink of its clips.

The treehouse. Its blue-green view of leaves and sky.

The tower too, the view from there of fields, river, woods, and roads.

The protestors.

Nonny. Nut. Ash. Big Ben.

Snow.

The house. The garden. Pond.

The sky. The light.

This whole upper land.

My mother.

A list of everything I have avoided loving for nine thousand years.

But there is one thing I must take, which I wish that I could leave.

The baby.

I have tried not to think of it and have managed, to a point, because my body seems to have forgotten it too. I have no symptoms. I am not showing. I have even begun to doubt that it exists. I am not bleeding but then I did not bleed for years, and it was never a sign that anything was growing in me. And if there is? It will bleed away into the dark. It will make no sound. Hades need never know.

But there is no way round it: in the next fifteen days, I have to say goodbye.

I start with Snow.

I sit up the treehouse with him in the evening. A slip of a moon is up, a silver bow, repeated in the pond. There is no need to tell Snow where I am going — he would not believe me, anyway.

'I'm going to miss this,' I say.

'Yeah. But there'll be other protests. Plenty more. The world's fucked enough to need them.'

'But I won't be there.'

'Shit. Sorry.' He drops his head. 'You know you can rely on Nut, or Nonny, more than me. They'll stick around to help you with the baby.'

I shrug.

'That's not the point.'

He looks relieved. 'What is then?'

'I wanted to say thanks.'

'For what?'

271

'Teaching me to climb a tree.'

He laughs. 'Any time.'

I touch the ink branches, snaking up his neck. He frowns, smiles.

'What's up?'

'In less than a fortnight, I'll be gone.'

'Probably,' he says. 'Might take 'em a bit longer to clear us out. But you should always do what you like, Pers. You're a free woman.'

I kiss him for not saying any more than that.

I do not contradict him.

The moon is thickening. I watch it grow, one sliver at a time. Twelve days to go. Eleven. Ten.

Seven.

I must talk to my mother.

The longer I have left it, the harder it has become. The dread of telling her I have to leave feels worse even than my dread of leaving.

It is familiar, this dread. We used to have scenes every summer's end.

'Love, you can stay another week — give your mother that.'

'You know I can't.'

Both of us in tears, more angry than sad. I should have been grateful — it meant that when the day came to leave, it was not hard — she made me want to punish her with winter.

But not this year.

No sighs from her. No looks.

At dusk, I walk with her back from the fire to her bed beside the pond.

She sits down on the bed.

'Need any help?'

'No thanks.'

She lifts her legs one at a time up onto the bed, leans back against the tree trunk, shuts her eyes.

It is easier to speak to her when her eyes are closed.

'Mother, we need to talk.'

'Do we?'

'Yes.'

'Why?'

'After the eviction, where are you going to go?'

She opens her eyes.

'Where are *we* going? You stayed — remember?'

'But. Hades —'

'No!'

She flares at his name. She is sharp, severe, as if I had been clumsy — broken a plate, tipped over a bucket of water from the well.

I look down at the bedcovers, my mother's patchwork quilt. I do not feel strong enough for this.

'Trust me,' she says, more gently. She pats my hand. 'After the eviction, if they manage to kick us out —'

'They will.'

'If they do, I have been thinking …'

I look up, relieved she has a plan.

'And?'

'We're going camping.'

'What?'

'Camping,' she repeats, smiling. 'We'll be nomadic. How I lived before I built the house.'

'Where?'

'Wherever we want. I want to wander, but I also want to stop. To listen.'

She gestures at a robin which has landed on the bed end. 'I've spent my life making my presence felt. But now …' She speaks in a hush, smiling, like it's a great secret. 'We'll leave no trace. We'll just go by. You. Me. The baby.'

'But the baby won't live!' I blurt it out. The robin flies off towards the meadow.

'Nonsense! I'm going to teach your little one how to listen to the world.'

This is too much. I crumple up on her bedspread. My mother puts her hand on mine.

'It will be okay, love.'

I need to try again. To find a way to say goodbye, without mention of my husband. For it to be only about me and her.

I look at her hand, cupped over mine on the bed covers. I speak slowly.

'In the hospital, I thought that you might die.'

'I didn't.'

'I know!'

'I won't.'

'But supposing you could.'

'Stop worrying.'

'This isn't worrying.'

'Sounds a lot like it.'

'It isn't! It's that — when you were ill, when I thought you might go, it made me want to say things to you, I wouldn't otherwise —'

'What things?' The sharpness is back in her voice.

'Wait — I haven't finished. It made me think, that might be the gift of it.'

'Of what?'

'Of dying.'

'You always were a funny girl,' she says, staring at me, but also through me, as if seeing a much younger child across the pond.

'But if you knew that you were never going to see someone again you'd say what really mattered, wouldn't you?'

'You're what matters, love. More than any words. You always have been.'

'I'm not! You are. Don't make it about me again.'

She frowns, leans back against the tree. She looks tired.

'I'm not sure I matter so much anymore.'

'Yes, you do! I love you mother.' But I sound angry, petulant, not loving.

'I love you too. Stop worrying. We're going camping.'

It is quite dark now. The crescent moon has risen, sharp and bright. I feel exhausted too, but I try one final time.

'When I first went underground, I thought you'd carry on —'

'I couldn't.'

'But now —'

'When you're a mother too, you'll understand.'

'— tell me that you'll carry on, whatever happens.'

She is quiet. A bat clicks past. An owl hoots.

'Of course, I'll carry on,' she says, 'For you.'

275

28

DEMETER

The moon is rising, round and red.

A blood moon. Rare as a blue.

A sign.

We must prepare for battle.

They, for their bailiffs.

Me, for Hades.

I can smell autumn. In the earth, the sky — the red moon reeks of it. Tonight, everything has purpose, everything sings with its own meaning, as easily as the robin flutters notes out of its throat, thoughtless as breathing.

I stand on my front doorstep, where I once stood to call her in, but she never came. Tonight, she is here, and I will keep her safe.

The house, garden, fields are full with my last guests. They have come here to protect my home. 'Defending Mother Earth', their banner reads. Yes, her. And her daughter. And her grandchild. All her children. From those who would possess them. Kill them. Eat them. Burn them. Rape them. Drag them down into the dark.

I think of the many eras that this earth has seen — of rock, of sea, of ice. I have been lucky. I have known it through a time of grass and grain. A green and golden time. What will come next?

I raise my arms, feel the pattern, older than any god, more intricate than veins in leaves, stretching out beyond the bloody moon. I do not know what will be next — that answer is beyond me — but I know my place.

I'm in a hurry to be down that tunnel.

He could be here any hour.

PERSEPHONE

I leave tonight.

Round the fire, I sit next to Snow. My mother arrives, settles herself in her chair, opposite. She has been giving out conker necklaces all day — for protection, she says. It helps that the day has felt final for everyone. When I have been tearful, people have understood. But this also makes it harder. I fit in. If I could be at odds with the world again, it would be easier to leave it.

'Let's go once round, so we're all clear,' Snow says. 'We need to be in position tonight — they could come early. Ben, Pers, and I are up the tower. Nonny, you're in charge of the lock-ons on the roof.'

In her lap, my mother has two conkers left.

'Nut, you take the treehouse. Dave, you look after the front garden lock-ons.'

My mother picks up one of the conkers and a skewer.

'Ruben's with the group in the house. Ash and Pete, you're down the tunnel. Any problems?'

'Yes,' my mother says, pressing the skewer through the nut.

'You'll be in the bed.' Snow is tense, but kind.

'I'll be in the tunnel,' she says.

I stare at her. I thought she would want to be up here, in the centre of things, where she has always been.

'I want to be in the bunker, at the end.'

The sharp tip of the skewer breaks through the skin of the conker in my mother's hand. The fire pops. Snow draws his hands together.

'I'm sorry,' he says, quietly. 'That's not possible.'

'Why not?' My mother twists the skewer, making the hole in the conker bigger.

'It's too dangerous.'

The fire hisses, slumps into redness. My mother studies the hole she has made. Everyone looks at her. She seems to grow bigger in the glow of the fire. The fire's glow becomes her, glowing. For a moment, my mother, the one I have known all my life, is back. She points at Snow with her good hand.

'You cannot tell me what to do.'

'The tunnel isn't safe.'

'This is my home.'

'Safe enough for Ash —'

'My house.'

'— but wonky enough to scare the bailiffs.'

'My garden.'

'It's my protest site.'

'Ours!' Ash says.

'Okay — ours.'

'None of you would be here but for me.'

'She's got a point,' Pete says.

'You can't go down the tunnel.' Snow looks away, back to the fire, as if the conversation is over. My mother lays the conker in her lap, snips a length of blue wool.

'I can chain you to the bloody bed and chain the bed to the

tree if you like,' Snow adds, angry, anxious. I should be backing him. It is madness for my mother to go down the tunnel. She shouldn't be allowed. But having resisted her for years, tonight all I want is for her to be free to do whatever she wishes.

'I can be down there too, man,' Ash says. 'And they'll take a fuck of a lot more care if they know there's an old lady down there than just one of us.'

Snow scowls. 'Look, basically, the tunnel could collapse. With you in it.'

My mother narrows her eyes to fit the wool into the hole in the conker.

'And even if you don't care,' Snow goes on, 'I do. About you. Your daughter. The whole fucking protest! Sorry to be brutal, but having a death on-site is not a good thing — for anyone!'

I know that Snow is right. I know that in all her wrongness my mother is right too. I feel inexplicably sad.

'It'll be okay,' I say to him.

Snow shakes his head. 'No. Just no!'

'It's not your choice,' I say quietly. 'Let it be hers, and if you can't let it be hers, let it be mine.'

'I'll stay near the entrance of the tunnel, and I'll check on her every hour. I've made it cosy down there,' Ash says.

'And we can make absolutely bloody sure they know,' Pete adds.

'You're all nuts.' Snow covers his face with his hands.

'Right,' my mother says. 'That's settled.'

She holds up the conker necklace, looks at me. I go to her — let her slip it round my neck, remember how she once decorated me with flowers. There is one last conker in her lap. I take it up, open my other hand. She gives the skewer to me. I set the point against the nut, make a hole, string it on a length of green wool. I put it on my mother, as if it will keep her safe. Everyone around the fire watches.

'Bed,' Snow says.

'Let me show you to your five-star accommodation,' Ash says to my mother. She smiles. She looks young, excited.

In the middle of the veg patch, we stand around the opening in the earth.

I look up at my mother.

I thought I would be able to tuck her into bed, beside the pond. I thought we would have one more moment alone before I slipped away.

But now, suddenly, this is it.

She is going down inside her veg patch and I will never see her again.

I have to say goodbye with Snow standing beside me, furious. With Ash also near, nervous. With others watching too.

'Take care, Mother,' I say.

I hope she can hear everything I am not saying.

Then I give her a hug. It is simple, ordinary, but I have never done this — not this way round, my arms going on the outside, palms across her shoulders, her arms on the inside, under mine. And for a wonderful, awful moment I feel her body let go, lean into mine. It frightens me. Her softening, this closeness — I want to pull away. But I will have forever to be far from her. So I hold her, and the conkers we are wearing, hers, mine, press into my chest.

And then it's over. It seems wholly inadequate, this hug. I give her my head torch, as if that is then enough.

'Don't worry, love,' she says, and I can hear there are things she is not saying, too. I hope they are the same as those I didn't say to her.

Then she lowers herself into the ground.

Once down, she looks back up, pleased. This will be my last image of her, crouched in the earth, grinning like a child. Then she tips onto all fours, into the tunnel, and disappears.

Once Ash has followed her, Snow and I slide the cover over the hole, heap soil on top to conceal it. We stand for a moment looking down at my mother's veg patch, with my mother in it.

'Right. Up the tower,' Snow says.

29

DEMETER

So, here I am again.

In the dark.

Beside a stone.

This time, no one swallowed me.

Now, I am the one in blankets. Last time it was the stone. My mother put a baby blanket round it to trick my father into eating it. Under the blanket that stone was smooth. This stone is lumpy — sand, gravel, concrete, bits of glass — rolled down here, fixed in the wall.

'If it's part of the shoring, it makes it even harder for them to cut you out,' Ash explains. He wants to help attach me to the stone.

'Which arm?' He asks.

'This arm's no good, anyway' I tell him, lifting my right.

But also, if I put my right arm in the stone, I will be facing the tunnel end — the way Hades will come.

'You know you don't have to lock on now — but I'll just show you how,' he says, frowning. He puts a loop about my wrist with a clip attached, settles the clip in my stiff hand.

'When you feel the bar within the stone, press like this on the carabiner — it'll open and should clip on. To unclip just reverse that.'

He slides my arm down the pipe, set in the stone. He is patient while I fumble, miss, then find the bar. I let go of the clip. He tugs on my arm.

'You're all set.'

'Good.'

'Here's the food bag. And here's your lavatory,' he says, looking down so that the light from his head torch falls on a saucepan — one of my best. 'To be emptied into here,' he says, lifting up a knot of plastic bags. 'Let me know if you need help.'

He is shy, serious.

'Here's your water.' He sets a big flask down. 'And last of all, here's your air.'

A black pipe comes out of the ceiling, runs down the wall, beside the stone, and then across the floor.

'There's a knife in the food bag,' he says. 'If anything collapses, you need to cut a hole in the pipe and put your mouth to it — can you do that?'

He looks anxious.

'I can use a knife,' I say, glad to have one down here.

'I'll check on you every hour,' he says, 'Though once they come for us, I'll nail the door down between us, so it's harder for them to reach you. Okay?'

'Okay.' I smile.

'Use these,' he says, turning on a string of fairy lights that run round the edge of the bunker. 'Save your head torch.'

He points back into the dark.

'I'm going further up the tunnel — going to nail down the cover. But just shout if you need anything.'

He tucks the blankets round me.

'Thank you,' I say.

'Sleep well,' he says. 'Just call.'

'Sleep well.'

Then he crawls away, and I watch him go, big-booted, into the dark.

283

And here I am. He expects me to unclip for the night, lie down. I do not bother. I arrange myself to fill the tunnel, as much as I can, lean against the stone. Keep watch.

For years I have stood in my veg patch, listened down. Tonight, I listen from within it.

Roots crackle and creak. It is soothing, like rain against a roof. Below me I can hear the hum of the hidden river via which Hades will reach the tunnel end.

I try to hear the surface too, put my ear against the pipe.

Screech of an owl.

Shushing of the chestnut tree.

Far up, faint but certain, like a set of footprints crossing the night sky — my girl, her boy. I listen to them for a long time. My eyes close.

And then I hear, think I hear, another heartbeat.

My father's.

I am back again, within him, one of five.

My two sisters sit and moan.

My brother, Poseidon, splashes about in stomach acids, as if he could save us from the inside.

My other brother, Hades, is quiet. Weeping, crouched beside the stone.

PERSEPHONE

Atop the tower, I wait until their breathing slows, deepens. First Ben's. Then Snow's. A single car passes along the Woodeaton road. I'd best be quick. I slip out of my sleeping bag, take a swig of water from Snow's water bottle, feel the cold run through me. It will not take long to leave. Soon, it will be over.

The moon has slid back from red to silver. The blood moon, terrible and beautiful, made me think of Hades, made me wonder, again, how much of this summer he will feel in me, when he holds me, takes his inventory. My bones, I think, are still the same.

I look at Snow's quiet face. I feel a pang, knowing his surprise at my absence when he wakes. But it will pass.

I keep my harness on for now, so I can be clipped on as I climb — soft, deft — down the tower. Across the roof, to the skylight, propped open tonight, but ready to be nailed down tomorrow. I climb past the lock-ons in the attic, down the ladder, along the few remaining floorboards on the first floor, past what was my mother's study, down the second ladder to the ground floor. I go past the empty kitchen, drop down on hands and knees to the hatch in the back door which will also be boarded in the morning.

'Goodbye,' I tell the house.

And I am out. In the cool of the back garden.

I hover near the veg patch. I look past the apple stump to the air pipe, sticking up above the earth. Part of me expects to hear my mother call out, for her to sense that I am going, bid me to stay.

I listen.

No call comes.

What will happen when I'm gone?

Not winter for the world forever more. Only, perhaps, for her.

But she promised me that she would carry on.

I turn, hurry round the house, to the front garden, steal past people asleep on mattresses, hiding lock-ons in the flowerbeds. I fit myself through a gap in the corrugated-iron fence up on the wall. I am in the silver fields.

I am leaving. I do not yet know how — the passage under the yew, in the woods, is gone, but I will head that way. Somewhere, if I keep walking, I will find another opening within the earth.

I cross the first field, walk past protestors' tents. Reach the stile, the single hawthorn tree beside it. Even though the rest of the hedge is gone, I still step up on the stile. In other years, this was where my mother, sitting in her study, had her final sight of me. No one is watching now.

I look out across the levelled land. Two trenches, set far apart, run in parallel, marking the road's width. And suddenly, I am glad to leave. Glad never to have to see a road run through the fields where my mother once grew grain. Leaving is horrible, but it is not hard. It is not hard to travel downhill, away from all the loss and grief up here, into the dark.

Usually, I keep walking, but tonight I allow myself to turn, to take a last look at my mother's house, standing tall and brilliant in the moonlight, with its tower and its banner, its garden walls like battlements. It looks proud. And lonely. Like a great ship.

I turn away. Go to climb down from the stile, but realise I have my harness on — I should have left it in the garden. I can't go back. It does not feel possible to undo a single step that I have taken from the house. I will hang the harness here, on the stile — someone will pick it up.

I loosen the straps about my thighs, start to undo the buckle at my waist.

I freeze. Hands on the buckle.

Under the waistband.

A scribble.

Like the tail of something as it disappears into the pond.

Then gone.

I listen, though it makes no sound.

There. Again.

Like a fish. A bird. A fluttering, swimming thing.

I am appalled by the monstrous truth of it.

There is someone else inside me.

The child is alive.

A moment ago, I could not take a step back to the house. Now, I cannot step away.

I am transfixed. Stranded on the stile.

I let go of the harness, clutch below it — my middle.

The baby will die soon. I knew this already. My husband is waiting for me. Now. Tonight. I promised him I'd come.

Still, I do not move.

I feel wonder, terror, and something else. Longing. Hunger. And, sharply, the memory comes of standing thigh deep in the flooded river underground, the press of water against me, the wish to cross it, the hunger for hunger I felt as I climbed up to the woods back in the spring. It is not a thought, not an idea — my body remembers, feels it and other things. Unbidden, I feel again the shock of my blood coming. I feel the ache in my arms climbing the oak, the ache through all of me of wanting to touch Snow. I remember the weeping I did, right here, beside this stile, after I told Snow about the deal. I remember the thrill of making the digger eat the earth in the field ahead. I feel the grip of my mother's hand, in the hospital. I feel the summer I have just left, the sense of being part of something greater than myself. And now this. I feel the baby, in me, quickening.

And slowly, as if wading upstream, through rapid water, I climb down from the stile, back into the first field.

To betray my husband, now, tonight, would be worse than my affair with Snow. Because it would be done openly, an indisputable breaking of our faith.

But something else has broken in me, too. It is as if, for all these years, I have been balancing on a walkway, a thin rope strung between my husband and my mother, and suddenly, with one small motion, it has snapped. I am no longer balanced on this rope but standing on the wide earth — I could go anywhere.

I remember the night of the storm, when Snow asked me what I wanted, when everyone waited for my reply, and I said nothing, could not find the words, looked to my mother for the answer.

Tonight, I know the answer, though there is no one now to hear it. It is clear as the moon. Unquestionable. It quickens in me with the baby. I want to be part of this world. I want to go back to my mother's. It does not feel like a choice. Nor like my fate. But something even deeper, older, stronger. Like the current of the river.

I take a step towards the house. Another. Nine thousand years too late, I head for home.

Such relief, such fear, run through me, as I run. I am back at the wall, back in the front garden. I pass the house. I am back by the veg patch, above my mother.

I break back in, climb through the silent house. I slip back onto the roof, the tower.

My heart, which has been racing all the way across the field, leaps again — Snow is awake.

'Where d'you go?' He asks, angry.

'Just to the loo. And to check on my mother.'

'You should have woken me. You mustn't go climbing down from here alone, unspotted, in the dead of night — that's bloody stupid. The real danger hasn't even started yet. Don't make extra!'

'Sorry.'

And then, I risk it.

'I felt the baby move just now. First time.'

He stares at me, then hangs his head.

'I didn't need to hear that.'

'I know. But I wanted to tell you.'

He fumbles in his sleeping bag, pulls out his phone, scrolls across the screen, presses something, hands it to me.

I look at the phone.

On the lighted screen is an app that describes the size of a growing foetus week by week, comparing it to different seeds, fruits. I look at Snow, amazed that he has put this on his phone. He will not look at me.

'How many weeks?' he asks.

I count it fast.

'Seventeen.'

I slide my finger up the screen. I pass a poppy seed, grain of corn, a bean, a fig, an apple, and then at seventeen weeks, I stop.

There, on the lit screen, is a picture of a round, red fruit — a pomegranate.

Both my hearts stop.

Then start again.

'How big is it?' Snow asks.

I make a fist, wrap my other hand around it.

For a moment, we both look at my hands.

'We need to sleep,' he says.

We get into our sleeping bags.

But I cannot sleep. I am still here. No one has given me permission to do this — not my mother, not my father, not my husband.

'You still awake?' Snow says.

'Yes.'

'Just promise me not to do anything stupid tomorrow. Don't give anyone a reason to get violent with you.'

'I won't,' I say, though I know it is too late — I already have.

30

DEMETER

I wake, with a start, to clamouring above.

Didn't mean to sleep.

No sign of Hades.

I press my ear against the pipe — stamping, thumping, shouting.

He has not come, though by the sounds of it everybody else has.

Ash comes crawling out the dark behind me.

'It's all kicked off up there. You doing okay?'

'I'm fine.'

'Right — I'll be back — Nonny's texting me news from the roof.'

On they crash, for hours — it could be the time of the Titans back again.

Why isn't he here? My son-in-law.

I start to feel cross. As if we had an appointment, and he is late.

I hear the drills begin — feel them even, a vibration through the ground.

'They've started drilling people out!' Ash comes to tell me. 'You okay?'

'I'm fine,' I lie.

I hear the engines thrumming, the machines, heavy-wheeled, roll over my roses. And as my legs grow stiff, my arm grows numb, as Hades does not come and does not come, I grow tired, sore, I grow unsure.

A pin, a needle of doubt.

I eat a biscuit. It crumbles in my mouth. Too dry. Too sweet.

Still, it is good that I am here, on guard, in case.

And my daughter and her boy are safe. Up in the sky.

I listen out for them, but I can't hear a thing with the racket that is going on. Keep the noise down, I want to yell, like a cranky downstairs neighbour.

I would know, would sense, if she were in any danger.

Or would I?

Did I know the first time? When he came for her?

I paused, that evening long ago, as the sun went down. I was carrying a salmon to the oven, but I stopped, by the window.

Why? To admire the sky, pink like the fish?

Or did I feel something — the splitting of the earth within the woods?

I had the fish to bake — I carried on.

And which is worse — not to have heard? Or to hear and shrug it off, hurry on with the preparing of the meal?

This last is worse, and this — I cannot hide it in this dark — is true. It was not part of my plan. I was, in my own way, greedy as Erysichthon. I covered her thin body with flowers, made her look the way I wanted her to look. I only heard the things I wanted her to say. And then I blamed her when she left.

'Ash!' I call.

He comes.

'I need to know Persephone's okay.'

'Sure. Let me text Nonny and Snow. I'll go back to the entrance to get a signal.'

He goes.

I wait. Listen. Someone is screaming, not Persephone.

After too long, he returns.

'No one's replying,' he says. 'Guess they're all dealing with the bailiffs on the roof.'

I stare at him, at his headlamp stuck to his forehead like a third eye.

'Don't worry,' he says. 'Snow will look after her. She's in good hands. I'll wait for a message. I'll tell you as soon as it comes through.'

He goes.

I wait an age.

No Ash.

No Hades.

The fairy lights fade, and then go out.

It is quite dark.

Last night I would have wrestled Heracles, as well as Hades. Today, I worry where my stores of strength have gone — they seem to have seeped away into the dark.

I twist to fumble for the torch my daughter gave me, can't find it, bang my elbow on the stone. More pins, more needles, and all at once, the ferrywoman's words come back to me — *next time you must come without that light, in darkness.*

That was the price she set.

But I was sure there'd never be a next time.

Could I have been wrong about that too?

Still the old fear.

Young fear.

Of a dark that eats.

A dark which breaks the body down. Dissolves it.

Yet I refused before. I stayed whole. I never even wept.

And now?

PERSEPHONE

We sit up the tower and watch everything: police and bailiffs setting up a barrier around my mother's home, breaking into her garden, swarming over it. Black uniforms. Dark-blue helmets with visors. Batons in their belts. Padded legs and arms. Hundreds of them.

I hold on to the cold scaff bars in front of me as, below, two men arrest a woman who was locked on to a barrel by my mother's lilac bush. She kicks and sobs. They drag her, one on each arm, out of the garden, across the fields, to the road, force her into a van, drive her away. Snow was right — it can, it does, get violent.

I am glad my mother is under the earth and need not witness it. I might never have seen it too.

Last time, years ago, I left, and the world ended — winter came.

Now, at last, I have stayed, and the world is ending anyway. Not from my mother's grief. But even now my mother manages to turn her garden white: when the bailiffs drill into her mattresses, laid over the lock-ons in the flowerbeds, a thousand feathers explode into the air. My mother made those mattresses, plucked the birds herself — geese, ducks, swans. Their feathers cover the earth. Some drift up to us, in the tower.

As I watch them, I feel the baby move again. I'd like to show it grandma's garden in a snowstorm of white feathers. But this thought frightens me because I have allowed myself to dream a future here. Time feels strange. I am cut loose from it, from how I have counted it for years. This is not my mother's time. Not my husband's. It is mine. How long I have, we have,

I do not know. Not long enough for anything so frivolous as feathers.

Early evening, generators shoot light into the sky. Cherry pickers extend their buckets on long arms, up level with the roof. Snow, Big Ben, and I put thick black bike locks round our necks, bolt ourselves onto the scaff bars of the tower. The keys are in our pockets, ready to be thrown away into the dark.

Someone has a music speaker on the roof — people dance and stamp on my mother's tiles. But already the bailiffs have had enough. They want to go home, have supper, watch TV. One of them — a large man, thickset — heads for Nonny, her arm deep in a block of concrete within the chimney stack. He grips her head, pushes it forwards, forms a fist and presses down behind her ear. She cries out.

'Unclip yourself, and we can get this done pain-free — okay?'

'No!'

'Unclip!'

Snow beside me, tenses. 'Bastard,' he says. 'Pressure points to save him having to drill her out — basically a form of torture.'

I watch, horrified, as the man pushes his knuckles into Nonny. She tries to pull her head away, to the side, so for a moment I see her face, eyes shut against the pain.

'Unclip,' he repeats, 'And we can all go home,'

'This is our home! Leave off!' Snow shouts down.

The man ignores him.

'Come on, dear — we both want this over.'

'Fuck off!' Nonny says.

'Talk dirty — you get dirty.' He shoves her head against the chimney stack, his knee against her ear, grinds her head into the stone. She starts to scream.

'Get off her!' Snow is shouting, unlocking himself, scrabbling down the tower. Another bailiff comes up to Nonny, bends down.

'There, there,' he says, rubbing her breasts.

'Shit. I'm going down too. You stay put.' Ben has his phone out, is trying to film what is happening while unlocking, downclimbing.

The moment Snow and Ben reach the roof, three bailiffs are on them. Snow lunges at the tower to climb back up, but they strike at his hands, pull him down.

One bailiff grabs a sleeping bag, left at the bottom of the tower, shoves it over Snow's head, pinning his arms to his sides. He is thrashing, hollering, but they have him now, slide him down the angle of the roof, push him into the bars of the cherry picker's bucket. The bailiffs inside drive him in, over the bars, keep the bag over his head. Ben is pulled in with him. Only as the bucket lowers does Snow get the bag off. I see him for a moment, hear him, hands on the bars, looking up, shaking, 'Shit, shit, shit,' but then they thrust him down.

Nonny has given in, unclipped, and is also carried off the roof, sobbing.

I am up the tower, on my own.

It starts to drizzle.

I watch the endlessly fine grains of rain falling through the beams the generators throw up into the night. Below, after pulling people off the roof, they start smashing a hole in the tiles to break into the attic. I am shivering. I put on a sweatshirt of Snow's that he used as a pillow last night. Right now, all I want is to lie down. I barely slept last night. They are concentrating on the attic — no one is looking up at me. I feel in my pocket for the key to the bike lock, unlock myself, slide into a sleeping bag, as much in shadow as I can, listen to the drilling and hammering below, and a music track that thuds up through the roof.

I curl up for warmth. I can smell beer, diesel, damp leaves. I think of my mother under the roots of the apple stump. I dream I can smell apples. Soft brown, wasp-eaten, mouldering.

The tower creaks. I snap awake. At the front, two bailiffs are leaning on the tower's base. I look to the back. I am clipped on — a short length of rope from my harness loops round the bar at the front so I cannot reach the back of the tower to check all the way down. I can see no one, but the banner, hanging on the side, obscures my view of the right-hand corner. Another creak. Someone is climbing up the tower.

I was stupid to unlock. I grab the bike lock, push it round my neck, press myself up against the scaff at the front, to lock on again. Fiddle with the key, hands too cold and slow. The bailiff is climbing round the front now, almost level with me. I give up on the lock, the key, kick out to keep him away. He grabs my foot, uses it to pull himself higher. Hand on my thigh, pushing up. Face in my face. Not a bailiff. Hades.

He stares.

I stare.

We do not touch.

Soon panic will come.

But now, like a wound before the pain has started, I feel blank, empty.

I see his tight, black pupils, wide irises, thin lips, wet, matted hair.

I see his hurt.

297

But seeing, looking, is not what we do. Not what we have done.

The eviction churns on under us, and he and I, at its highest point, are still.

Every other time that I have been with him spreads out below us, like the fields. When he watched the house from the corn, when he sat under the apple tree, when he opened the ground in the woods, led me down, lost me, found me, fed me six red seeds. Every year since. Every time he has studied me, sculpted me, made me, and made love to me. Now I study him. He used to seem ancient — like a fossil, a mystery, dug up. Now he seems only old.

He is quivering with hate. Love. They are so close. We are so close.

He has been faithful. True. His anger is not only terrible but righteous. The anger of the wronged. I know he feels deeply wronged. Deeply wrong. He has told me I am what makes him, the past, the dark, the dead, right. Now I am wrong too, and he is desperate.

He rises to take hold of me, his chest in my face, and the panic comes at last — a young panic, a memory of getting dressed, unable to find the hole for my head, the world gone. I pull back.

'You said you'd come,' he says.

'I know.'

'You're coming now.'

For nine thousand years, I have done what I am told.

'No,' I whisper. 'I'm staying here.'

Hades' face fissures, cracks, reassembles into a new stillness, hardness, a worse hurt.

I draw back and the ropes from my harness flick taut. I

cover my carabiners, twisted shut, but Hades has a knife, slashes the ropes. He pulls me to the platform edge, lifts me onto the bars below. He pushes his feet into my hands, forces me down the tower.

I reach the roof, busy with bailiffs and protestors. I have stood here, unafraid, all summer. But now I am unclipped. It is wet and dark. The roof's slope is steep, the edge is near, the fall is far. I imagine skidding down the tiles, smashing to the ground, my skull cracking on the front doorstep, the whole eviction stopping. Snow's voice in my head: 'Having a death on site is not a good thing.' I hold tight to the tower's base. Hades prizes my hands away, drags me to the ridge of the roof, across the back tiles, down to the ladder at the corner of the house, presses me onto its rungs.

The ladder bends, the give of it I loved before, my weight leaning on the long slant of metal, feels perilous now. Hades is above, pushing me down. Right hand. Left foot. I feel pathetic. Left hand. Right foot. Weak. But soon — at the base — I will have a chance. Right hand, left foot, last rung — I twist round, turn and run.

I sprint across the veg patch. I am by the apple stump. My head jerks back — he has my hair. His arm reaches under my arm, pulls at the neck of my sweatshirt — Snow's sweatshirt. I tilt forward, the top rips. Cold air on my chest, his hand on my breast.

I start to scream.

DEMETER

'Get off me!'

Her voice.

Straight above.

I jolt up.

'Let me go!' Her words, so loud they fill the tunnel.

'Persephone!' I cry.

But she is not talking to me. He has come.

Not from this tunnel.

Hades has found another way.

'Let go!'

Her voice and his animal smell, down the pipe. I smell her too, her fear.

'I'm coming!' I call out.

I twist, jerk towards the tunnel entrance. Go nowhere. My hand sticks in the stone.

The bloody stone.

Frantic, I try to find the thing that ties me to the bar inside.

Cannot even find my hand.

There. Found it. But it's useless. Fingers like a block. Unbending.

'Help me!' my daughter cries.

I try to yank my arm out.

Where are my stores of strength?

Panic beats through me.

Her screaming fills the dark.

'Ash!' Now I am screaming too. 'Ash!'

He comes, too slow. I hear him fiddling with the door between us.

'Persephone needs help!'

'I'll text Nonny.'

'No! Get out — go to her — now!'

'But the entrance is nailed shut.'

'Undo it!'

'Help!' she cries.

'Go! Now!' I yell at Ash.

'I'm going.'

'Help!'

Her voice is no longer straight above me.

Ash, hammering at the entrance.

'Go to the front garden!' I shout to him.

'Okay!'

'Please! Help!' Her voice, growing fainter, lost in the din of other shouts.

Soon they will be in the fields.

I try again to bend my hand, free it from the stone. I cannot do it.

'Ash!' I call. Silence. He has gone after them.

Her cries are fainter still.

Ash does not return.

Now I cannot hear them.

I pummel the stone with my free hand until it bleeds.

I force myself up. Legs bent, trembling, back pressed against the roof.

I kick out, hear the food bag fly. Remember the knife. The knife! I could cut off my arm. I would. I would do it. I reach towards where I heard the bag drop. Touch cold metal. Not the knife. The pan.

I try to smash the stone to pieces with the pan.

It dents the pan.

Ash has not come back.

I weep into the pan.

How could I have been so sure and yet so wrong?

Sure enough to tie myself in place.

Last time the stone was comforting. Now I curse it. I curse the world. The whole world, though it needs none of my curses, does not care.

I curse myself — stupid, useless old woman.

Shouting thumping drilling hammering above.

None of it matters.

They are gone. Hades has them — my girl, her boy.

I failed her again.

PERSEPHONE

He has me over his shoulder, as he runs through the front garden.

I am screaming.

But everyone is screaming. Everyone is being dragged out against their will.

He is past the smashed wall, already running into the field. His shoulder digs into my stomach. I reach my arms, desperate, back towards the house, my mother.

He nears the police fence.

They will stop him.

'Get him to put me down!' I yell at the officer by the barrier. 'He's not a bailiff!'

But the officer nods to Hades. He may not be a bailiff, but I

am a protestor — they are not here to protect me but to get me off
the site. He lifts and moves the fence aside to let Hades through.

Hades runs on. I pound my fists against his back. I lift my
head, see a man, heavy with tattoos, a can of beer in his hand,
looking my way — my last chance.

'Help!' I scream.

My father smiles, lifts his can. We got the story right at
last — the girl crying, her clothes torn, breast exposed, the man
carrying her away.

'No!' I call out, but he has already looked away.

Tears, snot, hair in my face. I hang down over Hades'
shoulder, make myself as heavy as I can. He staggers past the
single hawthorn, the stile.

We reach the road site where my mother and I dug. Now
levelled earth.

The sky too is flat, grey with buried light. Clouds hide a
moon, one night past full.

Hades sets me down, holds me fast.

We are both breathing hard. It is just us now. No one else
is watching, listening. He presses me to the ground, presses
himself onto me — he cannot wait. I do not want his hands on
me, his fingers round my neck, his breath in my face. He tries
to push his tongue inside my mouth. I lock my jaw, go rigid.
He spits. He would prefer distress. Prefer to have to wrestle
me down. He takes my wrists, drags me to one of the road's
trenches — he does not need to split the earth, as he did before
— the road workers have done it for him. He rolls me in, like a
body of which he is trying to dispose.

The base of the trench is filled with sand. Circular, hard,
black plastic covers, evenly spaced, stretch along the length of
it. Hades jumps down, drags me to where one cover has been

303

pulled aside. He kneels, leans me over the dark hole in the ground — a storm drain. They have used our lake, our digging, to build a drainage system for the road. This is the way he must have come.

I struggle but Hades holds me down. I have grown strong, but he is stronger. He lifts me, one arm pressing my legs together, starts to lower me, feet first, into the drain. I force my arms onto the ground either side of the pipe. I grip the sand — it comes up in my hands. I clutch the top of the pipe, tip my head back, see a dark circle of sky, suddenly clear of clouds, a scatter of stars — and then Hades is blocking my view, lowering himself in, his weight on me. My hands slip.

The drain squeezes my shoulders, hips. My arms are trapped above my head. I smell the new plastic of the pipe, fingers slide against it — hard, smooth, cold. I am used to the pinch and pressure of rock — this is worse — even less breath, even heart, thought, constricted. I cannot pull up, am being pushed down. The sliding stops. I am stuck fast.

A sudden thrust on my shoulders — Hades, from above, forcing me further. The skin on my forearms burns, rubbed against plastic. I shoot down, the world explodes, expands, turns to water, freezing, shocking. Heavy in clothes, boots. Rushing in my ears, pushing my eyes. Hades' hand in the dark, pulling me on.

Air at last.

I surface, not on the surface, but under the fields, out of the pipe, head pressed into limestone. No light. Hades leading me, bent double, wading through the stream that runs under the fields to the woods. I am shivering, crying, whimpering — everything I never did the first time. He pulls me through the dark, twisting tunnel, following the current, down.

31

PERSEPHONE

Only the knot of our hands in the dark. Like the first time. He was urgent then, too. I am terrified, as I was then — my heartbeat drilling through me — but this time I strain back up to the world as he pulls me down under it. He says nothing. I say nothing — no breath left for words, as I try to wrestle free of him, as he wins, as we descend deeper, as the water slows, deepens also. Above this, faint at first, like distant rain, I hear the dying. Like a radio with a hundred different stations, their voices crackle in and out of focus. Hums and hymns, lullabies and whisperings of things they wished they'd done, never said, blessings, sudden cravings. Every other year, on my way down, I have pushed ahead to the water's edge, tried not to listen. This time I cannot shut the voices out, but hear everything, everyone. Hades pulls me on, relentless.

Down we travel, for hours, until the tunnel widens and the darkness soars. Black sand underfoot. Sand in the air, in my mouth. The water roars through the chamber. It sounds even louder, swifter, wider than when I crossed it in the spring. Hades marches me towards it, past a hundred shadowy figures. We reach the water's edge.

When I first came here, the water shone. Now it is only black. A single point of light swings above the river — the lantern on the ferryboat, throwing giant shadows of the ferrywoman's arms over the water as they reach back and forth, pulling darkness into them.

Hades stands behind me, one hand tight about my wrist. I look down at the flotsam and jetsam at my feet — a set of keys, a single running shoe, a phone, plastic bags and bottles, rusting cans — the gifts of the dying tangled with the litter of the living. Beside me is an old man, confused by where he is. Next to him a young woman is crying. On my other side, a little boy crouches, silent, wide-eyed. I stare across the black water, and feel the baby stir. As if it were dreaming, turning over in its sleep. And suddenly, fiercely, the only thing I want is for it to live.

I do not feel the outrage I did in early summer, or the fatalism that came after. It isn't an idea anymore, to defend or to deny. It is a child. Mine. And in this moment, I understand that the first act of any mother is a leap of faith, of believing that the child will have its life, while knowing all the while, it may be lost.

Is it too late?

If there is any chance to turn, to run up the shore, the tunnels, back up to the fields, I will take it.

I wait. Quiet. Alert. Willing Hades to loosen his hold on me, if only for an instant.

The boat is sliding nearer. It is grey-white, like a half-moon rocking in the water, crusted with barnacles, as if the wood of it had long rotted away and it is now made only of ancient shells. I screw my eyes shut. I wish I could crawl back to the surface through the dark inside me.

I hear the boat swish over the silt, crunch on the shingle.

I hear the hushed songs of the dying, the roar of the river.

I hear the sigh of the ferrywoman.

I hear her say, 'Not her.'

I open my eyes.

She is pointing her oar at me.

Hades' hold on my wrist grows tighter still. He leans forwards.

'What do you mean?'

'She cannot cross,' she creaks, staring at me with her black, tear-filled eyes. 'I will not give her passage.'

The woman looks away through the crowd, searching. With his free hand, Hades grabs the conker that my mother hung about my neck, snaps it off, holds the hard seed out — 'Here,' he says. 'Here's payment.'

The ferrywoman shakes her head, looks away again. Hades wades into the water, pulling me with him, grips the side of the boat.

'You have ferried her across a thousand times before.'

The woman looks back, never hurried, even by the gods.

'I carry the dying,' she says, 'I can carry the immortal. I will not carry the living.'

Now I understand. Now I have a wild hope and desperate fear of what is coming.

On the night of the storm, I told Hades there was no one else.

All through the summer, I told myself that he need never know.

But now, he will.

He has always been the whisperer — my mother was the loud one — but now he is shouting out to the dark, the river, the ferrywoman, me: 'This is my wife! Queen of the Dead. She belongs here. Give us passage!'

His words hang in the air along with a million grains of sand. He goes to climb aboard, lift me inside, but the ferrywoman sweeps her oar to him, to bar his way.

'She is carrying a mortal life — she cannot cross.'

The river slides and spreads into the dark. The young woman near me, clutching a phone, climbs on board the boat. The old man and the boy follow. Slowly, my husband turns me round. He lifts his hand as if he might caress me, then strikes me hard across the face.

The force knocks me sideways, down into the water. He drags me back up, gripping my arm. His face is rigid. He stares at me as if he does not know me. A moment ago, he was abducting me. Now I am betraying him. For years, I have felt guilt for a wrong I did not do — because I never made the cold come. But this year, this crime, is mine. It is almost a relief. To have it in the open — sharp, clear, awful.

'Who?' he asks.

I think of Snow. Look at Hades. I do not know if it makes it better or worse that I have betrayed him for a man who does not love me. It could have been anyone, I realise. Any mortal man. I say nothing. The silence is terrible. Hades waits, hurts. But he too knows that it does not matter who, because then he asks, 'Why?'

A far worse question. My mother used to ask it. Why did I go? I never knew what to say.

Why did I sleep with Snow?

Because of the flooded river. The hunger. Because of the bleeding. Because of the trees, the treehouse, the climbing. Because of the coming road, the threatened woods, the changing world. Because of my mother, growing old.

None of these are reasons he will accept or understand.

'Because …' I begin.

'Because — what?' Hades pushes his face close to mine. 'I have been faithful to you. Have gathered precious stones, made gifts for you more beautiful than anything above. And now a summer too — down here — all for you. Things that will last forever. And you scorn this, me, for what? What does a mortal man have to give you I cannot?'

To this I know the answer. So does he. He has known it for years, before I ever came here — it was why he wanted me. He asks me the question that it will hurt him most for me to answer. And for a moment, even the dying lean in to listen, even the river, quietens, slows.

'Life,' I say. 'He gave me life.'

It is as if I, in turn, have struck him. He pulls his head away in pain, disgust, and, for a second, lets me go.

I turn, sprint back up the shore, but he catches me at once, by the wrist, drags me to the water, to the rim of the boat, is pulling it down as if he might capsize it, is stooping, lifting me, tipping me over the edge so that I land hard inside the boat. I scrabble to stand, to climb out, but he is climbing in, forcing me down. The ferrywoman raises the oar blades high in the air, clear of the water.

'I will not row her over.'

'Then I will,' Hades hisses. He reaches for the oar shafts, to twist them from her.

'Not with a life inside her.' The ferrywoman has her arms pressed down on the seat, her gnarled fingers fused with the wood of the oars.

'Do not worry,' Hades tells her, almost gently, 'It will not be alive for long once we have crossed.'

He tries, but cannot pull the oars from her, so his hands go to her hands. He jerks them upwards. The oar-blades scythe down, splash in the water. Hades leans back to pull the woman forwards. She resists, the hundred lines on her face tight with effort, arms bent to her chest. He forces her arms to lengthen,

309

her body to tip, and the blades to swing over the river. She locks her arms long — he presses them back, down, folds them into her, so that the blades slice through the water. The boat slides from the shore.

All my pain in crossing is in the pain of the woman's arms and face, as Hades forces her back and forth, against her will. He jolts her forwards, so far, so fast, that the tears which have stood forever in her eyes begin to fall. They splash down onto the trinkets and charms, lying like a strange catch in the bottom of the boat. As Hades presses her back, they run down the lines scored in her cheeks, glistening in the lantern light.

Midway, I cannot bear to watch the woman any longer, so I look away over the river. The current as we move out grows stronger. I spy a plastic bag, voluminous, white, billowing in the black water.

He said the child would not live for long once we have crossed. Does that mean it might live, for a little while? How long? And when it dies, will I know? Will I feel when it has? And will it stay a dead thing, inside me? Or must I birth a dead baby in the dead lands? Will it hurt? Will I be able to hold it? I watch the plastic bag floating, agitated by the current, and though I have no reason for hope, the stubborn wish stays — I want the baby to survive. I want us to escape. The bag catches on the blade of the oar which plunges it down and out of sight.

Rocks, black and ruckled, clear the flood water, marking where the shore once was. Hades steadies the boat against them, releases the ferrywoman's arms. She draws her hands, the oars, tight to her chest, like an injured child, recovering her dignity. The dead disembark. I squat in the bottom of the boat, as if I could stay there. A mobile phone, left on as a torch, gives off an eye of light.

Hades hoists me out, into the water, climbs out too but reaches back into the boat. He picks up the phone-torch. This frightens me. He has no need of light down here. What does he want with it? The little light is like an accusation.

We stand, thigh-deep in the water. It was beside these rocks he let go of my hand in spring. Now he may never let me go again. Now, I am meant to stay through every season of the year.

Hades sets off, leading me, wading through water. Now we have crossed, I do not pull back and up. I will not be dragged, crying. Instead, I quicken my pace, in case hope alone can keep the child alive for longer.

The dead sway as we pass. I used to find them graceful, but now I feel afraid of them, as though they might reach into me and lift life out. I will my heart to thud louder, strong enough to teach the baby's how to beat, even here. I breathe in extra air for both of us — it is cold and hurts my lungs. Hades holds the torch hanging by his side. Its reflection breaks apart with every step, sends light scattering. We cross into his flooded workshop, past the sculpture of me lying near the entrance. I do not want to see her. Part of me wishes that I could unsee everything that I have seen over the summer. If I could, then I could hide down here again, quiet, numb.

Hades wades on into the chamber where the pomegranate tree stands, huge and silent. Even here there is water underfoot, ankle high. He presses on, past the tree, further, deeper.

Slowly, the rock dries out. The tunnels narrow. On and on we go. I sense the weight of the earth over us, miles of rock. I smell my husband's sweat, feel it between our hands.

It is getting warmer. We must be so deep now as to be near the mantle of the earth, where rock turns soft, liquid, in the heat. For a moment, I fear he is taking me down to throw me in the fires of the earth. He is breathing hard. He pushes me in front, to crawl through another cleft. I emerge, Hades follows, stops, points out the little light.

We are in a small chamber. Before me is not the summer of stone I had imagined, but a garden made of glass. He has travelled far enough inside the earth to find the heat to turn his sands beside the river into glass.

It is everything he promised — a garden more perfect, beautiful, certain, than anything upon the earth.

Both spring and summer are here. There are snowdrops, stiff white hooded flowers with thin green stems. A honeysuckle bush — an intricate tangle of vines that coil and twist up to pale-yellow fluted flowers, stamens curving out of them, specks of golden pollen at their tips. Under the bush, I see a robin, glass claws splayed across the rock, black eyes glancing up. A stretch of deep-blue glass, ripples frozen in it, shines like water. A dragonfly on a lily pad has stained-glass window wings. Beside this, in the centre, rises a slender apple tree, fruiting with small swellings of green glass. There are roses of every colour, red poppies, and, in the far corner, tall spears of corn. A spider's web hangs between two stalks, a silver pattern of impossibly fine skeins of glass. He has done more, better, than he has ever done. He has dug deeper, gone further, made something down here almost alive.

I am amazed, afraid. I remember why I first fell for him, for his bitter, brilliant care. He shows the garden to me with his torch, as I feared, to punish me, though he had hoped to show me as reward. He darts the light from one wonder to another. He lifts his hand at last and throws the phone into the centre of the honeysuckle bush, so that for a split second the glass is lit as it explodes — a terrible, dazzling shower of shards. The phone clatters down — the light goes out.

Dark again. Hot dark. His hand, pulling me to him, striking me again. I cry out, drop down. He reaches for me through the dark, grabs my shoulders, holds me against him as if he either means to kill me or never let me go.

Minutes pass, maybe years.

I try to hold him as tightly as he holds me. To match his grip. I know I have forfeited the right to repeat any of our rituals. To track his spine. To recite that I am his. Our signs of being true. Now I cannot tell him that I love him, I discover that I do. Not for his skill, but for the tenderness it hides. If I were to tell him, he would strike me, call me a liar. So I say nothing, but know it, fully, in my bones, but also in my blood, in my lungs, in the soft spaces of my body as well in the hard, and know too that despite this, despite loving him, I have to try to leave him, to betray him, yet again.

Is there a way?

My hands ask this, wrapped about the ladder of his ribs, and his, in answer, wrap about mine tighter still, and by this, I think, hope, that there may be. Why would he need to hold me so, if there were no way out?

I listen down for any sign of movement from the baby. There is none. It may already be too late, but I must try.

At last, he speaks.

'You are my wife.'

'Yes,' I say, for this is true.

'You belong to no one else.'

'To no one else,' I repeat, but this, I realise as I say it, is a lie. Even though I may never meet it, I will now always also belong to the baby. At last, miles under the earth, I understand my mother. And I feel, perhaps for the first time, sad, instead of guilty, that I left her.

'You belong here,' Hades says.

'Yes.' Also, a lie.

He breathes out.

He feels up my spine, bone by bone, up to my neck.

I lift my hands to his skull, and for a second, he drops his forehead to my shoulder. I feel his tiredness. Like my mother, like my father, he too is growing old, though more slowly, for time is different underground. He has gripped me ever since he found me, far up in the world, atop the tower on my mother's house. He has carried me, pushed me, held me, by hand, wrist, hips, tight enough to bruise me, all the way from there to here, down near the mantle of the earth. And finally, in the heat, in my arms, he eases his hold a little, enough.

I pull away.

'I want to walk through the garden,' I say.

'No,' he says, but I am gone to do it.

I hear the broken glass crackle beneath my feet. I hear him after me. I move quick as I can, quiet as I can, hands held out. Fingers touch something round, small — a glass apple.

'Persephone,' Hades says.

I move to the right of the sculpted tree, feel for the far wall of the cave. My palms find the hot rock.

'Persephone!' His voice is angry, hurt again.

I feel my way round fast, to the cleft in the stone through which we came. I start to fit myself back through the rock — the slide of my trouser leg, grate of my boots, make a sound — he has heard me, is coming after, but I am out and in the next chamber, moving up.

'You cannot leave.'

He is urgent, close — I dare not answer — my reply would tell him where I am. I cross to the far wall and freeze. Silence. He has frozen too. We both wait. Both listen for the other.

We have been here before — in every winter — a game of hide-and-seek. This time, he must not find me.

If I speak, then move quick enough, quietly enough, I could confuse him. A risk. But there are no safe choices.

'I want the child to live,' I whisper, then move as fast as I dare away from where I spoke. He dives towards the sound.

'It won't!'

I feel along the rock, hit against boulders. I climb on these, reaching upwards, touch an edge, pull myself up into the next tunnel, run. I hear Hades pull himself up, close behind.

'You cannot cross the river,' he calls along the tunnel. 'The child belongs here now.'

I run on, one hand against the rock — the tunnel widens. If he knows where I am, and only has to run to reach me then he will — he is quicker than me still, though tired. I feel down at my feet, find a stone. I throw it back across the dark. It strikes a rock on the opposite side of the tunnel. I hear him go to it. I play this game as far and fast as I can. I throw out stones and words, try to confuse, confound him, to move away from where I speak, to leave a trail of sounds wherever I am not.

'You know the world is changing,' I whisper, slide down from a boulder, leave the words for him to find.

'The dead do not change!' he cries, running to the boulder. 'You can try to leave forever, and you never will.' His voice echoes up the tunnel.

I fear he may be right — I am playing a futile game. Maybe this is how the story ends — as some do — with a never-ending task, a pointless effort. I feel again the immense weight and structure of the earth's crust over me, the miles of granite, limestone, water, soil. But I do not stop.

'The deal is over,' I call. 'You told me so yourself!' I climb rapidly away, leave the words to skitter on the walls.

I keep moving. Once I feel his warmth, in the darkness, near my arm. I run, he runs. I crouch, throw a stone ahead of me, press myself into the wall, hold my breath as he runs past. I crawl back, try to find a different passage upwards, not the one he led me down.

At last, I do. I find another way up through the rock — a ledge that turns into a passage. I pull myself along it, flat against the stone, face to one side, until I feel air above me. I sit up. Listen. The dark does not hold its breath. I throw a stone. No one runs to where it lands.

'Hades,' I say softly, and move away. No one rushes to grip the dark about the name.

No way to know how long until he finds me. No way to know how long the child will live, if it is living now. I listen in my belly for any stirring and find, instead, hunger. I have never felt hunger under the earth, except for once, when my mother brought it and I ate the seeds. But now, here it is, though she is far away. I hope it is a sign I am still carrying a life. I wonder if I could starve, trying to tunnel upwards to the surface. I have never been this way, this deep, but the dark and the stone are in me now like an instinct, a pattern my body understands. I stand, hand to the rock and fly into the dark.

DEMETER

I breathe my own breath back in. Stale air. Stale thoughts.

Listen to the hammering as they break into my home.

Why did I think — again — that I knew best?

Too stubborn to let my daughter help.

I listened to the birds and spiders. Not to her.

Why?

Still too afraid what I might hear.

Gathering strength? I did the thing that took least courage.

A crash above as they ram through my kitchen wall.

Afraid her father was right all along — afraid she longed to leave me.

But, even though I did not listen — I heard her — a week ago — tell me that she loved me.

Saws whining now.

I hear the dull thud through the earth as they fell my chestnut tree.

And I understand too late where I went wrong.

Because I remember it now — not only the dark, but the terrible helplessness of the wait within my father. He was a violent man — nothing I could do, in the foul cave of his stomach, but sit and listen as he smashed up the world around him.

And afterwards I wanted to avoid both, at all costs — the dark, but also the helplessness.

I have been capable for years. So able she never stood a chance.

I thought to give my daughter everything I lacked — light, food, love — I forgot to give her freedom.

So eager was I for her story to be different, I never allowed it to be hers.

I hear the cackle of my hens, let loose.

Images come to me. Not of the clumsy, dreamy girl, who let her seedlings die, who slopped the water from the well. But of a woman, standing on a roof. Climbing down the chestnut tree to check on me. Feeding me. Or just sitting, by the fire, looking at the flames. Tall, willowy, strong. Why did I still think I was more capable than she?

And now?

Now I would let her be.

Now I would clear the ground for her, and not mind if she grew nothing there but just lay down on it to dream.

Now I would listen — never say another word.

I would shrink, small as a harvest mouse.

I would be smaller.

A seed.

Vanish to nothing.

'I would die for her,' I tell the stone.

Until now, I have made everything else die, year in, year out and called it winter.

I nearly killed the world for her, that first time, and called it love.

I could not live without her, I said, but I lived on all right.

My life has never been in question.

I have only ever been here.

Ever since I burst into the world that second time.

Always here.

My heart beats on.

I realise, too late, I am the hob. The thing left on.

The hurry. Milk boiled dry.

She asked me to carry on.

I said I would. Though I have carried on too long.

I hear them talk of the tunnel. Of how they cannot drive their machines over the back garden, must empty it first.

There is a woman down there, they say. The shoring is unsafe. Mine rescue workers are on their way, will help to pull her out.

They need not bother.

But I will carry on. Like the other gods. Mad, sad. Unable even to die.

I need to pee.

Piss in the pan.

This will be me.

Pissing in pans, eating from bins.

Frightening other mothers as I sit, slumped, muttering, outside the village shop.

I will go camping, as I planned. Steal a shopping trolley from the Tesco they will build beside the road. Push it to the woods — what little's left of them — sleep under it. Mother Earth's daughter.

And all the while she will be trapped down in the dark. Robbed of the life she should have had. Her baby, dead.

Who robbed her?

Not Hades. Not her father.

Me.

I will collect bags to hold all my regret and I will never have enough. And this will make me mean. Tight-mouthed, tight-arsed, tight-hearted. More bitter than winter.

Because I did not learn, in time, how to love.

How to let my child live.

32

PERSEPHONE

I have found my way to the cave through which the pomegranate grows. I recognise the snaking shapes beneath my feet, the sense of height, of space to either side, of something else alive inside the dark.

I raise my hands and walk out, feeling for the tree. Silent as I can. Hades may be near. Water at my ankles. The round hardness of a pomegranate by my foot. At last my palms touch bark, the wood I thought was stone when I first came here. I run my hands over its deep groves, rough lines, think of the ferry woman's face. I know Hades is right — I cannot cross the river. The ferrywoman will not take me back — the baby, she will say, belongs here now.

I lean into the trunk, too wide to hold. It is a kind of comfort to feel it, huge, unmoving, solid as rock but growing. In the dark, I see the summer's trees — the netted trees in Prattle Woods, yew, Snow's oak, hawthorns by the stile, my mother's apple, her chestnut — as if this buried tree were the root of every other. I think of Snow's tattoo — the tree inked into his skin. I think of the strange and terrible world above, of which I want to be a part. I feel wet between my legs.

I still have my harness on. Hands, frightened, fast, loosening it enough to touch the wet sliding down the inside of my left thigh. I know already what it is. I lift my hand, bring it to my tongue — blood.

'No!' I say it to the tree —

'Persephone!' — but Hades hears.

He is in the cave. His voice came from the entrance near his workshop. I hold in breath, tears, move away around the far side of the trunk.

My hands close on ridges in the bark, face pressed to them. Hades, splashing, running to the tree. Water rising over my ankles. Blood trickling down my leg. Everything is undone.

Except my hands, holding still.

I raise one foot out of the water, set it to the trunk. Suddenly I am bending, fighting with my boots, hauling them off, standing again, finding a hold in the bark with my hands, my toes, pulling up. Both feet off the rock.

'Persephone!' Hades calls out, by the tree now, but round the other side of it. I reach up with my right hand, find a grip, wedge my right foot into a new crack within the bark. I have spent the summer learning how to climb, yet never a tree like this. Never without being clipped on, never without light. But the feel of the harness round my waist and upper legs, gives me a reckless courage. I climb.

Swollen forearms. Toes crammed into crevices. The rapid look for each new hold, another game of hide-and-seek — the next place my foot, hand, can find. My right fingers reach a burr, a growth out from the bark. A solid hold.

'Persephone?' Hades' voice, under me. A question, flowering in the dark.

He does not think I would dare to climb this tree. I say nothing, less than nothing. Breathe without breathing. Send my left hand out. Read the braille of the bark. Fingers run over a surface that swerves towards the horizontal — here, perhaps, the tree begins to fork. It is smooth, wet with cold — nothing to hold. Place my palm flat on this new curve. Find a slit for my left foot, then right. No hold as solid as the one my right hand has — I have to risk a lunge up into nothing. And when I lunge, my hand, landing, will make a sound.

I push up, hand flying, slapping down, nothing to grip.

'Persephone!' A shout, aimed straight at the darkness where I am.

My hand clawing, torso flat against the curve, enough for my other hand to shoot forwards, grip a thin ridge, pull myself up.

'Come down!' Hades' words leaping up, as if I were a child, he, my mother. As if I were on the wall of the well, a steep, dark drop under me. Which there is.

I bunch up, curled in the crown of the tree.

'You cannot escape that way!' There is mockery, anger in his voice, but something else too — fear.

Of losing me.

To life?

To death?

His fear is dangerous. It gives me hope.

I stand on shaky legs. Feel many dark limbs round me — a forest in a tree. I brace myself between two branches, keep climbing.

Below, a short outbreath of effort — Hades, climbing after me.

'The baby will be dead already. You cannot save it!'

This, like a punch in the stomach — my foot slips — a horrible moment of hanging by arms only. I lift my feet to find the branch again. Climb on. No more blood between my legs but no motion either.

The branches grow apart. I have to choose one. Take the left.

I edge my way along it, massive as a trunk. No leaves, like

a tree in one long winter. The dark around me feels like water. Treacherous because it seems thick enough to hold me, but it won't. I grip harder, press closer, pull up.

'Persephone!'

Hades, climbing, higher, nearer. Impossible to tell his distance from me in this new terrain — not rock and tunnel. But wood. Tree. He may be close but on a different branch, and so still far from reaching me. Or not. He could sound far, be nearer than I know.

'Persephone!'

He is calling as when my mother called to me, over and over, as she came for me under the earth. My name, a way to claim me, even when he cannot touch me.

Minutes that are like hours. Me climbing. Him climbing. Him calling. I want to scream back. Scream for help, scream in terror, rage, grief. I say nothing. But he follows the sound of my breath, rub of my torso against the branches. Heart so loud he must hear it.

I find a fruit in a crook between branches, smooth-skinned, the size of the baby. I hold it, hope I can play the same trick as I did with stones through tunnels, send Hades a different way. I throw the fruit hard away from me. It slams against a branch, then drops, strikes on the rock below.

'Persephone!' I hear his panic. Smell it. For years I have reassured him. Now I terrify him. Whenever I find a fruit, I hurl it away into the dark.

He keeps calling — his voice frightened, angry, tired. I am all these things too. We climb the huge limbs of the tree. Older than any of us, he told me when he first brought me here. It will outlive the gods, he said. As I reach up, desperate to escape, I feel closer to him than I have for years.

323

I have struck stone. Rock at the top of the chamber.

But the rock has not stopped the tree — the branch goes on beyond it. Did the tree push through the stone? Or the stone form round it? I feel up for the edge of the rock, where the wood grows through. It crumbles in my hand. I take a carabiner from my harness, unclip it, hold it open — a metal tooth with which to dig. It makes a horrible scratching sound.

'Persephone!'

A lump of rock comes loose, falls.

A cry from Hades.

A jagged space left — tight, but it may be enough. I lie flat against the branch, push up — the stone tears at my back.

I pull through.

The branch goes on. Goes on branching. Unquestioning. I follow, also without question.

After a time — not long enough — I hear Hades find the hole, hear him groan, and then push through it too.

The branches split and split again, each a turn in a maze that may lead nowhere. They cut through layers of granite, chalk, limestone. Still no leaves — no light for them to breathe. No fruit now, either. Only these lengthening limbs, graceful, determined. I follow them, pushing up through cracks within the rock. I emerge a thousand times — hope for something — find only further dark. Raw fingers, shaking arms, weakening now.

I hear Hades follow, sometimes nearer, sometimes further, never far.

He becomes again what he was when I was a girl — a monster, god, man from under the earth coming to get me in the dark, but also — does he know this? — giving me courage, as he did when I first met him, when I kissed him, when I searched for him, when I went down into the earth with him. Now he gives me the strength to climb, keep climbing.

At last, he no longer calls. It is only the smell of him, his animal stench, following. The rub of his body, my body, against branch and rock. His breath. Mine. No other sound — the rush and drip of water gone.

Horrible hunger, like something climbing me. Taste of bile and bark. Thirst. I try to pull my breath back in, to drink the moisture that just left me. I lick dried tears — only salt, no water. I think of the baby, withering.

Still no sign of the surface, of my surfacing.

The branches are thinning, disappearing into rock, reappearing, more like roots — fine hairs sprout from them. Does the giant trunk lead only to these spindly threads? The rock is softening. I smell soil, moisture. I stop. Listen. Dream I hear the creep of water near. But the rock under me is dry, dusty. Not damp. It must be a mirage of sound my mind has made.

I scrabble through another gap, feel for the branch, root, thread within the ground. I cannot find it. The tree has tapered out.

Nothing left to follow. Only the dark. Dark in my hands. Dark in my eyes, ears, mouth. I drag myself forwards. Dark in my thoughts. Dark in my belly where the baby is, was. I knew it as a child. I knew it when I hid the ladle in the cellar, my mother's ladle, that she found too late, and only by mistake. She said that day and night were equal. I knew the dark was higher, deeper, older than the light. I knew one day that it would take me.

Now I wish Hades would catch me. I want his arms, someone's arms to hold me, even in violence. Even to kill me. I am more tired than I have ever been.

My mother's arms — I remember them as I pull forwards. Strong, young — swinging me high. Holding me close. Impossibly far away now, in space, in time.

Nothing but beat and breath left in the dark. And one simple want — my first, my last — for my mother's arms.

DEMETER

Scrabbling.

The rescue men?

The sound is not at the tunnel entrance.

But its end.

In front of me.

After waiting all this time with no one coming — someone is.

A fox? Frightened by the din?

No eyes gleam in the dark.

Something nears. Crawling.

I feel its warmth through the black. Hear its breath.

I draw the blanket round me, as if I might be eaten once again.

But it comes no nearer.

Cautious, reach out my hand.

Nothing.

Feel down, finger the cool ground.

Find hair.

Fine hair.

Feel further.

Brush a long neck. Thin, strong back. I catch my breath.

I stroke the face. Touch scratches on the skin, the lidded eyes, dry lips — feel feeble air pass from them.

'Persephone?'

She breathes.

Joy so sharp it stings.

Then I thank everything — worms, apple roots, pan, piss, soil, the whole aching world, more generous than I have ever been.

'Persephone!'

No reply.

She must have fainted, from effort, fright, or both.

I place my hand on her back, as far as I can reach, in the middle where it curves down. Bend to her.

'If there is any blessing left in me, any power, take it. It is yours now. And the baby's.'

A shout from behind me, near the tunnel entrance.

Now the mining men come, to rescue us.

But at the same moment, more scrabbling.

Who now?

Dread as heavy as the stone.

I may be wrong — I have been every time so far.

Quickly, I feel for my daughter's shoulder, slide my hand under her armpit.

I remember all the hauling I have done through all the years — the roots out of the ground, water up the well, sacks of grain back to the house. One-armed, I drag her, floppy, a dead weight. Pull her level with me.

Feel down, grab under her thighs, bend up her legs. I ball her up, twisting, bundle her behind me. Place my stiff right foot against her feet — bare, freezing — and push her from me. It is hard — her body rubs against the ground.

But now I am between her and whatever is coming.

And they are close. Panting, padding. It smells of animal — I hope it is one.

It stops.

We listen to each other in the dark.

A dull hammering from further down the tunnel.

I put out, again, a hand.

This time it meets another.

Another hand.

It clutches mine.

Fine fingered. Slight. Like a woman's. But not smooth. Its grip is fierce. I held it once before, but long ago.

At last, I got it right.

Hades has come.

'Persephone?' There is fear in his voice.

I try to keep mine steady.

'You are too late,' I say.

He jerks his hand from mine.

In the dark, we are close together — my daughter and grandson behind me, my son-in-law in front. Me, in the middle. Weak. Old. Cumbersome. But still, an obstacle.

'Where is she?' His voice, like the crackle of dead leaves.

'She has escaped,' I say and pray that this will give her time to do it. That she may come round, hear me, understand. 'She is gone up to the surface.' I say, loud as I dare. 'It is morning there.'

'No!' he says but does not move. For a moment we both listen to the day above — the churning of machines, the bailiffs' banter.

But then, my daughter moans.

'You lie! Let me to her!' Hades' hands, on my shoulders, he will force me back, tip me over.

I have nothing now. No harvest of strength.

I shut my eyes. See her. Tall, on the roof.

I pitch my body into Hades' hands.

I have this. My love. Given freely. And with it, I risk everything.

'Fight me for her,' I whisper. 'If you win, she's yours. If not, you let her go.'

'She's mine already!' His words hot in my ear. 'She has been so for years, but you would not accept it.'

'Not yours,' I say, 'Nor mine.'

His body, wiry, hard, against mine. His face in my face, the stink of him. Fearful animal — hurt man — god of dark. Everything from which I fled, hid. Everything I buried when I filled the well. He seizes me, forces my good arm down, my head into the pan of piss. The pan. I find its handle in the dark, strike up at him. He cries out. Urine, icy cold, spills on us both. Its sharp smell fills the tunnel.

He comes at me again.

But I am armed — beating off the King of the Dead with my best saucepan in the dark. He pounds my chest. He kicks my stomach. Pain spreads, branches in me but I stay put, striking with my pan.

Both of us, breathless.

He catches my wrist, forces the pan out of my hand.

'She chose me.' Triumph in his voice.

I pull my wrist in, draw him close.

'Yes, she chose to go with you.' At last, I admit it to be true. 'But now, she does not choose to stay.'

Hammering and voices echo down the tunnel.

'More plywood!'

'There's a door up here.'

'Another one?!'

'This is dodgy as hell!'

'We'll have to saw through it.'

'Hang on.'

A sharp bang, and then — light. A thin shaft.

Enough to see by. Hades' desperate eyes. His face, bleeding.

Behind me, my daughter moans again.

Hades lets go my wrist, no longer trying to attack me, only to get past. The dim light shows him how. He dives to my left. I strain out from the stone that locks me to the right-hand wall. Press with my left hand, leg, against the other wall, lean with my chest.

'Let her go.' I am pleading now.

'I cannot. I love her too much.'

'If you love her, you would not trap her in the dark against her will.'

For a second, something flickers through him — a memory, a fear — but then he is pulling my leg, my chest, from the tunnel wall.

He will pass me, reach her.

Unless.

Unless I move the stone.

I would move heaven and earth to save her, but all I have to do is shift a stone.

I have nothing left but this old body. Heart. Mine to give away — I need none of it back.

For one final moment, I must be strong as mountains. Sure as growing grain. I heave. I grunt. I wrench the stone loose from the tunnel wall.

Rough. Gritty. Grey. It rolls free.

The stone and I fill the tunnel.

Hades cries out, pushes against us.

Then, here we are once more.

My eldest brother, me, trapped around a stone within the dark.

'You could have her forever,' I tell him — urgent now — not much breath left. 'But she will never change who you are. Who we were. Remember this?' And I hold him with my one good arm.

Now he is not pushing past, but into me. Half in battle. Half in grief. I draw him about the stone. I know what it is to love my daughter and to find her gone. I know how it is to be near her and never have her. She has been escaping both of us for years.

There is a whining down the passage as they saw through the door. The light grows so that we can see her now — my daughter, his wife — lying, curled up on the ground. Pale, cut, bruised — alive. Hades strains after her. I hold him still, though I am weakening.

She stirs.

Hurry, love, I tell her. Hurry.

33

Persephone

Light enough to see my hands.

Stench of urine, sweat, fear. The smell of the shore beneath the earth. I must be back, waiting for the ferry boat. I climbed up high, only to arrive back here.

It seems that dying is like being born. Sensation is all there is. My head throbs, my stomach is filled with its own tightness. I hear hammering, that could be from inside me or from out. I roll my head to look further — it sets the half-light spinning. I see that it is raining underground. I am having impossible visions, as the dying do — I see my mother and my husband wrapped about a stone. My husband has his head bent to my mother's shoulder, but she looks up and out, at me.

Run along now, I hear her say, not say. As if I were a girl again. As if we were in the kitchen and she were making bread. As if it were a summer's day.

Go on, go out and play.

What do you mean?

The fields are waiting.

Why is my husband here?

Go on love, is all she says.

What about you? I ask.

I'll stay here. Run along now.

But I cannot run, cannot even stand. And suddenly I do not want to leave her — I never want to leave her again, whether we are in the kitchen, by the river, underground or under sky, and in whatever season.

I'm staying here with you, I say. I tell her what she has always longed to hear.

But she says nothing.

A whining noise starts up, behind me. I twist my head towards it, see no one.

I turn back to my mother, holding my husband. But now my husband's arms are lifted too. One is flung across the stone, the other is about my mother. It is still raining.

I must be dreaming. I must have lost my mind down in the dark.

I look between them, see a likeness I never saw before. In the structure of their faces. Their high, wide cheekbones, strong jawlines.

I used to know my husband by touch, my mother by sight, across the room or garden. This year, I have held her. I have seen him. Now they are holding one another, I know them differently again.

I want to move to them, but my head pounds and I am shivering.

The whining stops. Men's voices.

'Nearly there!'

'Quick! The roof's not going to last.'

And then I understand. It is not rain. It's dust, falling around us. I stare through it at my mother, her head now tilting down. She rests it on the stone, and then rolls it, so that it lies against my husband's chest. Her arm goes limp, slides from where it lay across his shoulders, so that he is the one left upright, holding her against the stone.

For a moment he looks out at me with longing, shock, but he does not move. He goes on holding the stone, my mother.

333

He looks to her. I do too. And as the earth rains down on her, my mother starts to change.

I may yet be dreaming. I hope I am. The skin on my mother's face is tightening, its lines sink inside it, like veins within a leaf. Her hair is turning brown-black, rich as earth, dug over. Her eyes grow clear. Her limbs thin and lengthen. My mother looks astonishingly young. So full of hope it hurts.

I cannot tell if she sees me anymore. Or Hades. But I see her, the girl, young woman, who she was before she had me.

The change moves through her, too quick to catch or stem. Her face is filling. Glowing. She is powerful — like the trees in summer. The mother I knew when I was small and it was always warm. I want to keep her like this. I want the change to stop. But it does not. The year, all the years, are sweeping through her.

Her hair greys again, the lines re-draw themselves across her face like furrows in the fields, her limbs slacken, soften. I cannot bear to watch, cannot look away. As autumn comes to her, my mother looks bright, defiant.

But she is growing paler now. Thinner. Her breathing becomes laboured, as it was after her stroke. It comes out of her in shudders, as if this last change will take effort.

'Mother! No!'

I look to Hades, holding her. He is staring down, afraid, as if the King of the Dead has never seen a death before, never held anyone as they died.

She promised me she never would.

'Mother. Stop!'

But she does not hear me. She is white. Cold and old and new as winter. Her breathing grows shallow. She stares up through the falling earth and her face tightens in pain. A sudden moment of surprise — and then — peace. Peace in the midst of winter — something she never thought that she would find. She sighs. And then is still. She does not breathe in again.

Where has she gone?

Of all those alive, I should know. But I do not.

The dead arrive at the river underground.

I do not know where the living go.

The tunnel shudders. It could be the hammering of the men, making the ground shake but I know better — it is the earth, weeping.

I reach for my mother, but Hades puts out a hand, as if he is protecting her from me, or me from her. He holds her, in her stillness, and for a moment, I see the father that he might have been, had his father not eaten him, had my father not cheated him.

He stares at me, through the falling earth. He looks almost as white as my mother. He mouths one word.

'Go.'

And then the roof caves in. Earth falls on me. A dark weight. Earth in my eyes. Mouth. On my legs. Chest.

I cannot move. I do not ever want to move again.

'Shit!'

'Where is she?'

A terrible pain in my middle, as if teeth are tearing me apart. I hug the earth about me, over me. I try to bury myself deeper. To bury the pain. But it is violent, livid, filling my whole body.

'Found her!'

Hands, digging. Pushing the weight from me. I fight them. Claw them off. Burrow back towards my mother. But the hands have me, drag me. A man — light strapped to his head — is gripping my shoulders, hauling me away. I try to tell him that I need to stay, but my mouth is full of earth. I reach for her.

'Oh no you don't.'

An arm about my chest, drawing me along the tunnel to the light. Still, I pull back to my mother.

'Fucking nutter — you're not gonna save the earth by getting yourself killed!'

He is lugging me further down the passage.

'Hey, Abe, get down here and help us. And get someone to call an ambulance — this one's for the hospital, not the station — pale as death, covered in cuts.'

I struggle, retch, point back, howl.

'You're bloody lucky, you know that? Ten minutes later and we'd have been too late.'

I am not lucky. I am shaking uncontrollably, and the pain stabs in my gut again, so sharp, so shocking that it winds me. I curl up. Press head into knees. It is getting lighter. I am being lifted, under my arms, lain on the surface of the earth, as if it were the spring. But it is not the spring. It is cold. The wind is up. And this is not the woods.

I open my eyes. I am in my mother's garden. I have no idea how I got here. They have pulled me out onto the veg patch, through the beans, to the corner my mother gave me once, where I never grew sunflowers or cherries. There are men in black uniforms, helmeted, yellow jackets, standing about the garden. It looks like a war zone — the earth is churned, covered with boot marks and trampled plants. A sign that says 'Beets: Early Wonder' lies near me, snapped off. There is a hole in the side of my mother's house — I can see into the kitchen. Dust, rubble, sheets of plywood, chainsaws, a ladder, spill across the ground. An excavator is parked beside the pond. The horse chestnut is down, lying on its side, its leaves worried in the wind. I see no other protestors. Only police, bailiffs, packing away, the battle done, won. And in between them all, my mother's hens, pecking in the mud for seeds.

I am shuddering, sobbing. One of the men comes over to me, puts his jacket round me, holds his fingers in my face — they smell of cigarettes. I gag. He asks me how many fingers he has, what my name is. I do not care about his fingers or my name, only about my mother — over there — under the apple stump. I ignore the man, crawl forwards. I tear at the ground, as if I could dig down to her with my bare hands. Soil under my nails. Men bending over me.

'What you doing?'

'Can she walk?'

I can't. They pull me up, away from this spot, and I do not have the strength to stop them. I want to tell them to get her out, but I am crying too hard to speak. They puppet me with limp legs, out of my mother's garden, away from the house, into the meadow, along the river. I turn my head back to see a hen, perched on the back-garden gate, astonished at its new freedom.

34

Persephone

Back in the hospital, but now I am the one in bed, surrounded by a thin blue curtain. A nurse presses on my inner arm to find a vein in which to slide a drip. I tell her I am pregnant. She shakes her head.

'Protesting down a tunnel is no way to carry on in that condition.'

'I had bleeding —'

'You'll feel a slight scratch.'

'Bad pain.'

'Hold still now.'

'I want to know if —'

'We're very busy tonight.'

'— the baby's dead.'

'The doctor will come over when she can.'

And then she goes.

The sheets, starched and white, creak under me. The lights in the ceiling buzz like insects. Footsteps, voices, passing. Machines beeping. Around me, above me, a building of people trying to live, or trying to die.

I am moved from A & E onto a ward. The doctor comes. I am dehydrated, under-nourished. My blood pressure is low. I ask about the baby. An ordinary stethoscope, she tells me, does not reliably pick up a foetus heartbeat before twenty weeks, and there is no one from the maternity ward immediately available. I am not registered on the system and must be so before they can book me in to see a midwife. If there is no further pain or bleeding, it is likely that the baby is fine and if not then, sadly, there is nothing they can do. I feel her silent accusation, recognise it — it is the same as my mother's used to be. I am thoughtless to have been on a protest site with a baby. Selfish, years ago, to have left my mother and not considered how it would be for her. I am trying not to think of her, I am trying to hold off thinking, feeling anything, until I know about the baby, as if I need to know the extent of my loss before I can allow myself to feel it. A woman in my ward keeps calling out for help: 'There's someone at the door,' she tells the nurse. 'Go and see who it is.' I roll away, face the wall, but see my mother, waiting for me at her door as I come in through the garden gate.

By the afternoon of the next day, I am on the system and am offered a scan. I want it over with, and I want to wait forever. As long as I am waiting there is still a chance. I lie, lift up my top, and a woman squeezes a cold, transparent jelly onto my skin with blue, plastic-gloved hands. She sits at a keyboard, with a computer screen above it. She is young, neat, with dark hair in a tight ponytail. The lights in the room are low.

'So we can see the screen better,' the woman says. She seems friendly — perhaps she has not read my notes about having spent a night underground in an eviction. She swipes a nozzle back and forth over my belly. On her screen a dark image appears, with streaks of light inside it. The image is set within a triangle, that bulges at its base in an outward curve, like the bottom of a boat. Within the curve lies another — the curve of a body, a luminous outline of a head, a grainy torso, one limb bent up. It is as if someone has begun to scrape away the dark to make the shape of a baby, as if, like a wood carving, the image grows from removing matter, not adding it. It looks like it is by the river, underground, drifting in the dark.

'It's dead isn't it?'

In answer, the young woman sweeps over my stomach, presses down onto one point. On the screen appear four dark spots, like a track in sand made by an animal, but it's moving — it is the animal, not the mark it left. It ripples and blinks. The lady presses a key and suddenly there is sound, fast, furious, like a dog's tail, thwacking against a wall.

'That's its heart,' she says.

I stare at the screen.

'How?' I say.

'What do you mean?'

'I had a rough time.'

'It will have taken what it needed from you. Babies are set up to be selfish. Quite often, mum can be in a terrible state and baby will be just fine. I'll check through everything else. Shut your eyes if you don't want to know the sex.'

I shut my eyes. Relief, and with it, at last, grief. Right now, they are the same — I cannot separate them. Children are selfish — both me and the baby. The baby is alive. My mother is not. These things seem impossible, miraculous, except miracles are meant only to be joyful. I wish I could perform some magnificent gesture, like my mother. I would get up from here, walk out, make the trees in the hospital car park blaze up with leaves of red and gold, then watch them fade and fall. Instead, I have to hold everything within myself, this body.

In the scanning room and every hour after, I miss her. It is a physical pain, sometimes sharp, sometimes dull, but one for which there is no remedy — I understand why my mother never accepted it, never healed. How can anyone heal from the pain of something that isn't there?

'Going home tomorrow then, I hear,' the nurse says as she does up the band that squeezes my upper arm, to check my blood pressure.

'Yes.'

This nurse is a big woman, like my mother was, maybe a mother herself. I do not tell her that I no longer know where my home is. I ask instead if she can help me contact the baby's father.

'He's likely to be at the police station,' I say. She rolls her eyes but agrees.

'And can you pass on a message for him to bring me some shoes and extra clothes?'

'The young!' she tuts.

Later that day, Snow comes.

'Your boyfriend's here,' the nurse announces. I am nervous as if he were, as if this were our first date. He looks nervous too, and tired. He has brought me a bag of clothes.

'I'll see you in the waiting room.'

I get changed in the bathroom at the end of the ward, out of my white hospital robe, into some leggings of Nonny's, her old trainers, a T-shirt and sweatshirt of Snow's.

The waiting room is like the one we met in before, after my mother's stroke. It has a TV up on the wall — another young couple are viewing another old house.

We hug. He no longer smells of wood smoke but of other, indoor places I do not know.

'Let's not stay in here. You allowed out for a breath of air?' he asks.

341

'I think so.'

'C'mon. Let's go.'

We take the lift down to the sliding doors of the entrance, walk out into the early evening. Patients and visitors stand around outside, waiting to be collected, chatting, having a smoke. There is nowhere to go but round the car parks, between the big, white, square buildings, with their many floors, death under them all — I saw it in the lift — the morgue is in the basement. The road going through the grounds is busy with cars, taxis, a bus going to Oxford city centre.

We walk without talking yet, through car park one, two, out to a corner of car park three. We sit down, side by side, on a strip of green, facing a privet hedge that runs along one side of it. Two grey metal posts grow out of the grass behind us, supporting a sign that lists the parking charges. A crow lands on the sign, waits, hoping for crumbs.

'You'd better fill me in — the bastards kept me in and took my phone away. Are you okay?'

'Yes.'

'And the baby?'

'I had a scan — heard its heart.'

Snow tugs at his beard, tilts it up at the white sky.

'I never thought I'd say this but, thank fuck.' He grips my forearm for a moment, lets it go.

'And how's your mother?'

I am ready for this. I remember his words, around the fire, about how it isn't good to have a death on site.

'She's okay. How about you?'

But I am too light, too quick.

'Where is she?' he says.

'Camping in the fields.'

'What?'

'It's where she wants to be.'

Snow swings himself right round to face me.

'What's happened?' He takes my wrists. 'You've got to tell me what's happened.' There is violence in his voice.

'Okay.' I take a breath. 'I ended up in the tunnel with her. She died down there. They pulled me out. They didn't know about her.'

He stands and slams his hand into the parking notice. The crow flies off. He lifts both arms to the sky.

'Fucking hell. I fucking knew it!'

Several people, hurrying to their cars, turn their heads.

'I told you. I told you she shouldn't be allowed down there. No one fucking listened.' He drops to his knees. I feel sick, like a child, who has done something very wrong.

'Look. I'm sorry,' he says. He pushes out air in a long stream. 'It's your mother — it's awful — but have you any idea how serious this is?'

'Yes. It's why I tried not to tell you.'

'You can't not tell me and think that's going to help!' He is up again, pacing. 'There'll be an inquest —'

'Stop.'

'The battle over who's liable will go on for bloody ages —'

'Listen!'

'It'll have massive repercussions for future protests.'

'But I'm not going to tell anyone!'

'What the fuck do you mean?'

'I'm not going to register the death.' Now I am calm and clear.

'You can't do that.'

'A long legal battle is the last thing she would want.'

'I know — none of us want it — but you can't pretend it hasn't happened.'

'Think of her as if she's not been evicted — she's down in the tunnel, still protesting.'

'That doesn't work, Pers. Nice story — load of shit.'

'It's not your fault.'

'So what? So what if it's not my fault?'

'We don't need to tell.'

'But I can't keep it a secret just because it doesn't suit me, and it's going to be a fucking nightmare!'

'She wanted to go down there.'

'Not telling anyone is behaving like a bloody murderer!'

'She chose it.'

'She didn't know what she was choosing.'

'She did. She knew.'

'Shit.' He is down on his knees again, head pressed into the grass. 'This is everything I feared.'

'Stop it.'

I say it loud enough that people turn their heads again, attracted by the idea of a row. I drop my voice, kneel down.

'Listen to me. She had no birth certificate. No passport. No bank account. No driving licence. There is nothing, except me, and the ruin of a house to say that she existed. Why should her death be registered by pieces of paper in a way her life never was? Her life was registered by fields, corn, birds, by an apple tree, by everyone who ate a meal at her house, by every season of the year, and by every myth told in her name. Let her death be registered that way as well.'

'You can't,' he says, but softly, as if maybe I can.

'Look.' I point up. As the sun sets behind the hospital

buildings, it is bleeding into the sky, turning it red, pink, gold. The evening star is out.

'There,' I say, as if the light has settled it. I am surprised at my certainty. I sound like my mother. I realise this will happen now. Because she is not here, the ballast of everything will change, is changing. The things in her from which I recoiled are different now that she is gone. I can be self-assured, grand even. I feel Snow see it in me, as he looks up from the grass.

'You're fucking mad,' he says.

'It's what she wants.'

'Look, I need to sleep on it.'

'Sure,' I say, knowing he will leave it now.

He stands, comes to me, holds me, underneath the parking sign.

'I'm sorry for your loss,' he says.

'Thanks.'

We let go of each other. I take his hand and we walk back up through the car parks, as the red and white lights of the cars move along the road, the yellow streetlights come on, and the sky turns orange from the city's glow — so many lights, as if the whole world has grown frightened of the dark.

'What are you going to do?' I ask him when we reach the entrance.

'I've a court date in a month. And it's not exactly over, is it?' He points with his beard to the field of cars in front of us. 'I'll probably hook up with some of the HS2 protest sites.' He looks down. 'I did warn you about being a shit father.'

'You did.'

'But I can help find you somewhere to stay — Nut or Ash, or one of the others, will have a room.'

'That'd be good. I'm coming out of here tomorrow.'

35

PERSEPHONE

I climb over the railings, into the field by the bridge, follow the river back. It is one of the first cold days there has been this winter. I did not want to go back on a mild, wet day, of which there have been many.

The baby is fast asleep as I walk, tucked up in Berry's old sling, snoring like a cat. Nut says Berry has outgrown the sling and I can keep it. He is warm against me. He is always warm, as if he had summer stashed away inside him. The ground is hard, and the grass squeaks underfoot. Frost-edged trees fork into the white sky like black antlers. I am startled by the beauty of it. It is easy to feel powerful on a day like this — there are brittle puddles which crack when I step on them, and my breath rolls out of me in plumes. Although he is only three weeks old, already I want to give the boy these things — winter — the one I read about, dreamt of, the one my mother made. But this kind of cold is old-fashioned nowadays. Over Christmas, before the baby came, I walked through the village and was amazed how many different kinds of snow I saw: paper, polystyrene, cotton wool — none of frozen water. Grief too — the hard, relentless kind, to which my mother was committed, is also out of vogue. I am meant to soldier on, recover quietly. I begin to think better of my mother's bitterness. I have been low, thinking I should be high, to be up here, alive. Mrs Casey, Nut's mum, thinks I have post-natal depression, but it is not the birth or the baby that depresses me.

I look down at the lad as I trudge on beside the river. He is frowning in his sleep. He looks like my mother — her almond eyes, her wide forehead, big cheeks. It is strange to look down on her as he is feeding from me. The only resemblance I see to his father is that he is bald.

Snow has been as absent as he promised. He was around for a month, before his court date. We went back once to the site together, to retrieve what we could — my mother's savings from under her mattress — and we managed to catch two of the hens and bring them back to Nut's. Snow settled me and the hens there, and then was off. He has not met the baby yet. I do not mind. He has left me and the boy his fleece, which is big enough that I can fit it round us both — zip the little man up in it while he is in the sling. Little man is what I call him — I have been slow to find a name. I want to get it right. It will be my first gift to him. I am not sure I gave him life — I think he took it for himself.

I slide my hand across the curve of his back, watch my breath. One more field to go. According to my mother's story of my birth I was slow to come. My son showed no reluctance to be born. I had to hold him in, sit cross-legged in the car as Nut drove me to the hospital. I couldn't have him in the house — Mrs Casey's home is too clean, too white for all that blood. And there was a lot. Nine and a half pounds at birth, and keen to keep on growing. He has tall men to follow.

Crows circling. The sound of traffic. One lonely dog walker across the other side of the field. One more stile, and then we will arrive. I wish my mother could have seen him.

I had thought the house would be gone by now, the road already built, but Snow says it takes years to build a road. They clear the route in a great rush, evict houses, but then leave them boarded up, abandoned for months before they get round to completing the demolition. I can see from the edge of the meadow that my mother's house is still standing, but they have smashed in the roof so that it is no longer weatherproof.

I walk away from the river, over the frozen meadow. I bang my hands against my legs — my gloves, borrowed from Nut, are thin black wool. My toes are numb. I am glad of the baby's warmth.

As I near the house, I spy something in the grass, beside what is left of the back garden wall. I go over, squat down. It's a dead animal. A fox, a vixen — I can see her teats where the red fur thins. Her body is stiff, with frost, and death. Her fur is matted. I wonder how long she has been there.

'I'll come back,' I tell her, my words making white shapes in the air.

Then the little man and I go on into my mother's home.

With the roof gone and a great gash in the back wall, the birds have claimed the house. The floors are covered with their droppings. My mother would approve. My mother invented homes, and now hers is sky-high again, its doors flung open upwards, like an invitation.

'Grandma lived here,' I tell the baby. He squirms in his sleep. I go back out.

Beyond the apple stump, the pipe that led down to the bunker is still there, as if she might shout up a greeting.

I go back past the pond, clogged with leaves, ice at its edges, and find the vixen.

It is hard to move her. With the baby on my front, I cannot bend far forwards. I have to half-drag, half-carry the body up the garden. I place her near the apple stump, her sharp face pointing to the pond. The movement wakes the baby. He complains. I set him suckling inside the sling.

'We've work to do,' I tell him. I, we, go gathering. This afternoon there is not much in bloom but near the river I find silver pussy willow in long spears, a hazel, with its tiny, red star flowers. I pick a length of both. I need to keep walking to stay warm and it feels good to be out — I have hardly left the house since the birth. In the fields, I find a blackbird's feather, a celandine and then — under the hawthorn — a snowdrop. I carry them all back, lay them on the vixen too. Evidence that spring will come, even though neither I, nor my mother, bring it.

I gather black, wet horse chestnut leaves beside the pond and pile them round the body. The baby is getting restless. I jump up and down to settle him. I realise I am happy in a way I have not been for weeks. I start to cry.

I miss my mother. I miss my husband too. All those years I thought I was travelling a great distance from the dead, back to the living. Now here I am, shocked to find how close they are. Not poles apart but back-to-back. Snow may be off, fighting to save the world, but meanwhile, Hades is near. Not a threat now — the deal is undone — but he did not die down in that tunnel, only held my mother while she did. I feel a kind of painful pride in her, remembering suddenly how she declared to me, beside her beans, that no one would make her move from here. Well, no one has.

The baby is crying too. I unzip the fleece, take him out of the sling, hold him against me. I kneel.

'Time to give the fox back.'

With one hand I push the black leaves over the body. I rock the boy, watch my breath puff up into a white sky, think of my father. He is out there, somewhere, in a sorry state, not sorry for any of the things he's done, unable or unwilling to help.

My husband, though, is still waiting for me under

everything. The fox may even be a gift from him. I think down through the veg patch, buried bulbs, the thick roots, and thin threads, down through the thousand branches of the pomegranate tree, into the dark. All that Hades told me last year, about this changing world, is true. He cannot lie and, unlike me, he never learnt.

The baby's hand pulls at my face.

'Don't worry. It will be okay,' I tell him.

Will it? I am not sure. I am the Queen of the Dead, up among the living, and I wish I had more answers.

The baby whimpers.

'Shhhh,' I say. 'Your turn now.'

I take off his hat, my gloves. He quietens. I lean out and touch the leaves covering the vixen, and then I touch his head.

'I call you Fox,' I say into the cleft in his skull where the bones are not yet fused. In honour of the digging and the dead. In honour of my husband, the boy's other father, who has my mother now, whom I still love, and to whom, one day, I will return. But I don't tell the baby this — not yet.

'I call you Fox,' I say, 'because, in the world that is waiting for you, you're going to need your wits about you.' I kiss him, put his hat back on.

I put Fox into the sling again. We get up to go. The sky is blueing with the evening, and as we walk away the crows begin to come. They fly in long lines from the fields, the roads, from Otmoor and from Noke, cawing, circling, congregating at my mother's — her empty house must be their winter roost. They keep coming as we walk away, hundreds of solemn, black birds, as if every evening of this winter is a service, held in my mother's honour.

We go back one more time.

A blazing July day. The river is green with weed. Fox is in a sling still, but on my back. At six months, he is a lump already — he has his grandma's appetite.

I climb into what was my mother's meadow and stop.

There is nothing there. No garden wall. No garden. No pond. No house. Everything gone. Only a level, raked stretch of earth. The demolition has been carried out at last.

Nothing prepared me for this. The starkness of it. Under a blue sky, too. It takes my breath away. Fox squirms on my back.

'It's okay,' I tell him, lying. I know now that this is what mothers do — step lightly over horror, smile, as if it were no more than a dropped stitch. I hum for Fox, but I feel desperate. I want to find some evidence at least, some sign of my mother.

I walk up the meadow — what is left of it. I search the area. Fox is hot, impatient.

'All right. I'll let you down.'

I set him on the earth — he can sit up on his own now. I look at him, looking at me for a moment — he gazes up at me as I must have done at her, thinking I'm a goddess.

I keep hunting. I want there to be a sapling horse chestnut, growing from the conker that I placed about her neck, something stubborn that they could not chop down. I can see nothing. I look back at the boy.

'Oh Fox — no!'

He has his fat fists round clumps of earth and his mouth is full of it. Crumbs of soil on his chin and down his front. I run to him.

'No, love.'

I go to scoop the dirt from his little tongue, and he gives me a black, toothless grin, as if this is the best thing he has yet eaten.

Acknowledgements

I am going to start, not with an acknowledgement, but a confession.

There were many times during the decade that it took for this book to come into being, when I slipped into a fantasy about writing its acknowledgements. There were three reasons for this. First, because it would mean I had done it — got to the end, found a publisher, produced a book. Second, because writing about those who had helped me seemed a good deal easier than writing the book itself. And third — linked to the last — because there were so many people, at each stage, without whom I could not have got as far as I had, that I wanted to start thanking them right away, and to contest the idea that a book is made alone, by an author, sitting at a window, awaiting inspiration. This book, at least, was not made that way.

This book was made by many people.
But it began with a single word.

Back in 2011, the space in which I wrote had no windows, but instead I had a bag beside my desk. It was a 'word-bag,' created under the instruction of Lynda Barry, whom I met for one week, in deep January snow at Goddard College, Vermont, and who taught me how to write by hand again. Barry told me to keep my pencil moving, across the page, no matter what. Without learning this skill, I would never have even got going.

There is a section in Barry's book *What It Is* (p. 178–9) in which she explains how to make a word bag. You copy a long list of words — mainly nouns — onto small rectangular pieces of card — one word per card. I painted mine in thick black ink. You put each card into an envelope and put each envelope into the bag. When you come to do your writing practice, you put your hand in the bag, pull out an envelope, open it up, read the word, and begin.

One morning, in April 2011, when I had just found out that I was pregnant with my first child, I walked to my windowless seat, and pulled an envelope out of the bag. Inside the envelope, the word on the card read: 'spring.'

No Season but the Summer began in the spring. It was that time of year and that word that summoned Persephone up, from under the earth, and precipitated her climb towards the surface.

She would, however, never have seen the light of day, without the mentorship of Sally Cline, with whom I worked through the Gold Dust scheme, in my days of early motherhood, and whose kind and persistent encouragement, in the cafe at the back of the British Library, teased my stilted prose pieces out into something resembling a novella. I thank too, the faculty members at Goddard College who worked with me on this early draft within the context of my MFA: Richard Panek, Rebecca Brown, and John McManus.

After that, things got tricky. Or rather sticky, and then downright stuck. I had a novella that wasn't quite working. I also had, by this point, two small children. I had precious little time and energy. Thankfully, I had a large dose of stubbornness too — I wasn't prepared to abandon Persephone altogether. But I needed help.

I had, by now, founded an initiative called Mothers Who Make to support people like me to sustain their creative identities, alongside their caring roles. It was through a campaign I was running for this, that I made contact with the novelist and writer Nicky Singer, who also happened to be the big sister of one of my oldest friends, Jackie Singer. I wrote to Nicky: would she consider taking a look at the draft of a book with which I was struggling? I offered to pay her. She wrote back and said she hardly ever did such a thing, she never did it for money, and it almost always ended in tears. Desperate as I was, I accepted these stringent terms and conditions and sent her my draft. That was in 2017. I am still awaiting the tears. And the end.

The story you are holding in your hands would never have made it into book-form had Nicky not taken me on, with incredible generosity and unfailing insight, and taught me how to write a narrative, with an arc, rather than only a series of nice, budding spring images. She has made the last five years of working on it joyful and helped me remember why I wanted to write in the first place — because of the particular kind of friendship and love, at once intimate and formal, which can grow from words on a page. She told me, early on in our exchange, that once the book came out (one of the many miraculous things she gave me was her steadfast belief that it would), she would be the first in the queue to acquire it. She shall, accordingly, be the first person to whom I send a copy. She got to the front of the queue before anyone else — in fact when there *was* no one else — and, what is more, stayed there. For this, I will be thankful to her through every season, evermore.

Once Nicky had set me on track, I also sought help from someone with whom I could work face to face. My background is in theatre — I wanted some rehearsal room time, or its writing equivalent. For stepping brilliantly into this role, I thank Angela Clerkin, whom I met on a show about another Ancient Greek

God — Pan — in which we were both woodland nymphs. My exchanges with her, out in the woods, were also invaluable.

Next up —the activists — all those I encountered in researching the story. Thanks first to Charlie Kronick for reading, writing, talking, putting me in touch with others, and always taking me seriously, even when— truth be told — I felt like a joke. Thanks to the men and women on the ground, and in the trees: Dr Andy Letcher, Phil Pritchard, Rumi Mohideen, Hannah Martin, Paul Morrozzo, and Kate Evans, whose book, *Copse*, was beside me throughout my writing. Lastly, big thanks to Mike Schwarz, for generously sharing his extensive expertise on all things legal in relation to the protestors in the story.

For inspiration, I want to name David Almond, and in particular Mina, in his prequel to *Skellig*, who stamps on the earth and shouts encouragement down to Persephone, imagining her struggling over rocks and roots under the ground, trying to return. It was Mina that brought Persephone to mind when I looked at the dark word 'spring' on my rectangle of white card back in 2011. But there is a stack of other books, as tall as me, on which this book rests and without which I couldn't have written it: *The God Beneath the Sea* by Edward Blishen and Leon Garfield, *Underland* by Robert Macfarlane and, *The Bloody Chamber* by Angela Carter, to name but three.

And then there are those who just offered friendship to me and the writing — though 'just' is wholly out of place in this context. I thank Julia Gwynne for our letter exchanges. I thank Christine Rose for keeping a folder for the novel, patiently waiting in her home. I thank Mika Rosenfeld for her support, for lending me her pottery shed, and minding my daughter, while I did last minute edits. I thank Lizzy, Rebecca, and all of the participants in the Mothers Who Make online peer support meetings for cheering me on. And I thank Jackie, not just for having a brilliant big sister and activist husband, but for being herself and helping me when the book, and life, were stopping my sleep.

Thank you to my agent, Laura Williams, at Greene & Heaton, and to my editor at Scribe, Molly Slight, for believing in this story, even though, or especially because, it doesn't fit into the box that other classical retellings do, and who together enabled me, finally, to do this thing which I have dreamt of for so long: writing my acknowledgements, for a book that is going to be published.

And last up — my family. They made this book, too. I thank my husband, Phelim, for giving me the space to write for ten long years, even when I had nothing concrete to show for it. For letting me make all manner of unconventional choices, as a mother, and wife, along the way. Thank you to my children, Riddley and Tenar, who loaned me their bedroom floor on which to write, who had far more screen time than is generally considered to be wise, who designed several early book covers and did some excellent proofreading. They also taught me what it is to mother, and how hard, and a sense of what Demeter must have gone through.

And, lastly, I thank my own mother, who is the real heroine, or goddess, now quite ancient, behind the whole process. In her role as Granny, almost all of the hours I had for writing are thanks to her — even now, on this autumn afternoon, she is downstairs with my daughter, playing 'Cat and Dog'. But even more than the time she has given me, I thank her for her faith: though I have dragged her to the underworld and back more than once in my life, she never gave up on the possibility of spring.

357